coming

back

to me

coming

back

to me

Caroline
Leavitt

st. martin's griffin
new york

www.stmartins.com

Design and title-page photograph by Lorelle Grafeo

Library of Congress Cataloging-in-Publication Data

Leavitt, Caroline.
    Coming back to me / Caroline Leavitt.
        p. cm.
    ISBN 0-312-26937-4 (hc)
    ISBN 0-312-30554-0 (pbk)
    1. Medical care, Cost of—Fiction. 2. Infants (Newborn)—Fiction.
  3. Married people—Fiction. 4. Runaway wives—Fiction. 5. Sisters—Fiction. I. Title.

PS3562.E2617 C66 2001
813'.54—dc21   00-045962

First St. Martin's Griffin Edition: September 2003

P1

For Jeff Tamarkin

and Max.

I love you.

acknowledgments

This book could not have been written without Rochelle Jewell Shapiro. She took time from writing her own novel to read endless drafts, and to comment and critique even the conjunctions. She calmed and cheered, she was the perfect critic and the perfect friend, and she cared about this book as much as she cared about me. Thank you, thank you, Rochelle.

For years I've seen the name Gail Hochman praised in acknowledgment after acknowledgment of my favorite books, and I'm so thrilled that now I get to do the same. I couldn't ask for a smarter, funnier, warmer, and more completely wonderful agent, champion, and friend. My gratitude is boundless, my devotion absolute.

A multitude of deepest thanks to Jennifer Weis, Joanna Jacobs, and everyone at St. Martin's Press.

My gratitude, too, for the support and kindness of Nancy Lattanzi, Lindy Judge, Jo Fisher, Jane Praeger, Linda Corcoran, Peter Salzano,

acknowledgments

Andrea Valeria, Micky Pearlman, and Fatima Bayati; and for my mother, Helen Leavitt, my sister, Ruthy Rogers, and Hillary and Jonathan Rogers, too.

I'd also like to thank Dr. Steven Ordorica, Dr. Henrietta Lackner, Dr. Kenneth Hymes, Dr. Robert Wallach, Dr. Francis Adams, Dr. Steven Hoffstetter, Dr. Elliot Newman, Dr. Steven Rosen, and every single person at Mount Sinai-NYU Medical Center. I would also like to thank Dr. William Bell of Johns Hopkins.

More thanks and love than I can say to Jeff, who took infinite, loving care of me and this book both, who read every single night with thought and attention, even as his own book deadline loomed, and who lived these pages along with me.

And for Max Henry Leavitt Tamarkin, who's the reward.

coming

back

to me

prologue

Gary and the baby sit at the Tastee Diner. Otis is only three weeks old and lies swaddled in a soft blue-striped blanket on Gary's lap. This is what Otis knows: the red leatherette seats; the soft blur of sound coming from a jukebox in back, which is usually something by Patsy Cline or Dolly Parton, something country; Gary; and for three whole days, Molly. Three days so far, Gary reminds himself. *So far.*

Every night Gary orders the same thing: black coffee and a cup of hot water to warm Otis's bottle. Otis is always in a new outfit. Today he's wearing blue and gray stripes with a matching hat and booties. Four changes every day because he christens each and every thing with spit-up and formula and rivers of drool. It doesn't matter. The supply of clothing is endless. Every day presents arrive in the mail, packaged in silver, laced with ribbon, tied with cards, wishing them luck, sending them prayers. Otis looks great in whatever Gary puts on him. Stripes, polka dots, and, Gary's personal favorite, a tiny red stretch jersey printed with black singing Elvis Presleys. Otis is small and creamy as a pearl and already he has the same mop of black hair that Gary does, the same huge slate eyes as Molly's. He's got lashes so long they leave faint shadows on his cheeks.

He's so brand-new, yet he has what Gary would call wise eyes, making Gary feel it is perfectly okay to talk to the baby as if he were an equal.

"So, what would you do if you were me?" he asks, bending his face down, breathing in the clean powdery scent. Otis regards him gravely and yawns deeply. Gary's neighbor, Emma Thorton, a deeply religious woman who goes to church three times a week, has already told Gary with great authority that newborns come into the world knowing everything. "Only gradually does the world take that knowledge away from them," she insisted. "It's a mysterious, sad thing."

Gary laughed when she told him. "The world probably has to take it away or they'd go insane," he said, and then he felt a vague sort of shame when Emma's face telescoped shut.

"This is not a joke," she said. "It's true. Who knows what wisdom we could learn if we could only speak the language of children? 'And a little child shall lead us,' that's what Jesus said, after all. It's in the Bible. It's true."

Gary nods, but he doesn't know what is true or not true anymore. God. The universe. He looks for order and can find none. How could he when his life has no framework anymore, when nothing makes sense to him?

Gary used to have a married couple as friends, atheists who raised their daughter, Stella, not to believe in anything more radical than herself. No Santa. No Easter Bunny. And certainly no God to make sense of things. When Stella was five, a bright, pretty girl with a storm of mustardy curls, he had asked her, "So, now that you're a big girl, what do you miss most about being a baby?" All the adults had waited, smiling at Stella as she peered up at Gary, her eyes shimmering with thoughts.

"I miss talking to God," Stella said finally, nodding her head for emphasis.

"Excuse me?" said Stella's mother, startled, but Stella turned busy, plucking at the hem of her dress, twisting one damp finger into her curls. "Who do you talk with?" Stella's mother asked her again, but Stella popped her finger in the side of her mouth, making a popping sound. "Cluck, cluck, wuss a bus the duck!" she sang. At the time Gary had thought Stella's—and her mother's—response was hilarious.

Now, though, he thinks a little differently. He thinks if he were Stella's parents, her response would have stopped him in his life, just for a moment. He would have pivoted. He would have somehow been changed. He's lapsed Jewish, but he would have been willing to try religion, to see just what might happen. *You never know,* he thinks, and depending on where you are in your life, that statement could either ease you or put you in torment.

Gary doesn't know what he believes, but he's willing to give anything a try now. He doesn't know what possessed him, but yesterday, on his way to the grocer for more formula, Otis bundled in the blue denim Snugli, a soft, sure weight against his heart, he had walked into a church. It was filled with rows of pews in deep, dark woods, and brilliantly colored stained glass, and a few chipped statues of Jesus and Mary and some saints he didn't recognize. It was empty. As soon as he walked in, his feet echoed on the polished floor, and Molly had blurted into his mind like a shout. He sat in the back row, looking up at the mural on the ceiling, pastel angels filmed with gold and white cottony clouds, and then, as soon as he was settled, he realized he didn't know any prayers. *Please* was all he could think of to say. *Oh, please.* And he didn't know if that was enough, if it carried any power or weight.

Otis stirs now, his round, damp mouth moving, his hands as perfect as tiny stars you might wish upon. "Hey," Gary says, and bends and kisses his son. He can't kiss him enough. He gets drunk on the touch of him. He loves the baby's clean scent and can't help himself from sniffing Otis's neck, his round belly, his head, his hands. Gary kisses Otis once more and then checks his watch. Time to feed him, his son who was breast-fed for three days, who was held against Molly's heart, and he looks around for a waitress for another glass of hot water to warm Otis's bottle.

He knows the waitresses by now. He doesn't have to look at their name tags, shaped like clocks, with names he suspects aren't even theirs but are given to give the place a sense of atmosphere, the snap and sheen of style. Doreena. Darla. Donna. And his favorite name, his favorite waitress, a new one, Patsylu. Patsylu is tall and thin with green eye shadow and a bubble of bright bottle-blond hair tied back in a black velvet ribbon, and she has a soft spot for Otis. "Well, aren't you just the piece of blueberry pie?" she says to the baby.

Every time she glides by, she strokes back Otis's hair, and though Gary knows you aren't supposed to let anyone touch a newborn without making them wash their hands first, he hasn't the heart to criticize someone so kind to his son and to him. She brings him refills without even asking. She always smiles and she never once asks him a question, Where are you from? Who do you know here? Why did you come here? What do you want? *Everything*, Gary thinks. *What I had, which was everything.*

Tonight, Patsylu comes by with eggs. "Made them myself," she says, her voice low, soft, and sweet as music. "I even cleaned the grill so there isn't an ounce of bacon grease." He smiles up at her and thinks she would be pretty if she scrubbed her face, if she let her hair go natural. Simplification is the theme of his life now that everything is so complicated. She taps him on his arm. "You eat," she says, making it a command. "You eat that and you won't have to worry about protein for the rest of the day." She sets the plate down, a cheery bright red festooned with a flowered rim. The eggs are cooked hard into rubbery yellow buttons, the way she knows he likes them. They're freckled with coarse black pepper, sprigged with parsley, and he'll do his best to eat at least some of them, pushing the rest to the side of his plate to make it look like he did a good job, an old trick he learned way back in grade school.

He hands Patsylu Otis's bottle and lays one hand on Otis to calm him. He feels his son's steady pulse, he feels the late hour, growing later still. Already he knows that Gerta, the live-in baby nurse he's hired, will be good and pissed at him when he gets home. "You don't take a newborn out at night," she'll scold. "What's the matter with you?"

Patsylu comes back with the bottle warming in a glass of water. She shakes her head at his plate. "You have to eat more than that. You've got to start thinking about nutrition. You're a family now." She sets the glass down; she moves to another table.

A family. My God. An orphan, he doesn't know anything about family except he is almost one. The only things he knows about his own parents are the stories that his aunt Pearl, who raised him, told him. Pearl was a lean, hard woman living on her husband's Social Security and her teaching pension, and she loved Gary as much as he loved her. "I'm sharing my retirement with you," she told him. "What could be better than an old lady and a little boy?" Pearl had snowy white hair she tied up with a rhinestone clip. She wore satiny suits in ocean colors and she let him wear whatever he wanted. She never cut his hair until he told her it was in his eyes. She loved him. They went to plays and movies and she baked him pies and cookies and told him tales at night, and some of them were about his parents.

"Your folks were wildcats," she said. "They didn't have room in their hearts for anyone but each other—and you."

He has photos of them, his mother pale and luminous, her hair spun sugary blond, pinned up with a flower, or skating down to her shoulders. In one photo, his favorite, she's lifting one hand against the sun, but it looks to Gary like she's beckoning to him, like she's calling, *Come here, come here, come here to me.* His father is tall and thin with a slick of dark hair and a toothy grin. He always wears suits and ties and a fedora at a snappy angle. His shoes are shiny and his fingers look like they are snapping to the beat of music. Pearl said Gary's parents took him everywhere, to restaurants and movies and department stores, to ball games and roller rinks and walks on the beach at night. "You were good as gold," Pearl said. "Portable as a box of popcorn." They took him with him the day they were killed.

They were grocery shopping, carrying brown bundles of food, maybe something special for dinner, maybe something romantic like chocolate cake or oysters or a half-decent bottle of red wine. They were wheeling Gary in his blue stroller and it had started to rain. Lightning sparked the sky. Thunder boomed. His parents were struggling with the stroller and the groceries. The brown bags were tearing, spilling food across the damp ground. They were trying to get the stroller and Gary up the steep front stairs to their apartment and finally they must have decided to take him out, just until they could get their bearings. The car was parked in front, a turquoise Plymouth with cream trim, and they sheltered Gary in it, laying him across the front car seat, shutting the door. Just for a moment. Just to protect him. And then they both put their hands on his stroller, to get the groceries packed underneath, to collapse the carriage, and the only thing wrong was that they touched the shiny silver metal handlebars the same exact moment the lightning did. "Freak accident," Pearl told Gary, rocking him in her arms, soothing his hair as he tried to imagine it. The spark and fire of life. The brilliant sudden sizzle. Did they think about Gary or did they turn and see only each other or did they think nothing at all but the quick shock of it all? They died instantly, but he, Gary, had slept in the car for two hours, lulled by the rhythmic pounding fizz of rain. It took a neighborhood kid, running home without his red rubber boots and duck-printed umbrella, to find Gary's parents, and then to find Gary, small and compact, and perfectly asleep.

He has photographs, but no memories. Pearl died four years ago, and now Molly and Otis are all the family he has. *Has*, he says. Present tense. *Has*. He feels himself rustling like leaves.

"How about some ice cream to top that all off?" Patsylu says. "We've got peach, fresh as a June day."

Gary starts to say, *Oh, I'm dying for some*, and then stops. A phrase as simple as that, and he can't say it. It feels as if a layer has been pulled off his life. He's scared all the time. And he keeps thinking: *What happens now?*

But the thing is, no one knows what is wrong with Molly. She went in to have a routine delivery of Otis, and three weeks, five operations, and two near deaths later, still no one knows. They keep her anesthetized so she won't feel what is happening to her. Sometimes when he comes to see her, he wonders if she is imagining that he's left her, if he's dead, because she hasn't seen him, not for days, not for what seems like months, when the truth is, he is always there. "Honey," he says. Her eyes flutter open and then shut again, and she doesn't hear him, she doesn't see. It is as if there were a wall separating them, a wall he would smash with his own hands if he could just find it.

"I'll wrap some pie up for later," Patsylu suddenly says. "So you can have something sweet later."

Gary pays Patsylu, overtipping her as usual, and bundles Otis up in his arms. "Bye, bye, sweetie pie," Patsylu says, and for one moment, he can't tell if she is talking to him or to the baby. He opens the front door, careful of Otis, and steps out into a nudging unseasonable chill.

chapter

one

G ary Breyer had first fallen in love with Molly at the Tastee diner. He was not a man who fell in love easily, but he had always hoped he might. People had always told him that he was smart and funny, and although he didn't consider himself very good-looking, women, to his great astonishment, found him handsome. They touched his heavy lashes, his thick mop of black hair curling into the collars of his jackets. They found his sloppy way of dressing in flannel shirts and tees, in faded jeans and high-top sneakers, endearing and boyish.

He almost always had dates, photographers he worked with, a cellist he had met at a concert, a pharmacist who had filled his antibiotic prescription, and once even a hand model who had put a skin of cold cream on her hands before slipping them into her white cotton gloves every night. Sometimes the women fell in love with him and sometimes he fell in love back, but in the end, nothing ever took, his relationships slowly drifted apart, and he never quite understood why. His girlfriends told him he was too intense, or sometimes not intense enough. "The fit isn't right, that's all it is," Emily, his last girlfriend, had said two days before she left him to go back with her ex-boyfriend, a ski bum living in Utah who seemed to fit her just fine. Sometimes, though, he was the one who broke off the relationships. He fell out of love with a nurse because she hated to talk about her feelings. He stopped seeing a book editor after she came home from a two-week business trip and he suddenly realized he hadn't missed her.

Gary began to feel a great, deep sadness, a restless longing as if love were a season that had somehow never arrived for him. He tried to keep busy. He had a job he loved, designing book jackets at Treasures Press in Brooklyn, and he didn't mind working long hours or late at night. He lived in bookstores and at the movies, and he had a network of friends who opened their homes to him Thanksgivings and Christmases and New Years. But gradually, as he and his friends all started getting older, their twenties nudging into their thirties, his friends began marrying and having kids. He rented tuxes for their weddings, he gave fluid, funny toasts and flirted gallantly with all the bridesmaids, and gradually, he even began to attend the christenings and birthday parties, the pint-sized celebrations filled with small, buttery voices calling him Uncle Gary. Uncle. Family. He was and yet he wasn't. And as his friends moved farther and farther away from him, out of his Chelsea neighborhood and deeper into the suburbs or out of New York entirely, he saw them less and less, and when he did, his friends' conversations were peppered with names and places he didn't recognize; their kids sometimes couldn't remember who he was.

He couldn't help but envy his friends' lives. He stood in his married friend Bob's kitchen in Massachusetts, leaning along the adobe tile wall, watching Bob and his wife, Rayanna, cooking, the two of them teasing, every passed spoon so intimate an act, Gary felt like a voyeur. He walked to films in Ithaca with Allan, a copywriter he had worked with and befriended, and Allan's girlfriend, Peggy, but Gary walked alone with his hands deep in his pockets, while theirs were twined together. His friends saw how silent he sometimes got; they tried to keep including him in their lives, they handed him phone numbers of women they thought he might like, they tried to generate romance. "Maybe you want too much," Allan finally suggested. "Maybe you should be more realistic. Stop expecting miracles."

* * *

Gary began to feel weary. He began to tell himself that peace and solitude were not such bad things, that a person could be happy in his own company. He began taking drives, exploring, and he began to eat more and more of his meals at a tiny New Jersey diner he discovered, a black-and-chrome shoe box called the Tastee.

The Tastee had chrome tables and soft leatherette booths. There was a rotating neon clock that took up a quarter of the far wall. The diner was fairly crowded, and there were four waitresses bustling around, white aprons snapped about their waists, name tags pinned to their breasts. One of them, a middle-aged blonde with a name tag that said Donna, nodded toward the back. "Spicy fries are good today," she urged.

"Okay. And coffee, too," Gary said. Glen Campbell was crooning on the jukebox about being a lineman for the county. It was one of those corny songs Gary was embarrassed to admit he liked. Gary made his way to the back and sat down in a booth and looked around. There were lots of families here, mothers daubing napkins at their kids' faces, fathers in business suits, leaning forward, talking earnestly to their teenaged daughters who were rolling their eyes or staring blankly off into space. There were some couples, a few groups of elderly women, and there in the back, sitting alone, eating soup, was the most beautiful woman Gary had ever seen.

Her hair was a fiery tangle of curls spiraling down her back. She had a constellation of freckles dotted across her nose, a small pointed chin, and eyes as clear and gray as slate. Her white overalls looked a size too big for her, her white sweater underneath was unraveling at the elbow, and her left high-top sneaker had a blue paint scribble on the toe. She was curved over, one hand cupping her chin, the other on her book, reading so avidly, she seemed to be eating her soup blindly, raising the spoon slowly to her mouth, not taking her eyes from her page. He liked it that she liked to read, that she seemed so at home by herself. He liked it, too, that she didn't act like it was a failing that she didn't have a guy with her or another girlfriend, but rather that she was enjoying herself completely. He watched her for a moment, waiting, seeing if there might be an opening for him, but when she didn't look up, when his fries arrived, he turned his attention to them.

He told himself she could be married. He didn't see a ring, but that didn't mean anything. She could be in love or on her way to France on the next flight out. He ate a fry, crackled with pepper, spiked with garlic, jolting his appetite, so that he was suddenly starving. He pronged a couple more fries on his fork. Beside him, two teenagers in identical blue turtlenecks and jeans got up and began to slow dance to an old Bruce Springsteen song. They crowded the aisle, slinging their arms about each other's shoulders. One of the waitresses was laughing, a high, roller-coaster peal. "I gotta get past you guys," she warned, edging around the dancers, pushing them closer. Gary watched the kids swaying, all that heat and energy and young love, all that promise and purpose, and then, because he couldn't help himself, he glanced over at the redheaded woman again. She turned a page, half smiling as she read, so deep in thought she didn't notice when her sleeve dipped in her bowl, making a wobbly soupy star on her elbow. Gary grinned to himself. He couldn't help watching her a second more, and then he suddenly wished for a book for himself, too, a sketch pad. Next time, he told himself.

He grabbed another fry. He didn't know what it was about this woman, why every time he looked at her, why every time she moved, he felt a change in the atmosphere, a charge. It was ridiculous. He didn't know anything about her, who she was, what she did, whether or not she was smart or funny or even remotely interesting. She could be moody or psychotic. She could be simple as a pane of glass. He couldn't see what she was reading, though he half hoped it was a classic, or something new and good, anything other than a celebrity bio or a lurid True Crime, that was engaging her so much that she didn't look up and see him, she didn't feel his interest.

Maybe he'd go over to the redheaded woman's table, ask to borrow the salt or the pepper, start a conversation and see what happened. People met people anywhere. In movie lines, at supermarkets. He had had one friend who had met his wife when he had stumbled on the street, reaching up to grab something to steady himself, and he had grabbed her, instead, ripping her skirt hem, tumbling her down with him. "I beg your pardon," she had said, and two months later, they were married. What did Gary have to lose?

He grabbed up one last fry, studded with pepper, intensely salted. He got up, taking the fries with him, and walked toward her table. Outside, it had begun to snow, damp, heavy flakes that clung to the glass window. He could see bits of gold glinting in all that red hair. He could see her paperback, the title like a beacon. Truman Capote. She read Truman Capote. Something tightened and pulsed, zipping up his spine. She was smart. He was about to introduce himself, to ask if she'd like to join him, when she looked up. Her eyes were flickering with light. "Hey, I know you," she said.

He smiled.

"Don't I?" Her voice was low and rich. She leaned forward, nearly toppling her glass, water sloshing from its lip. They both reached for the glass at the same time, and his fingers touched hers. A jolt of heat moved up through his fingers. She looked up at him, waiting. "Don't you want to sit down?"

Her name was Molly Goldman and as soon as he sat down, he couldn't stop talking to her. He told her about growing up without his parents, about growing up with Pearl, and about his job. She told him she lived in Elizabeth, New Jersey, where she taught third grade.

"A teacher!" he said. It tickled him. He could just see her in the classroom, paint on her clothes, chalk in her hair. Kids clamoring at her feet.

She looked at him curiously. "Is that a funny profession to have? You're smiling so hard."

"No, no, it's perfect. It's a great thing to be."

"I think so. I mean, I really love it. The only thing about it is that sometimes it's a little insulating." She looked happily around the diner. "That's why I come here. The noise. The commotion. Seeing different people. Especially adults. You come here enough times you start feeling like family. I know all the waitresses here. And they don't care if I read or work here half the night and order only grilled cheese." She told him she had thirty kids and while most of them were working-class baloney-sandwich-and-milk type of kids, some of her students had more money in their bank accounts than she ever would, and they all knew it. She laughed. "Last Christmas two of my students came to my house in a caroling group and I invited all of them in. They kept opening the closet doors, sure there must be another room in there and not just my old moth-eaten coats."

Gary laughed.

"I admit it, I fall right in love with my kids. I worry about them and champion them and I start feeling like they're mine. And I always forget that they're just on loan. That they only love me for a year, then they move on and change and fall in love with their new teacher and bang—I'm history. It's sort of sad."

"But they must come back and visit, don't they?"

Molly shrugged. "Sometimes. Some of them do. But it's always just to reminisce. I'm not a part of their lives anymore. Which, I guess, is the way it should be." She looked over at his fries. "Can I have some of those?" she said, and he pushed the plate over and she picked one up with her fingers. "Anyway," she said. "It's a weird universe, teaching. The other teachers I work with are mostly married women and they drive me crazy always trying to fix me up." She reached for another one of Gary's fries. "They're always trying to push me together with this guy Jack, who teaches kindergarten. They keep saying, 'Oh, you make such a cute couple! You look so good together!' One of the teachers even bought me this joke T-shirt she said I ought to wear so Jack might get the hint. TEACHERS DO IT WITH CLASS. When I finally took Jack aside and told him, he laughed. 'Gee, should I tell my Andrew?' he said."

Gary laughed and took another spicy fry from the plate, his fingers brushing hers.

By the time Molly and Gary were on their fourth cup of coffee, the snow was so heavy you couldn't see out the windows, the radio was predicting a state of potential emergency, and Gary was so enraptured by Molly he didn't care if it snowed forever. The lights flickered and went out. "Oh, hell," said the waitress.

"Is this okay, staying here in all this snow?" he asked her.

"I like dramatic weather."

The waitresses lit candles. Customers got up, putting money down on the bill, bundling into their coats, their hats, pulling the brims down low. The waitresses glanced at the clock.

Gary looked at Molly. "Could I call you some time?"

Gary told himself to take it slow. He hadn't been lucky in love before. The best thing to do would be to give them both room and not rush into anything. He had her home and school phone numbers tacked up on the bulletin board in his office in his apartment. Today was Monday. He didn't want her to think he was crazy or desperate. He'd wait until Wednesday, maybe even Thursday to call her.

He tried to bury himself in his work. He came in early to find Ada, his secretary, setting something up on a tray. Ada was young and pretty and anorexic-looking, with a blaze of blond curls, and nine times out of ten she was dressed in blue because she claimed it was a calming color for her. She grinned at him and held up the tray. Brownies were arranged on it. "Carob brownies today," she announced. "Fruit juice sweetened." She waited, expectant.

Ada was macrobiotic and was always trying to gain converts to her cause. A week didn't pass when she didn't bring something in, and even at the end of the day, when all her goodies lay untouched, she didn't get angry or depressed. She took them home, whistling. She came back the next week with more.

"Try one," Ada pressed. Maybe it was thinking about Molly, feeling as if something were sparkling inside of him. Maybe it was feeling so good. But Gary took a carob brownie from Ada. She looked at him, shocked and delighted. "Why, Gary!" she said, "good for you!" and he took a bite.

The brownie broke apart in his mouth in dry little pebbles. He couldn't swallow. Ada's smile grew. "What did I tell you?" she said happily.

"Mmm," he said, and excused himself, shutting the door to his office. He grabbed a Kleenex, spat out the rest, and tossed it, along with the rest of the brownie, into the trash, burying it under a shelf of paper. He searched his desk for the cough drops he kept around and tucked two into the side of his cheek to kill the papery taste.

All that day, he couldn't stop thinking about Molly. He ran out for a quick lunch at a local sandwich shop, but as soon as he sat down, he saw a flash of red hair from the corner of his eye. He looked around for Molly, confused. A woman with glasses was walking past, balancing a tray. A deeply tanned woman was waving to a friend. The red hair—and Molly—were nowhere to be found. He suddenly wasn't hungry anymore. He got up and went back to work and stared at his layout for the cover of a boating book called *Ships Ahoy!* The information he had on the book itself was sketchy, but he knew editorial wanted something streamlined, something technical-looking, despite the dopey title. He bet the marketing V.P., a recent MBA graduate fond of catch phrases, wouldn't like the bold typeface he wanted against a bold design. "All bold is no bold," she'd admonish. He crumpled the layout up and threw it in the trash. He clicked the computer on again and made a pale gray screen. *Molly's eyes are gray*, he thought, and then, despite himself, he picked up the phone and called Molly at school. "Is this an emergency?" the school secretary asked him.

"Why, yes, I believe it is."

As soon as he heard Molly's voice, he was grinning again. The words seemed to spill out of him. "I know we just met yesterday. But what about dinner tomorrow night?"

She laughed. "I thought you'd never ask."

He wanted to talk more with her. He could have stayed on the line all afternoon, but she interrupted him. "Gary, listen," she said hurriedly. "We're not supposed to get personal calls. They really frown on it." Her voice lowered. "But listen, too, I know this great place we can try for our dinner. The waitresses sing opera. They're absolutely terrible, but that's what makes it so much fun."

He promised he wouldn't call her at work, that he'd see her for dinner, six o'clock so they could catch a movie afterward. "Or two," Molly said. "Two's okay with you?"

"Two's great."

*　*　*

He tried not to call Molly again, but by four he wanted to tell her about Ada and the horrible carob brownies no one would touch, even after she told everyone that Gary had found them delicious. He wanted to tell Molly that the new hiree in copy had started that day only to leave two hours later with "I Quit" scribbled across a pad of paper on his desk. And he wanted to tell her what it was like to think you might be falling in love when you had never hoped such a thing might happen for you. He picked up the phone.

The school secretary sighed in exasperation when she heard his voice. "Hold on."

"Stop, please, you'll get me fired!" Molly complained when she got on the line. "I had to leave thirty little kids with glue and colored paper and only the not-so-watchful eye of the next-door teacher. There's no telling what I'll come back to!"

And so, reluctantly, he had stopped calling so often. Every time he thought of her, every time his hand reached for the phone, he got up and went to the snack machine and got chips instead, and they lay on his desk uneaten. He talked to Ada, to the copywriter down the hall, and he even asked Brian a question he didn't really need an answer to. An hour later his phone rang.

"You never call me anymore," she said.

It was Tuesday. He was going to finish early, run home and shower and change and go get Molly when he heard the click of Brian's shoes coming toward him. He looked up.

Gary tapped his computer screen, at a shining planet Earth suspended in a bright field of blue sky. "I think it works great. It's simple, it's direct, it's clean."

Brian frowned. "Well, I don't like it. And I'm the one you have to impress." He frowned. A thin line of brown hair fell over his forehead and he blew up a puff of air to get it out of his way. "It doesn't scream environment to me."

Gary studied his drawing. "I think it does," he insisted. "It's the planet."

Brian shook his head. "But does the planet mean the environment? You might think it does, but will the average Joe? I don't think editorial's going to go for it. And marketing's going to say it doesn't talk to the customer."

"That was last month's catch phrase."

Brian ignored him. "I'd like to see something more environmental. Maybe something with the weather. Or with rocks. Try a few different approaches we can present." Brian put his hands on Gary's desk. "And, Gary, I need them on my desk tonight."

Gary grew still. Brian was always at the office late. He liked to work, and he liked to use the company phone to call his girlfriend Candy in L.A., an airbrushed-looking blonde whose photo hung prominently in his office. "First thing in the morning." Gary tried to make his voice sound positive.

"Tonight."

Gary slumped back in his chair. He'd never finish three versions by six, let alone by eight, or even ten, if he were lucky.

He watched Brian wandering back to his office, saw Brian lean back in his chair, lifting his boots up on his desk, picking up his phone. He hummed "Sugar, Sugar," vaguely out of tune. "You are my can-dee girl!" He punched down emphasis on "candy," the name of his girlfriend. He'd be on the phone with Candy for hours and as far as anyone knew, Brian had never actually met her. Every time he had planned to go out there, something had come up. She had the flu. She had an audition. It wasn't a good time.

Gary picked up the phone to call Molly.

"Oh." Her voice sounded flat, disappointed, when he told her he had to cancel. "I understand. But I can't go out tomorrow night. Parent-Teacher Night. Can we do it the night after?"

The night after. Three more days. "Sure we can," he said.

He worked until midnight, leaving five minutes after Brian did. He drove home, and then he didn't know what was going on, what was driving him, but no matter which direction he turned the car, it started moving him back down her roads, back into Elizabeth. She had told him where she lived, she had described the house, but he had never been there before. Her neighborhood was so silent, he could hear his own heartbeat. He parked in front. The house was small and boxy, painted a pale adobe color. It had a square scrubby front yard and a winding flagstone path up to her door. There was one light on in the front of her house.

He was sleepwalking. He was so exhausted, he wasn't thinking clearly. Someone else was opening up his car door and walking to her front door. Someone else was ringing the bell, not caring that it was past midnight.

He tried to compose his thoughts, to figure out what he could say that wouldn't scare her away. He tried to think of a good enough reason why he was showing up here to see her. The door opened. She was in black sweatpants and a white T-shirt, her hair flopped over one shoulder. "I was just in the neighborhood—" he said lamely. He felt like a fool. He stopped and took a breath, shaking his head, trying to clear it. Sudden heat rose like a cloud around him. He swore he saw lights and then she took two steps forward and she studied him, her face grave, and then, abruptly, she kissed him soft and full on his mouth. She stepped back, pulling him inside with her, into the warmth and light.

In the morning, everything had changed, and they both knew it. When he woke up, she was sitting cross-legged in bed, the sheets in a tangle about her. She was watching him, smiling, burrowing into a navy velour robe.

He looked happily about her room. The walls were as pale peach as her skin, the floor was gleaming wood, there were books everywhere, and every time he spotted a title—John Irving, Emily Brontë— he felt happier, because he either knew and loved the book, or he wanted to read it himself.

There was a trophy on one of the bookshelves, a golden figure of a girl. He reached over the bed for his boxer shorts and pulled them on.

Then he got up, and went over to look at it. He held it in his hands and peered at the inscription: Miss California Beaches. Delighted, he turned to Molly. "You won this!"

She shook her head. She got out of bed. She pointed to the inscription. Angela Goldman. "My mother."

She pivoted him to another wall of photographs and pointed. "That's her on the wall." There was one big photo of a slim, lovely woman in a two-piece, laughing into the camera, tossing a tumble of stormy black hair. He stood up to look at it. "She's beautiful," he said.

He turned back to look at Molly. She looked at the photograph of her mother. "She was," she said quietly. "She died."

"Oh, God. I'm so sorry."

"My father was one of the contest judges. He took one look at her, gave her the prize, and married her. And then, three years later, shortly after I was born, he disappeared."

"God."

"It's all right. My mother would never talk about him except to say we were all better off. And it's hard to miss someone you never knew. She used to say that was a real survival skill, not knowing."

"I know what it's like to be an only child, to be orphaned."

Molly grew quiet. "I'm not an only child. I have a sister."

"You do?" He looked at her, surprised. People with siblings were always threading the names of their brothers or sisters casually into their conversations, but Molly hadn't mentioned a sister at all. Not until now.

"Suzanne. She's three years older. She ran away when she was seventeen and I haven't seen or heard from her for a few years now."

"Are you serious?" Gary shook his head in astonishment. If he had had any family at all, a brother, a sister, even a cousin, he would have made sure that they lived next door to him for life. He would have been on the phone with them every day. "Years," he repeated. Molly looked distractedly off in the distance. She bent to pick up a stray sock, to straighten a magazine on the table. There were things that people didn't want to talk about, and usually he respected that. Usually, he let people keep their secrets or take their time revealing them to him. But Molly wasn't "people." Not to him. "How come?" he persisted.

Molly stopped bustling about the room. She tapped the sock against her hand.

He gave her a loopy smile, trying to make her feel more relaxed. "I won't tell anyone."

She looked at him as if she were deciding something important, and then she slowly put down the sock. She walked over to a table and picked up a clear acrylic box, pieced together like a puzzle, with four steel balls rolling around on top. Inside was a piece of paper folded over. She handed it to Gary.

"What's this?" Gary said.

Molly half smiled. "Suzanne's unlisted address and phone number. You have to get all these balls into this hole to open the box and get the paper. I know it's kind of silly, but I put it there anyway, like a symbol, just to remind me she's still present in my life. And to remind me to think twice before contacting her."

"I'm good at these things." Gary reached for the box, and Molly snatched it back toward her.

"No. Don't you dare." She put the box back on the dresser. "It's a whole long story."

"I like long stories."

This time she smiled back at him, considering. "How about we get to know each other a little better before we talk about Suzanne?"

Gary looked over at the rumpled bed. "Wait a minute! We don't know each other now?"

She laughed. "Well, we do, and we don't."

"Well, then we'd better start changing that. How about dinner and a movie? You name the day."

chapter

two

Molly Goldman couldn't stop thinking about Gary. How easy he was to talk to. How funny. How smart. How much he seemed to like her already. After he left, she rushed to get to work. She kept seeing his face, kept feeling his hands sliding across her body.

She didn't want to blow it. She was a little worried, though. She had seen the look on his face when she said she didn't want to talk about Suzanne. She had seen that look before. People got suspicious of you if they found out you had a sister and didn't bother with her. No matter what the story was, they blamed you for not being loyal, for not being forgiving. "It's a sister, after all," they said. Molly knew that. Molly knew that better than anyone.

There was a time when she and Suzanne had been real sisters. When they had been happy together. It was back when they lived in California, crowded with their mother into a tiny rented house in La Jolla, a mile away from the beach.

They were pretty much on their own back then. Angela was a single working mother, and although she managed to find cheap sitters for them when they were babies, as soon as they both were in grade school, she gave Suzanne keys to the house and a little pocket money and instructions to watch Molly and to try not to burn the house down. "I'll be back by five," she promised, and she was.

Molly liked the way things were. She had invitations, but she didn't really care to go home with her friends because their mothers always looked at her with a peculiar sympathy she didn't understand. They were always coming at her with a sandwich she didn't want, an extra sweater they had got on sale, and would Molly, perhaps, like it? She didn't envy the way her friends couldn't blast their music in their own houses, or stomp their feet, or even choose when and what they wanted to eat. Her friends' mothers could look at her with compassion all they wanted, but Molly knew she had something better. She had a kind of freedom. And she had Suzanne.

Every day after school, Molly would run outside and find Suzanne leaning along the fence, waiting for her, her choppy black hair blowing into her face, her eyes bright with excitement. "Come on, let's run wild," Suzanne said, a phrase one of the girls at school had told her was the reason why her mother wouldn't let her play with the Goldman girls. They hightailed it to the beach and swam. They roamed the dunes searching for valuables people might have dropped. They ran over to the duplex theater and paid for one movie and halfway through snuck into another, gorging themselves on popcorn and stale candy, laughing and making so much noise, other people would always tell them to shush.

Molly remembered money wasn't so tight back then. The bills were kept in check by Angela's job, and there was often enough left over for small surprises. A new dress now and then. A new portable radio. Everyone helped out, and to Molly, it seemed kind of fun. Dinnertimes were raucous and noisy, the radio blasting, spaghetti boiling in a pot, a store-bought, sugary cake for dessert. Afterward, Angela did laundry or cleaned the house while Suzanne helped Molly with her homework. And then, they all watched movies on TV or took walks, and by ten each night, all of them were yawning. "Who's tired?"

Angela said, stretching. "I've got work tomorrow and you girls have school."

The girls had twin beds, pushed to opposite corners of the room. Molly loved sharing a room with Suzanne because Suzanne was so strong and capable and unafraid of anything. Suzanne didn't think twice about shooting out into the backyard in just her nightgown and bare feet to check out a sound. "Any robbers out here?" she shouted gleefully. "Any bad men?" And she wasn't the least afraid of the dark. Not the way Molly was.

To Molly, the dark was a living, breathing thing, with a personality you didn't want to mess with. It waited for Molly. It stalked her. And Molly saw things at night. Shadows that changed their shapes even as she looked at them. She heard things. Deep, throaty growls. Insect whines, the beating of wings, everything getting closer and closer. Molly arranged the sheets so that only her nose poked out. She jumped at every noise, rustling the sheets, so that Suzanne finally sat up. "Do you think you could keep me awake a *little* more?" Suzanne said acidly.

"Did you hear a noise?"

Suzanne sighed. "No one can get in. It's safe. Now shut up and go to sleep."

"Do you think there are ghosts?"

"No. Go. To. Sleep. Now."

Molly lay in bed, listening, staring at the ceiling. Finally, there was silence. If Suzanne was asleep, Molly was totally unprotected. "Suzanne?" She sat up, bundling the covers about her. She shivered and made a noise with her feet knocking against the footboard. Silence. She did it again, louder this time, and then she looked over and there was Suzanne sitting up, glaring at her.

Suzanne didn't say anything. She stuck her arm out, her fingers reaching for Molly across the divide that separated their beds. "Go to sleep," she said. Molly shut her eyes. Five minutes later Molly opened them, and kicked her legs on the footboard again. Suzanne's eyes flew open. Suzanne sat up. "Oh, for God sakes," Suzanne said. She sounded disgusted. She got up and headed for the door. Molly cursed herself and then Suzanne suddenly turned and came back and stood beside Molly. Her brow was furrowed as if she was thinking of something. She folded her arms across her flowered nightgown. "So are you going to give me any room or what?" Suzanne said, and climbed into bed beside her.

Molly fell asleep next to Suzanne in two seconds, not waking until morning, the birds fussing outside the window. That morning was the first time, in a long while, she felt rested. She rubbed her eyes. There was Suzanne already up, pulling on her dress, sliding into her shoes. "Don't think this is an everyday thing," Suzanne told her. "Don't get all cocky about it." But that night, and every night after that that she needed, all Molly had to do was look across the room at Suzanne. She didn't have to say a thing. Suzanne rolled her eyes. She sighed. And each and every time she got out of her bed and into Molly's, and she stayed in that cramped little bed with Molly until morning.

Molly was nine and Suzanne was almost twelve when Angela's company was sold to a conglomerate in Elizabeth, New Jersey, and if anyone was willing to relocate, they could have a job—and with slightly better pay. That was all Angela needed to hear. "We're going," Angela said.

The day before they were to leave, the girls went to the beach for the last time. It was night, clear and cold and there was no one on the beach except for them. Molly didn't know how she felt about the move: strange and scared and a little excited, too. "Do you think we'll like it?" she asked Suzanne. She thought of tall, needlelike buildings. People rushing by so fast you could be knocked over in a minute. Winter and snow.

"Everything's going to change now," Suzanne said seriously. They were in their pastel flip-flops and shorts, their T-shirts flapping in the salty wind. There were signs pitched into the sand. Undertow. There were rumors that a Scotty dog had been pulled in and all that had been left was his rubber bone, floating up, along the waves.

Suzanne abruptly began tugging off her top, her shorts, stepping out of her flip-flops. "What are you doing?" Molly said.

Suzanne was in her white panties and T-shirt. She sprinted into the water. "Stop!" Molly called, but Suzanne kept going, all flashing white arms and legs and long black hair.

"Suzanne!" she screamed.

She ran down to the water. A wave splashed at her feet, so icy she felt panicked. "Suzanne!" she screamed. She scanned the water and then suddenly she saw her sister's head, bobbing up, slick like a seal's. Suzanne's mouth was moving and then she went under again and Molly dove, unthinking, into the waves.

She had never swum over her head in the ocean. She wasn't even that good a swimmer, but she wouldn't let herself stop. She took in great gulps of salty water, pinwheeling her body around to search for her sister. "Suzanne!" she cried, frantic. What did an undertow feel like? Did you have warning? Could you pull yourself free? Would you die? "Suzanne!" she screamed, and then she saw her sister's head again, bobbing up, one hand gliding up out of the water, like a strange delicate flower, just inches from her and Molly lunged and grabbed onto it. She pulled Suzanne around.

Suzanne was laughing. Her eyes were round blue marbles. "Isn't this great?" Suzanne screamed. "Isn't this the best?"

Molly's hands dug at the water. Her legs felt like anvils. The cold was like a thousand stabbing needles.

"Your lips are blue," Suzanne said. "Let's go back."

By the time Molly made it to shore, Suzanne was already pulling her clothes back on, twisting the water from her long hair.

"Dope. You swam in your clothes," Suzanne said. She rubbed Molly's arms with her own. She took care of her, the way she always did. "Rub yourself down," she ordered.

Molly was so freezing she could barely clap her arms about her body. "I thought you were drowning," Molly blurted, trying to stamp warmth into her feet.

Suzanne snorted. "You would. Ha. Like I need rescue. You watch out for yourself that you don't catch a chill." She rubbed Molly down with her hands a little more.

"You can't get sick from being cold. That's an old wives' tale."

Suzanne ignored her. "We'll go home, get hot showers, and no one will be the wiser."

The next day, the only sign that the girls had gone to the beach at night was a fine spray of sand in the hallway of the house. Molly was fine, but Suzanne came down with a flu so virulent she was sick for weeks after.

Both girls had hated Elizabeth on first sight. It was too gray, too faded, and the air had a strange metallic smell to it. There was no beach to run to, the shopping district was run-down, and the people seemed more sour than exotic. Even Angela complained. "This house is so small," she said. She roamed the rooms, looking caged. She kept shaking her head.

Almost immediately, it was clear that things weren't better the way Angela had promised. Molly felt lost in her new school. She had had friends before, but here she felt as if all the other girls were speaking a foreign language. They seemed to know things she didn't, about makeup and clothes and how to act. And they took one look at her frizzy red hair, her knees like teacups, and treated her with casual disdain, a California girl who didn't have the sense to at least look Californian. In the cafeteria, she sat with the other outcasts, girls with sloppy ponytails and bad skin and braces, girls who stared at her as furiously and resentfully as she did at them, because they all knew if there were anyone better to sit beside, they'd be there. The only times she felt happy were when she passed Suzanne in the hallways. Suzanne walked alone, too, but she wasn't hunched over the way Molly was. Suzanne whistled and bounced, and when she saw Molly, she winked broadly at her.

Angela began coming home later and later. She was working for a wolf-faced man named Lars whom she claimed never stopped riding her because she was a minute late, because she had made a single typo, because she had gone to the wrong room for a meeting and held everyone up. "Just because he looks like that, he doesn't have to take it out on me," she said. She mimicked his walk, stiff-legged, hands swinging like a soldier, making the girls laugh. "Oh, Miz Gold-mun," she rasped. "Please could you do more slave labor? Oh, Miz Gold-mun, please could you work every single second of your life, not even taking time to breathe?" She began bringing some of her work home. Just to keep up. Night after night, she grabbed dinner standing up, a cold cheese sandwich, a hot dog, a burger. Weekends, Angela spread out piles of work all over the house. And as Angela's work grew, so did the piles of laundry, the dirty dishes stacked in the sink, the dust floating like a pollen in the air.

One day, Molly and Suzanne came home to find a big black chalkboard hanging in the kitchen with a list of things on it. Laundry. Shopping. Wash floors. Clean bathroom. Dust. Angela tapped the board and pointed to Suzanne. "A house is like a business, and what we need here is a little delegation."

"A little what?" Molly frowned.

"Delegation. Parceling out the things I don't have time to do to someone else. Someone like Suzanne."

Suzanne blinked at Angela, astonished. "Mom—" she said. "You're kidding, right?"

"We have no food in the house. We have no clean clothes. The dust bunnies are turning into rabbits even as we speak. You're a big girl. It's time you help out around here."

Molly watched Suzanne's face darken. "What do I do?" Molly said. She was almost afraid to find out.

Angela considered. "You take out the trash and do your homework and listen to your sister. Someone has to be in charge, run the ship. And Suzanne's the oldest." She looked at Suzanne. "And you watch Molly. I don't want her here alone."

"But, Mom . . ." Suzanne's voice trailed.

Angela's voice grew sharp. "Don't look at me like that. I'm still your mother and what I say goes."

It was a lot to ask a young girl. Molly remembered Suzanne was always flying around the house, always busy. After school, Suzanne had to come right home now because she had to do the shopping or the laundry. Suzanne bought the groceries from lists Angela left her, she cooked the dinners and did the laundry, and she took care of Molly, rustling her out of bed mornings and taking her to school, picking her up to get her home, and bossing her into bed at night. Molly picked up some laundry and Suzanne knocked it out of her hand. "It'll just take longer if you help," she said, panicked. Molly was still with Suzanne all the time, but now everything felt different. Going to the market wasn't the same as going to the beach. Suzanne stopped joking, she stopped running for the door with Molly when Angela's key rattled in the lock and instead waited in the kitchen, tense, as Angela looked around the house, inspecting. "The clothes folded?" Angela asked Suzanne. "Did you get to the bathrooms the way I asked?" Angela checked off each thing on the chalkboard. "What about the dusting? Did you do that?"

Molly loved her sister, and she knew Suzanne loved her, but sometimes, when Molly looked at Suzanne, she saw the same anxious look on her sister's face that Angela wore when Angela thought no one was looking, as if someone were chasing her, starting to gain ground. It was a look that made Molly want to shut her eyes and never open them again.

One morning, Molly bolted awake from a bad dream. The house was still dark. Suzanne was still sleeping, the covers bunched about her head. Molly squinted at the clock. Six. Almost time to get up anyway. She padded out of the bedroom. The house was so quiet for a moment, she thought her mother had left. She felt a flicker of anger and then, there in the kitchen, she saw Angela standing in the middle of a pile of papers, staring out the back window, looking so lost and hopeless that Molly felt like grabbing her mother around her knees and holding on. "Mom?" she said, and Angela turned, smiling wearily. "Well," she said, overly hearty, joking, "like my new filing system?"

"I can help you—" Molly said.

"Scoot," said Angela. "Go get ready for school."

"Are you okay?"

"Of course I am."

But that evening, when the girls came home, Angela was quiet. She didn't speak through dinner, hotdogs and frozen french fries, not until Suzanne got up to clear the table. "There's got to be another way out of this," Angela said.

A few evenings later, Angela came home, dumping her work on the kitchen chair, heading straight for her room. The girls trailed after her, sprawling across Angela's bed, plucking at the chenille tufts on the spread, watching Angela as she shucked off her suit and then squeezed into her one good dress.

"Are we going out somewhere?" Molly bounced on the bed. She leaned over and plucked up a book she had left there and leafed through it.

"You're not. I am," Angela said. She smoothed the bodice of her dress. "There's a nice new hotel that has dancing that some of the girls at work were talking about. And right now there's a dental convention going on, filled with lots of nice single dentists."

Molly frowned. "No," she said.

"Please, don't look at me like that," Angela said. "I'm doing this for you girls."

Angela spritzed perfume on her hair. "It's drying on your hair, but the scent is worth it." She fluffed her hair with her fingers.

"Mom," said Molly. Suzanne stared sullenly at the wall.

"I can't stay home," Angela said. She bunched her hair in her hand and tied it up with the same rhinestone clip that had won her the beauty contest. "Believe me, I'd like nothing better than staying here with you, and Lord knows I have plenty of work, but what other choice do we have? It's no good for any of us to go on this way. I can't even take you to a lousy movie. Don't you want something better? I do."

"You could take us to a movie if you were home," Suzanne said. "If you really wanted to."

Angela studied herself critically in the mirror, and then took her hair down, cascading it across her back. She tightened her belt to show off her tiny waist. She hiked up her skirt and dipped her neckline. "I still have what it takes, don't I?" Angela said, but her voice sounded doubtful.

Suzanne stared glumly at Angela. "Can't you stay home?"

Angela looked around the house and made a comical face. "I don't see any eligible bachelors around here, do you?" She ruffled Suzanne's long, shiny hair. She kissed Molly and tried to smooth some of her fizz of red hair. "You think I like working so hard? You think I want a husband for any other reason other than to make it easy for you girls?" She took the book out of Molly's hand. "You read too much," she said. "You're going to ruin your eyes."

"They're already ruined." Molly took the book back, holding it close against her chest.

"Zip me up," Angela ordered Suzanne.

It became a pattern. Angela would hear of some event at some hotel. A convention. A dance. She'd leave perfumed, poured into her dress. And a few hours later, she'd come home tense and quiet, not wanting to talk. "Didn't you meet anyone?" Molly asked.

"I met plenty," Angela said, kicking off her shoes. "Just the wrong kind of plenty. And I'm not stupid enough to fall for that twice."

"So don't go anymore," Molly said. But Angela was already looking past her, thoughtfully scratching one leg. "Maybe I'd have better luck at the Marriott," she said, brightening.

One evening, Angela was just getting in past ten when the phone rang. Angela shucked off her coat and flung it wearily over one of the kitchen chairs. She didn't even stop to say hello to Molly and Suzanne, but plucked up the phone. The girls could tell it was the office by the strange new tone in Angela's voice. "Yes, I did," she said, tugging off her glittery earrings. "I worked through lunch on it. And both my breaks. Yes. It will be on your desk by nine," she said. "Of course. No problem." As soon as she hung up, she leaned along the kitchen wall and shut her eyes for a moment. When she opened them, she frowned.

Angela stared angrily at the kitchen counter and then went to the stove and noisily filled a big pot full of water and set it to boil. She got out a plate and slammed it on the table. She yanked open the silverware drawer and grabbed a fork and knife and clattered them by the plates. Suzanne gave Molly a warning look. Angela flung open the cabinet and then stopped, staring. "Where is it?" she shouted. She flung open another cabinet, riffling through it, knocking cans off the shelf, letting them roll across the floor. "No spaghetti!" she yelled. She tugged another cabinet open, and then another and another, and then in a fury, she picked up a can of green beans and flung it across the room. She whirled around, flaring at Suzanne. "There's no sugar! There's no tea! Didn't I tell you to buy paper towels?" Her voice got louder and louder. "What is wrong with you? Don't you have any brains? Didn't you read my list? I can't do everything around here on my own!"

Angela lifted her hand. Suzanne stiffened and then ran from the kitchen.

Angela lowered her hand. "I have to know I can count on you!" Angela shouted after Suzanne.

It was in New Jersey that Suzanne turned fifteen and became beautiful. Away from the hot California sun, her skin grew pale and luminescent. It made her blue eyes seem bluer. It made her black hair seemed even blacker, glinting with light, and because there wasn't money for haircuts, it spurted to her waist in a silky curtain, but Suzanne swiftly became something exotic, a star.

Being suddenly beautiful did something to Suzanne. It gave her a kind of power, an entry through a door that Molly couldn't begin to pass through. And both of them knew it.

That year, Suzanne began to pull away from Molly. Maybe because she could. She didn't have to get Molly up in the morning anymore, or take her or pick her up from school. Molly was old enough now to fix her own meals, if she wanted one, to stay at home by herself, to decide for herself how she'd spend the long, boring hours when Angela was gone.

Suzanne put down a line of white tape on the floor of their bedroom. "Cross and you die," Suzanne coolly informed Molly. She put signs on her desk drawers. KEEP OUT. THIS MEANS YOU. Suzanne began to dress differently, too, in shorter, tighter dresses. She began to stain her mouth with color, to line her eyes in kohl black. She spent hours in front of the mirror, and she began to look at Molly more critically. "Do you have to wear that dress?" she said, pained. Molly's hands flew to her polka-dot dress.

"What's wrong with it?" she said, but Suzanne just shook her head.

"If I have to tell you, then you'll never get it," Suzanne said.

"Do something about your hair," Suzanne told her. "Wash your face." She ordered Molly about, but even when Molly braided her hair back and put on her wheat jeans that Suzanne liked, Suzanne still didn't want to have much to do with her. "Why would I want to hang around a baby?" Suzanne said disdainfully.

Molly began to be grateful that her junior high was on the other end of the city from Suzanne's high school. She had a few friends now, and her teachers all liked her because she was smart, but she and Suzanne were in different orbits. She was glad she didn't have to witness the triumphs Suzanne sometimes told her about in a kind of blow-by-blow wonder, the boys jumping all over each other to flirt with her, the most popular girls wanting to sit next to her. Things that would never in a million years happen to Molly.

At home the phone began to ring and ring, and it was always a boy, and always for Suzanne, but she was never allowed to do anything about it.

"Forget it. Fifteen is too young to date," Angela told Suzanne. "If you can just keep yourself back a few years, till you're eighteen, say, you'll have more sense. No one will take advantage of you."

"Eighteen! I'm not waiting until eighteen."

"Listen to me," Angela said. "I learned so you don't have to. You stay home and help out with Molly. You run the house for me instead of gallivanting all around. You'll see. When the time is right, some great guy will show up on our doorstep for you. And he'll be the right one. A college guy, maybe. Someone with a future."

"Yeah, right," Suzanne said.

"I can look after myself," Molly said, offended.

"I've been taking care of things since I was seven. She's *twelve*."

"No. Case closed." Angela strode out of the room.

Suzanne glared at Molly.

"It's not my fault," Molly protested.

But Suzanne's cold look didn't soften. Molly followed her to their room. "Suzanne—" she said, and Suzanne drew an invisible line across the room. "My side. Your side. I can't hear you. I can't see you," Suzanne said. Suzanne flopped on the bed and put on her headphones and turned up her Walkman, ignoring Molly.

Molly turned and went out of the room. The hours stretched ahead of her. She went into the bathroom and picked up *A High Wind in Jamaica*, one of four books she was avidly reading at once. She ran her hands along the cover. She was glad to have the book, glad to have something she could count on. She took the book and sat in the hall and read. And then before she knew it, the house disappeared. There was only a stormy sea and pirates.

She was still reading that night when she heard noise from outside. Suzanne came out of the room, stepping over Molly as if she weren't even there. Molly heard the front door open and close, and she ran into the bedroom, to peek out the window. There were three boys standing outside on the curb, knocking against each other, all arms and legs and hair, and as soon as Suzanne came out, they seemed to snap to attention. They socked one another in the arm. They tried to touch Suzanne, who danced away, laughing. Suzanne tossed her hair and threw her head back. She acted as if they were the funniest guys she had ever met. Molly pressed her ear against the pane, trying to hear what they were talking about, but they were too far off.

Finally, the guys left. Suzanne started back up the walk, a strange, secretive smile on her face, and then she suddenly looked up. She spotted Molly at the window. She stopped and looked at Molly, and then the glow about her switched off as abruptly as a light.

That year, Angela was home less and less, and when she was, she seemed different. She didn't have to go to the hotels or conventions anymore, because she had started dating Lars, her boss, a man she said she had been all wrong about. Neither one of the girls could understand it. Every time the phone rang, she jumped, and Molly could tell it was Lars just by the way Angela began speaking. Her voice took on a kind of music. She laughed louder and longer than she usually did.

"You like this guy?" Molly demanded. "I thought you said he looked like a wolf."

"Not everybody can be gorgeous. And don't you know that Jefferson Airplane song 'You're Only Pretty As You Feel'?"

"I thought you said he had a pole as big as Toledo up his butt," Suzanne said.

Angela waved her arms. "Oh, that was just the way he was at work. And he had to be that way, to get things done. Outside of work, he's a lamb in wolf's clothing." She turned and looked at the girls. "He won't let me pay for anything—not even a pack of cigarettes. Can you imagine?"

Suzanne mimed putting her finger down her throat and gagging. "Yuck!" she said. Molly snorted, trying not to laugh.

"Fine. Make fun," Angela said. "But he's turning my life around and that will turn your lives around with it. And then you'll both thank me. You really will."

Angela kept promising they would all have dinner together to get to know one another. That maybe they would even take a vacation. "He's dying to know my family," Angela said. "And he knows some very classy restaurants." But there never were any dinners. Never any vacations. Usually, Angela and Lars went to dinner right after work, and then someplace else. The only times the girls saw Lars was the few times he came to the house to pick Angela up.

The first time Molly saw Lars, she thought he looked even worse than Angela's description. Everything about him was long and narrow and dark, as if he were in perpetual shadow. He was in a heavy brown suit and white shirt and his tie was a neon yellow. His hair was thatchy and gray and his eyebrows thick and unruly. When he looked at Molly, his eyes seemed to bore right into her. "Hello, you must be Molly," he said stiffly. His smile was one long tight line.

"Pleased to meet you," Molly forced herself to say.

"I'm Suzanne." Suzanne stepped forward and then Lars's face changed, but he wasn't focusing on Suzanne. He stepped past her, his smile widened. "Angela, you look lovely," he said warmly, and Suzanne stepped back, stung.

It didn't take Molly more than two minutes to see how smitten Lars was with Angela. He couldn't take his eyes off her, couldn't stop leaning toward her, as if she were a magnet and he was iron, irresistibly pulled.

"We hope we'll know you a lot better," Molly said, and Lars turned from Angela and looked at Molly with a kind of surprise, almost as if he had forgotten she was there.

Molly watched Angela and Lars leaving from the front window, her nose pressed up against the glass. Lars held Angela's arm as if she were a piece of spun glass. He smiled when he talked to her. Angela's laugh was so loud you could hear it through the window. She kept touching Lars, too, faint, tentative taps as if she might be getting shocks. She kept looking at him as if she had to make sure he was really there. When they got to the car, he stopped and cupped her face in his hands. And then he opened the door and helped her in, and the car drove away.

It was the year Angela disappeared from the house even more, and the year, Molly thought, that Suzanne did, too. Suzanne now balked at doing the housekeeping. She frowned and sniped at Molly. "You buy the damned groceries," she said. "You pick up the dry cleaning and tend the house. I did it long enough." She left the grocery lists, scribbled in Angela's hand, for Molly to take care of. She let the laundry pile up, six overflowing bags every few days, and pointed Molly toward the detergents. Molly stared at the bleach, at the soaps, at the complicated-looking dials on the washing machine. "How do you do this?" Molly asked, but Suzanne waved a hand. "You know how to read. The directions are right there in front of you. Just separate the darks and lights or Angela'll get pissed."

Molly fumbled with the laundry. She carried four loads up and down the stairs and by the time she was finished she was so exhausted she could barely move, and there was still more to be done. How did Suzanne do this? How did anyone? She did the shopping and cleaned the house, scrubbing at the floors furiously, slamming groceries into the cabinets. She was now so busy all the time that she didn't have time to call her friends, who got tired of her not even being able to gossip with them a little, who began to fade away from her, to close their ranks. She had to leave books half read for so long that by the time she picked them up, she forgot where she had left off.

When Angela got home, Molly was indignant. "I did four loads of laundry," she complained. "I didn't even do my homework yet."

She thought Angela might get angry at Suzanne, she thought at least Angela would thank her or praise her, but instead, her mother seemed preoccupied. "Next time, use starch on these shirts," Angela said.

Suzanne stopped coming home for dinner. She didn't come home at midnight, even though Molly waited up for her, staring out the window, worried, wondering what had happened, so exhausted she couldn't see straight, and so anxious she couldn't have slept if she'd wanted to. Suzanne usually managed to make it home minutes before Angela. She'd whisk into the house. "You still up?" she said to Molly. Suzanne threw off her clothes and flopped into bed. She turned her back to Molly, facing the wall, dreaming.

One night Molly heard a great roaring outside. It was past midnight, about the time Suzanne might be coming home, hours before Angela would show up. Molly went to the window and there was this bruised old car, the doors open, and leaning on it was this beautiful black-haired boy, and he was kissing her sister Suzanne. Molly held her breath. She touched her own mouth, the roaring sounding deep inside of her.

His name was Ivan. He had just moved to town and even though half the girls in Suzanne's class were in love with him, he loved Suzanne and Suzanne loved him back. Molly found all this out snooping in Suzanne's room, reading the love letters he wrote to her that Suzanne didn't even bother to hide. She traced her fingers over Ivan's words.

Molly looked at Suzanne with a new kind of wonder. Love had done something to her sister. Suzanne seemed perpetually flushed, as if heat were shimmering from her skin. She was always half smiling, as if she knew this great and wonderful secret.

One day, while digging around in Suzanne's things, Molly found a silvery locket, a heart as big as her fist. She put it over her head, and then opened it. There was Ivan staring out at her. There was Suzanne's picture next to it. Molly slipped the locket over her head, took it off, and then hid it deep in her purse.

That night, Suzanne went crazy looking for her locket. She tore the house apart, flinging everything out of her drawers, and the whole time, Molly sat quietly, her heart pounding. *Just one day*, Molly told herself. *I just want to wear it one day.*

Suzanne left early for school the next morning and Molly spent the time cutting out a tiny picture of herself and squeezing it over the one of Suzanne in the locket. Molly wore Suzanne's necklace to school, and almost instantly things began to happen for her. It was almost as if some of Suzanne's power had rubbed off on her through the locket. She could do anything now. Nothing scared her. Karen O'Brien, who sat beside her in English class and even though she had the biggest mouth in the whole school never said two words to her, came in and suddenly nodded at Molly. "Cool locket," she said, and Molly looked up. Karen was still watching her. "So, whose picture is in there?"

Molly flipped it open. Karen sucked in a breath. "Holy moly!" She looked at Molly with new respect. "Who is *that?*"

Molly hesitated for only a minute. She drew herself up, breaking into a triumphant smile. "My boyfriend," Molly said.

By sixth period, it was all over school. That big frizzhead, that knock-kneed Molly Goldman, had a boyfriend like you wouldn't believe. Suddenly, people wanted to know her. Cora Fisher, the head cheerleader, stopped Molly in the bathroom. "I love that shade of lipstick," she said. Michael Sherman, who had broken up the whole homeroom the other morning by loudly asking Molly if she took double her dose of ugly pills that day, nodded pleasantly at her. "How ya doin', Molly?" he said.

Molly didn't mean to lie, and sometimes she worried, because what if someone knew Ivan or a friend of Ivan's, what if it got back to Suzanne? But it felt so good to have people wanting to talk to her, and after a while, she got so good at telling stories, it began to feel real to her.

Molly began to look at the locket as hers. She wore it every day, taking it off blocks before she got home, stuffing it deep in her purse. She created a whole life for herself and she now had plenty of time to do it because Suzanne wasn't coming home until two or three in the morning, and Angela sometimes wasn't coming home at all, and when she did, she had a new faraway look on her face Molly didn't recognize.

"How's Lars?" Molly said, to be polite.

Angela smiled. "He made me pancakes this morning. All I did was mention I liked pancakes two weeks ago, and I woke up to them today. Fresh blueberry pancakes. He wouldn't even let me carry the dishes to the sink, let alone do them." She shook her head. "They were the worst pancakes I have ever tasted, but they were also the most delicious. Do you understand what I mean?"

"Maybe *I* would have liked some pancakes," Molly said, but Angela was yawning, heading for the shower.

Well, so what. Molly told herself she had Ivan. Ivan didn't care that Molly was younger, he thought she was mature for her age. Ivan took her dancing. He wrote her love letters and bought her gifts. Molly talked so much about how Ivan loved her, that after a while she was in love with him herself. Anything could happen, she told herself. Suzanne was fickle and in great demand. She could change her mind and be in love with someone else already. Ivan could come to the house pining for her. He could look up at her window and see Molly and be suddenly struck. *My own true love*, he might think.

But Suzanne kept her same dreamy look, and no one ever came to the window except an occasional squirrel. And then one night, Molly was woken up at five in the morning to hear Suzanne and Angela arguing on the front lawn. Molly looked outside. Angela was shaking her head in disgust, screaming at Suzanne. "Don't you ever make me call the police again! Don't you ever make me worry like that!" Angela grabbed Suzanne's shoulders and shook her, but Suzanne was looking beyond Angela, and Molly followed her gaze. She tugged back the curtain so she could see better, and there, like a shock, was Ivan, jumping into a green car and driving away.

There were days of terrible fights. Angela had to leave work four different times to go see Suzanne's principal because Suzanne had skipped so many days of school, she was in danger of not graduating. Angela had had to talk to the manager of Woolworth's because Suzanne had been so lost in reverie about Ivan that she had walked out with a scarf in her pocket and they had nabbed her for shoplifting. Angela and Suzanne shouted and screamed at each other, while Molly sat in her room with her hands clapped over her ears. "To think I had to talk to your principal! I had to talk to Woolworth's Security!" Angela shouted. "The way they looked at me! The way they talked!"

"What's the matter, it eat into your busy schedule?" Suzanne shouted back. "It stop you from trying to bag your precious Lars? You want to ground me, then you'll have to stay here, too, and you can't stand it either."

Angela kept shouting, but Suzanne slammed into the bedroom, ignoring Molly, pulling on her Walkman and the headphones, turning it up so loud Molly could hear the bass, and then Suzanne would squinch her eyes shut and dance, wildly waving her arms, stomping her feet, her face so set and angry, it worried Molly to see it.

One night, Suzanne didn't get home until four in the morning. Angela was beside herself. "Where could she be?" she cried. She called the police, Molly sitting beside her on the kitchen stool. "They said they can't do anything for fourteen hours!" Angela said. She went to the front window and peered out and then she came back to the kitchen and called the local hospitals. "Suzanne Goldman?" she asked. Nobody knew anything. Angela was so terrified she couldn't sit still. "You can't imagine what can happen," she told Molly. "She should be home, the way she belongs. If she would just listen to me . . ." her voice trailed off. She threw open the front door and stood out on the dewy grass in her bare feet and robe, straining at the road. "I'm calling Lars. He'll know what to do—" she started to say, and then, there in the distance, swinging her pocketbook, taking her own sweet time, was Suzanne.

Molly had never seen her mother so furious. Angela strode to Suzanne and grabbed her by the shoulders. Suzanne's head snapped back and forth. Her hair flew into her face like an angry black cloud. "Are you trying to kill me?" Angela shouted. "Are you trying to drive me insane?"

Suzanne wrenched free. A light flickered on in a house across the street. "What do you care?" Suzanne cried. "What business is it of yours what I do?"

Neither one of them saw Molly running out, trying to get in the middle of them. "Will you two please stop?" Molly screamed.

Angela blinked at her as if she had just noticed her there. "Get in the house," Angela said.

"Mind your own damned business. It has nothing to do with you—" Suzanne said. She whipped back around to Angela. "I hate you—" she started to say and then Angela struck her, and Suzanne's hands flew to her face. She bolted back, shocked.

"Don't—" shouted Molly.

Angela struck at Suzanne again, striking her on the shoulder, her back, not caring when Suzanne tried to shield herself with her hands. Angela kept hitting Suzanne, again and again, her words emphasizing every blow. "I'm sick of this! When you're eighteen, you can do what you want. But as long as you live in my house, you play by my rules!"

Suzanne was so silent, it terrified Molly. Suzanne straightened up, letting her hands fall back down to her sides, staring at Angela, who was panting, who had finally stopped hitting her. Suzanne turned and walked out into the night, turning a corner, not once looking back.

Molly couldn't move.

Angela violently started back to the house. "I thought I told you to get inside," she ordered Molly. She yanked open the door. She violently turned the lock, and then she whipped around to Molly. "You go to bed," she said.

Suzanne didn't come home. The next morning Angela went to the cops with Lars, but once they found out that Suzanne was seventeen, they stopped being so interested. "She'll come back," they said. "They always do."

But Angela didn't listen. She kept trying to find her. Molly heard her mother calling Suzanne's friends and teachers, her voice cracking with strain. She heard Angela calling Lars. "Help me think what to do," Angela pleaded.

Lars was there when Angela called Ivan's parents and the whole time she was on the phone, Molly was gripping the necklace. "I see," Angela said. "Well, that's fine and good, but I don't appreciate your tone."

"What? What?" said Molly.

Lars lifted a finger, shushing Molly. "Let your mother handle it," he said.

Angela frowned. "Nevertheless, I'd appreciate it if you'd call me if you get any word."

She hung up the phone and sat in the chair opposite Molly and

Lars. She looked suddenly old to Molly, and it frightened her. "She left with Ivan," Angela said. "His parents have washed their hands of him."

She swiped her hands wearily across her eyes. "This is just what I didn't want for her! She'll get trapped young, the way I was." She rubbed her eyes again, smudging rings of mascara on her face. She shook her head.

"Angela," Lars said. She stopped. He reached for Angela and made her look at him.

Angela leaned her head against Lars's shoulder, shutting her eyes. "I don't know what I would do if I didn't have you."

Molly left the kitchen. She went outside the front door and sat on the porch. Angela had Lars. Suzanne had Ivan. And Molly had no one.

Molly took off the locket and buried it deep in her drawer. She'd never wear it again. She'd never think of it if she could, but the next day at school, Mara Tushin, who won Prettiest Girl three semesters in a row, stopped her. "Hey, wait a minute. No locket today?"

Molly shrugged. Mara put one hand on her hip. "So how are things with you and Ivan? What are you two lovebirds up to these days?"

"We broke up," Molly blurted.

"No way! But that's awful!" Mara shook her head. "He do it or you?"

"I did it," Molly said. "And I don't want to talk about it."

Mara looked at her with great understanding. "I was exactly the same way when I broke it off with Wayne. And I agree totally. It's enough you hurt them. You don't need to spread salt in their wounds by jawing off about it. It's so much classier to just be quiet."

By sixth period, the news of Molly's breakup was all over school. The girls were solicitous. They didn't press her to talk. They looked at her with a new respect.

* * *

Molly waited. Every time the mail flopped in the slot, she ran to get it, sure there would be at least a postcard from her sister. Every time the phone rang, she jumped, her voice bright with expectation. She couldn't believe Suzanne wouldn't at least call her to let her know she was okay. "What if something happened to her?" Angela worried, but Molly just shook her head. She knew her sister. Knew nothing bad could ever happen to Suzanne.

And then, one night, when Molly and Angela were eating dinner, the phone rang. "It's probably Lars," Angela said, grabbing for the phone, and as soon as she spoke, her face changed.

"I should have guessed. California, the promised land," Angela said wearily. "Two wet-behind-the-ears kids. What are you living on, love?"

"Is that Suzanne? Let me talk to her!" Molly tried to grab the receiver, but Angela held it away. "What's she saying?"

"All right," Angela said. Her voice was calm. Steely. "I'll tell you what. If you can show me you know how to behave, you can come home. We can start from scratch." There was silence and then Angela quietly hung up the phone.

"Wait! I wanted to talk to her!" Molly cried, grabbing the receiver, but the line was gone, the wires hummed. "What did she say?"

"She hasn't learned. That's what she said," Angela said, leaving the room.

Molly grabbed the phone. She dialed the number Angela had scribbled on a pad by the phone, but she didn't get Suzanne. Instead, she got the machine, Suzanne's voice raspy from cigarettes saying that she and Ivan were out.

Molly kept trying to make contact. She wrote letters to Suzanne that Suzanne never answered. *I am sleeping with a boy,* Molly wrote, thinking that might get a response. *I think I may be pregnant.* It surprised her how much she missed her sister, how you could miss and yearn after a person who had stopped being around. Some nights, Molly lulled herself to sleep, she felt less alone by imagining that Suzanne was just outside the window, coming home from another adventure.

Finally, one day, Molly got Suzanne on the phone. "I want to come visit," Molly said and Suzanne laughed. "Visit where? We live in one room."

"Then come home."

Suzanne was silent for a moment. "I am home," Suzanne said quietly.

Molly had just gotten into college when Angela married Lars in front of a justice of the peace and right up until the last minute, everyone expected Suzanne to show up. Molly was in a new white dress, her hair held back with one of Angela's rhinestone clips. Molly couldn't get over how her mother looked. Like a young girl. As if she were dipped in powdered sugar.

Angela was fine until right before the ceremony. And then she suddenly excused herself. Molly could see her on the phone, shaping the air with her hands, talking, and then hanging up. Angela looked at Lars, and then shrugged. "Never mind," Lars said, taking Angela's hand. "I don't even want to know the excuse." He took Molly out to dinner with them to Chinoise, which was supposed to be the best Chinese restaurant in town, but Molly had no appetite. She fiddled with her chopsticks. She rearranged her sweet-and-sour prawns on the plate, her gluey brown noodles, and she kept thinking about Suzanne.

Angela and Lars were going to move to Florida, where Lars was going to go in with his brother on a gift shop. Angela gave her the house, putting it into Molly's name so "you'll always have something." Molly had never seen Angela more happy. She seemed to dance instead of walk. Her voice lilted. Glints of light sparked off her hair. She looked like the girl in the Miss California Beach photo. "From now on, all I'm going to work on is my tan," Angela announced.

Lars, polite and distant to Molly, petted her awkwardly on the shoulder. "We'll have an extra room for you. Anytime you want to come and visit."

"You'll come this winter," Angela said, "or the spring." She looped her arm around Lars, tugging him close to her. *Visit*, Molly thought.

Maybe this winter. She nodded brightly. She acted like that was the best idea she had ever heard of.

It wasn't a bad life. Molly went to school, became a grade-school teacher. She had the house. She was happy enough, content, and so busy she didn't really have time to think about how lonely she was. She spoke to Angela every Sunday on the phone when the rates were cheaper, when Angela might be at home instead of out on the golf course or at the beach or shopping with Lars, and although Angela always seemed happy enough to hear from her, when she mentioned Molly visiting, she was always pushing the date ahead. The next summer. The next fall. Winter, when Molly could really appreciate that wonderful Florida sun.

Molly called Suzanne, who was friendly and distant and who never once called her. And then, in her first year of teaching third grade, she got a phone call from Lars. "My poor Angela," he said, weeping, and then he stopped talking. He sobbed. Molly froze.

Angela had died in a car crash. She wasn't even going that fast, just from the condo to the supermarket to pick up some suntan lotion when a truck simply plowed into her. She was killed instantly.

"I'll get the next flight out. I'll call Suzanne—"

"No. I'm not having a service. I'm not burying her. I'm not scattering the ashes." He snuffled into the phone. "Let them cremate her. I won't be a part of it."

Molly called Suzanne, who cried helplessly.

"Please, come here. I need to see you," Molly said. "I can't get through this by myself." Suzanne was silent. "Or I'll come there. I can take some time off school."

"No, don't come here. Look, maybe I'll come there. I'll call you."

Molly waited. She roamed the house, she wept, but Suzanne never called. And when Molly, desperate, wanting to talk, called her again. Suzanne's line was disconnected. Molly stared at the phone in disbelief. How could Suzanne do this? How could she be this way? How could she leave Molly so alone with this?

Molly called Lars a week later. He barely spoke, and finally he said that talking to her was just too hard. "You understand," he said. "Sometimes it's better to just forget everything. And everyone."

Angela had left a little money. Five thousand Lars had invested for her, half for Molly, half for Suzanne. The house was Molly's. And if Molly was sometimes lonely, if some nights she grieved for her mother so hard she thought she was going mad, she told herself it wouldn't always be that way.

She kept waiting for Suzanne to call her, veering between fury and need. A few times she sent her sister cards to her old address, always with the words "Where are you?" scribbled across them. She was careful to write her return address, and the cards never came back, but she never heard from Suzanne, either. Not until the spring, when Suzanne called her.

In the background, Molly heard loud music. "Where were you?" Molly said.

Suzanne gave an odd, dry laugh. "What do you mean, where was I? I've been right here."

"Your line was disconnected!" Molly accused. "You never answered my cards!"

Suzanne was silent for a minute. "I was suffering, too," she said quietly.

"But you had Ivan. I was all alone here."

"I don't have Ivan. He left."

"Ivan left—?"

"I don't want to talk about it," Suzanne interrupted. She drew in a breath. "Anyway, what's important is that I'm calling you now, right?"

"Right." Molly knew better than to try to push Suzanne. She wrapped the phone cord around her hand. She waited.

Suzanne hesitated. "Listen, could I borrow some money, do you think?" Her voice rushed on. "It's not that much. I'm going to Beauty

Culture School now and I'm a little short on tuition. Five hundred would do it."

"But what about Mom's money?"

"That was gone a long time ago."

"It's gone?" Molly said, shocked. "All of it? How could it all be gone?"

"I have expenses," Suzanne said stiffly. "It's very expensive here. I didn't get a house the way you did. Come on, I can pay you back."

Molly mentally added up her expenses for the month. Food. The car. Heat and electricity. She needed a new winter coat desperately.

"Please. I'm really desperate, Molly."

Molly made a final calculation. She could swing it. "I'll put it in the mail tomorrow."

Three weeks later, Molly was writing spelling words on the blackboard, listening to the musical groans of her class when a monitor, a sixth-grade girl in a red dress, came into the room and handed Molly a note. "*Personal* phone call at the office." Molly put the chalk down. Her class hushed, watching her with interest. Mrs. Daisy, the principal, hated personal phone calls. "Be right there," Molly told the monitor, and then went to open the door between her room and the next, to beckon to the teacher to please watch her class.

The school secretary sighed when she handed the phone to Molly. "Keep it short," she told Molly.

"Oh, thank God you're there!" Suzanne cried.

"Could you call me at home? We're not supposed to get personal calls at work——" Molly said, loud enough so the secretary could hear.

"No, no, I can't! My rent is already three weeks late. I have to give them the money by this Friday. Please. Just this once. It's just five hundred. That's all."

The secretary loudly stapled papers together. She looked pointedly at her watch and then at Molly. She looked over at Mrs. Daisy's open office door.

"Okay, okay," Molly said. "I'll send it. Just call me at home from now on."

Molly gave Suzanne the rent check, and though she waited and waited, though she sorely could use the money, Suzanne never paid her back. And Suzanne began calling more and more, and always for money. Five hundred dollars there. A thousand for a collection agency. Two hundred for a dental bill insurance wouldn't cover. "Just until I finish school," Suzanne said.

Molly sighed. She reached for her checkbook, glancing at the balance. She had never let herself get this low before. She'd have to fudge a few bills this month. Pay a little portion so they wouldn't hound her so much. And she'd have to forget about the new coat she needed. She'd have to make do with what she had.

Molly's finances were getting screwy. She had a second notice on some bills. She even had a notice from a collection agency. She began to worry. It was just her, all alone; what if something happened? She was a new teacher without tenure. Already, Mrs. Daisy had intimated that Molly's review could suffer if she kept getting personal calls, if the calls kept disrupting her class. She could be fired, and then what would she do? It wasn't so easy to get a teaching job, especially if you had lost one. She had read in a magazine that you should have money in your account, enough to last a year if you had to, if you were fired, and Molly now had barely enough for three months, and it began to worry her. Because of all the money she was loaning Suzanne, she was late on the gas bills, on her car insurance, and her car was making funny noises. And she was beginning to get a little scared. She knew Suzanne was in trouble, but she couldn't let her pull her down with her.

Late one night, the phone rang. Startled, Molly picked it up.

"Listen." It was Suzanne, clear-voiced, bright and happy. "I'm going to open my own shop!"

"That's great—"

"I'll start small, and then expand with the business. I already have people lined up. If you can loan me just a little money—"

Molly had barely scraped by this month because of all the money she had loaned Suzanne. Her savings were next to nothing. "Suzanne. I can't."

"Five thousand. That's all. I know teachers don't make that much, but five thousand is nothing."

"No, it's not that I won't. I can't. I can't pay my own bills. I don't have five thousand. I don't even have five hundred." As soon as she said it, she felt sick. How could she manage on just five hundred?

"Molly, I took care of you for years. I did everything. You know I did. You remember. Can't you help me now? I'll pay you back in six months at the latest."

"Suzanne, you've never paid me back ever before! Not even a part! I must have given you thousands of dollars!"

"Now, wait a minute. That doesn't mean I'm not going to—"

"No," Molly said, "I can't—"

"Or you won't," said Suzanne bitterly, and then she slammed down the phone.

For weeks, every time the phone rang, Molly tensed. At school, every time a monitor came into the room, Molly felt frozen, but it was always just a message about milk money or recess duty. Suzanne never called Molly back. And after another while, Molly began to realize that she wasn't tense at night anymore, that a hall monitor could come into her room and she didn't instantly freeze.

Suzanne had an unlisted number. Molly wrote it on a piece of paper and put it into an acrylic puzzle she had and snapped it shut. She thought suddenly of what Lars had said about Angela. Sometimes you needed to forget. Sometimes you needed a little distance.

When they were kids, Suzanne's recklessness had always drawn her like a magnet. Molly had wanted to be like Suzanne, a beautiful, glowing flame. Brave, strong, a girl who flung herself headlong into danger and came out on top. Just being near her had made Molly feel she could survive any trouble, too. Or if she couldn't, that Suzanne could save her from it. But now Suzanne was wildfire. And if Molly wanted to survive, she would have to get out of Suzanne's path.

She began to put away money again, to like her life again. She thought it was a good one. She was taking care of herself. There was just her, but it felt okay. It felt safe. She had thirty kids she loved and a few friends at school, and a house. Nights she began going to the Tastee because the waitresses let her stay there as long as she wanted. No one bothered her, and she liked the light and the noise. She could sit there and read and listen to the music and get fat on ice cream. And that could be enough.

And then she had met Gary, and everything had changed all over again.

chapter

three

Gary bought a cheap camera and began taking pictures of Molly. He stashed photos of her in his apartment, in his pocket, in his office desk drawer so every time he'd go to grab a pen, he'd see her face, every time he opened a cabinet, there she was before him. He called her four times a day, not at school where he might get her into trouble, but leaving long funny messages on her machine at home, waiting for her to pick up, to call him back on one of the school's pay phones.

He even came to her school once, taking half the day off to pick her up. He got there early, when she still was on bus duty, but he stood outside his car and watched her. The other teachers were standing together, their hands burrowed into their pockets. They looked weary. But Molly was zooming up and down the bus lines, flashing smiles, joking with the kids, her wild hair like a parade unfurling behind her. She didn't see him, not yet, but she saw a little woeful-looking boy standing apart from everyone else, his hands balled into his pockets, and she strode over to him and crouched down and said something to him, and he suddenly threw back his head and laughed, and then she laughed, too. She zipped upright, bounding toward another group of children straggling into their bus, and Gary saw how the boy's eyes followed Molly, how they wouldn't let go.

Gary held Molly's hand during dinner, on their walks, and once in the subway, on a crowded E train. The doors slid open and a man barreled through, dislodging Gary's grip. He reached back his hand for hers, twining his fingers into those of a surprised old man while Molly, in the corner, watched laughing. At night, he hooped his arms about her, he held her. She sighed and stretched and she looked so suddenly tiny to him, so childlike. He put one hand gently on the top of her hair. He held it there. She turned and looked at him, sleepily. "What are you doing? Is my hair too scratchy?"

"I'm protecting you," he told her.

They planned to get married in the fall, in a judge's study in Manhattan, with just a few friends present. By then, they were living out of each other's houses, but Molly was superstitious and wanted to go home to dress. "It's bad luck to see the bride before the wedding." She laughed. "I'll meet you there."

They spent the night before their wedding at Gary's place. In the morning, he woke to find Molly already up, sitting in the kitchen, nursing a cup of tea. Her face was thoughtful, a little sad, and he sat beside her. "What's wrong?"

"Oh, I was just thinking about my mother's wedding. The thing I remember most was Suzanne not being there."

Molly started to take a sip of tea and then put the cup down. "Do you think I'm awful for not inviting her? For not calling her?"

"No. I don't want anything or anyone to hurt you. Or us. And anyway, she should have called you."

"I guess you're right," Molly said, but she still sounded doubtful. She got up and put her cup in the sink, and when she turned back to him, she was smiling. "Well, I had better get going." She leaned forward to kiss him playfully. "I'm getting married today!"

Molly went home and he dressed, in his best navy jacket, his good black pants. Six people from his job were coming, a few teachers from

Molly's school, and a few friends of Gary's: Bob and Rayanna, Peggy and Allan. He grabbed for his tie, thinking about Molly at her mother's wedding, Suzanne not being there, and then he glanced at the photo on his dresser: his aunt Pearl, in blue jeans and a sweatshirt, laughing into the camera, her arms circled about his shoulders, the two of them leaning on her car in an empty supermarket parking lot. He remembered that day. He had been ten and upset about not making the soccer team at school. "Oh, posh," Pearl had said. "Anybody can play soccer. But how many people can *drive* at ten?"

"Not me," he said, and then he saw the look in her eyes.

"We'll see about that," she said and held up her car keys.

She had taken the camera to commemorate his first lesson. She had let him drive around and around the parking lot until he was laughing and then she had set up the timer and taken the shot.

He touched her face in the photo and he suddenly felt pained. He wanted her to be at his wedding. He wanted his parents or a relative or a sibling. He thought of Molly, the way she had looked at the photograph of her mother, the hard yearning way she had just spoken about her sister. He wanted family there with him, too.

He was five minutes early to the judge. He stood, nervous and awkward, and then Molly rushed into the room.

He felt stunned by the sight of her. She was in a long, shimmering column of pale blue velvet, her feet were nearly bare in thin black high heels, and she had braided bits of tiny blue flowers throughout her hair. Her face was flushed and she looked at him, and then away, suddenly bashful.

All through the ceremony, he was aware of her beside him, like a force field blocking everything else out. He couldn't hear a word the judge was saying, couldn't hear the chamber music they had arranged to play on a boom box. Instead, he heard Molly breathing. He heard the rustle of her dress, the sound her shoes made on the floor whenever she made the slightest move. Her hair rippled along her back. Her fingers curled and uncurled about his, and he heard his own heart pulsing toward hers. And then he heard the judge say, "Go ahead and kiss," and the words were like a shock in the silence and Gary moved through the force field toward Molly. Her eyes were clear and wide open and suddenly it didn't matter at all that Pearl wasn't there or Suzanne or Angela or his parents, because Molly was right there before him. She was all the family he would ever need.

Molly sold her house in Elizabeth. He had thought it might be hard for her, because it had been her mother's house, a last vestige of family, and when he noticed her standing in the rooms, one hand tracing a wall, he came up behind her and slung one arm about her shoulders. "Did you want to stay in this house?" he asked. "We could probably squeeze in here."

She shrugged. "It's just a house," she said quietly. "We'll have our own."

With the money she made from the sale, and his own savings, he was certain they could find something close to the city. They spent weekends scouring Manhattan, not being able to afford even a studio. They went farther out to Brooklyn, to Park Slope, and finally began looking back in Jersey City in New Jersey.

It was a changing area. Hardscrabble, but pocketed with good houses, with lofts. Artists were moving in, writers, Wall Streeters. And it was only a seven-minute PATH train ride to the city. And not a bad commute to Elizabeth and Molly's school.

A realtor showed them twenty different houses, and two lofts, and all of them were way out of their price range, and finally, just as they were about to give up, she showed them one house they could afford and bid on, a two-story row house in need of repairs. "Ah, the miracle house," he overheard the realtor say to herself, but Gary wasn't sure whether she meant it was a miracle they had found it or a miracle the house was ever sold, and he could never bring himself to ask.

The house was painted the same bright blue as the house attached to it. It had two baths, a mahogany staircase, and four big rooms Gary and Molly counted out. "Our bedroom," Molly said, stepping into the biggest and sunniest.

"Office," Gary said when he was in the smallest.

They walked over to the side-by-side smaller rooms. Molly turned to face him. "Baby's room," he said, making her smile. She looked at the other room. "Guest room," he said, but Molly shook her head. "Another baby's room." Their grins widened.

The kitchen was old, with boxy yellow cabinets and pink linoleum. One of the two bathrooms had three kinds of pastel-colored tile and green plaid wallpaper. Molly ran her hand over the silver foil wallpaper in the hall, over the yellow plastic light fixtures and wood paneling. There was wall-to-wall blue shag carpeting, lowered acoustical ceilings, and a claw-footed tub painted pink.

"It's just cosmetic stuff. We can fix it," Gary said. "We have all the time in the world."

Their neighborhood was predominantly Italian, a mix of brownstones and row houses painted over in violet and pale green and blue, hung with awnings, festooned with flags. There were small front yards and stoops to sit on, and square backyards that were large enough for a garden and a deck. The realtor had told them that people had lived in these houses their whole lives, they had married and raised children right in the confines of three or four blocks, and even though Manhattan was seven minutes away, most of them never left the neighborhood, never thought or wanted to. Manhattan could have been a foreign country. "You know what they call the bad side of town here?" the realtor had confided. "Brooklyn."

The first day they moved in, three weeks before Halloween, the neighborhood seemed empty. Almost every house had a stoop or a porch, but no one was there. The windows were heavily curtained, the doors were firmly closed. But signs of life, Halloween decorations, were everywhere. Paper witches hung in the windows. Scarecrows positioned on the roof, gaily waving in the wind. Blinking orange and black lights circled the doorways and slung along the iron railings. Across the street was a six-foot-tall stuffed Dracula complete with drips of red blood. "Must be a lot of kids," Molly said.

But they didn't see any kids, didn't hear the shouts and squeaky bicycle wheels and bumping balls that went along with children. In fact, the only person they saw was a young woman in a black leather jacket and jeans, who stopped to watch the movers. She waved and introduced herself, her stubby brown ponytail bobbing behind her. "I live on the far end of the block," she said. "Lisa Jordan." She worked in marketing in the city, her husband Timothy was a lawyer. She loved the neighborhood, but hated the nosiness of the neighbors. "You can't sneeze without one of the neighbors commenting on it."

"What neighbors? Where? We haven't seen a soul yet," Molly said, and Lisa laughed.

"Ah, but they see you," she told them, rolling her eyes. "You just wait. They know everything and they'll comment on it, soon enough."

Gary did his best to find other neighbors, to connect, but more and more, he began to feel that he was lying in wait. He was watering plants in the living room when he happened to look out the window and see a middle-aged woman and a man he assumed was her husband emerging from the house on his left. Watering can still in hand, he pushed open the front door and stepped outside. He waved and said hello, he introduced himself. The woman blinked doubtfully at him. "Emma Thorton," she finally said. "This is my husband Bill." They were polite, guarded. They looked at him as if he were somehow dressed wrong.

"Would you like to come in and have coffee?" Gary asked.

Bill tapped at his watch and then took Emma's arm. "We have to go. We're late as it is."

It bothered Gary. He thought of his friends Bob and Rayanna in Boston, where every month they had a different block party. He remembered Allan's chunky white house in Ithaca, his big backyard where he threw barbecues in a neighborhood so safe, he swore he left his door open and never worried once about it. Even Gary's old neighborhood in Chelsea had been friendlier than this one.

* * *

Finally, one night, when he and Molly were coming home from a movie in the city, Molly suddenly pointed. "Look." He followed her finger. A group of neighbors were sitting on the porch next to their house, lazily talking. "It's showtime."

"Hello," Gary called. The neighbors looked up. They grew suddenly silent, watchful, as if they were studying him. Gary recognized Bill and Emma, but there was a surly-looking teenaged girl there with them, her hair dyed white, a rooster shelf combed high on her forehead. There was a woman with short black hair and a flowery dress, a bald man in a brightly patterned shirt chain-smoking.

"We've been hoping to meet all our neighbors——" Molly said.

The woman in the flowery dress nodded. "Theresa," she said. "Theresa Morella." The bald man was her husband Carl, a retired factory worker, and the surly girl was Emma's sixteen-year-old daughter Belle. "Where did you live before?" Theresa asked.

"New York."

"Cool," Belle said. Her face softened. She pulled up from her slouch and looked hopefully at Gary. "Where? In the Village? In SoHo?"

"Chelsea."

"I've been to Chelsea."

"When have you been to Chelsea?" Emma said sharply.

"I'm from Elizabeth," Molly said.

There was another long silence, and because he felt awkward, Gary began to ask questions. "Where's the best place to get groceries?" he wanted to know, even though he had already found a Korean greengrocer's he and Molly liked. "Where's the nearest PATH train station?" he asked even though he took it every day to work.

"Are you leaving the house the way it is?" Carl asked suddenly.

"Pretty much——" Gary said.

"Because the people who moved in across the street gutted a perfectly good house, changed it all around. The fumes were so terrible, Theresa was throwing up, I had headaches."

Theresa touched one hand to her head. "It took me months to feel better."

"I don't think we'll be doing anything with fumes."

Bill nodded. "There was construction going on for almost a year. You couldn't park anyplace. You couldn't breathe the air. The Dumpsters took up four parking places. Then as soon as the house was done, they sold it." He snapped his fingers. "Just like that."

"I never liked those people," Emma interrupted. "They put on airs. And they never had curtains in their windows. And that music. Remember that music?"

Belle rolled her eyes. "Big deal. Classical music." She looked at Molly and mock whispered, "They were from *New York*."

"Don't you be so fresh." Emma said.

The talk wound down, the neighbors became silent. "Well, we'd better be going," Gary said finally. None of the other neighbors made a move to leave. Theresa stretched out her legs and scratched at her knee. Carl lit a fresh cigarette and handed one to Bill. "Nice to meet you!" Belle called. As Gary and Molly were leaving, she fanned her fingers in a good-bye wave, five, four, three, two, one, closed fist.

They had called Lisa once or twice to invite her to dinner, but each time she had always called back to cancel. "Work. You know how it is." She hung up without asking for their number and the next time he spotted her, on her way to the train, swinging a black leather briefcase, she waved vigorously with her free hand, but didn't stop. "I'm late!" she mouthed.

Gary and Molly painted the inside of the house a soft clear white. They polished the light fixture back to the original brass and took up the carpeting and the paneling. He had spent most of his life living in apartments, and it surprised him how different a house could feel, and how much he loved it. He and Molly sat out on the back porch and had breakfast. She looked so content and lovely that they both began to take their time getting to work, and Molly was late so often that the principal had called her into the office to reprimand her. Evenings, Gary couldn't wait to get home. She met him at the train station sometimes so they could walk home together, a bouquet of dandelions in her hand for him. And when she didn't get to the train, she was always waiting on the front porch, sitting alone, sometimes with a pint of ice cream with two spoons crisscrossed in the center.

They both kept trying to be friendly. Every time they encountered a neighbor, they tried to make small talk, to offer an invitation, and every time it was refused. Gary told himself it didn't mean anything, it was just a kind of shell they had to penetrate. Gary even brought home some of the kids books he had done, handing them out one evening to Bill and Carl. "For your grandkids," Gary said. Carl flipped the book over and over in his hands, frowning, as if he didn't know what to make of it, before grudgingly accepting.

The neighbors might have seemed disinterested, but Gary couldn't help noticing that every time he and Molly walked outside, a curtain would move. Every time he came home and grabbed a kiss from Molly or swept her hair from her face, a group of women down the street would go silent, considering them.

One afternoon, Gary had left the front door open to get something out of the trunk of the car, which was parked out front, and when he came back inside, he found Carl in the living room, looking around, scanning the walls, picking up a glass bowl on an end table and calmly studying it. "Something I can do for you?" Gary said, astonished.

"Just wanted to see how you changed things." Carl craned his neck, staring at the ceiling. "You put in new drywall?"

Gary tried to be polite. He let Carl examine the kitchen and the living room. He didn't say anything when Carl turned the new kitchen faucet on and off. "Cheaply made," Carl said. He tapped the cabinets. "You changed the knobs, too, I see."

Carl wound his way to the front of the house, rolling his palm thoughtfully on the wooden banister, staring critically at the bookshelves, at the bare wood floors. "Wood floors can be cold. We like to carpet."

"I like the wood."

"Well, you can always carpet later." Carl squinted up at the moldings on the ceiling. "You've done all you're going to do with this house?"

"Well, we might do a little more," Gary said. "You know, cosmetic stuff."

They were at the front door when Carl suddenly seemed to notice Gary's front windows. "Is something wrong?" Gary asked.

"You're not putting up any Halloween lights?"

Gary tried to be tactful. "I suppose if we had nieces or nephews or kids, we would."

Carl blinked at him. "What do kids have to do with it? It's decorations. It's beautifying. Used to be the whole neighborhood was blazing. Every holiday, too. Prettiest thing you ever saw in your life." He shook his head angrily, as if Gary had insulted him.

Gary let Carl out, but after that things seemed to change. Carl never seemed to forgive them. He began to find more and more wrong with everything they were doing. When they sandblasted the blue paint from their brick house, Carl called the police complaining of toxic fumes. "It's making Theresa ill," he complained, though Molly had spotted Theresa in the backyard just that morning, hanging up her wet wash, humming something low and deep in her throat. When they put up a six-foot wood fence in the backyard, instead of a short, open wire one the way everyone else did, Carl called the housing inspector to demand a stop, and when that didn't work, he tried to get a petition going in the neighborhood as a protest, sliding a scribbled list of names under Gary's door one night. Gary stared at the names. Mrs. John Storelli. Stan Lorenzo. He didn't recognize any of them. The fence stood, but for weeks afterward, they found tiny surprises on their porch. Cigarette butts when neither one of them smoked, candy wrappers, trash. And once, a small dead sparrow.

When they passed Carl and Theresa on the street, Molly would always smile. Theresa wavered, looking unhappily from Gary to Molly. "Hi, Theresa," Molly said, and then Carl began to whistle, something jangly and tuneless, and Theresa's gaze shot down.

"Theresa! Carl!" Gary called, but they kept walking, moving past them as if he and Molly were invisible.

*   *   *

That winter, the neighborhood blazed with Christmas lights. It snowed so heavily, the cars were buried. People put on skis to walk down the street, if they walked at all. The whole neighborhood seemed to be in hibernation, and it was that winter that Molly became pregnant, that spring when she began to show, and the neighbors began to take new notice of her.

In April, paper Easter bunnies and pastel eggs filled the windows, and the neighbors brought out brightly colored plastic lawn chairs and set them up near the sidewalks. Nights they would sit outside talking, sometimes having cups of lemonade or store-bought cake on paper plates, sometimes a radio playing beside them. A few kids ran around on the sidewalk, playing balls, shooting by on skateboards.

One day, Molly was sitting with Gary on the small front porch, her belly little more than a speed bump. Four months pregnant with a little boy they wanted to call Otis, when Emma came outside. She stared at Molly, as if she were trying to figure something out. "Hi," Molly said, the way she usually did, and this time Emma looked at her and then smiled. "It's a kind of gift I have, or maybe it's more like radar, but I can always tell. You're having a baby, aren't you?"

Molly grinned happily, put one arm about Gary, and then nodded.

"So you two are staying then?"

"Staying? Of course we are," Gary said.

"The Riders didn't stay. They gutted their whole house and redid it, but soon as their kid was old enough for kindergarten, they moved to Montclair. Same with the Morans. Only they went to Short Hills. Take my advice and don't listen when people tell you the schools here aren't good. All of my kids went to these schools and turned out just fine. This is a good place to raise a kid, to build a family."

"Well, we want to," Molly said.

Emma nodded at Gary. She leaned on their gate and talked to them. She looked down at Molly's belly. "You're carrying so high, I bet it's a girl. I'm almost never wrong."

"Boy according to the doctor." Molly had a sonogram photo of the baby she carried in her wallet, a small white foot pointed upward, a tip of a nose, a presence.

"Ha. Doctors don't know everything," Emma said. "They told me Belle was going to be a boy, too. Maybe it would have been better if she had been."

"Well, we have an extra bedroom, all painted pink, so if this one isn't a girl, maybe the next one will be." She laughed.

"The next one!" Emma nodded at her, pleased. Emma was so friendly that when Theresa walked by, Emma flagged her over. She put one arm about Molly. "She's having a little baby! Look at that sweet belly!"

Theresa exchanged glances with Emma.

"They're staying," Emma said.

Theresa sat down on the porch, stretching out her legs. "I don't think we've ever had the chance to really talk."

The neighborhood women never really became Gary and Molly's friends. They never invited either one to their bridge games or to sit in the park or over for dinner. No one ever asked Molly or Gary what they did or what book they might be reading or what movie they had just seen. But the whole time Molly was pregnant, they warmed to her as best they could. When they saw her, they called advice. "Stay off your feet," Emma told her. "Drink peppermint tea," Theresa advised and came over with a blue pitcher full of it, so sugary sweet Molly felt light-headed. The women stroked her belly, they praised her weight gain, they noticed the slight swelling in her ankles. Theresa wanted to know what names they had picked out, and when Molly said Otis, after Gary's favorite singer, Otis Redding, Theresa looked blank. "Well, isn't that nice," she said doubtfully. They were vociferous in their disapproval that Molly's doctor was not only a woman, but that Molly called her by her first name, Karen, and worse, that Karen was at Mt. Sinai in Manhattan. "Manhattan, are you insane? Why do you have to go all that far away for?" Emma said.

"No, no, it isn't far. And she delivers almost all of her patients' babies. Most of the other doctors have associates."

"Well, I don't know," Emma said. "You change your mind, I have a good doctor for you, the same one my niece used. Dr. Howard Crabbe. I don't know why you have to go all the way to New York when we have perfectly good doctors here."

The women never tired of talking to Molly about her pregnancy, although they never talked to Gary other than to warn him not to let Molly do too much. "She looks beautiful, your wife," Theresa told Gary. "Look at that belly on her." Her hands shaped form. The men wouldn't let Molly carry a grocery bag if they saw her, but they ignored Gary, especially Carl, whose whistling grew louder and more insistent. Only Belle seemed somewhere in the middle. She began to hesitate when she saw Molly, to stare, but she never said anything at all, and in the end, she kept walking.

Family, I have family, Gary exulted. He couldn't stop touching Molly's belly. At night, in bed, he lifted up her shirt and gave the baby advice.

"Always expect the best," he whispered. "Always try to be happy."

Molly threaded her hands through Gary's hair. "You big fool," she said affectionately.

He took photo after photo of her, of the house, sending copies to Bob and Rayanna, to Allan. "Now you have to come visit us," he wrote them. "We'll be the ones with a backyard barbecue this year, with bottles boiling on the stove." He kept a changing roster of her pictures up in his office, so all he had to do was look up and see her. His life seemed to shimmer in front of him, to sparkle.

He kept buying things for the baby. Teddy bears in T-shirts, plastic rattles and trucks and a tiny leather jacket that was so absurdly expensive he had to check the price tag twice before splurging on it anyway. Suddenly it didn't matter so much that the neighbors were still a little distant, that Carl's only response to them was still a sullen whistling. He had Molly. He had the baby. Every time he watched her walk down the hallway, swaying a little with her new weight, he felt dizzy in his happiness. He couldn't take his eyes off her, he couldn't keep his hands from her belly, from her hair, from the arch of her back.

But Molly suddenly began to worry.

She was six months pregnant when he found her at the kitchen table staring at books with titles like *Doctor, Is My Baby All Right?* and *When Things Go Wrong.*

"Molly, is this really necessary?"

She looked up at him helplessly. "I know the amnio was fine," she said. "And I know it's probably just hormones, but I can't help it."

"Molly, come on." He lifted the books from her hands. He made her come with him and take a walk. She tried to act light about it, but he saw how she began to be more and more careful. At dinner that night, she pushed aside her chocolate cake without tasting it. "Caffeine," she said wistfully. She rubbed at her temples. "Headache," she said, and when he reached for the aspirin bottle, she shook her head.

The next afternoon, he came home to find the counter was lined with vitamins, with teas with names like Babyease and Calciyummy and Pregnant Protection.

At night he woke up to find her sitting up straight, her hands on her belly. "PROM," she whispered to him.

"Excuse me?"

"The umbilical chord rushing out of you. The baby gets damaged."

"Molly."

"Cystic fibrosis. It can happen during birth, if there isn't enough oxygen."

"It's not going to happen."

"What if it does?" She had a list of terrors. Failure to thrive. Choking. She had heard two pregnant women in Karen's waiting room talking about a woman whose doctor had been on vacation and his associate doing the delivery had panicked during delivery and strangled the baby with the cord. "You can't go on vacation," Molly warned Karen. "You can't even go away for a weekend."

Karen half smiled. "Does the dry cleaners count?"

"Wear your beeper at all times."

Karen sighed. "Molly, you should just relax."

But the fear still lived in Molly, wild and restless, beating against her ribs. She kept a skittery list in her mind of all the things that could go wrong when she delivered. There would be a traffic jam in the tunnel. The car would break down, and she'd have to deliver it in a ditch and there wouldn't be enough oxygen for the baby to survive. She made Gary take the car for a tune-up even though he had had it checked months back. She made him buy a beeper. She bought books on home delivery that she studied at night as if she were taking a test. She knew three different kinds of breathing and a few exercises for self-hypnosis to help her relax. She quizzed herself, she quizzed Gary. "How many seconds between breaths?" she asked him. She wanted to be prepared.

"Everything is going to be fine," he told Molly. He lifted the T-shirt she slept in and kissed her belly. He reminded her how well she ate, how she had given up sweets and fats and salt.

"You haven't even had a cold," he reminded her.

She loved teaching, but she began to be glad the school year was ending. The school threw her a baby shower, her class made her thirty different cards, most of them with crayon drawings of storks on them *Come back*, they all said. *Come back to us next year.*

She stayed home, busying herself with projects. "The nesting in-stinct has kicked in big time," she told Gary. She began fixing up the baby's room, painting on a tiny border of zoo animals, hanging cur-tains. And then one day, he found her sitting on the front porch with Belle, and Belle was tying a blue rope bracelet about her wrist. "It's for luck," Molly said sheepishly. "Everyone at Belle's school wears them." She pulled at the bracelet, she tightened the knot.

In September, the week Molly was due, the neighborhood was cele-brating the Feast of Saint Ann. "Grandmother of Jesus, patron saint of motherhood," Emma explained to Gary. "The woman's saint." It was already four and growing dusky, and three different blocks were closed

off to traffic. People were crowding the streets, sitting on curbs, standing on the sidewalks, filling the porches. Emma had two small TV
trays set out on her porch filled with paper plates of zeppoles she kept
urging on neighbors. "Saint Ann, Saint Ann, send me a man," Emma
crooned, handing a pastry to Gary. A small parade had already come
by, ambling down the center of the road. Two dozen little girls in
blue satin costumes were tossing batons and high-kicking their tiny
white boots. A marching band was playing a horn-heavy, only slightly
out-of-tune serenade. Six men boosted up a life-sized statue of Saint
Ann, a pale, dark-haired woman, robed in blue, and pinned all over
her robe, like exotic flowers, were dollar bills. Emma nudged Molly.
"Go, put one on her. It's good luck."

"I can hardly walk," Molly said. She was wearing one of Gary's
-shirts over a black stretchy pair of pants. She fiddled with the brace
Belle had given her. An old woman in a black coat, a black kerchief
about her head, gave Molly a long, hard look, and then abruptly
crossed herself, spitting noisily three times into the street. Shocked,
Molly recoiled.

"Oh, no, no, don't look like that," Emma said. "She's keeping the
Evil Eye away from you."

"Oh." Molly looked uncomfortable. "The Evil Eye."

A woman with a newborn baby in a carrier strode by and waved
at Molly. "Don't worry, they do come out!" she called.

Emma dug into the pocket of her red pants. She put a dollar into
Molly's right hand and curled Molly's fingers over it, giving them a
little pat. "Go," she said. "My treat. Put it on Saint Ann. She'll give
you an easy labor."

Gary had stood on the porch, among the neighbors, watching
Molly, magnificently large, trailing into the crowd. Instantly, hands
were on her belly. She stumbled back a step.

Theresa's front door opened and Carl came out, two children lag-
ging behind him, a man Gary had never seen before, all of them carrying
boxes. "Here we are! Fireworks!" Carl announced.

Molly parted through the crowd. "There, now, don't you feel
better?" Emma asked.

Molly rested her head on Gary's shoulder. "I'm tired."

Carl waited until the parade had passed by and then he crouched and began to pull out the firecrackers, long red sticks that Gary stared at. He knew these kind. He had seen kids shooting them off in the Village, and once in his neighborhood in Chelsea, the explosion so loud, the cops had come to put a stop to it. Fireworks like these were illegal, but you could get them for the asking in Chinatown, you could buy them by the Holland Tunnel, hawked by kids.

"Carl—" he said, but Carl lighted one and the street boomed with noise. There was a flashing shower of red and green. Blasts of debris flaked onto the sidewalk, smattering like tiny bones. "Jesus," Gary breathed. Molly came to stand beside him, leaning against him, her hands soothing her belly. "I don't like this," she said.

The man Gary had never seen before, who had Carl's same crooked nose, his same beefy lower lip, pulled out a handful of firecrackers and handed one to a skinny boy in a plaid jacket. "Thanks, Dad," the boy said. The man took one step into the street, and there, a foot away from a car, set off a few. "Good one!" he called to Carl.

Carl bent down to pick up a firecracker. "Are you crazy?" Gary grabbed at Carl's sleeve, stepping back, away from the roar and color and light. "You can't set these kinds of fireworks off here. You can't let a kid shoot them off!"

The boy, firework fisted in his hand, glared at Gary. Carl jerked his arm free. "Are you going to start with this, too? We've been doing this for twenty years. My whole family, my grandkids, come for this. Just who do you think you are?"

Gary gestured. A little girl in overalls was running into the street, a firecracker in her hand. "There's little kids here. There's cars!"

Molly looked up at the maple tree in front of their house. She touched one of the branches. "You'll ruin the tree."

"Now you're being ridiculous." Carl snorted. Another toddler ran out into the street, a firecracker exploding above him. There was a sharp snap and pop and a wild fluttering of red and blue and green flying along the phone lines, raining down on the cars.

"This is madness!" Gary said. "You're going to hit someone's car, someone's child—these kinds of fireworks are illegal—they're dangerous—" He looked around. "Aren't there any police around here?"

Carl's face hardened. Emma and Theresa began to look uneasy. Carl started to say something, words hidden in the next booming explosion, when Emma touched Gary's elbow and pivoted him to Molly, who was suddenly sitting down on the porch, her hands cupped on her belly. Molly looked up at Gary and before she even said one word to him, he knew.

He didn't feel scared. Not then.

He ran for her hospital suitcase, packed with a new nightgown and robe he had bought her as a surprise, with the baby's first outfit, a green and white polka-dotted onesie with matching hat. She had packed a rubber ball and clean warm socks, and a lollipop, all the things the pregnancy books had suggested. He grabbed a still camera and helped Molly stand. A firecracker exploded over her head, raining rainbow streamers over the trees. Molly craned her neck. "It'll kill the trees."

"Good luck, honey," Emma cried. Carl moved deeper into the street, farther away from him. The women formed a half circle, waving at Molly, calling things to Gary that he couldn't hear because the firecrackers kept exploding. Colors crackled and popped around them.

The car was parked two blocks away, and even from there, he could still hear the bombs. The atmosphere seemed to shudder. He helped Molly in beside him. "How are you doing?" She nodded, her face tense and white. She leaned forward and jammed a fist against her back. "Back labor," she said.

The car glided. There was no traffic in the tunnel, the roads were clear, and he made it up to the Upper East Side in less than twenty minutes. "First labor is long," Karen had told them. "Some of my patients from Connecticut could walk here and be in time." As soon as he parked, he helped Molly into the hospital, where they got her into a wheelchair and set her up in a labor room, a small pale green room with no window. Molly grimaced. She started to do her Lamaze breathing. "Ha ha, hee hee. Please. I need an epidural." The nurse laughed and handed her a blue johnny. "Put this on."

Molly struggled with the cloth. "The epidural—"

They settled her up on a high bed with a monitor and a chair for Gary, the door wide open so the nurses could hear her. A tall nurse with a pixie haircut came in, smiling and laughing. "I'm Cat, your labor nurse." Her voice chirped. Her eyes were green marble. She tapped Molly on the shoulder. "Oh, now, come on and put that sad face away! You're going to get a baby out of this! I want to see nothing but smiles in this room!"

"Get her out of here," Molly whispered to Gary. "Don't make me have to kill her."

Cat hooked Molly up to the monitor. "I'll be back, sweetie."

They watched the contractions on the monitors, jagged mountainous lines. They could hear the other women, in other rooms nearby, moaning and shouting, calling out names. Ralph and Roy and John. "Get away from me! I hate you, Bob!" one woman shrieked. The women screamed for their mothers, for their fathers, for drugs and relief. One woman was screaming out the periodic table, punctuating it with tiny harsh intakes of breaths.

"I can't do this!" Molly, panicked, sat up. "I changed my mind."

A doctor in green scrubs came in, his hair hidden, his face smattered with acne. He looked fifteen, too young to be a doctor, and Molly shrank from him. She caught Gary's eye. She shook her head. The doctor smiled, showing braces. "Where's Karen?" she asked.

"Let's get you your epidural," he said and she suddenly relaxed. She smiled back. "There is a God," she said.

He turned her around. "Don't look." He wagged a finger at Gary, and Gary looked anyway, at the long skinny needle sliding into his wife's spine. He winced at the exact moment Molly sighed in relief.

When she turned around, her face was smooth, her breathing even.

"I'll be back to give you boosters. You just holler if you need me." He winked at Gary.

Molly slept through most of her labor, lulled by the epidural.

When she woke up, resurfacing as if from under deep water, she blinked at him, and then sleepily smiled. "It's not too bad," she told him. "It's not too bad." And then a contraction would grab at her, and she would bolt upright, straining for him, gripping his hand so hard, she left marks. She gritted her teeth. "I can do this," she insisted. "I can do this."

She had been in labor for three hours when she asked him when he was going to take pictures.

"Are you sure?" It had seemed like such a good idea documenting the birth, and now he wasn't so certain. He felt too nervous to focus the lens, his hands were too sweaty, his grip too loose. Molly posed, one hand behind her head. "Shoot."

He was giving her the camera, letting her take his picture, when Karen came in. She scooted beside Gary, leaning down. She was in blue scrubs, a shocking pink T-shirt poking up underneath the blue, her dark hair held back with a spangly red barrette. "Cheese," said Karen.

Karen turned and examined Molly. "Eight centimeters." She stood up, shaking her head, and patted Molly's knee. "Not yet."

Karen left the room and the teenaged-looking anesthesiologist entered. "Booster?" he said, and Molly nodded.

The epidural made her sleep again. Gary, though, didn't sleep at all. He didn't know what to do with himself. He found himself talking to Molly, even as she slept. "It's all right," he told her. "It's all right."

By three in the morning he began to hate everything in the room. He hated the narrow bed, damp with his wife's sweat. He hated Cat's cheeriness, the way she laughed at Molly and teased him. "This is a wonderful time!" she said. He felt like hitting her and seeing how wonderful she thought things were then. He hated the noise of the monitor, the numbers whirring and clicking, and most of all he loathed the clock planted on the wall right where he could see it, marking out the minutes, dragging the hours. Molly's hair was pasted down her back. Her lips were caked dry but when he asked Cat for some water, she shook her head and cheerfully handed him a cottony swab tipped with lemon.

*   *   *

Nine hours later, Molly still hadn't dilated more than eight centimeters, two less than she'd need to push. She was so worn out that when Karen suggested a C-section, Molly nodded. "Let's do it," she said. Karen made Gary get into starchy green scrubs, a cap, a mask, a long gown with ties in the back. Molly blinked at him. She half smiled and touched his sleeve. "You look hilarious. I have to get a picture of this." She made him stand against the wall so she could snap him.

Cat came in and helped Molly onto a gurney. Gary's legs suddenly were jelly. His back had no bone. He tried to compose himself, to grip onto his breath so that he might seem calm and strong and so capable Molly didn't have a thing to worry about. "Coming through," Cat said, wheeling the gurney out of the room and into the corridor. Gary raced behind. He grabbed blindly for her hand. He held on tight.

The delivery room was big and bright with light. Four or five people in green surgical scrubs, their faces masked, were already standing around in a kind of lopsided semicircle, casually waiting. Cat slid Molly onto the table. Molly craned her neck and helplessly locked eyes with Gary. He was coiled with nerves, but he rubbed her shoulder, he made himself smile. He looked around for Karen, for a face he recognized and trusted, a voice that might soothe him. "Excuse me." Cat moved briskly past him and began stretching Molly's arms out to the sides, strapping them in with leather strips.

"Wait, what are you doing?" Gary looked at Cat in disbelief.

"Don't tie my arms!" Molly insisted. She looked alarmed; she tried to rise up and Cat patted her arms.

"Oh, now. We can't have you helping out with the operation, can we?" Cat said.

"Don't tie my arms——" Molly said again, panicked, and Karen suddenly strode into the room. She patted Gary on the back. She leaned over Molly. "It's to keep you steadier." Karen's voice was calm. "Hold Gary's hands," she suggested. Molly's fingers waggled open. Gary sat beside her, breathing through the starchy cotton of his mask.

An IV snaked into Molly's arm. They set up a tall green curtain, a screen bisecting her. "Stop!" Molly cried.

Circled around her, the doctors talked about their vacations. "Don't go to Key West," Karen said. "The surgeons go there. The gastro people." They talked about which restaurants made the best steak. They argued the merits of SoHo and Chinatown. "Best Italian food isn't in Little Italy," said the anesthesiologist. "Right here. East Eighty-fourth. Paulo's." He leaned over Molly. "How're you doing, kiddo? Need another boost?"

Molly shook her head. "I don't feel a thing except scared." She looked over at Gary. "What's happening now?"

A med student, a Chinese girl with a big nose and a wide middle part, stood in the back, peering curiously at Molly. "The incision will be here?" she questioned. "The stitches will be here?" Everything she said was a question. "Good pasta is at Eighty-sixth and Madison?"

There was a loop of talk and so little of it was about Molly that it began to make Gary nervous. He was about to ask Karen a question, something, anything to get her back on focus when she suddenly snapped upright and the conversations stopped. Everyone seemed to be looking at Karen and waiting. The room seemed to pulse.

"Here we go," Karen said. Her voice had changed. It was different, threaded with steel, boned with authority. She even looked different to Gary, like someone he had never seen before, and it made him even more nervous. "Karen?" he asked.

She nodded at Gary. She snapped her hands into gloves. "I'll tell you when to look."

Molly looked dazed, her skin felt clammy to him when he touched her, holding her hand. In back of the curtain, the doctors worked. He watched their heads, bobbing and dipping. He watched Molly. "Gary—" Karen said, motioning, and then he stood up and looked down over the curtain.

"What?" Molly said, her voice sliding. "What's going on now?"

Molly was opened up, her skin peeled back from her like a strange exotic fruit, and when he looked down, for just a second, he could see the baby curled inside of her, knees tucked up, head bent, skin a flush of pink. Astounded, he stepped back. He stumbled. He caught at his breath.

"Gary?" Molly said. "What's going on? Gary?"

"Back you go." Karen nodded at him and he stepped back, astonished, and immediately, despite himself, he started to weep. He swiped at his eyes with his free hand, and he held Molly tighter.

"Gary." Molly tried to hoist herself up. "What's wrong?" She was struggling to sit up, to move, her face was tight with alarm and he kept crying. "Something's wrong. Something's wrong!" she cried. "What is it? What's wrong with the baby?" Her arms wrestled against the ties.

"Nothing's wrong. Look and see." Karen held up the baby. His eyes were wide open. He was covered in vernix and blood. He was like moonlight. Molly, stunned, stopped moving. Gary gripped her hand.

"Baby boy, coming through," said Karen, and lifted him back over to the table, for swabs and tests and cleaning. The Chinese medical student hovered by the table. Then Karen came back to Molly. "Just some finishing up to do, and then we're done."

"Here?" said the Chinese student and Gary bent and kissed Molly, here and here and here, and she sighed and shut her eyes.

"He's brilliant, score nine on the Apgar," Karen said. "Ten's only for other doctors. Professional courtesy." Someone unstrapped Molly's arms. She flexed her fingers. The baby was lowered into her arms.

"She's wrong," Molly said to Otis. "You're ten. You're *perfect*."

Gary had wanted to sleep in the empty bed beside Molly, but the hospital wouldn't let him. "That bed has somebody else's name on it," Karen ordered, placing a friendly hand on his shoulder. "Kiss your wife and let her be for a while. She did hard work." Karen paused. "So did Otis. And so did you."

Gary was so exhausted, he listed on his feet. He felt unmoored and exhilarated, as if every cell in his body were somehow prickling.

I'm a *father*, he kept repeating. A *father*. We're a *family*. He laughed out loud.

Gary bent and kissed Molly very gently on her cheek. She smelled faintly of sweat. "I'll see you both soon."

As soon as he got home, he couldn't sleep. The neighborhood was dark. The front of the house was littered with debris from the fireworks. Threads, paper parachutes. The tree in front, the one Molly had worried over, had two broken branches. Nobody had bothered to clean anything, but he didn't feel angry. He felt like ringing doorbells, waking up Emma and Bill and even Carl, who had asked him who he thought he was, making them all come over and celebrate with him. He didn't care what time of night it was. *I have a son.* he thought, amazed. *I have Otis.*

The house was clean. Everything was ready. It was the first time since he had married Molly that they had spent a night apart and already he missed her. He went into Otis's room and sat in the wood rocker he had bought.

He got up and went into the living room. With a section, Molly and the baby wouldn't be home for another three days, but he couldn't wait. He felt like a little kid, jumpy with excitement. He wanted everyone to know. He went to the kitchen cabinet and found the blue balloons he had bought the day he found out their baby was a boy. He was going to string them on the front railing, the only decorations he'd ever put on the house. He sat in the middle of his living room and blew them up, gulping, blowing long deep puffs. Two balloons down and he still wasn't out of breath, he wasn't in as bad shape as he sometimes thought. Maybe he and Molly could have a little party, too, invite friends, some neighbors, celebrate their son. Son, he thought, and reached for another balloon.

He thought about all the things they might do. He had a little vacation time left, they had money saved, enough for two months. He was going to stay at home with Molly so both of them could do nothing but be full-time parents. The first time he had mentioned that to Bill,

Bill had looked at him as if he had suddenly started speaking Swahili. "Molly wants you to do that?" Bill said, perplexed. "Your boss okays that sort of thing?"

He'd read all the books along with Molly. He'd talked to Otis through Molly's belly when he was little more than a pinpoint. He'd sung to him. Ada at work had warned him how exhausting a newborn could be. She told him horror stories about her sister's kid, how the lack of sleep and endless neediness of a newborn had made her sister feel cannibalized. A newborn had no personality, Ada insisted. They didn't even smile until they were six weeks old. "My sister asked the doctor if he'd take the baby back," Ada said, "and she wasn't kidding." Ada had petted him on the shoulder. "Maybe your kid will be different. And if not, I guess we'll see you back at work sooner than you think."

He had no intention of going back to work earlier than he had planned. He had never thought of Otis as a blob, even when he was no more than a blue line on Molly's pregnancy test. He couldn't wait to be sleepless and bleary-eyed, to be facing a mountain of diapers and laundry breeding in the corners of the rooms because neither he nor Molly could get around to it. He couldn't wait to sing to his son, to lie on the bed with Molly and the baby and feel like a family.

He suddenly thought of Pearl. She'd hate to hear him thinking about the future, thinking ahead even five minutes was a sin to her. "Don't you dare waste the life you have now thinking about a future you know nothing about," she had always told him.

He finished the last balloon and went outside. It was the middle of the night. He tied the balloons onto the railing. Soft washed blue, they floated and bobbed. At this time, the neighbors had wanted them to put up some decorations, and now he had. Then he got the camera and took a picture of the front of the house. He didn't want Molly to miss anything.

He couldn't wait to get to the hospital the next morning, to see Molly and his son. He couldn't stop smiling, couldn't stop the wild exhilaration tearing through him. His son! He loved the sound of it in his throat. His son! He wanted to pepper his conversation with it, to tell everyone at every chance he had. He dropped off the film from the night before. "Pictures of my *son*," he said. He went to the florist and bought wildflowers in a green paper cone for Molly. "My wife just had a *son*," he told the cashier, who looked at him, bored.

When he got to the hospital, Molly was calmly walking around her room. She was attached to her IV pole, rolling it noisily across the floor. Her ankles were puffy, and her nightgown, new and pale green and sprigged with pink flowers, didn't fit quite right. "You look beautiful," he said, and kissed her. There was a sudden sound, like the mewling of a cat, and Gary froze.

Molly laughed. "It's Otis. Go say hello." She pointed to the other side of her bed.

Otis, in a tiny white cap with a blue pompom, was lying in a bassinet, half swaddled in a striped blanket, lifting his fists. Gary stared at his son in fresh astonishment. The baby looked mischievous to him. His eyes were dancing with light. Gary touched Otis's apricot skin, his tiny fingernails, his blush of hair with a kind of reverence.

"What, are you hungry again?" She bent, gently lifting the baby up, sitting with him in one of the chairs. She raised up her shirt. "Welcome to the Milk Bar. We're always open and your credit is always good." She settled Otis against her breast. "This feels so completely weird."

A nurse strode in, bright-faced and very blond, carrying a thermometer. She motioned to Molly and popped it under Molly's tongue. She shook her head at Molly. "Will you look at her?" she said to Gary. "When I had my C-section, I couldn't sit up for two weeks, and this one is doing laps around the halls." The thermometer blinked and she took it from Molly, scanning it. "Vital signs all great. Let's just check this C-section." She lifted the sheet. "I have never in my life seen a cut so low. You could wear a microkini and not give anything away." She stood up. "I wish the other day nurse were here. She'd get a kick out of that scar." She gave Molly a pat on her head. "You, my girl, are putting us all to shame."

Molly laughed. "This really wasn't too bad," she said. She looked suddenly mischievous to Gary, the way he thought she must have looked at six or seven, when she had snuck a frog into the house or cut her doll's hair. "I could see myself doing this again. Maybe two more times again."

He grinned back. "Two more times?"

"A baby brother for Otis. A little sister he can spoil rotten and fix up with all his friends."

He bent and kissed her. "Well, then we ought to start practicing. As soon as you get home and are able."

Molly was fine, itchy to go home, complaining that every time she turned around, a nurse was coming in, hounding her, asking her if she had peed, if she had passed gas, if she had eaten the rubbery Jell-O or drunk enough juice, and her answer was always no, no, no. She wanted to start doing some simple exercises to get back in shape, to feel more energized, but she said the only thing they would let her do was to stride around the halls, her IV racing behind her.

By four, when Gary was going to go home for a bit, a new nurse came in. "I'm unhooking you from the IV."

"Thank the Lord." Molly lay on the bed, watching. She rubbed absently at her stomach. "You know, I don't feel like this is going down very much."

The nurse closed up the IV on Molly's wrist. "Takes time."

Molly frowned. "It looks like it's getting bigger."

"Doubtful." The nurse started out of the room, taking the IV pole with her.

"Fat and tired, that's me," Molly told Gary.

Gary soothed her shoulders. "Come on, you look beautiful. And you want tired? Wait until it's just us and no nurses with the baby at home."

"Can we go home now?"

*   *   *

When he left that day, he kept thinking how much he actually liked the maternity ward, that if you had to visit someone in the hospital, this was the place to be. Everything so brand-new: babies and parents both. He wasn't stupid enough to not realize that even here, things could go wrong. He had passed one room where a young woman was weeping, a man helplessly stroking her back. He had seen stunned disbelief on the face of a man talking to a nurse. But the odds were in your favor here. And the atmosphere was giddy with anticipation.

There were all these young happy women striding down the halls in pretty robes, their hair held back with colored ribbons. Women were kissing their husbands with loud smacking sounds, laughing out loud. There were balloons and stuffed toys and the floor felt electrically charged. One of the nurses had told Gary that there was a three-year waiting period to be an obstetrical nurse, and watching the nurses, he believed it. They moved with a kind of grace and calm and undeniable sunniness here. Maybe it was just because he was a brand-new father, but he swore there was a kind of music here, an audible kind of joy you might never tire of listening to.

She was supposed to come home her third day in the hospital, but when Gary arrived, Molly was glumly lying in bed, one hand rocking Otis in the bassinet beside her. "Guess what. I have a blood clot."

He stood, stunned, but she waved her hand. "No, don't look like that, it's nothing. Karen told me it's common with sections. The way they have to move everything around. It happens. They just need to go in and clean it up. I'm just depressed because it means I have to be here two or three more days." She pulled her nightgown over her belly. "See how huge? How hard? That's the clot. It got bigger." Gary tentatively rested one hand on her stomach. It was a hard, moving swell under his palm. "It hurts, but I won't take a painkiller because I'm breast-feeding."

Molly lifted her arms and then let them flop back on the bed. "I'm tired and depressed. All the other mothers who delivered when I did are going home."

"You'll be going home soon." He stroked back her hair, then he bent and picked up Otis. His son's head wobbled against his palm. His body felt nearly weightless. He carefully sat on the empty bed beside Molly and then spread out, resting Otis on his belly. Molly yawned and turned her head. "He's something, isn't he?" She smiled and yawned again.

Gary couldn't take his eyes off his son. Otis flexed his hands and frowned and drooled and then fell asleep on his stomach. "Molly, look—" he whispered, but when he turned to her, she was sleeping, too, her eyelids fluttering in dreams.

He couldn't sleep. He kept imagining Otis rolling off his belly and onto the hard floor. Instead, he gently hinged up. He carried Otis, still sleeping, back into his bassinet and gently lowered him in, tucking the layette blanket about him. "Pleasant dreams, everybody," he said. He walked outside and went to find Karen, who was standing at the nurse's station, laughing. He touched her elbow. "So. Should I be worried?"

"It's nothing," Karen said. "Pure routine."

He was late to the hospital the next day. He had already spoken to Molly, who told him triumphantly that she had changed Otis's diaper that morning, that she swore he had winked at her. They were going to operate at ten and she had begun to hurt more, enough so she'd reconsidered her no-painkiller rule. "Get here before they knock me out," she told him. "I want a good-luck kiss."

He had left early, stopping only to pick up the photographs, leafing through them hurriedly in the car. Molly. There she was, beautiful and exhausted in her blue johnny. There was Otis, lying in the bassinet, half swaddled, one arm reaching out as if to greet them. And there he was, too, a brand-new father with a glad, goofy smile, his hair too long, the edges of it poking out of his scrub mask. He laughed out loud. He put the photos on the seat beside him.

He should have made it to the hospital in a half hour, but there was an accident in the Holland Tunnel and traffic was backed up for over an hour. He stared at his watch. Beside him, in the other lane, a woman was putting on mascara, staring critically at herself in the rearview mirror. Behind him, every once in a while, a man in a white Cadillac beeped his horn. Gary glanced at his watch again. He'd never make it to Molly in time. She'd wonder where he was, she'd worry, she'd probably call the house. Now, she wouldn't be out for another few hours. He thought of Emma telling him they should have had a doctor in New Jersey and then he settled back, turning on the radio. The Rolling Stones sang about Brown Sugar, and he tapped the beat out on the steering wheel.

He didn't get into the city until nearly eleven. He'd wait for Molly in the waiting room. He'd stop and buy a magazine or two downstairs in the gift shop. They had a great selection.

Later, he strode down the halls, half hidden by a giant bouquet of yellow jonquils. Her room was empty, her bed carefully made. Blinking in the bed next to Molly's was a woman with brassy hair, a set of twins in her arms. "You don't look like my husband," she chimed.

Gary backed out of the room, excusing himself. He set off to the nurse's station and suddenly spotted Karen, a stubby yellow pencil tucked behind one ear, her hands folded across her white coat. "Karen!" he called, but Karen, when she turned to him, didn't smile. He fanned the photos and her face looked pale and distant to him, waning.

"Have you seen this woman?" He held up the best picture: Molly sitting up, sucking on a lemon swab. Karen suddenly averted her face. She swiped a finger across her eyes, and he suddenly felt a pulse of uneasiness.

Karen turned back to him. Her eyes looked damp. She put one hand on his sleeve. "We've been trying to reach you."

Gary sat in an empty waiting room, unable to move. Karen was leaning forward, hands flat on her knees.

"I don't understand—" he said, and Karen shook her head.

"Either do we," she said. It was a bleed, she told him, not a clot. They had opened Molly up and there had been so much blood. No one could remember having seen that much blood before. And it wouldn't stop. They had scooped out what they could. They had sewn her back up. With that kind of bleeding, and the kind of pain that went along with it, they were keeping her anesthetized.

"What are you telling me?" Gary stared. "Is she going to be all right?"

Karen looked away from him. "She's critical."

"Is she going to make it?"

"Gary, I don't know."

The room swam around him. Karen was speaking, saying something, but he couldn't grab on to it, he couldn't hear. "Wait——" he said. "Wait just a minute."

She stopped. "Gary," she said, and then she began speaking, and this time he could hear her. She had already called in a critical care specialist, a hematologist, and they needed Gary to sign a paper authorizing more surgery. Molly was filling up with blood too fast. They had to open her up again, drain some of it out, try to take another look and see what was happening.

"When?"

Karen handed him the paper and a pen, "Tomorrow. We really can't wait."

He signed his name, he handed the paper back and then stood up. "Can I see her?"

The hospital had moved Molly from the maternity ward to the surgical intensive care unit, two floors down. Karen rode the elevator with him and as soon as they got off the floor, as soon as he started to follow her, to move deeper onto the floor, he noticed a difference.

He was used to crowded hallways, but here there were fewer patients walking around, and the ones he saw looked as wrung-out as damp washcloths. A man on crutches winced as he passed Gary. A woman, face drawn tight as a change purse, held on to her husband, who was intently whispering something to her. In maternity there had been a doctor here and there, but on this floor, there seemed to be teams. One doctor leading an entourage, a bundling of white coats and green scrubs and rapid-fire talking. In maternity, the doctors strolled, but here, they strode, covering ground, veering suddenly into rooms.

Karen stopped in front of a room. SICU. Surgical Intensive Care. "You can go in, but only for a moment, now," Karen said. He peered inside. Three nurses were sitting at a station, scrolling down on a computer. One of them, small and wiry and frowning, looked up at Gary. Karen placed a hand on Gary's sleeve. "You should prepare yourself a little."

"For what?"

"She's going to look different. It's all the blood pooling up inside of her. And there's some tubing. To help her breathe. She's anesthetized. In a deep-sleep state."

Gary didn't know what to expect when he entered the room. It was one big room with four beds in it, each one positioned like an island, connected up with blinking monitors and IVs and tubes and a nurse's station with three nurses whisking around. There were four patients, and none of them moving. It was a mistake. He didn't see Molly, and then Karen gently touched him. She pointed. "Over there."

For a moment, he didn't believe it was Molly in the bed. At first all he saw were the tubes and the IVs, and then he saw her, swollen and thickened, her long thin neck the size of a football player's, her eyes shut, her skin red, as if she had rusted. One of the machines she was hooked up to made a noisy, rattling sound. It flashed a series of fluorescent green numbers and none of them made any sense to him. There was an orange leatherette chair by her bed and he pulled it closer to her, he sat down. "Molly." His voice sounded funny to him. "Molly," he said again. He took her hand. It was warm. It didn't move.

Gary felt as if he were sleepwalking. He didn't know what to do, where to go, except that he couldn't go home, couldn't leave Molly here. He sat beside her bed, watching her, staring, marking time by the nurses who came to check her pulse, to adjust a tube, to tell him to go home and get a thing as simple and as impossible as some rest.

He was keeping his vigil when Molly's machine suddenly whirred and buzzed, so loudly he sprang to his feet, terrified and sick. "Nurse!" he shouted. Instantly, a nurse appeared. "Something's happening—" he said, but the nurse seemed calm. She looked at the machine, tapped it on the side, pressed a button, and the buzzing stopped. "It happens all the time," she told him.

He felt himself snapping, like a rubber band. He got up to walk the halls, to calm himself, and he stopped at the nursery. There was one other man there, older, with a full white beard, a shock of hair. Someone's grandfather, he guessed, tapping at the glass. Gary stared in at his son, who was sleeping, swaddled in a blanket, unaware of him or Molly or the sudden new danger crackling and glinting.

Two hours later, he finally left the hospital. As soon as he got to the house, the balloons bobbing on the railing made him sad and helpless. He didn't know what to do. He didn't think he could bear to see them inside the house, floating toward the ceiling. He didn't want to see them deflating and he couldn't bring himself to puncture them, so instead, he untied them, he jerked them free. He opened his hand and let them sweep across the sky.

Inside the house, he couldn't concentrate, couldn't sit still. He called the hospital. "Critical," a voice said, and he told himself that at least that meant she was the same, she was no worse, things could change for the better at any moment. He went into Otis's room and looked around. He wished he had family. He wished he still had Pearl. When he was growing up, all she had to do was look at him and know that he was sad or lonely or feeling unsure, and she had always seemed to know just what to do about it. She used to pluck him up and take him places, the roller rink, the theater. She helped him get his mind off his troubles.

Well, he didn't have Pearl anymore. He didn't have brothers or sisters or anyone but Molly, and he couldn't reach her. So he did the next best thing he could think of. He called a few friends of Molly's: Cinda, a second-grade teacher she liked; Jack, who taught kindergarten. He called Ada at work and Allan in Ithaca and Bob in Boston.

He didn't know what to say, and every time he opened his mouth, he felt as if he were standing outside of himself watching, listening to this poor awkward man stumbling over his own words. The people he called were always shocked, horrified, numb. No one knew what to do or what to say. "I'll have my class make cards," Jack offered, and Gary didn't want to tell him that Molly wouldn't know if they sent cards or not. Cinda cried on the phone, so long and hard Gary ended up comforting her. "I'll visit every day," she wept. "We'll cry on each other's shoulders."

"Molly can't have visitors," he blurted.

Ada told him he was under stress. "Let me cook you dinner," she said. "Tempeh, pickled plum—all excellent for stress."

"I can't eat," he told her. "But thank you."

Three seconds into each call Gary made, he was immediately sorry he had picked up the phone at all because the more people tried to help, the worse he felt, the more panicked, more unraveled. His terror became more real, more immediate, just by saying what was happening out loud, and by involving another person in it.

"I have this great natural healing book at home," Ada said. "I'm going to look Molly's symptoms up and get back to you."

"I'm sure it's nothing," Bob kept repeating.

"I can be up there in two hours," Allan told him. "Stay for a four-day weekend."

"Come here?" Gary felt baffled. "I'm at the hospital all day. I just wanted to talk."

"No, no, you're in no state to know what you need. You need someone to take over. I'll help out. I'll clean the house. I'll be there to talk to when you get home."

He felt exhausted talking to Allan. "No, no, please don't come up. I'm fine." He tried to sound reassuring.

"You sure? You'll be okay?"

He was drowning. There was no oxygen, no light. "I'm fine," Gary insisted.

"You keep me posted, then," Allan told him. "She won't die, I know it. She won't—"

Gary cut him off, hanging up the phone. He felt grateful for the silence of the house. He left the phone and went into the bedroom. He'd sleep, he'd forget. He'd get up in the morning and maybe things would be different. Maybe it would all be a bad dream, like one of those stupid cliff-hanger TV shows where the hero suddenly wakes, and the fact that the hero could even imagine himself in some sort of terrible situation or tragedy is all a big huge joke everyone can laugh over.

He bunched up Molly's pillow against him, trying to form it into Molly's slender weight, but as soon as he smelled her fragrance on the case—ocean and rose—he felt himself unraveling again. He jolted up from bed. He went upstairs to his computer. Work, he could lose himself in work. But as soon as he logged on, he ignored all the files for the environmental series, for the new Reading Rider series, and instead he got on the Internet. He searched for medical forums, for the names of doctors, experts, anyone who might know something. He found the name of a hematologist. Dr. Steven Ribor. He buried his head in his hands. He looked up and typed in a query, a message in a bottle, a plea for rescue. *My wife gave birth and is suddenly seriously ill. The bleeding won't stop.* He looked at the words. He kept typing. He started out slow and full of purpose and within minutes he was begging shamelessly for papers, for information, for help, pleas flung out across the wires. He wrote down his phone number, his address, his name. *Call anytime, day or night,* he begged. *Please,* Gary typed out. *Respond. This is an emergency. Please.*

He fell asleep at the computer, deep and dreamless, and in the morning, he woke with a start, his head on the computer table, his back coiling with cramps, his neck stiff. He hinged himself slowly upright and blinked at the computer. He had two pieces of E-mail. *Turn your washer into a cash cow!* and *Answer to your question.* He deleted the cash cow mail and clicked open the other. It was from a doctor in Los Angeles. "Hemorrhage after childbirth could be from the uterus failing to contract," the doctor wrote. "Sometimes removal is necessary. I need more information to be more specific. Please keep me posted. This sounds like an interesting case."

An interesting case. Gary felt a flicker of rage. The doctor wanted more information. Well, maybe that was the problem, because Gary didn't have any. Gary got up and reached for the phone to call the hospital, thought better of it, and instead went to get dressed to go and see Molly himself.

Gary paced the halls, trying to steady himself, and every time he passed the SICU, he grabbed for a glimpse of Molly, making sure she was still there, making sure the nurses were watching her. He walked and walked, wired, too terrified to sit down for a minute. He would have kept walking except a doctor, a lean, bony man in a long white lab coat who looked as if he were sucking on a piece of slightly rotted fruit, stopped him. "Are you Molly's husband?"

Gary nodded.

"I'm Dr. Price, your wife's hematologist."

"What's wrong with my wife?"

"We're running some new tests right now."

"But what do you think it is? You must have some ideas—"

Dr. Price gave him a hard stare. "I will tell you my ideas when I see the test. It would be foolish to be premature." He strode out of the room, as if it were somehow Gary's fault, as if Gary were to blame.

On the way out, Gary stopped at a bank of pay phones. A woman next to him was laughing into the phone. "An itty-bitty cyst!" she cried happily. A man on the other side of Gary was nodding glumly. Gary dialed Brian, his boss. The machine picked up on the second ring.

"It's me," Gary said. He cleared his throat. The laughing woman beside him giggled and tapped the phone.

The line buzzed and crackled. Something beeped. "Hold on," Brian said. "Let me get rid of this other call." Gary waited and then Brian came back on. "Emily in Accounting. She never gets the hint not to leave a message, to just call me until she gets me. I never return calls to subordinates. It puts me on their level." Brian took a breath. "Hey, Gary, so how does it feel to be a dad?"

"Ada didn't tell you?"

"Ada? Ada's a secretary."

Brian said nothing the whole time Gary was talking. He was so silent that for one moment Gary thought he might have hung up or been disconnected. "Are you there?"

"Of course I'm here. You take all the time you need," Brian said. "I can get you more unpaid leave if you need it. Don't you worry about anything."

Gary hung up the phone the same time the laughing woman did. She gave him a big smile, but he couldn't manage to return it. It didn't matter. She wasn't really seeing him anyway.

Molly came back from the operation, four clear plastic drains attached to her stomach, a new tube tracked down her nose. He couldn't bear to look at her. He couldn't bear to look away. He wanted to get up on the bed and lie against her, nest among the tubes. *I'm right here. I'm with you. You breathe. I breathe.*

Dr. Price strode by with another doctor he didn't know, a small, round man with a Band-Aid on his nose who introduced himself as Dr. Kane. "The surgeon."

Gary waited. Dr. Kane looked uncomfortable and then cleared his throat. "We cleaned up a lot of the bleed. But she's still bleeding."

"The blood work is still not good," said Dr. Price. "Normal hematocrits, the red blood counts for a woman her age, are thirty-five to sixty. Hers are nineteen. Not good at all. I want to start a transfusion."

"What does she have?"

"We're doing more tests," said Dr. Price. "CAT scans. MRIs. Nuclear medicine. We can perhaps track the bleeding with isotopes, find the source. If need be, we can glue the veins closed."

"What?" Gary felt as if he were dreaming.

"I like it because it's nonsurgical. You go in with catheters."

"But what does she have? Why can't you tell me anything?" Gary felt a knot of anger forming. A headache took on speed behind his eyes.

"Because," Dr. Price said, "we don't know yet."

The days took on an eerie kind of rhythm. He had his routine. He checked in with Molly first, sitting by her bed as long as the nurses would let him. He never knew what to do, what might be the magic thing that could unlock her to him. Sometimes he held her hand. Sometimes he talked to her, trying to act normal, as if that might force things back to normal themselves. "It's freezing cold outside," he told her. He told her jokes and riddles that he had once thought were funny. "I love you," he said. Her eyelids flickered and opened, making him bolt to his feet, but all that happened was her eyes rolled upward and then her lids shut again. "I love you," he tried again, but her lids stayed shut this time.

Sometimes he brought in the newspapers and loudly read her horoscope to her. *Stand up to your boss and you'll see great results.*

"See?" he said to her. "Tell those doctors you're fine. Stand up from the bed." He urged her upward, he made his voice rich with enthusiasm, fluid with love, and when she didn't stir, he began to read the baby's horoscope. "Get active now. Go for a ride in the country." He laughed, despite himself. He never read his own fortune. He was too terrified to find out.

He read aloud to her from a novel he had picked up. He turned on the boom box. "Sing along with me!" he ordered. He sang along to the Monkees, to the Beatles, he hummed to Vivaldi. She never moved. A nurse glided by, her hair tied in a small bun on top of her head. She stood in the doorway watching Gary. "I don't know what you're doing, but keep doing it," she said, nudging her chin toward a monitor that kept flashing a series of numbers. "I like her numbers."

Gary glanced at the numbers. "Those are good?"

"Uh-huh." She gave him a smile.

Gary watched Molly's numbers, making sure they stayed at those levels for at least an hour before he got up to see his son in Maternity.

The nursery was at the far end. There were always fathers and grandparents and relatives pressed up against the glass waving at the babies, sometimes a new mother in a robe, her hair tied back with a ribbon, and the happiness felt so new and brilliant, Gary felt blinded by it. Today, there was only one other man there, about Gary's age, a lean, horse-faced blond with a scrubby mustache. The nurse behind the glass noticed Gary and held Otis up. He had a white cap on with a bright green pom-pom. Across the side it said, *I got my first hug at Mt. Sinai Hospital.* Otis blinked gravely at him and for the first time, he saw Otis had Molly's eyes. Stricken, confused, he stepped back from the glass, bumping into the man next to him.

The man patted Gary good-naturedly on the shoulder. "Don't even tell me about it. Lack of sleep. Me, too."

Gary looked at Otis again, at Molly's eyes studying him in that small perfect face. The nurse grinned and lowered Otis back into his bassinet.

The other man disappeared and there was Gary, alone in front of the glass, watching three nurses move among the babies, holding them up, nuzzling them, cradling those sweet, lovely faces, those perfect tiny bodies. The nurses clowned around. They made the babies wave their tiny hands, like small, brilliant star bursts. They combed the hair of the babies who had hair into tiny marcel waves, into parts in the middle, far on the side. One of the nurses looked up and noticed Gary. He waved weakly. She bent and picked up Otis again and then she motioned to Gary to come around the side. Puzzled, he walked over.

"Listen," she said in a low voice. "Mr. Goldman, I'm so sorry about your wife. Would you like to hold your son and feed him his bottle? There's a private room back here."

He felt weak with gratitude. "Yes. Yes, please, I would."

He followed the nurse to a small sunny side room. He sat in a chair and she gently put Otis into his arms. "He's the king of the road in there," she said. "I swear all the other babies ask him for advice." She held up one finger and whisked from the room, returning with a bottle. "There you go," she said, handing the bottle to Gary.

She bent over the two of them. She was young and lean and coffee-colored, with dreadlocks that bobbed whenever she moved. "Here's Mr. Handsome," she said, guiding the nipple into Otis's mouth. "I told him I'd wait for him to grow up so I could marry him. He's got great manners. He doesn't fuss when the lights go out to sleep. Good personality. He doesn't scream for his bottle, but waits politely, and he never, ever pees in my face when I go to change his diaper." She waggled a finger at Otis. "Do you, honey?" She laughed. She gently repositioned Gary's grip. "Hold him close," she advised. "Later, I'll give you a diaper-changing lesson, but for now I'll just leave you two alone for a while. Let you get acquainted."

Gary felt as if the world were breathing, expanding and contracting around him, pulling him with it. He thought of Molly and he felt something breaking inside of him. He looked down at his son. Otis felt so sturdy. He smelled like powder and milk and a bottomless ocean. Gary buried his nose against Otis's neck, making the baby squirm. Otis felt and dozed and fed again in his lap. Gary could look at his son forever, at his tiny nose, his hands, his perfect feet. He felt an astonished rush of love, and then a deep, wrenching hurt. What did babies know? Did Otis feel abandoned by Molly? Abandoned by a father far less jolly than the one who had told him bad jokes when Otis was still in the womb? "I'm so sorry, pal," Gary said, tickling Otis's chin. "I don't know what else to do." Otis sighed and stretched. Gary didn't want to move, even when the muscle in his left leg began to cramp. No, he waited, as still as a crib bed until the nurse reappeared and took the baby from him, and as soon as she had, his hands felt empty, useless weights in his lap.

Even when Gary left the hospital, he felt as if he were at the hospital. He went outside and he swore he smelled disinfectant. He got in his car and he heard the monitoring machines from Molly's room whirring and clicking, an undertone to the sounds of the car engine. He turned on the radio, and a girl group sang about loving someone forever, about never letting go, and he switched it off again. The whole drive home, he kept staring at the people walking around, living their lives, in stupefaction. *How can you?* he thought. *How can you?*

He watched a couple sharing sips from a bottle of soda. He saw a man in a business suit link hands with a well-dressed woman. All those little moments. That timing. But then he thought of how when he had first met Molly, he had wanted to take it slow. To get it right. To prepare. And he hadn't been able to stop himself from rushing ahead with her. Who knew what might be happening now if he had gone slower? If he hadn't gone to Molly's house that night and spent the night, if he had waited for the third date or the fourth to sleep with her? If he hadn't been in such a hurry to make a family for himself, to be in the best possible place? What if the sum of all his choices had added up to this—Molly in the hospital, Molly dying?

He found a parking spot near the house, and when he got out, when he saw the empty neighborhood, the empty house in front of him, he suddenly couldn't go back inside there. Not alone.

He climbed back into the car. He didn't know where he was going. He kept driving and driving, getting on the Jersey Turnpike. He just kept going.

He drove until it started to get dark and then, too exhausted to continue, he turned around and came home. He parked two blocks from the house. For a minute, he rested his head along the steering wheel. And then he pulled himself up. He got out of the car and he walked back. None of the neighbors came out of their houses.

He got to his front porch. He was about to get his key, to jiggle it into the lock when he saw a small white card tucked into the front door, his name scribbled across the front of it in red ink. He stared at the card for a moment, and then slowly opened it.

Hallmark. Or what he called a drugstore card, the kind Pearl had loved. A basket of violets was on the front, a white kitten, curled like a comma about the basket. He opened the card. *Best wishes from the neighbors*, it said. The handwriting loped across the page. He couldn't tell whose it was. He folded the card shut, put it in his pocket, and went inside.

He left early each morning and came home so late the streets were dark. Gifts began appearing, always with hopeful cards, some of them signed by people he couldn't remember telling about Molly. Get well soon, they said. Some of them were from the neighbors. How could they know? Maybe they called the hospital and asked. Maybe they just assumed, with Molly not coming home, the balloons down. He opened the cards and presents to have something to do, pulling out tiny red-striped outfits, a glittering vest, books, and booties. There were usually nine or ten messages on the machine. Molly's friends wanting to know how she was. Cinda, weeping on the phone, making him feel so shocked and frightened he deleted the message before it played itself out. Every time he heard a voice, rich with concern, dizzy with fear, he felt worse. He felt overwhelmed. He didn't want to have to call them, to say any of what was happening out loud. Instead, he wrote out E-mail. Progress reports he sent out over the wires.

He was numb. There was no respite, not even at sleep where he dreamed he was in blue scrubs entering a great dark operating room, calling out, "Hello? I can't operate in the dark here. Hello?" He heard the soft sounds of a machine breathing for a patient he couldn't see. "Hello?" he called again. No one answered and he began to get more and more agitated and the operating room loomed larger and larger and the machine seemed to sputter in panic and then he heard this great loud ringing in his head and he bolted awake, sweating. The phone was ringing. He glanced at the clock. Two in the morning. He stumbled for the receiver.

"Hello, is this Gary?" A woman's voice, soft and serious.

"Yes."

"You doing okay?" There was a pause. "I read your request on-line for information. Is it okay that I'm calling so late? You did say it was all right to call."

He pulled up from bed, swinging his legs onto the floor. He turned on the light, looking for his pen, his pad of paper. "Please. Yes, it's fine, it's fine. Tell me what you have."

"I have steak."

"Excuse me?"

"Steak. You like steak dinner? Wouldn't that make you feel better, help you to be stronger?" There was a rustling in the background. "I don't live too far from where you are. And I'm blonde." She paused. "All over. Collar *and* cuffs."

Gary put the paper down, he let the pen roll from his fingers onto the wood floor. "This is supposed to be about blood."

The woman laughed, deep and throaty. "I think I know how to make it boil," she whispered and he hung up.

He couldn't move. He didn't know what to do. If he wiped his name from the message, he might not get any more crank calls, but he might not get the one call from someone who did know something, who might have even gone through the same thing.

The phone rang again, making him start. The blood boiler, he thought. Or maybe it was a psycho wanting to come over and rob him. *I can't do this*, he thought, and then he picked up the phone, not speaking, waiting.

"Gary? Are you there? It's Karen."

He didn't know suddenly whether to feel relieved or more terrified. "I'm here," he said finally.

"We're going to do another operation. We need you to sign an okay."

Gary couldn't speak.

"Gary? Are you there?"

"How many operations are you going to do? Why do you have to do them?"

"She's young. She can handle this one."

He got up. He drove to the hospital and signed the papers without even reading them, because what was the point, what was he going to tell them, no, don't operate again on my wife, no, don't save her life? They could have told him they were transplanting the head of a monkey onto her feet, and she would be fine, and he would have agreed to it. "Do whatever it takes," he said. He waited for the operation to be over. He slept in the waiting room. How is she, he kept asking every time a nurse walked in, how is she? And in the end, despite the operation, it was always the same, the same, the same. He was sitting on the long orange couch in the waiting room and this time Dr. Kane and Dr. Price walked in, both of them so drawn-looking and serious, Gary bolted to his feet.

"We cleaned out the excess blood," Dr. Kane said. "The uterus looked infected so we took it out."

Gary stared. "Wait—you—"

"We *had* to. She wouldn't have survived." Dr. Kane's scowl deepened. "We thought it might be infected, that that was what was causing so much bleeding."

"An infection?"

"We thought there might be. It seemed indicated. In any case, there was so much bleeding, and now there is, at least, less."

"At least, less— What are you telling me?" Gary shook his head.

The doctors wouldn't look at him. "I have an idea," Dr. Price said suddenly. He usually stood when he talked to Gary, but this time, he sat on the couch beside him, he let himself sink down. "I think something isn't showing up in the tests we're doing. The blood is following the model, it isn't changing over time the way it seems like it should, so it's indicating nothing to me about why it's not clotting. I want to do another kind of test. I've seen it work once before with a young hemophiliac I was treating."

"What kind of test?"

"We wash the platelets. It's very involved and very expensive and very hard for the lab to do properly." He shook his head. "They won't like to do it and I'm sure they'll give me trouble." He shrugged. "But it's a very subtle and sophisticated test that will show if there is something present, an inhibitor protein that might be destroying her blood's ability to clot." Dr. Price stood up. "The blood has many problems, and I think Molly's is with her Factor VIII. I think her body might be producing an inhibitor against it."

"But why would it do that?"

Dr. Price held up his hand. "Who knows? No one sees anything like this. Maybe one case in a billion comes up. Sometimes in postpartum, things precipitate autoimmune disorders of all kinds." He frowned. "But we don't even know if that is what your wife has."

"But if it is?" Gary said.

"And then, we take it from there. We figure out what to do."

"There's something to do then—" Gary said.

"We'll talk about it later." He patted Gary's shoulder. "You hang on," he said.

Gary sat in the waiting room alone. An image kept flashing in his mind. Molly, the day Otis had been born, the way she had been peeled open before him, how he had seen her uterus, the baby inside of it. "I could do this again," she had said to him afterward. She hadn't been able to stop nuzzling Otis. She hadn't been able to keep her hands from him, that was how gleeful and happy she had been. How amazed. He had gone home that day and thought about a little girl with Molly's face, a little boy tagging after Otis. A whole brood trundled into a station wagon because their car would be too small. He ran one hand over his face and started to weep. Ghosts. The rest of their children were ghosts. And Molly was dying.

Molly began to acquire more and more doctors.

He could tell which group of doctors belonged to what specialty in minutes, though. Karen always showed up alone, or sometimes with one or two students. They were quiet, gentle, even though Molly, anesthetized, wouldn't feel a thing.

There were two different surgical teams, groups of six, who strode quickly in, all of them talking rapid-fire, volleying questions. The surgeons zipped off Molly's sheets and prodded and poked at her as if she weren't there. They argued among themselves.

The hematologists came alone. They were the most quiet. They stood for a long while standing in front of Molly's bed, as if they were contemplating her.

Gary could never remember the names of any of the doctors. He tried nicknames, plays on words. Dr. Pather, one of the new surgical team, he'd remember by calling him Dr. Paper. Dr. Verm, a critical-care specialist, was the wormy guy, but even then it backfired, because his brain was so foggy, he was so exhausted, it was all he could do to remember just the nicknames.

"Mr. Goldman," the doctors all called him. It was Molly's last name, not his, but he didn't bother to correct them. It was the only thing they did he found comforting.

The nurses, though, were a different story from the doctors. Maybe it was because he saw all three of them every day, because they always made time to sit and talk with him, or maybe it was just because they seemed somehow more hopeful to him than the doctors, less terrifying, but he never forgot any of their names. And there were two he really liked. Annie and Grey. Annie was big-boned with a toothy grin, and her husband Nicky was also a nurse. Grey was small and birdlike, with a soft, serious voice, and she dated a resident she said looked just like Jeff Goldblum. She made Gary come into the hallway with her one day so she could point him out. "See? Didn't I tell you?" The resident was tall and dark but other than that, he didn't look like Jeff Goldblum at all to Gary. "The spitting image," Gary said to Grey, and she beamed.

Gary liked the nurses. He saw Annie bending over Molly, brushing her hair. He watched Grey giving Molly a sponge bath, stroking the water across her arms, talking to her the whole time. Grey sometimes sang to Molly. Annie tickled Molly's toes. Gary watched them moving from bed to bed. He never saw them look anxious or disturbed or even distracted. He never saw one of them look helplessly at the other, and it made him feel calmer.

One day, Gary walked into the room and heard a strange whining music. At first, he thought Molly was singing. Excited, he moved closer to her. "Come on, honey," he said, but she was silent. He looked at her and saw the sheets faintly moving. He lifted them up and there, encasing both her legs, were soft blue plush stockings pulsing rhythmically about her. He put the sheet down.

"Circulators." Gary turned around to see Grey. "We want to keep her from getting bed sores. These stockings help."

"I thought she was singing," Gary said helplessly.

He was in the elevator, going to Maternity to see Otis. It was crowded with people, a few doctors in lab coats, a group of women with big leather purses. He felt someone staring at him, but he couldn't turn around, he didn't know who it was, and besides, he had gotten so little sleep. He was probably imagining it. He looked around the elevator. There was a large sign posted behind him that showed two doctors in a football kind of huddle and a large, interested-looking woman eavesdropping on them, her head cocked, one carefully manicured hand fanned out around her ear. SILENCE IS GOLDEN! RESPECT PATIENTS' RIGHTS! the sign said. The elevator stopped and three women got out. The doors whooshed shut. The ride continued. Beside him, a doctor he had never seen before suddenly leaned deliberately toward him. "You look tired, Mr. Goldman. I urge you not to neglect your rest."

"Excuse me?" Gary said, but the elevator door hissed open again and the doctor strode out.

His life was divided. Back Then and Right Now. None of it was right. He spent hours sitting beside his wife, talking to her. He spent hours with his son, feeding him, holding him, talking to him, too. He talked to the nurses, to the doctors, to the other people on the floor.

Otis was already bigger than the other babies. His eyes followed

Gary around the room. His face filled with light. "Daddy loves his boy," Gary sang.

He was diapering Otis when the dreadlock nurse came over to him. "I know this is bad timing, but have you been thinking about taking this baby home?"

"Home?"

"He can't stay in the nursery here forever. It's not good for him and it's going to cost you a fortune."

He hadn't thought once about insurance or cost or what he might do. The nurse nodded at him again encouragingly. "Do you or your wife have family?" He shook his head. "We are the family," he said.

"Then you need a baby nurse," she repeated.

"We wanted to do it ourselves." he said, and then immediately felt stupid. Molly had made fun of baby nurses when Ada had suggested it. "Who can tend a baby better than his parents?" she had said.

"Otis's immune system needs to strengthen. You don't want to bring him to the hospital with you when you come to see Molly. They won't let him into the SICU anyway." She folded her arms. "You need someone good and not too expensive, because insurance usually won't pick up the tab."

Gary nodded, dumb.

"Remarkable Baby Nurses," the nurse said. "That's the name of the agency we recommend."

chapter

four

R emarkable Baby Nurses answered on the third ring. A woman, her voice bright and lilting, announced herself as Mrs. Teasdale, and began to pepper him with questions. "How old is the baby and how long do you think you'd like one of our nurses?"

Gary fumbled. "My wife——" he said and then swallowed.

"Will this be live-in or live-out?"

He lay his hands along the counter. He studied his nails, the fraying threads of his shirt cuffs. "Newborn. My wife is hospitalized." He swallowed again. "Live-in," he said finally. "A month. Maybe more."

"For live-in, it's a thousand a week." Her voice was pleasant, calm. She acted as if this was a perfectly reasonable request.

He sat down on the kitchen stool. He had no vacation pay, no sick days left. He had known his insurance wouldn't cover a baby nurse, but he hadn't thought it would be this expensive. But he had the money they had banked for him to stay out. He'd have to use that, he'd have to not think ahead. "All right."

"And the nurse usually gets her own room."

"All right." They had a spare room with a small bed already in it.

"What kind of a nurse are you looking for?"

"Excuse me?"

"Strict, easygoing, a Dr. Spock or a Dr. Brazelton——"

Gary felt something cramping up along his spine. He had spent most of Molly's pregnancy reading baby books, but now he couldn't remember which doctor was which. "I don't know—" His mouth felt scratchy, dry. "A good one," he said finally. "I need a good nurse."

There was another clip of silence. "A good nurse," Mrs. Teasdale repeated slowly. "All right. I'll tell you what. It's very short notice, but we do have one woman I can send over tomorrow for you to meet. She's very good. Very experienced. Her name is Gerta Simmons. You talk with her and then you decide. If you don't like her, I'm sure we can find you someone else. How will that be?"

"All right. But I need to be at the hospital by noon at the latest. Can the nurse come early?"

"Is tomorrow at nine all right?"

He cleaned the house. It seemed important that the nurse didn't think he was sloppy or uncaring. He dusted and mopped and vacuumed, and for a while, the mindless action soothed him, lulled him into not thinking about anything more than the dust sparkling under the bed, the grime layered under the toaster oven. He swept the spare room, straightened books and papers, and as soon as he was through, the clean house filled him with despair because it didn't look as if people lived in it anymore.

Otis's room was spotless. He looked at the daybed by the window, at the new soft blue quilt Molly had special-ordered, and it hurt so much to see it that he bent and swept it from the bed. He stuffed it into the laundry closet.

Gerta Simmons, he thought. He had no idea what a name like that might produce, and he didn't really care, only that it was someone who might be warm and efficient and caring, someone who might know all the shortcuts he didn't. It was funny. Molly and he had planned for three people to be in this house, only now it seemed like it was going to be the wrong three.

He ran out and bought a small coffee cake from Swenson's Bakery.

He bought freshly ground coffee and tea. And then he came home and showered. He dressed in a clean shirt and jeans. He combed his hair as neatly as he could and then he waited to make a good impression on Gerta Simmons.

At ten-fifteen, the doorbell rang. She was late. He stood in the center of the living room for a moment, and then strode to the door and opened it. *Here we go*, he thought. To his surprise, Gerta was much older than he expected. Sixty, he thought. Maybe even sixty-five. She was trim and wiry, with a small foxlike face. Her hair was snow-white and clipped so short and straight, it seemed starched to her head. It was still warm outside, but she was bundled into a floor-length white coat. Her skin was so pale she looked as if someone had taken a gum eraser to her. She wore tan stud earrings, small as freckles. "Gerta Simmons," she said in a clipped voice. She had a faint German accent. "How do you do?"

He let her in. She stamped her feet on the rubber welcome mat outside the door. She unbuttoned her coat, handing it to him carefully. She was wearing a starchy white uniform, which startled him. She looked around the room, her gaze measured, and then back at him. "Well," she said. "They told me the baby isn't here yet. They told me about your wife. I'm sorry."

She sat opposite him on the couch, her hands folded in her lap.

"Would you like some coffee cake?"

She gave him a queer look.

"Tea? I have coffee? Water?" He felt like a fool.

"It's not necessary." She shook her head, and he sat back down on the sofa.

She riffled in her purse and handed him a thick envelope. "References," she said. "All of them good." He glanced at the first page, a line of print jumping out at him. *Never in my life have I met anyone as wonderful and as caring as—*

He blinked up at her. "I came to America from Germany twenty years ago when I got married to an American," she told him. "I have been tending babies since I was sixteen. I know them. I talk to them. I understand them." She leaned forward. "And they understand me."

Gary nodded. She was looking around the room again. He remembered something Mrs. Teasdale had said. "Do you favor Dr. Spock or Dr. Brazelton?"

"I favor Gerta Simmons. I believe in schedules and a firm, clear tone. I would never hit a child or raise my voice. I keep a notebook telling you when each feeding is, when each diaper change, and what was in it. And, very important, I know baby CPR and get recertified in it each and every year. Your child will be safe with me."

"That all sounds fine—"

"I have to have my own room," she announced. "And a decent bed with a firm mattress."

"Of course."

She seemed to relax a little. The silence wheeled around them.

"I tended triplets my last job," she said. "The family wanted me to stay but I don't like to stay too long because you get too attached to the babies and that's not good for anybody, is it? You don't want to spend your life missing people."

Gary flinched.

"I know you must worry about your wife. But now you don't have to worry about the baby." She was so sure and calm and still, he felt suddenly relaxed. There was no real reason for him to, but he trusted her.

"When can you start?"

Gena smiled for the first time since she had entered his home, her mouth a semicircle of pink, her teeth small and even as corn Niblets. "Tomorrow afternoon."

Bringing Otis home alone was the hardest thing Gary had ever done. It was nothing like the way he and Molly had planned, the way he had imagined and thought about and wondered over. The pint-sized polka-dot onesie, the matching hat and booties they had bought as a homecoming outfit, was still tucked in Molly's hospital suitcase. He couldn't bring himself to get it. So he pulled something out of Otis's drawer instead: a second choice, a yellow coverall with a tiny hood.

He had always planned to bring a video camera, to film Molly dressing the baby, Molly carrying Otis to the car and into his car seat for the first time. The instant camera was loaded with color film. He had bought a brand-new video camera and read the manual cover to cover. He left both cameras at home.

He spent all morning at Molly's bedside, watching her chest rise and fall, watching the lighted numbers change on her monitors. He talked to her in a loud strong voice, as if she could hear him, as if things were normal. "I'm taking Otis home today." He watched her, half expecting her to stir, to wake, to stay his hand and tell him, "Oh, no, wait, you can't do it without me——" But she stayed motionless.

"Gerta seems fine," he told her. "You'll see for yourself." He stayed, holding her hand, and then at noon, he bent and kissed her good-bye. He stopped being cheery. "I'm so sorry," he said, and then he went to the nursery, Otis's change of clothing balled in one hand.

There was a nurse there he didn't recognize, but to his surprise, she seemed to know him. She waved vigorously. "So today's the day, is it? You're taking our Otis?"

The nurse grinned. She was tall and pretty. She had a wide gold band on her finger, and he thought: *She's happy. She has a husband. Maybe a family. Maybe the only thing she worries about is whether or not she'll get a refund at tax time.*

"It won't be the same without him. Who's going to show all the new babies the ropes? Who's going to teach all to cry and fuss and jam as many fingers as they can into their mouths?"

She put a hand on Gary's shoulder. "You have a car seat, right? He's not going anywhere without a car seat."

"Brand-new."

"You hold on, then." She bent and picked up his son. She fit Otis into his arms. Otis stretched and yawned and blinked up at him.

She helped him put the clothes on his son. "Well, aren't you the cutest thing." She gave Otis a resounding kiss. "I'll miss you, honey bunny," she whispered to him. Then she gave Gary a pat. "Wait," she ordered.

She was gone for only a minute, and when she came back she handed him a small blue case printed with yellow smiling rabbits. "Our goody bag. Diapers, formula, even a pacifier and an infant tee. Everything you need to get you started." She gave him a half smile. "I put in some extra surprises. Nipples. Bottles. Changing pads and receiving blankets. Now you go ahead and take him before the other babies know their leader's missing."

In the elevator, two very pregnant women smiled and cooed at the baby. Their fingers floated up in greeting. As soon as Gary stepped outside the hospital's revolving door with Otis, he felt the air clamp around him. "Here we go," he said.

Otis was silent when Gary gently lowered him into the car seat, facing backward by law, which disturbed him because how could he tell if his son was all right if he couldn't see him? He seemed too small for the car seat, sinking down, his head lolling. Gary tried to prop the baby up better. He tightened the straps.

Gary usually drove a neat, zippy speed, darting in and out of other cars, taking chances, but now he drove so slowly and carefully that the other drivers became annoyed. They honked their horns, they shouted at him. But Gary kept going slowly because even though his son was buttressed in a padded car seat, he was taking no chances.

Gary was halfway home when he began to be worried by Otis's silence. Didn't newborns cry and fuss and carry on? Was this normal for a newborn to be this still? Was something wrong that the hospital had missed? He began to feel a twist of fear, and then abruptly, he veered to the right, pulling over, the other cars whizzing past him. His heart knocked against his ribs. He jumped out of the car and opened the back door and leaned into the backseat of the car, over the car seat, ready to pull his son out, to give CPR or rush him back to the hospital or whatever else he needed to do, and there was his son, peaceful, mouth open, asleep, his tiny chest rising and falling.

*   *   *

Gary got home fifteen minutes before Gerta was to arrive. The neighborhood was empty except for Belle, jumping into a car, who didn't see him.

"Here we go," he said to Otis, trying to sound hopeful because he had heard somewhere that babies could read the emotion in a voice. "Home sweet home." He bent to open the car seat, to pick him up, and as soon as he did, Otis's small perfect face bunched into a scream.

Inside the house, Otis was inconsolable. His face pinched in misery and grew red. His hands fisted. He screamed. Gary checked his diaper, which was clean. He patted his son's back and tried to rock him, but everything he did seemed to make Otis shriek even more. Desperate, he turned on the radio. Opera flooded the room. Verdi. He turned it up, hoping the music might soothe his son, he sang to attract his attention, but nothing seemed to calm his son's squall. When the doorbell rang, Otis's wails rose another decibel.

Juggling Otis, he opened the door. There was Gerta in her white coat, carrying two blue plaid suitcases. She looked from Otis to Gary and back again, and then she said something in a voice so low he couldn't hear her. She stepped inside and clapped her hands at him. "Give him to me."

Otis stiffened. "What should I do?" Gary said, panicked. "Should I get a bottle?"

Gerta ignored him. Instead, she reached for Otis. She started to murmur something low and soothing and pretty. She cradled him closer to her.

"What's that?" Gary asked.

"German lullaby. Babies love it." She looked around. "Shut off that opera, please."

He clicked the radio off. She swayed with his son, back and forth, keeping time to the lullaby she was whispering, and after a while Otis's screams began to slow into sobs and then into whimpers. His fists relaxed, the red in his face began to fade into pink. She nodded at Otis. "Yes, I agree wholeheartedly," she said. Otis whimpered once and then suddenly seemed to take note of Gerta. His eyes, grave and gray, grew rounder. He stared up at Gerta and then, to Gary's astonishment, he yawned, and his lids fluttered shut. He slept in her arms.

Gary was astounded. "What did you do?"

Gerta glanced over at Gary. She sat down with Otis on the couch. "Babies pick things up. You were getting more nervous, so he got more nervous. I was simply calm. I am always calm."

She stroked Otis's hair. "And I listen to what a baby tells me. This one has told me many things already."

"He has? What things?"

"That he needed stillness."

Gary smiled dumbly. "How did he tell you that?"

Gerta looked down at Otis. "Babies have their own language. I just know how to translate." She rocked Otis in her arms. "We are going to get along just fine."

The first morning Gerta was there, the commotion in the kitchen woke him up. He felt funny about appearing before her in his robe, so he quickly showered and dressed and came into the kitchen to find her, in her nurse's whites, which troubled him because they reminded him of the hospital. She was feeding Otis his bottle, settling him on her lap.

"Good morning." Her voice was clipped and serious.

"Hey, how are you, Otis?" He bent to see his son, but Otis's eyes were on Gerta.

"You don't have to keep wearing the uniform if you don't want to—" he started to say, but she looked at him as if he had suggested she fly to Mars.

"Certainly I do. It's professional. Cleaner."

He nodded. "I'd like to hold him." Gerta frowned, but she pointed to a chair. "Sit." She lowered Otis into his lap, and fit the bottle into his hand. "Don't tilt the bottle up too high." She stood in the kitchen watching Gary and his son, her arms folded, and then abruptly she turned to the sink and began noisily washing bottles.

He wanted to be at the hospital by ten. It gave him only a few hours with Otis, and when the baby fell asleep in his arms, he couldn't help feeling a raw despair that they were wasting time. Gerta leaned over him and picked Otis up. "He's a good sleeper. I can tell already." She rocked Otis for a moment in her arms. "Let's take you to your crib."

Gary didn't know what to do with himself while Otis slept. He didn't want to leave after seeing his son for only a half hour. He went upstairs to his office and tried to do some work, but he couldn't concentrate. He kept listening for Otis's wake-up cry. He kept straining to hear, and in the end, he clicked the computer off. He came back downstairs. He'd come back for lunch. He'd call and see if Otis was up.

He went to find Gerta, who was in the kitchen boiling bottles. "I'll call you from the hospital."

"Everything will be fine."

"There's a spare set of house keys hanging in the kitchen," he told her. "And please, make a list of what foods you'd like for yourself, what things you might need, and I'll pick them up for you."

"I will be fine."

The whole way to the hospital, he felt nipped with guilt for leaving his son. He felt eaten away with worry. What if something happened? What if Gerta stopped being concerned the moment he was out of the house? People snapped like dry twigs.

A car behind him honked and he speeded up. *You're being an idiot*, he told himself, but he couldn't help stopping at a convenience store, running out to a bank of pay phones and dialing. There was a pebble of pink gum wedged up along the metal.

"Just checking." He tried to sound cheerful.

"Everything is fine. Otis woke and had a wet diaper. Just as he should. I'll take him to the park later." She was silent for a moment. "He knows you are at the hospital seeing his mama."

"Excuse me?"

"He tells me, Mama is sick. What can I do? He is so little, it's frustrating for him."

After Gary hung up, he rested his head against the phone. His legs buckled beneath him and he gripped the phone for balance.

Gary called Gerta two more times that day, once when he first got to the hospital, and later when Molly was wheeled down to get another CAT scan. Each time he called, Gerta answered on the second ring, sounding more and more annoyed. "I'll be home around one to see Otis. Will he be up, do you think?" Gary asked.

"It's possible."

At one, Gary drove home. He didn't know what to expect, but as soon as he opened the front door, he nearly stumbled. She had spread a sheet across the living room, and lying across it was every single toy of Otis's. "Hello?" he called.

Gerta came out, Otis on her hip. "I washed and sterilized the toys," she said. "I aired out his room and washed his baby blanket."

"You didn't have to do that."

"Germs."

"I want to take Otis for a walk."

She nodded. "I'll get him ready." He trailed her into the baby's room. He stood watching her put on Otis's little jacket, his tiny shoes, and then he followed her out again and watched her put him in the stroller. It wasn't until she began pulling on her coat that he realized she was coming along, too.

"Please, take a break. You must be tired."

"Oh, no, no. I have to stop and pick up a few things at the market anyway. Plus, it looks like such a nice day. I'd like to get out."

She put her hands on the stroller. "I'll do it," he said, taking the stroller from her, but as soon as he did, she moved closer to him. He felt her watching him, as if any moment she expected he might do something wrong.

He didn't relax until Gerta stopped in front of the Thrift-T-Mart. "We'll wait out here," he told her. She hesitated. "It seems a shame to take him out of the fresh air."

She nodded, considering. "I won't be long," she said.

Gary wheeled the stroller to a green bench and sat down, angling the stroller so he could see his son. "Let's live dangerously." He bent down and unhooked the straps. He lifted up Otis and held him in his lap. "Here's Daddy." Otis blinked at the sun. He scrunched up his face and waved his hands. Gary held the baby close to him. Molly had stopped wearing perfume because she said it confused babies, they needed to know their mother's scent. He hadn't put on aftershave that morning. He'd do without it from now on.

"Oh, Daddy's a fool for his baby—" he sang and then suddenly, there was Gerta standing in front of him, a plastic bag in one hand. "How are we doing?" he asked her, teasing, trying to be light.

She studied Otis. "You're holding him too tightly." She reached forward, trying to adjust his grip, and Otis suddenly spit up, a rivulet of cream down his sleeve. "You see?" Gerta said.

"He's a baby. Babies spit up," Gary said, but Gerta bent down, examining Otis's diaper.

"He's soiled his diaper. Didn't you notice?" She took Otis from him. Otis belched, loudly and noisily. Gerta smiled. "Oh, that wasn't you, was it? That must have been the baby next door who burped so rudely."

She turned back to Gary. "Babies tell you things. He probably made a small face, or didn't seem comfortable. You are going to have to learn to pay more attention."

Gary had expected there would be an adjustment, a getting used to each other, to the house, but Gerta seemed as if she had never lived anywhere else or been with any other baby. She didn't ask Gary where the bottles were, the nipples or the toys, because she somehow seemed to know. She snapped about the house, talking constantly to Otis, singing, and when Otis slept, she cleaned bottles or napped herself in her room, the door firmly shut.

Every morning at exactly seven o'clock Gerta got up and she fed Otis and then he had his nap and then each and every time she gave him a bottle, she marked it in a little notebook. There were pages and pages of times and ounces and none of it meant anything to Gary except that Otis had been fed.

She criticized everything. "You have the wrong bottles," she warned.

"I do? What's wrong with them?"

"You have to get the kind made in Germany. With a knob instead of a loop so the baby can't grab on to it and fling it to the ground." She hated the diapers he chose, with the Velcro close. "Cloth is handier, cleaner, and more economical." She even distrusted the bottle warmer, preferring warming the bottles herself in a pan of hot water.

"You talk to Otis wrong," she announced one evening. "Your tones are too low. Children like high sounds, you should raise your voice." She shook her head. "In Germany, children are raised better. We know they try to get things over on us, and because we love them we don't permit it. Even a newborn is manipulative. Look how little Otis cries to be picked up. You think he doesn't know his tears can move mountains as well as hearts?"

Gary looked over at Otis who was having a sudden squall. "I think he knows only he wants to be picked up."

"Wrong," Gerta said triumphantly. "This baby, he understands what is going on. He knows his mother is sick. He knows you are upset. He wants to help but he knows he is just a small baby and cannot do much of anything. He tells me these things."

Gary thought of his friend's child Stella, balancing on her stocking legs, casually sucking her thumb as if it were fine wine. *I talked to God*, she had said.

Gerta nodded vigorously. "This baby prays for his mama. I hear him at night. Come home, Mama, he says. Get well and come home. I miss you, Mama."

Gary blinked at Gerta.

"You want me to pick him up, I'll pick him up," Gerta said. "But you're wrong. And you're starting a bad habit."

"Pick him up."

"In Germany, things are better."

Then go back, Gary thought, but he didn't say it. He couldn't risk offending her. Another nurse might be better, but she might be worse, too, and he couldn't take that chance.

He let her do what she wanted, gave her free rein. She came back with new pacifiers, diapers, wipes, and formula. She was methodical, humorless. He couldn't help himself, he knew it was terrible, but sometimes, watching her, he had the urge to ask her what she did during World War II, how exactly she had served the Fatherland.

Gerta kept to herself. As soon as she put Otis to bed, she went to her room and watched comedies on TV or talk shows. She was addicted to the Home Shopping Network, the jewelry and the exercise gadgets, and although he never heard her order a thing, he could hear her intakes of breath, her pleased, lingering sighs. "Oh, look at that!" she cried.

One night, Gary was coming home, bounding up the stairs when he suddenly noticed two blue casserole dishes on the front porch. There was a small white card attached to one of them. He crouched down and plucked it up. There in firm red lettering it said, "Bake half an hour in a hot oven (425 degrees)." There was no signature. No sign of whom this might be from. He picked up the casseroles, balancing them in both hands, and brought them into the house.

Gerta was in the kitchen making Otis's bottle. Otis was napping in the bassinet beside her. "What's that?"

"I don't know. Neighbors must have left it." He lifted the lids. Macaroni and cheese. Baked ziti, it looked like. "I guess it's dinner."

"I've eaten already," Gerta said.

Gary heated up the baked ziti casserole and ate because he thought he should. The pasta was overcooked, the sauce too salty. The food warmed him. It made him feel less alone.

* * *

It began to happen more and more. Evenings, when Gary came home, there was always a covered dish on the front porch. Blue glass with an aluminum-foil lid, flower-sprigged Corning Ware with a tin pie top. There were never any notes, never anything more personal than cooking instructions.

He walked around and around the neighborhood, hoping one of the neighbors would come out. They know everything, Lisa had told them, so why didn't they know he was walking the sidewalks with his son, that he wanted to thank whoever had given him the food?

He looked for signs of life. The neighbors had sat out nights in the summer, but now that it was fall, the street seemed empty. He could ring a bell if he saw a light. He could make some excuse.

He was walking around the street for the second time when he saw a car pull up. He took his time, he waited for the door to open, and then a burly man got out, someone he didn't recognize.

When he came back inside, Gerta was watching Home Shopping Network, staring at a woman in a red evening gown. "Do you ever see the neighbors?" he asked Gerta.

She kept watching the TV. "Sometimes. They comment on how beautiful this baby is, they ask for Molly, and for you."

He felt a flicker of surprise. Gerta talked to the neighbors. "Really? Who do you talk to? What do you tell them?"

She waved one hand. "I don't remember. The woman on the right. A man down the street. I tell them everything is under control. They wanted to know who I was, what I was doing here. They were suspicious." She looked away from him, glancing at the clock. "I'm too busy to stop and chat."

Nothing was under control, Gary thought. Everything was flying away. "Will you thank them for me for the food? Will you tell them I want to thank them myself?"

"The people don't want to be thanked," Gerta told him.

He never knew what to do with the dishes. None of the neighbors ever called to ask, "So, did you like that turkey noodle stew? Did you finish the pie?" None of them knocked on his door, apologetically asking, "Say, are you done with my blue casserole dish because I could use it to roast a chicken tonight." The few times he spotted one of the neighbors outside, the most they ever did was nod, so swift and sure and sharp that he didn't feel he could walk over to them and ask if they were responsible for such kindness. "You don't want to embarrass someone who has been kind and doesn't want to be thanked," Gerta told him. "And worse, you don't want to embarrass someone who hasn't been." Gary washed and dried the casserole dishes and the pots and set them out, empty, onto his porch. Sometimes they disappeared; sometimes, if they remained on his porch for a week, he kept them; and every time he saw them in his cabinet, he flinched because it was another unknown, another thing he had no control over.

Gerta might have had her routines, but so did Gary. His days had a kind of rhythm, a sameness he found himself clutching at. He knew what nurse would be on duty when he got to the hospital. He knew when he went to the cafeteria to get a sandwich he couldn't eat, there would be the same three kinds of cheese, the same yogurts, the same chicken wings. And he began to notice a kind of sameness in the visitors, as well.

While Molly was having tests, he sat in the waiting room. The waiting room at Intensive Care had regulars, and Gary started to know them all. There was a tall thin blond woman who Gary guessed must be in her early forties. She always wore high-powered dark suits and heels so high and sharp they could be used as weapons. She made Gary, who barely raked his hands through his hair, let alone a comb, who sometimes put on the same faded jeans and sweatshirt he had been wearing all week, feel like a cast-out. How did she have time to do laundry? There was a young couple who held hands, who nodded apologetically at Gary, as if his being there was somehow their fault. "My brother got in a skiing accident," the woman blurted. "It was so stupid. Parachute skiing. Who does such a thing? Who in their right mind?" She waved one hand.

"He's going to be fine," the man said. He tapped a finger to his forehead. "I know these things." His voice was so sincere that Gary felt like asking him if he knew anything about Molly.

An elderly man came in every day at five. He always dressed carefully in a suit and fresh shirt and tie. He told Gary he came to see his wife, who had just had triple bypass and wasn't doing very well. He leaned toward Gary and showed him photographs every time he came in. They were always of his wife when she was young, posing in white floppy shorts and a T-shirt, one hand angled behind her head, her dark curly hair ruffling about her. There was one of her rising from the sea, in a snow-white shirred bathing suit, her hair slick against her shoulders, her teeth flashing. "Ain't she a beaut?" he said.

"She's lovely," Gary said.

There was a kind of etiquette in the room. No one dared to ask anyone why they were there, who they were waiting for, but if people volunteered information, then you could have a conversation. You could swap symptoms and prognosis and even make a joke or two about the doctors, though that was considered dangerous, like tempting fate. Gary listened to a man named Aaron telling the couple that he himself had had many skiing accidents and had emerged better than before. "I won my first ski race after I healed from breaking both legs," he told them. Gary knew the rules. You didn't have to believe what anyone told you, you only had to believe the feeling infused in the words, to try to hang on to it yourself. Anything could be hope. The way a doctor held his stethoscope. A change in hospital menu.

Gary was still. "Who is here?" the old man asked. He was breaking the rules.

"My wife," he said finally. "She got sick after she gave birth." The old man's gaze was steady and serious. "They—the doctors—don't know," Gary admitted.

"I consider that a positive. When they don't know, there is room for hope. My brother Abe had cancer five years ago and beat it," the old man said emphatically. "None of the doctors thought he would make it. Every day they told me to give up, but I never did. Now he has a relapse. And you know what? He'll beat that, too."

*   *   *

When Gary went back to see Molly, there was a bag of thick cheesy-looking material hanging from her IV. He stared at it in confusion. Her electronic monitors flashed numbers he didn't understand. He didn't know what to do with himself, what to do for her. "I'm here." His voice cracked. "I'm right here."

"Good. I wanted to talk with you."

Gary started. Dr. Price, his white lab coat thrown open over a blue T-shirt and scrub pants, strode toward him. He never made eye contact with Gary anymore, which bothered Gary in some deep, undeniable way. Instead, Dr. Price looked at the IV. "We know what she has."

Gary waited.

"In postpartum, the immune system can go a little haywire. Things for the mother are always compromised to protect the baby. In her case, she formed a protein, an inhibitor against a factor in her blood that clots it—Factor VIII. We can perhaps transfuse human Factor VIII into her to start things working again, to tip the balance against the inhibitor." Dr. Price put his hands in the pockets of his lab coat. "I would like chemo."

"Chemo. But this isn't cancer, is it?"

"No, but chemo works on many things. And we are talking about mild chemo."

"Excuse me. *Mild* chemo?"

"Cytoxan. Not any sort of compelling dose."

Gary shook his head. "What kind of a drug has toxin in the name?"

"Tox-*an*. Very short-term. We could do steroids very long-term, but with the doses we'd need, we'd see all sorts of problems we might not like. And there is the factor of time." He stared at Gary. "Chemo works fast."

"I don't know."

"I recommend we start immediately." He smiled at Gary, suddenly friendly, as if things had been settled. "I have your okay?"

Gary felt numb. *It works*, he told himself. *It works fast. A little mild chemo.*

"I feel it is best," said Dr. Price. "Works in no time. With a minimum of side effects."

Gary shut his eyes. *In no time. No time.* He nodded. "Do it," he said finally.

That night, on the computer, at three in the morning, Gary did a search for Cytoxan. It popped up, filling two screens, and he scrolled down to read. Chemotherapeutic. Can cause massive bleeding. He stopped. Why would they give a drug that could cause bleeding to a woman who was already hemorrhaging? He printed the page out and then clicked the computer off, sick.

Frantic, Gary tried to call Dr. Price. He got the answering service and left a message. He paged him every five minutes. He didn't care. He got to the hospital in the morning, the printouts in his hand about Cytoxan, and then he paged Dr. Price again. He used the pay phones and then a phone at the nurse's station. He paged and paged until he saw one of the nurses picking up the phone, nodding at him, lifting one finger, trying to get a word in edgewise. Five minutes later, Dr. Price was striding down the floor. "What?" he said, furious.

"What were you thinking? Why would you give a drug that can cause bleeding to someone who can't stop bleeding?" Gary flapped the printouts in his hands. He gave them to Dr. Price, who glanced at them and then sighed, exasperated.

"Look, this drug does good things. But it's complicated. It doesn't know not to do bad things in order to get the job done. This was a good thing. The chemo seems to be helping."

He folded up the paper and handed it back to Gary. "You don't have to bring me a paper. I'm well aware of what each and every drug we give Molly does."

* * *

Gary stood in Molly's room. She didn't look any different, any better. But, he told himself, she didn't look any worse.

Three days later, Molly was hemorrhaging. The Cytoxan was stopped. She was rushed into surgery for an angiogram, a catheter threaded through her artery, glue on her veins because they couldn't risk cutting her open, couldn't risk more blood.

For five hours, he waited in the solarium, afraid to move. It was empty except for the woman with a cell phone, and for the first time that he could remember, she was speaking into it. "No one knows," she said.

He was staring at a newspaper he had already read three times when Dr. Price and a new doctor he didn't know came into the room. "Dr. Swen. I did the operation," he said. "She's stable now. What we do now is watch her, and wait." Dr. Price looked right at Gary, his face smooth and impassive and blameless. "We'll go with the steroids after this."

Gary couldn't move. "And we're putting Molly on memory blockers." He nodded at Gary, pleased.

Gary looked at Dr. Price, astonished. He had never heard of such a thing. "But she's anesthetized," he said finally. "Karen told me she was in a deep-sleep state. Why would you need to make her forget?"

Dr. Price was silent for a moment. "People rouse up from sleep. They rouse up from anesthesia. We're trying to minimize trauma. Would you want to take the chance of her remembering?"

"They rouse from anesthesia?"

Dr. Price was silent, waiting. "Think of it as a precaution."

Gary felt glued to the floor. He watched Dr. Price stride down the corridor. Good, he thought, then good. She wouldn't remember the tubes shimmying through her. She wouldn't remember the drainage or the pain. Sleeping Beauty. And then it hit him, with a force so terrible, his legs buckled under him and he had to sit down. She wouldn't remember him, either, the way he was there beside her, holding her hand as if he might never let go. She wouldn't remember that she wasn't alone in all this, not traveling by herself down dangerous unmapped land, full of minefelds. He felt consumed with guilt and grief, furious at himself. And he wanted to kill Dr. Price.

That same morning, at home, while Otis napped, he called all the hospitals he knew. The Mayo Clinic. Johns Hopkins. He asked for the names of the heads of their Hematology Departments, for the phone numbers. He always got secretaries, nurses. "You're not a patient?" they said. They didn't want to put Gary through. They didn't want to even take a message, not until he pleaded, not until he told them what it was Molly had, and then there was silence. "Hold on," the voices said. "Hold on."

He spoke to five different doctors, and all of them told him something different about treatment. They all had particular likes and dislikes and the more they talked to Gary, the happier they seemed. Two liked chemo and said Molly probably hadn't been given enough. One liked interferon. Another liked steroids. All of them seemed to Gary to be clamoring to take Molly's case, to see her, to consult, to take a look. They offered appointments, they gave out their beeper numbers. "Dr. Price," the doctor from the Mayo Clinic sniffed. "I know Dr. Price. I've met him. Kind of a sledgehammer of a guy, isn't he? Intractable. No sense of humor." But Gary, listening to the Mayo Clinic doctor talk about longer, stronger doses of chemo, didn't feel comforted. "This is a really interesting case," the doctors all said. But none of them said a single word about cure.

It was afternoon. Gerta had taken Otis to the park. He wanted company. He wanted a calm presence telling him everything would be all right. It was Sunday. Maybe someone would be home. He dialed a few people he knew but he kept getting answering machines. Finally, in desperation, he called Brian.

"Brian."

"Gary. What's up?" Brian's voice was sleepy. *What's up,* Gary thought, baffled. *What's up?*

"Molly just had another operation."

Brian was silent. "You feel like grabbing a bite with me?" Gary said, trying not to make his voice a plea. "I could use the company." He knew as soon as he said it, it was probably ridiculous. Brian didn't socialize with the people he worked with. He held court. He organized company picnics no one wanted to go to, and the one time Gary hadn't gone, Brian had called him into the office the next day to reprimand him. "So where were you?" Brian demanded. "Do you know how bad it looked that you weren't there?" When morale was particularly awful, Brian made everyone go to lunchtime pizza parties, all of them herded into an overheated conference room when all anyone wanted to do was get away from work for a while, maybe have a nice quiet lunch. Gary included. But now, all Gary wanted was company. Even Brian's. "So what do you think?" Gary said.

There was silence again. He could hear the TV blaring in the background. Sports, it sounded like. Brian must be watching the game.

"Sure, what about tomorrow?"

Tomorrow might be too late. Tomorrow might be busy. He couldn't think that far ahead, but he was glad and grateful that at least Brian hadn't mentioned work. "I was thinking now."

There was a brief swell of sound from the TV. Brian sighed into the phone. "Okey dokey. You come here. We can watch the game."

Brian lived in Montclair, in a big, roomy house surrounded by trees. Gary had been to Brian's only once before, for an office Christmas party, before he had met Molly. Brian had money and the area was wealthy, but Brian's house had an unfinished feel to it. It was filled with plasterboard furniture, pull-out sofas, ready-framed prints.

Brian answered the door in navy-blue sweats, a mug of beer in his hands. As soon as he stepped inside the house, Gary wanted to leave. "Sit," Brian said. "Green Bay Packers. They're creaming the Dolphins." Gary didn't tell Brian he had never much cared for sports, but he sat down on the scratchy plaid couch. Brian nudged a bowl of chips and dip in front of him. "It's good," he said, but Gary shook his head. In the corner of the room were two boxes. CompUSA. "New equipment?" Gary pointed.

"It's a PC for Candy. I'm sending it out as a present."

Gary nodded. "Nice present."

"She needs it. Last time I called, she was a little depressed. She hadn't gotten an acting job she thought she had. I'll probably set it up myself when I get out there."

"You going out there soon?"

Brian stretched and reached for another chip. He stared hard at the TV. "Nice move!" he shouted, and then turned back to Gary. "Soon."

For two hours, Gary sat on Brian's couch, the game blaring about him. He couldn't concentrate. Every few minutes Brian would slap his thigh or jump up or simply holler at the TV. "Isn't that just the damnedest?"

"Yes," Gary said. "It is."

He had hoped to talk to Brian, but the only time Brian really spoke to him was during the commercials, and even then the look Brian gave him was so guarded and worried, it seemed like a warning to Gary. He had been there an hour and a half when Brian finally, reluctantly, turned to him. "So how's Molly?" His voice deepened in concern. "How are you holding up? I don't know how you do it. I've been calling Candy twice a day now because you're on my mind so much. I keep thinking, what if it were me and Candy, and then my mind just slams shut."

"It does that for me, too."

"That's why I have to get out there and see her," Brian patted him on one knee. "Well, listen, I was thinking. Since you have your computer at home and all, think you might have a minute to do a mockup of a math textbook cover for us? Just the cover? Should be pretty easy. Just numbers. Something graphic. Right up your alley."

Gary couldn't speak. "You want me to do work?" he said finally.

"No, no, I just know that in my times of trouble, I personally always find work helps me keep my mind off things. Helps me stay focused. Gives me a purpose."

"I have a purpose. I go to the hospital, I see my son, I try to cope."

Brian turned away from the TV. He looked at Gary with new interest. "Gary—" Brian's voice lowered confidentially. "I thought long and hard about bringing this up. I've decided that I would be highly remiss if I didn't at least mention this to you. The word from up top is that layoffs might be coming. I know how awful that would be at a time like this, and I certainly would fight tooth and nail for you. I go to bat for you each and every day. I always say, 'The best ideas are Gary's.' You know that."

Gary was silent.

"It's important to stay visible." Brian cleared his throat. "Walk the halls, I always say, walk the halls, pop your head into every office, give them something personal to remember you by. I can say your name until I'm blue in the face, but sooner or later someone's going to notice the body isn't there—or the work."

Gary nodded, numbly. "So just get in some layouts," Brian said, and then turned back to the television.

Gary didn't know why, but he stayed at Brian's for two hours, lulled into a kind of stupor. Finally, when he knew Otis would be awake, he stood up. He jammed his hands into his pockets. Brian looked at him expectantly. "I'd better get going."

"Don't you want to stay and see how the game ends up?" Brian looked surprised. "The Packers are winning."

Gary wound his scarf about his neck. "I'm beat."

Brian nodded. He kept his gaze fixated on the television as he walked Gary to the door, opening it. "You drive safe now—" he started to say and then whooped at the TV. "Go, go!" he cried.

Gary stepped out into the cold. "See you, Brian," he said, and walked to his car to go to his son.

* * *

A week later, Gary hadn't touched the layouts for Brian, and Molly was still critical. There were new doctors to talk to: Dr. Monroe, the critical-care specialist who was monitoring Molly for infections; Dr. Herm, another new surgeon. He began to see Dr. Price, the hematologist, more and more. Gary always felt like laughing when he heard the name, but he knew it was mostly nerves, anxiety flying up and crashing against his ribs.

"We're going to try transfusions," Dr. Price told Gary. "We've had some good results in the past. If we can stabilize her, we can start to lessen her drug dosage."

"What does that mean?"

Dr. Price half smiled. "It means we can stop the memory blockers. It means we can try to wake her."

Gary sat by Molly's bedside, holding her hand. Her eyes stayed shut, her chest rose and fell in awkward rhythm. Her hair was greasy and tangled and there were new white threads spun through it. Molly's lips were chapped.

"Molly."

He sat with Molly, bringing the bread to her nose. "Smell," he ordered, but she was still, her face turned from him. He told himself it didn't matter that she didn't show a reaction. Who knew what was going on in her mind? The night before he had looked up stories on the Internet about coma, although he knew it was not the same thing as being anesthetized. An endless sleep. What did you know, what did you feel? Did Molly rise up as if from deep water and hear his voice? Was she dreaming?

There was nothing on the Internet about anesthetized states, so he operated as if she were in coma. Kids had been brought out by their pet dog, smuggled into a hospital in a backpack, licking their bowners' faces. Husbands had been brought out by a vial of their wife's perfume set by the bed. People showed no sign of motion and then suddenly, abruptly, sat bolt upright and asked a question as if it were an ordinary day. Did you put an extra quarter in the washer? Did you start dinner yet?

* * *

He came home to find Gerta watching TV, the baby asleep. "All is fine," Gerta told him.

He went to Otis's room. "He's sleeping," Gerta warned, but suddenly Gary didn't care. He wanted to see his son. He opened the door to the room and as soon as he did, Otis stirred and blinked up at him.

He came downstairs with Otis dressed in a jacket and hat. Gerta's mouth formed a line. "We're going to the park," he said. "Alone."

He told himself he didn't need Gerta with him, but it was astonishing to him the things he was unsure about, the things he didn't know how to do. When Otis cried, Gerta usually could stop him in seconds, with a bottle or a diaper. He fumbled with a pacifier and Otis spat it out. He tried to stroke his son's head and Otis screamed louder.

There were only a few other people there: an elderly woman in a blue coat reading a newspaper and eating a muffin, and a young woman with cropped black hair, a Walkman clamped to her head. She was in sweats, stretching, getting ready to run.

He tried to reposition Otis on his lap, but the baby screamed more, so loudly the woman in sweats suddenly looked over at him. She unplugged her Walkman and walked over to him. "Burp him," she said. Her hands flapped. "Pat his back. Bounce him a bit on your knee," Gary bounced Otis, who erupted into a burp, and then yawned. "Told you," the woman said. She smiled. She brushed at her hair. And then she looked down at his hand. "Oh, sorry, wedding band," she said. "Thought you were a single dad. Just my luck, the nice, nurturing ones are married."

He stayed out until dinner and then he took Otis to the Tastee, where he had first met and fallen in love with Molly. The waitresses made a fuss and he stayed for an hour, Otis on the leatherette seat beside him.

Gerta was furious when he came home. She plucked the baby from his arms, as if she were inspecting him for damage. She whispered to Otis. She cocked her head. "He's telling me he was tired, that he didn't want to go out, but you insisted, and he had no choice," Gerta said. She whispered to Otis again. "He said he is worried now about you, and it is too much for a baby to worry about his father and his mother both." She held up her head, as if she were listening to Otis. "Yes," she said. "I understand completely."

Gary was coming home from the hospital the next day, when, to his surprise, he saw Gerta sitting on the front porch with Otis, talking with Theresa and Emma. It was the first time he had seen the neighbors, but more amazingly, it was the first time he had seen Gerta so animated. Her eyes lit like sparklers. Her free hand fluttered as she chattered, and she was relaxed. She seemed as if she was old friends with the neighbors.

As soon as Gary approached the porch, his hands awkwardly at his side, the talk stopped. The women all looked at him, expectant, and then Emma suddenly got up and came over to Gary. She wavered. Her mouth moved as if she wanted to tell him something and then she took two steps toward him and hugged him. "A million times I wanted to come over, ask what I could do, but I didn't want you thinking I was interfering." She nodded at Gerta, who sat there, placidly rocking Otis. "Gerta's been keeping us all posted on how Molly's doing."

"On how you're doing, too," Theresa blurted.

Gary looked at Gerta, but she was adjusting a button on Otis's blue striped shirt.

"We're all so concerned," Emma said.

Theresa nodded. "I've been praying for her. For all of you. Saint Jude. Saint Ann. Every day, I light a candle."

"You tell us what you need," Emma said. "Don't hesitate."

Gary looked from one face to the other. "The casseroles were so delicious."

Theresa flushed, pleased.

"Thank you for the cards."

Theresa nodded. "Wasn't it a cute card?"

"Please stop. You don't thank neighbors," Emma said quietly.

*   *   *

Seeing the neighbors together like that seemed to unlock something. Where before they were hidden, they now seemed to be everywhere. He ran into Emma at the greengrocer's. And although Theresa still didn't speak to him when she was with Carl (and as soon as Carl saw Gary he burst into a determined, tuneless whistling that didn't stop until he was a block away), when Gary saw her alone, as if to make up for her husband, Theresa was effusive. She always hugged him. She always kissed Otis. "How's our baby?" she said, "how's our Molly?" and he felt such a ridiculous flush of gratitude for the "our" that he could have wept.

At the grocer's, he saw Emma's husband Bill, squeezing grapefruits. He nodded at Gary. He didn't ask how Molly was. He didn't bend and admire Otis, but he held up a grapefruit. "This one is ripe. Why don't you take it?"

Gary didn't know how to repay any of the neighbors for their concern. He tried once to invite Emma and Bill to dinner, but Emma looked uncomfortable. "That's my night to play cards," she said, but that night, around the same time he had invited her to dinner, he saw her later in her backyard, taking wash from her line.

The next day at the hospital, Dr. Price came into the room. He had a suit on under his white lab coat, which startled Gary a little because he couldn't imagine what it meant. Dr. Price nodded at Gary. He lifted the sheet from Molly and probed at her stomach. He whisked the sheet back over her and then frowned up at the bag of blood hanging from the IV pole.

"I don't like her numbers."

"Is she worse?"

"We're going to try something else," Dr. Price said. "Porcine Factor VIII. Sometimes it works when the human factor doesn't. The problem is that each vial has to be separately checked, code numbers matched up. And we need so many vials, it could take a few hours for each transfusion." He frowned again. He looked so disturbed it made Gary uneasy.

"There's not time?" Gary finally said, and Dr. Price shook his head. "Oh, no, there's time. The problem is there's no nurses. They can't spare staff, especially two nurses, to take two hours to double-check the vials, but they'll have to spare one. You'll have to hire another nurse, a private one. It can be pricey, especially if we need to transfuse for any length of time, but I'll talk to the insurance company, see if we can get them to pay for it."

"Anything she needs," he said.

"Good. I'll get a nurse in here for you. We need to start the transfusions right away."

The private nurse they sent in was a tall, silent black woman. She wore a long blue scrub belted like a dress, and tiny red glass earrings and white running sneakers. She ignored Gary completely, bending to study Molly. "Okay, honey, I'm here." Her voice was soft and smooth. Most of the time, she simply sat by Molly's bed, reading from a stack of magazines she brought, sometimes leaning forward and looking intently at Molly. Four times a day, she got the porcine transfusion ready.

It took her and another nurse an hour and a half to start the transfusion. They set out vials, they read off code numbers and double-checked them, and then Gary left for the evening.

The next morning, Dr. Price came by with a team of two other doctors. They talked outside the door, their voices threaded together, tightening, and no matter how Gary strained, he couldn't hear a thing. They came into the room and looked at Molly and then Dr. Price took Gary aside and told him there was a problem with the insurance. "I'd fight them on this," Dr. Price told Gary. "They don't like to pay for what they consider beyond the normal range of things. I spoke with them myself. I told them this was hardly a normal situation." He pushed his hands into the pockets of his lab coat. "I'll be willing to bet they'll pay for at least eighty percent."

"All right," Gary looked down at Molly. "Is it working better, the porcine?"

The other two doctors looked awkward. "It's too early to tell," Dr. Price said finally.

That night, Gary sat in front of his computer and switched it on, waiting for the green blinking cursor, for the screen saver he had recently put on: Molly, nine months pregnant in a white dress she was stretching across her belly, her head thrown back, laughing. Her hair like a long flame about her.

He was about to go onto the Internet, which he did every night, to look and see if he could find anything new about Molly's condition, when the phone rang. He picked it up. No one would call this late except the hospital, who thought nothing of calling in the middle of the night. Sometimes they wanted him to sign papers for another procedure, another operation, sometimes they just told him what they were doing. Half the time he didn't recognize the doctor calling him. "Gary Breyer." His voice sounded strange in his own throat.

"Gary! Did you get my messages?"

Gary slumped back in his chair. "Brian. I didn't see any messages." The chair rolled on the floor, and he stopped it with his feet. He remembered the work he was supposed to do for Brian, work he hadn't even thought of.

"Oh, I left them on the machine, I thought. Maybe it didn't pick up." Brian's breath moved like a slow tide. "Hey. It was good to see you last week."

"Yeah, me, too."

"What a game, right?"

"Yeah."

"How's Molly?"

"The same."

"Oh." Brian was silent for a moment. "Well, listen, I really hate to do this over the phone. But maybe there's no good way to do it."

"Do what?"

"There have been cutbacks. Downsizing." The line popped and hummed. Brian cleared his throat. "I got to have people I can depend on here. I'm firing you, Gary."

Gary heard his breath moving in and out of the phone.

"Look, if you want, you could think of it as a blessing. Now you have the time you need to tend to your wife."

"You really have to do this now?" Gary said.

Brian cut him off. "Hey, don't put this all on me," he said, his voice taking on an edge. "I gave you a chance, Gary. I told you to get the layouts in. I told you what was going on here. Be reasonable."

Reasonable. Brian was still talking but Gary couldn't hear what he was saying anymore. He lowered the phone, gently replacing it in the cradle.

Math texts, he thought. Environmental series. He thought of the ocean. He thought of a fish, bright and silvery and ready to spawn, a gleaming hook caught in its throat, rushed into a hospital and saved by modern medicine, brought back to his family in their ocean home. He saw suffocating nets. He felt salt water choked into lungs that could no longer breathe air or water or earth.

Survival rates are not optimistic. He clicked the computer off. He cupped both hands over his face.

He went to the kitchen to make himself some tea. Strong and hot enough to burn the fear from him. He put the kettle on. In the other room, he could hear the Home Shopping Network. "Isn't that lovely?" a woman's voice throbbed. "Wouldn't you want that in every color?" He clicked on the dishwasher, which whirred and fretted and whined and died. He opened the door. Water pooled along the dishes and sloshed onto the floor. He took the dishes out and did them in the sink, and shut the dishwasher. He mopped up the water with a dish towel. He couldn't afford to fix the dishwasher. He didn't know what he was going to do.

He looked out the window. There wasn't another light on in the whole neighborhood. There wasn't a house he could go to and bang on the door. He couldn't ask his friends for money. They had wives and families of their own, they had bills.

Bills, he thought. The mail was on the table. He hadn't even thought to look through it yet this week. He sat down and siphoned the mail into piles. Junk mail, bills, letters, glossy magazines. The bills were the largest stack. The mortgage. Gerta. The private nurse. The hospital.

He found his bank statement in the pile and tore it open. They had saved ten thousand dollars for them both to take time off to be with Otis. Their mortgage was two thousand a month; the rest of the bills, credit cards, utilities, were another three thousand. They had thought with careful planning, with some freelance they both could do, they'd be fine. But now, there were other things. Gerta was a thousand a week. The private nurse was five hundred a day and the insurance company didn't want to pay for her. And he had no money coming in except for unemployment, which would barely keep him afloat. He couldn't go and get a full-time job when he had to spend most of his time at the hospital, with his son. Who would hire someone who could only work at odd hours in the middle of the night, who, even then, had to be on call to leave at a moment's notice? Well, he wasn't proud. He'd do anything if someone would only let him.

He stared at the bank statement. There was only four thousand left. He couldn't afford Gerta anymore. He couldn't even afford this month's expenses.

The kettle whistled. He shut off the gas. He left the kettle on the burner. He took all the piles of bills and muddled them together. He put them back into the mail basket, and then, panicked, he stood in the center of the kitchen. He'd have to do something. And fast.

He tried to think, but his mind seemed to be caught in a stopper. His friends. Which of his friends could he call? Allan was having some money problems himself. Ada worked. The neighbors all had family of their own. Who? Who? It was like a drumbeat in his head, growing louder and more insistent.

Cinda, Molly's teacher friend. She was single. She worked only three days a week teaching music. She always used to call Molly complaining how bored and lonely she was, how teaching wasn't enough for her. Maybe she could help out, spell him here and there out of friendship. He cleared his throat. He hoped she wouldn't weep on the phone the way she had the last time he had called to tell her about Molly, that she wouldn't keep apologizing, as if Molly's illness were her fault. "I need your help," he told her.

Cinda didn't cry when she heard his voice, but her voice began to lose its lilt. She spoke in a hushed, reverential tone. "I'd love to help out. You know I'd do anything for Molly. But I work," she said. "Maybe I can baby-sit a few hours after school—" she said doubtfully. Then she brightened. "I know some real good baby-sitters."

"But that's the point. I can't afford the nurse anymore. I can't afford baby-sitters. I need friends."

"Maybe you just need to get a group of people together," she said cheerfully. "Have a kind of round robin of free baby-sitters."

"Why, what a good idea," he said flatly. He felt disgusted. He could kill Cinda. He hung up and tried to think what to do, but all he saw was his bank account dwindling, the baby needing food and diapers and Molly needing him. And then suddenly, a thought blurted into his head. He knew what he had to do. The only thing left.

He went into the bedroom and crouched down to Molly's dresser and yanked open the bottom drawer. He dragged out the blue box, tossed off the lid, and grabbed out the acrylic puzzle. There inside that small white strip of paper was Suzanne's phone number and address.

She was Molly's *sister*, no matter what Molly said, no matter what had gone on before. Surely that mattered. He'd scrounge up money to pay her airfare. If she was with some boyfriend, well, he could come, too. Anyone could come, her cats, her dog, anyone, as long as they got here to help him.

He pivoted the acrylic puzzle cube in his hands, moving some of the pieces experimentally. The steel balls zinged to a corner and stayed there. Goddamn. He didn't have time for this. He jerked at the cube. It was a kid's puzzle. It shouldn't be so difficult. He had figured out the Rubik in less than two weeks; surely he could figure this out. Gary studied the acrylic block. He moved the puzzle so one of the balls got into the hole. He felt so nervous, as if this were some great test he had to pass. He moved the cube, trying to roll another of the balls toward the hole, and then, just as he almost had it, the first ball spilled out again.

He bolted up. No. He yanked at the cube, getting more and more frustrated. He was sweating, his hair prickled. He tried to roll the balls toward the hole again, and they all suddenly flew in different directions.

He stared at the cube.

He went into the kitchen and banged open one of the drawers and grabbed out the big utility hammer. He set the cube on the floor and then he lifted the hammer and smashed and smashed at the cube until it broke open, Suzanne's number unfurling before him like a sail.

The phone rang six times, and then just as he was about to give up, a woman's voice, raspy, exhausted, sounding nothing like Molly's, said, "Yeah?"

Gary swallowed. "Suzanne?"

"You got her. Is this for an appointment?"

"This is Gary. Molly's husband."

There was a clip of silence. "And——" she finally said.

"I'm calling because—because Molly's really sick. She's in the hospital."

There was that silence again. Gary was suddenly furious. He didn't want to be doing this in the first place, and she wasn't helping him. Why wasn't she asking a million questions? Why wasn't she asking what was wrong with Molly or if she was going to be okay? "She had a baby."

"A baby," Suzanne said flatly. "So how come she's sick?"

"Her blood's not clotting. She's comatose."

He could hear Suzanne's breathing now. Harder. Sharper. But still, she wasn't saying anything.

"I know things haven't been right between you two," Gary said, "and I wouldn't call if I had any other options. I'm at my wit's end.

I need someone to watch the baby so I can be at the hospital. Look, I'll fly you in. I'll pay for you to come here. You won't have to spend a dime the whole time you're here." He felt the panic rising in his voice. "Please." He was begging now. "I'll do anything. Please."

She was quiet again. "Please," Gary repeated.

"Wire me the money," Suzanne said abruptly. "And I'll come."

He hung up the phone. His heart was beating so fast he stood up and then sat down again. Suzanne would come.

He waited until the next evening to tell Gerta. Gerta had finished putting Otis to bed. She was scrubbing bottles in the sink before boiling them. "Gerta?"

She kept washing the bottles. "Yes, I can hear you."

"I'm not going to be needing you after this week."

She shut the water off and turned to him. Her hands were dripping and she wiped them off along the sides of her uniform.

"I'm not doing a good job with Otis?"

For the first time that Gary could remember, Gerta looked vulnerable. Her lashes flickered, her mouth twitched at one corner. "You're doing a wonderful job. Otis loves you."

"But you don't like me? You'd prefer someone else?"

"No, it's not that—" he said, and then realizing what that sounded like, shook his head again. He tried to clear his throat and felt something stick in it.

"It's money. I don't have any to pay you," he said finally. "I haven't worked. I don't have vacation or sick days. The bills are piling up. I don't know what to do."

Gerta blinked and stayed silent.

"I don't have money coming in," Gary said.

"Who will care for Otis?"

"My wife's sister. I'm flying her in. She's coming in two days."

Gerta's shoulders untensed. Her spine lengthened "Ah, family," she said, nodding, as if that explained everything. "That's all right then."

"Am I leaving you in the lurch?"

Gerta straightened. "I'm always in demand. The agency will have something for me."

By the next afternoon, Gerta already had a new job. "Twin baby boys," she exulted. "I start in two weeks, so I can have some time at home with my husband."

"You'll stay until Friday, when Suzanne arrives?"

"Absolutely."

Gary watched her. Now that she was leaving, she slowly, slowly began to disengage. She stopped washing Otis's toys every night. She grew laxer about scrubbing his bottles. Even her voice, when she talked to Otis, was more distant. "I expect great things from you," Gerta told Otis.

That night, when he was upstairs at his computer, he heard her feet on the stairs. She appeared at his door, a little out of breath. "Otis needs to be fed soon. You should make up his bottles." She leaned against the doorjamb. "It's better to keep Otis with what he is used to."

She stood over him, watching, scolding him when he didn't leave the bottle in the warm water for the full seven minutes. She monitored the way she held his son, she adjusted his grip, and when he was finished, she told him she was leaving him her notebooks. "Everything you need to know is in there," she said. "When to feed him, when to get him to sleep, I wrote down all my trade secrets."

The Friday Suzanne was due to arrive, Gary left the hospital at five. In the car on the way home, Diana Ross wailed about her Love Child. If Gary had a time he liked the least, it would be driving home from the hospital. It was always the hardest because then he felt himself to be in a kind of limbo, neither with his wife nor with his son. The car didn't handle right. He had never been in an accident in his life, but now the wheels skidded, the steering wheel felt jerky. Gary clicked on the radio. "Because you care—" a voice, deep and sonorous, intoned, "1-800-REST IN PEACE." Gary snapped to another station.

Gary pulled into the drive. He fit the key in the lock and opened the door. The house felt yellow with light. Gerta appeared, an old blue apron of Molly's tucked about her. *Because I'm the Cook. That's Why* was scribbled across the front in bright red embroidery. The house was fragrant with garlic and the sizzle of meat, which shocked Gary because he never once saw Gerta eat anything, other than a cracker, and because he was a vegetarian. "As of right now, I no longer work for you. So now, you can eat with me."

Gary was dumbfounded. He wasn't hungry at all, but he followed her to the dining room where she had set the table with a red cloth and matching napkins and good china service for two, where there were the pewter candlesticks and two white candles already lit, and even a small startling bowl of yellow flowers.

Gerta folded her hands across her belly and for the first time, Gary noticed she wasn't wearing her white uniform. No, she was in a blue printed dress with a matching belt, and small gold hoop earrings. Her hair was faintly curled about her ears. She had put on perfume, too. He could smell the scent, lily of the valley. "Well, it's a special occasion," she said to him.

"Dinner smells terrific," Gary lied.

"Lemon chicken," she said proudly.

Gary didn't have the heart to tell her he didn't eat meat, that he was too nerved up to eat anything. He sat down, unfolding his napkin. "I can't wait," he said.

"Otis is sleeping." Gerta said. She dashed into the kitchen and brought out a steaming white tureen, ladling big chunks of chicken onto his plate. Gary knew enough to realize how difficult it must be for Gerta to not only have cooked in his house, but to dine in it as well, and to dine with him. He told himself to think of it as the mock yam concoctions some of the Chinese restaurants in the city served. Think of it as tofu, pounded and dried, masquerading as meat. He took a bite. It won't kill you, he told himself, and tried an old trick he used to ply as a boy—not breathing while you ate, which rendered any food tasteless.

Gerta took a voracious bite, smacked her lips, and said, "It's good, isn't it? My husband Benjamin loves it."

"Delicious," Gary said. He looked at Gerta. "It must be hard for your husband when you're on a job."

Gerta shrugged. "It's sometime good for couples to be apart." She picked at her dinner. "Sometimes."

Gary ate, knowing he'd probably be ill later, the way all vegetarians are after they chance meat, but he didn't care. He cut the meat up in tiny pieces and tried to fork it to the edge of his plate. "Otis is so quiet," Gary said.

"He's been sleeping so much today. He knows I'm going and he doesn't want to be awake for it. He might be angry for a few days, but let him express it and then it will pass."

For dessert there was apple pie, flaky and delicate, clouded with cream. He wolfed his piece down and Gerta stood up, gathering plates.

She wouldn't let him help her clean up. "No, no," she said, when he started to bring his dish to the sink. "I like to do them." She got a soft dish towel out of the drawer and lay it along the counter. She put a skin of plastic wrap over the leftovers and set them in the freezer, and when she was finished, the kitchen smelled of lemon cleanser and Fantastik. It looked as if no one had ever been in it at all, let alone cooked an entire meal. She rubbed her hands briskly together and glanced at the clock. Nine-thirty. "Your Suzanne is late," she announced. "And I had better go call a cab."

She went upstairs, got her suitcase, and came down to call a cab.

"Ten minutes, he said," she told Gary. She gave an odd little smile and then thrust her hand forward and slid something into his palm. "My number. You call if you need advice on anything." She nodded. "You don't forget. Otis is a good little boy and he knows what's going on. He tells me. Every night he prays for his mama and a baby's prayers go right to God before anyone else's. Even the pope's."

Usually Gary would have rolled his eyes, but this time, he stepped forward and hugged Gerta. At first she was stiff, but he kept holding, and then her body relaxed and swayed against him, and then, to his surprise, she lifted her arms and hugged him back.

"Well," she said, disengaging. "Don't forget the things I taught you and you should be fine. You have the notebook." She straightened. "You relax, you listen hard. Otis is speaking to you, too."

He nodded dumbly. "I need one more look at my boy," she said.

He followed her into Otis's room. Otis was on his back, a striped blue blanket about him, a pacifier in his mouth. Gerta leaned over the crib. She whispered something he couldn't hear, something that sounded German, something he couldn't be privy to. And then she glided out of the room, and he followed her, and it wasn't until they were both back in the light of the hallway that he saw that her eyes were damp.

chapter

five

S uzanne got out of the cab, staring around her. Oh, God. This was the *boonies*. She had forgotten what an armpit New Jersey was, how the whole state made her want to scream. Those squatty houses in those weird pastels, the scrubby trees and the stupid plastic orna-ments on the porches, the cloth flags. *I'll have to kill myself*, she thought. *I won't last a day here, let alone months. I'll die. Unless I'm driven nuts, first.* There wasn't even a dog on the street. Did people here still think if you weren't in your pajamas and in front of the TV by eight that there was something wrong with you? She suddenly thought of this cartoon she had once seen, the caption on it: Houdini fleeing New Jersey. Well, she wanted to run, too, but she was no magician. It wouldn't be so easy this time.

The driver finished dumping her things on the sidewalk. "Forty bucks," he said. Suzanne cursed under her breath and dug into her purse. Gary had sent her the plane fare. He should have sent her cab fare, too. Maybe he would have if she had told him she was being evicted, that she hadn't had a head of hair to cut or color in nearly two months.

Jesus. She was freezing right down to her toes. How could she have forgotten how cold it got here? She shivered, blowing on her hands, turning up the collar of her blue cotton coat, stamping her feet.

Suzanne blinked at Molly's house. One of those two-story deals with a black iron gate. It looked better than anyone else's on the block and she had to admit it beat her crummy little studio by miles and miles. A house. God. Suzanne hadn't cared when Angela had given Molly the house in Elizabeth. Suzanne certainly hadn't wanted it, especially if it meant coming back to New Jersey. But now that all of Suzanne's money was gone, the thought of having a house—even a New Jersey one—made her feel a little prickly. It made her wonder, how did Molly get to have a house and she didn't?

Gary had told her he was in dire straits, that there really was no money anymore. Anyone would have heard the begging in his voice, anyone would have believed him, but that was on the phone, and here was this whole house, with those pricey-looking blinds and that fancy carved door.

What she believed about Molly was a whole other story. How could Molly be as sick as Gary said? How could she possibly believe that? When they were kids, Suzanne was the one always dosing up on antibiotics. Molly never missed a day of school—not that she would have, even if she had had the Bubonic plague.

Well, maybe Gary was exaggerating about Molly, the same way he was about his money. Maybe he was playing her for a fool, wanting a free nursemaid, a free housekeeper, the way Angela had. Blood didn't mean anything. Family was a cheat. She had learned that lesson early on, and she wasn't about to forget it now. She blew on her fingers again. What did it matter? She had no other place to go.

She rang the bell. Musical chimes. So corny they made her wince. The front door opened and a man came out onto the rim of the porch. So this was Gary. He wasn't much. She'd pass him on the street and not look twice. Certainly not anyone she'd want to be with. Not like Ivan. She saw Ivan's beautiful face, his hair, black and soft like a wing of a crow. She shook her head until his image disappeared from her mind.

"Suzanne?" His voice was hoarse and deep.

"In person." She tried to sound upbeat.

He looked past her, his smile fading. She felt a flash of shame. She knew what he was looking at. She could see the gears in his mind whirring away when he saw all her stuff: the five big battered suitcases, tied shut with rope, the taped-up cardboard boxes. Everything she had managed to grab from her apartment except the furniture and the roach motels.

He opened the door wider. "Please. Come in." He ushered her inside, helping her with her coat. He hung the coat on a padded hanger, buttoning it at the throat, as if it were worth something.

It took him four trips to drag her things in. He never once asked her to help, and she never offered. He was panting when he was finished, all red in the face like a half-ripe tomato. For a moment, she and Gary just stood there looking at each other, and then he awkwardly motioned to the couch. She was still freezing. She looked around for the thermostat, rubbing her arms. "Could you turn up the heat?"

He knotted his brow. "Can I get you a sweater?"

"It's really freezing in here."

He stalled for a minute and then walked over to the thermostat and turned it up. She heard a little flare, like a match striking. The pipes banged. The heat hissed on. She had forgotten all the sounds a house made. Creepy. Like the house was alive, breathing down your neck. Waiting for you.

She sniffed. The house smelled, too. Milk and powder and dirty diapers. She wrinkled her nose and dug around in her bag for a cigarette, pulling up a rumpled pack from the bottom of her purse, a fold of matches. She was down to her last four cigarettes but she held the pack out to him, thinking she'd start off on the right foot. She'd be polite. Generous. "Luckies okay?"

"Actually, could you not smoke in the house? We don't smoke, and with the baby . ..." his voice trailed off.

"Sure. Of course. Only outside." She dropped the cigarettes into her purse. She had only vaguely wanted a cigarette, but now that he told her she couldn't, she was dying for one. No cigarettes in the house. She was going to have to be locked up.

She looked around. Her whole apartment was only slightly larger than Molly's living room. Molly used to be so neat, you'd think she used a ruler to line things up. But this room was just as cluttered and messy as Suzanne's studio. Dirty plates were stacked on the coffee table, laundry piled on a chair.

Gary followed Suzanne's gaze. "It's usually tidier," he apologized, "but the baby nurse just left."

A baby nurse, she thought. How could you afford a baby nurse one week and not another? "Nice place."

Suzanne looked past the shelves of books (she had never been much of a reader herself) and saw a wall of photos. She got up to look at them: Gary and Molly. Gary and Molly. Kissing. Holding hands. On a beach. At the park. Hallmark stuff. And then a single black and white photo swam out at her, startling her.

She knew this photo. She had grown up hating it. It was a picture of Angela, the year she won the beauty contest. Thin and beautiful in a little two-piece, laughing like she didn't have a care in the world. Like her whole life would always be apple pie and ice cream. Angela always made everyone who came into the house admire it. She'd fish for compliments and then she'd sigh and say how entering that beauty contest had really been the worst thing in the world for her because if she hadn't, maybe then she'd have been able to make something of herself. To be someone, other than a child bride, a struggling single mother stuck in suburbia. "Don't get me wrong, I love my girls—" she always added, her voice trailing off. That was the part that always hurt Suzanne the most. Almost as much as seeing the photo now.

She scanned the wall again. Not a single picture of herself up there. Just as well. She'd never be that beautiful again. People used to stop her on the street just to comment on her long black hair. Her clients used to beg her to make theirs look like hers, with its glints of blue and plum running through it, its mirror sheen. Now, Suzanne's black was from a tube. She didn't have to look in a mirror to know she had faded from too many worries, too little sleep, and too many cigarettes. Suzanne blew a puff of air up toward her long bangs. They used to make her eyes look as big as soup bowls. Now, they just hid some of the tiny lines that had begun to etch their way into her skin like they were a road map to Nowhere. Well, at least she was still thin. Maybe too thin.

"Otis is sleeping," Gary said. "We don't have to whisper or anything because he seems to like noise. He'll be up in about an hour and then I'll show you all about the care and maintenance of a newborn. He's really very good." He rubbed at his forehead. "You've been around babies?"

"Yup," she lied.

"Come on, let's have some tea."

She shuddered. She hated tea. Angela used to have Suzanne make big pitchers of it because it was cheaper than juice or soda. Supermarket brand, the same bag used for three cups, so what you ended up with always tasted like boiled socks.

"Do you have coffee?"

He led her into the yellow kitchen and dug around the shelf. "No coffee." He shook his head. "No lots of things. I need to go shopping."

It was just as well. If she even smelled coffee she'd probably jump out of her skin.

He stopped. "Maybe when I'm at the hospital, you could take Otis and pick up some things. Some days I could leave you the car."

"The car?" Her mood brightened. She could get away, drive places. She could plunk the baby in the stroller and maybe he'd snooze while she window-shopped.

"You just tell me when you want to go see her."

"Tomorrow," she said. "Or the day after."

He was quiet for a minute. "I really appreciate this. I know you and Molly haven't been exactly close these past years."

Whose fault was that? she thought, but she didn't say it. She could just imagine what Molly had told Gary about her. That she was selfish and a terrible person. That she had broken Angela's heart and taken all of Molly's money. But did Molly tell Gary about the last time Suzanne had called, desperate, pleading, weeping for another loan, and Molly had flat-out refused? Did Gary know that Molly had never even once called Suzanne back after that to see if Suzanne was managing, to ask whether or not Suzanne might need something other than money?

Suzanne bet Molly didn't tell him how she had practically raised Molly all by herself. How by the time she was twelve, she was baby-sitter, maid, cook, and laundry lady, doing just about everything because Angela was either working long, crazy hours or trying to land a husband, because Angela had put her in charge and Molly was no help. Suzanne had had to say no to more parties than most people were ever invited to in their whole life. That was the way her life had been, right up until she had met Ivan, and then all that stopped. She shook her head again. It had been five years already. When did you stop loving someone, when could you hear their name and not feel so sick inside you wanted to die?

"Suzanne?"

She looked up at Gary, waiting.

"The baby's crying."

"He is?" Suzanne didn't hear anything. Gary was still looking at her, like he expected her to take care of things, even when he was home.

Gary started walking, then he looked back at her, waiting. "We'll get a bottle." He went into the kitchen and took a bottle from the refrigerator, running it under the tap for a while. "There. That ought to be warm enough, now. Come on."

Suzanne reluctantly trailed after Gary. The baby's room was in the back of the house.

Gary put his hand on the door, bright yellow with blue stars, and Suzanne sipped in a breath. *Here we go,* she thought. Molly's kid was on the other side. He opened the door. It was a kid's room all right— white furniture, puffy clouds on the ceiling. A small braided rug. She could hear the baby, baaing like a lamb.

"Come here." Gary motioned her forward. Reluctantly she came closer. She looked into the crib. The baby's face was scrunched up. His hands were tiny fists. Oh, yeah. He was crying all right.

"What's wrong with him?" Suzanne asked.

"He's hungry." Gary bent and picked him up. "Right?" he asked the baby. The baby's pajamas had a big damp spot down the front. "Sit," he said to her. "I'll give you a feeding lesson."

She looked around. She stared hard. There was only one chair in the room. The white rocker from Angela's bedroom.

The rocker was like new. A friend of Angela's had bought it for Angela when Suzanne was born, but Angela had never used it for anything but decoration. "It's a Whistler's Mother kind of rocker," Angela always pointed out. "And I'm hardly the Whistler's Mother type." Suzanne's throat knotted. Leave it to Molly to take this thing. Suzanne wouldn't have taken anything from Angela's. She would have burned the whole stupid house down and everything in it.

He placed the baby on her, upright, so his head lolled against her. The baby felt like a bag of soggy fruit. Gary lowered him on her a bit, and then she saw the soft spot on the top of the head, moving, like it was breathing. Like it was alive.

Gary handed her the bottle. "You can breathe, you know."

Suzanne didn't even realize she had stopped. She sucked in air. She tried to look at anything but that terrible breathing spot on the baby's head. The baby worked greedily at the bottle, his mouth tugging like a leech, his eyes squinched shut. His whole body felt like it was pulsing against hers. All she wanted to do was get this over with and get the baby off her.

Gary watched her for a moment. He frowned and looked confused and then he held up one finger. "Was that the door? Be right back."

"Wait—" she said. "I didn't hear anything—" but he was gone. Great. Just dandy. He didn't seem to her like he really knew what he was doing, either. At least the baby did, busily stuffing himself on the formula. But she couldn't get comfortable and her nose began running like there was no tomorrow. She had a tissue in her pocket, but getting at it was something else. As soon as she lifted one hand from the baby, he startled, the bottle jumping from his mouth. He slid down her leg. She panicked, grabbing him about the belly, hoisting him up, closer to her than before. Suzanne shoved the bottle back in his mouth.

"Jesus. Sit right." She sniffed and then she couldn't help it. She sneezed loudly, and the baby suddenly stopped feeding. He looked at her with interest.

"False alarm. No one there." Gary came back into the room, watching her. "Getting the hang of it?" He bent and repositioned the baby, perching him up on her shoulder, so that his soggy mouth was right up against her blouse. He drooled and gummed at her neck. She recoiled. It felt as if he were trying to burrow through her.

"Pat his back," Gary said.

Suzanne moved her hands in an awkward circle.

"Harder."

She pressed her hands in. The baby burped, like a popped cork, and suddenly she felt a puddle of something wet and disgusting on her shoulder. She jerked back.

Gary quickly grabbed something from the changing table, a small white cloth he handed her. "Burp cloth. I should have put one on you before you fed him."

She couldn't take this another moment. She lifted up the baby and Gary, thank the Lord, finally took him from her, holding him as awkwardly as she had. She daubed at her shirt with the cloth.

"You think you'll be okay with him?" Gary asked. The baby began to move his head side to side. Suzanne stared. *God Almighty. He's saying no.*

"I'll take the night shift, mornings and evenings when I get home." Gary gave her a pleading look.

"Piece of cake," she lied. She didn't really have a clue. And Gary didn't seem to know all that much either. Well, she'd do what she had to do. What she always did. Fake it. Take her clues, trial and error, from the baby. He, at least, seemed to have a good sense of what he wanted.

"You look exhausted. Let me show you your room. Try to get as much sleep as you can. You'll need it."

I'll need a sanitarium, Suzanne thought.

* * *

The room was too pink for Suzanne's tastes. Like a facial tissue. And it looked unfinished, as if it were waiting to become something. The bed looked too big for the room, as if it had been thrown in as an afterthought, and the dresser looked too small—like a child's dresser. Even Gary seemed uncomfortable in the room, leaving almost as quickly as he showed her in. Still, it had a door she could shut, and it faced out to a backyard, the one thing Suzanne had never had unless you counted alleys and concrete and brick walls. The silence made her antsy. She was used to car alarms and yowling stray cats and drunks screaming out the names of the people they loved enough to want to kill.

She was still freezing. She had changed into the warmest thing she owned, her jeans and a sweater, which were about as comfortable to sleep in as an iron lung. She shifted under the comforter. She took away one of the down pillows on the bed and then put it back again. She wanted to shut her eyes, to not have to think about anything. There had been nights like that in California, but then she had squeezed herself into some spandex, sprinkled glitter through her hair, and gone to a club. All the light and noise and male attention had made her forget that she was lonely, that she hadn't heard anything from Ivan, that she had grown so shamelessly desperate she had even left notes taped to his front door. *We have to talk.* Or: *We can work this out.* Or simply: *Please.*

She got up, pacing, feeling caged. If she didn't have a cigarette, she'd die. She looked out the window and touched the glass, which was ice cold. No way was she going to go outside to smoke. Screw it. She'd do it in here. What Gary didn't know wouldn't hurt anyone. Especially her. She smoked two cigarettes, one after the other, waving away the smoke, tapping the ashes into an empty vase. She began to feel calmer. Thank God for cigarettes. You could tell her about cancer all you wanted and it still wouldn't stop her from smoking.

She opened the window a crack to toss the butt outside. She threw it far into the bushes, and then she suddenly saw a woman in the next yard, staring up at her. The woman had on a flowery blue bathrobe and her hair was in pink curlers, but she bent and disgustedly picked up the butt and lobbed it into her trash can. Then she straightened and glared accusingly over at Suzanne, who pulled back from the window. Great. Would that old biddy tell Gary?

Suzanne shut the window and then crawled back into bed. She put a strand of hair in her mouth, something she hadn't done since she was a kid. When she and Molly had lived in California, they had been friends. They used to romp on the beach, and she could boss Molly around and Molly could make her laugh. They used to work for hours making sand sculptures. A woman with a big belly and big breasts in a bikini. A murderous-looking octopus, scallop shells pushed in for eyes, a growling seaweed mouth. And they always went to the movies.

At night it was Suzanne who gave Molly supper and washed the dishes. She did some laundry and swept up and then took her shower, and as soon as she stepped out of the bathroom, Molly was at her. "Let me comb your hair," Molly begged. Suzanne rolled her eyes, but she always let Molly do it. Sometimes she told herself she let Molly because she felt a little sorry for her sister. Molly's hair was so wild and curly, you couldn't even get a comb through it. No matter what you did with it—braids, hot combs, curlers—it still ended up a tangled mess.

Suzanne sat on a kitchen chair, her long wet hair spread out over the chair back. Molly stood on a hassock to reach. Suzanne arched her back, leaned back her head. Molly used her fingers to free some of the tangles. Her touch was so gentle, Suzanne slowly shut her eyes. Molly drew the comb lightly through Suzanne's hair and Suzanne shivered with pleasure. The moment Molly finished and took her hands and the comb away, Suzanne wanted them back.

Suzanne chewed on her hair. She thought about Molly and she felt suddenly scared. What would she do when she saw Molly now? What would she say?

The baby began crying. Suzanne rolled over on her side. Gary didn't expect her to go to the baby, did he? Not her first night. She waited, but she didn't hear Gary, and the baby gradually calmed himself down.

And then she heard Gary's voice. "Molly Goldman."

She opened the door and peeked at him from around the corner. He was on the phone, leaning against the wall, in gray sweatpants and bare feet, in a faded black T-shirt. "Yes," he said slowly. "Thank you." Then he hung up the phone, turned, and saw her.

"Still critical," he said quietly, and then turned and walked away from her.

Critical, Suzanne thought. Critical wasn't like the phone call she had gotten at two in the morning when Lars had called to tell her Angela had died, his voice flat as a pane of glass. Suzanne had barely been living with Ivan for two years when the call came, and as soon as she heard she had started weeping on the phone. "Baby?" Ivan said, lifting up from bed, grabbing her to him. It was the first time she couldn't feel him touching her. She couldn't grab hold of his scent. She suddenly couldn't remember how furiously she had left, how she had vowed to never come back. Instead, she remembered when she was six and had had an earache and Angela had picked her up, big girl that she was, and held her in her arms all night long. She remembered, too, long after she had run away, a day when she had been shopping at Macy's and she had followed a woman through three different floors just because she looked like her mother, because the woman had turned and smiled at Suzanne for no reason at all.

Suzanne had cried to Lars so hard she couldn't speak. "I—" she said. "I always meant to come back."

"You don't need to come," Lars interrupted. "God. How you hurt her."

"How I hurt her?"

"She was fine without you while she was alive. She's fine without you now." He was silent for a moment. "We all are."

Two days later, Suzanne and Ivan had had to move to a cheaper apartment. She hadn't called Lars ever again.

Suzanne turned from Gary and went back to bed, pulling the covers over her head. Critical was still alive.

* * *

Suzanne dreamed a baby was crying. She bolted awake. The house was quiet. She put her feet on the floor, and popped them back up with a shock. Jesus. Had Gary turned the heat back down again? Well, Gary was going to be at the hospital all day, and as soon as he left, she'd crank up the thermometer until the house felt like Florida.

Still, she'd be lying if she said she wasn't more than a little unnerved about Gary not being here. What was it going to be like taking care of a baby? She remembered a client named Liza who had three little kids. "What's it like?" Suzanne had once asked. Suzanne was just making conversation, trying to make Liza comfortable. She wasn't even all that interested.

Liza had laughed at such a question. "Here's your answer," she said and then she suddenly grabbed Suzanne's wrist, her hand a steel trap.

Suzanne, startled, had tried to pry Liza's fingers from her, but Liza held on. "Cut it out," Suzanne said.

"This is kids," Liza had said with a smile. "Forget career, forget a life, forget a lover. This is it."

Suzanne wrung her hand free, shaking circulation back into it. She waggled her fingers. "How do you not go nuts?"

Lisa had laughed. "Believe it or not, but when I feel the grip loosening up, that's when I begin to feel crazy."

But Suzanne didn't get the appeal. She and Ivan had wanted to grow old together, but they had never wanted kids along for the ride.

"Can you see me as anyone's father?" Ivan said. "I come home from gigs at three in the morning. I'm not going to want to deal with poop and spit-up. Kids tie you down. They sap the strength right out of you. They want everything. I mean, name one great rocker who has kids."

Suzanne could name a bunch, but it was kind of a moot point, because she didn't want kids, either. She hated it when clients didn't even ask her, but just brought their kids along, expecting Suzanne to be all surprised and thrilled about it, to think they were the cutest things in the whole wide world. The babies cried and carried on, jangling her nerves, ruining her concentration. The kids grabbed for her expensive Japanese scissors and spilled her homemade shampoos all over her floor.

Suzanne plucked up her clothes and dressed. She passed Gary's bedroom. He wasn't there. The patchwork comforter was thrown back on Gary's side. A pillow was horizontal on Molly's side, bunched to form a kind of body.

Gary was already in the kitchen, wearing the same faded flannel shirt and jeans, listlessly spooning cereal from a bowl. He looked even worse than he had the day before, like he hadn't bathed yet or even tugged a comb through his hair.

Gary got up and put his dish in the sink. He handed her keys on a Daisy Duck chain. "House keys and car keys." He yawned. "Oh, and good morning. I'm so tired I'm forgetting my manners."

He dug into his pocket and gave her a handful of bills and a long folded-up piece of paper. "I made you a grocery list."

"A list?" Suzanne liked roaming the aisles, throwing in whatever caught her eye, or whatever she thought she could afford. Suzanne hadn't used a list in years, not since Angela had made her shop, leaving her lists so long they might have been a book. Suzanne had to buy all the groceries, even Angela's embarrassing personal things like those huge boxes of sanitary pads or the special scented douche that Suzanne had to sometimes ask for. It made Suzanne want to die. She averted her head, hiding her face with her hair. She couldn't make eye contact, and even though no one paid her the least bit of attention she still burned with shame. There were always more items than there was money for them, too, but Angela didn't care. She'd raise hell if Suzanne so much as forgot a single thing. She'd make her go right back and get them. "I don't have time for this," Angela warned her.

"I'll call you if there's any news," Gary said.

As soon as Gary left, Suzanne decided to get some news of her own. Good news. The first good news was to crank the heat up. The second was to have a cigarette.

Then she headed straight for Molly and Gary's bedroom and began to snoop. She wanted to know what she was in for, and she knew you could tell a lot about a person by their stuff. Everything meant something. Everything told a tale. She had snooped on all her boyfriends, except for Ivan, because she had been fool enough to think she knew everything about him. Maybe if she had snooped, things might have turned out differently.

She picked up Molly's hairbrush, a soft bristled brush she could have told Molly was the exact wrong kind for Molly's hair. Suzanne rummaged through the dresser drawer. She pulled open the top drawer. There wasn't much interesting. A sewing kit. A baby book she pulled out only because it was open, some of the words highlighted in yellow.

Congratulations! Your baby's beautiful, now what about you? To look and feel your post-baby best, start getting back in shape as soon as you can! Flex your feet in the hospital bed. Make circles with your arms. And think about sit-ups as soon as your doctor okays them!

Oh, Jesus. Suzanne shut the book and looked at the title. *Surprise, You're a mom!* Right. Big surprise, Suzanne thought, tucking it back in the drawer.

She went to the dresser and pulled open the bottom drawer. There was a big blue box and she pulled it out and opened it.

Her breath stopped. The locket Ivan had given her. A bright silvery heart, as big as the real thing. So heavy it used to bang against her chest when she walked, and when she finally took her clothes off at night, sometimes she'd find a faint blue bruise on her chest where the locket had bumped against her. How had Molly gotten it? Suzanne went crazy when she couldn't find it. She had hurled clothing out of her drawers and her closets. She had retraced her steps until she was so exhausted she couldn't walk straight anymore.

Suzanne lifted up the thick chain. She slid the locket over her head. *I'll never take it off,* she had told Ivan. It was the nicest thing anyone had ever given her. She had been terrified to tell Ivan she had lost it, and when she had, weeping, he had merely shrugged and kissed her. "Oh, you're always losing something," he said. She had thought he was wonderful, being understanding like that, but she should have

known what that shrug meant. She should have realized that the something she was losing wasn't just the locket.

She clicked the locket open. His image struck her, like a slap. And
there her face was, too, young and beautiful, and so stupid, it was a
crime.

Suzanne clicked the locket shut. How *had* Molly gotten this? And
why had she kept it? Suzanne didn't think Molly even knew Ivan. At
least not really. Ivan had only come to the house once or twice, and
then it was just to get Suzanne or to drop her off—and all of it was
as quickly as possible because Suzanne didn't want to spend a minute
at home she didn't have to. And then after a while, Suzanne was with
Ivan all the time and she had stopped coming home altogether. She
had stopped caring what might happen if the laundry didn't get done,
if the groceries weren't bought and put away, if Molly were alone in
the house.

The first time Suzanne saw Ivan, she had been fifteen years old. It
was a bright, shiny hot summer day, and Molly and Angela were at
the dentist. Suzanne had two loads of laundry to do and the kitchen
floor to mop, but as far as Suzanne could see, she really had the whole
day to herself and she was going to make the best of it. She could get
home before Angela and Molly did and splash water on the floor. She
could say the washer was on the fritz again, buy herself some time.

She had put on her shortest cutoffs. She had tied a red kerchief
around her chest like a halter top, and spritzed herself with Angela's
perfume, and slathered on sun block because she liked her pale skin.
She stared anxiously at herself, wondering if she was really pretty, the
way all the boys were suddenly telling her. No one had ever told her
she was pretty before they moved to New Jersey, but now, to her
astonishment, boys followed her all over school and cars beeped when
she walked down the street. She kept thinking this was like some great
gift, this beauty, that she could use it so she wouldn't be lonely, but
to her surprise, the other girls treated her with distrust or with cool-
ness, as if she were competition they couldn't afford to be too friendly
with. The boys saw her glossy hair, her luminous skin, but they didn't
see her. They never asked her what she thought or what scared her

or what she might want more than anything in the world, and every time she tried to talk about any of it, the boy she was with would get all glassy-eyed. "Shhh. Don't talk," they always said and then they'd kiss her and touch her, and tug her close, and Suzanne would feel more alone and lost than she ever had in her entire life.

She hightailed it to the park, where some bands were playing. Everyone was going to be there, and by the time she got there, they were. The whole field was dotted with blankets, swarming with kids and mosquitoes. Guys were prowling around, their shirts off, their feet bare. Frisbees, like kamikazes, whizzed dangerously close to Suzanne's head. Everything smelled of suntan lotion and sweat.

Suzanne stretched like a cat. She flipped her hair back and tugged it forward back over her shoulders. She recognized a few faces, and someone even waved at her, but she kept to herself. The band playing now wasn't so hot. They got off the stage to a smattering of applause. She was thinking she might sit down, or maybe she'd go get herself a soda. Or maybe she'd just find someone with some spare sun block because it was getting so hot she almost couldn't stand it, when suddenly a voice boomed out, "Let's hear it now, one more time, for Ivan Troon and The Touch!" The world exploded. A wave of people stormed the stage. Girls began screaming. An ankle bracelet zipped by Suzanne's head. "Oh, my God, that's him!" a girl shrieked.

Curious, Suzanne got closer. And there, on the stage, was the handsomest boy she had ever seen. He wore black sneakers and black jeans and a black T-shirt with a white dot right where his heart would be. His hair was a slide of black silk to his shoulders, his skin was sweet cream, and his eyes—my God, his eyes were this eerie electric blue she had never seen before and she couldn't stop looking at them.

A tide of people moved and pushed against her. Hands waved in the air, feet stomped. Suzanne stood perfectly still.

The girls screamed again and Touch began playing and the handsomest boy Suzanne had ever seen began to sing, so that a jolt zipped through Suzanne. She felt as if he were singing right to her, telling her something important. "Surrounded by people, and lonely as glass—" he wailed, and a tremor ran through Suzanne. She tried to move closer, so she could see him better. So she could hear more. "Don't you ever feel like the wind is in your soul?" he sang. He leaped up and slid back across the stage; he threw his head forward and back, tossing that glorious hair. Suzanne couldn't take her eyes off him and if anyone had told her that you couldn't fall in love at first sight, she would have told them they were nuts, because that was exactly what was happening to her.

The girls behind her pushed her another step forward, and then another, until she was in the front lines, and then suddenly, the boy's blue eyes shone on her like a spotlight. There was just him and her. She could no longer hear the music, she could no longer feel all the kids trying to crowd her out of their way.

The music snapped off. The boy dropped down to a crouch and sprang back up, his hair flicking back. The crowd screamed "More! More!" Someone shrieked out, "Ivan! Ivan! I love you, Ivan!" and then the emcee came out and waved his hands. "See ya next week!" he called. "That was Ivan Troon and The Touch!"

The band began packing up. The kids dispersed, and for a moment Suzanne just stood there, the spell breaking up all around her, just like shattered glass. Things felt ordinary again. Boring. She noticed her arm was jeweled with mosquito bites that itched. She had a sunburn, sun block or no sun block. Her white sneakers were scuffed with dirt. Maybe she had just imagined him singling her out. Maybe his eyes weren't that great. Maybe his hair was ordinary. Just because someone sang something that got to you, didn't mean they really felt it themselves. She sighed, turning away, when suddenly she heard, "Hey, there! You with the long black hair!" It was a voice full of Texas, and she turned to see the boy and all the miracle of him came right back at her. He smiled, making her feel bathed in light. "Ivan Troon," he said. "So, you need a lift?"

She got into his blue Chevy. It smelled of cigarettes and had a tiny plastic key ring that said TOUCH ME hanging from the rearview mirror. She started to lift her hand toward it and then let it flop back down on her knee. He looked at her and smiled, as if he knew something she didn't, and then he dug in his pocket, pulling out a rumpled pack of Luckies. He tapped two out, put them both in his mouth, lit them, and then handed one to her. "It killed me when I saw this in an old movie," he told her.

Suzanne pretended she knew what movie he was talking about. She didn't watch movies much anymore, and she had never had a cigarette in her whole life. Had never wanted one, really, preferring sugary candy and salty snacks, if you wanted to know the truth. But the cigarette in her mouth had been in his mouth just seconds before. It seemed as intimate as a kiss, and she sipped in a breath of smoke. Her lungs crackled like paper. They burned. She coughed, nearly spitting the cigarette out, and felt instantly mortified.

Ivan laughed. "Not your brand, huh? Sorry."

He drew the smoke deeply in, watching her, even as he drove, which made her a little nervous. His hair kept sliding into his face, but he never once pushed it back with his hands. Instead, he tilted his head up, as if he were contemplating the stars, let it fall away all on its own. He had a scent to him, too—pine, she thought—and it was making her feel so crazy she didn't know what to do.

And then he began to sing. "Struck down by you," he crooned. His voice was clear and full of feeling and she could have listened to it forever. He glanced at her sideways, grinning, waiting. "Struck! Down!" he abruptly wailed, throwing his hands up dramatically, startling her, so she inadvertently jumped. She blushed. *He thinks he's the cock of the walk*, Suzanne thought, but it didn't make her like him one bit less. It didn't change anything.

"That's so pretty."

"You like it?" He beamed. "I wrote it." He made a right turn. "Maybe I wrote it for you."

"Me? You don't even know me."

"That's what you think."

"What do you mean? How do you know me?"

"You haven't seen me around school?" His gaze washed over her. "I've sure seen you."

She looked at him, confused. "You go to my school?"

"I go to the Voc," he said defensively. "Transferred in a month ago from Dallas."

She nodded. The Vocational School. A whole separate building set back from the school. Fifty kids at a time, just about all of them guys. She had heard the stories. Everyone said the Voc was for kids who were too stupid to attend the regular school, the remedial programs. Everyone said the Voc was for kids who were misfits. She was like everyone else. She walked past the Voc on her way to school, past the kids hanging outside when the weather was good, working on cars, wiping their hands on their greasy coveralls. They could wire your whole house if they felt like it. They could take apart a whole car and put it together again. She didn't give any of them a moment's thought. Not until now.

She gave Ivan a sidelong glance. He wrote songs. He had a clear beautiful voice that could break your heart just to listen to it. No one in a million years could ever call him a misfit. No one could ever call him stupid.

"So, you didn't see me?" he repeated.

She shook her head.

"Well, my very first day, I saw you. Right in front of the regular school. Surrounded by guys."

Suzanne flushed.

"I knew none of them was worth your little finger. I knew none of them understood anything about you."

"How'd you know that?"

"I'm an artist. An artist watches things. He observes." Ivan tapped his head. "I saw you, so completely beautiful I was getting a heart attack just looking at you. But there was something shy about you, too. Something unsure. The way you were standing. And none of those guys was noticing. They were just getting louder and louder, when really, they should have shut up for a minute. They should have given you a little silence. A little respect."

Suzanne blinked at him. She thought of all those guys, flirting with her, cracking lame jokes, laughing too loud, flirting so hard it was a wonder they didn't explode in front of her. Ivan pointed a finger at her. "You——" he sang, his voice rolling up. "Strike me dow-own!" He grinned and put his hands back on the wheel. "This song, 'Strike Me Down.' It was like a dream the way it came to me. I was just sitting there thinking about you and the words just spilled out. Like you were my muse or something."

"I bet you have lots of muses." She felt ridiculous as soon as she said it. It was like saying, I bet you say that to all the girls, but his face was serious.

"No. I don't," he said simply. He frowned. "A lot of people don't even understand about music. They don't get it. Like my parents. They've never been to one of my gigs. Not one. When I ask, my father says"— Ivan made his voice deep and gravelly—"'Get an A on something, then I'll be impressed. Get into the real high school, not the goddamned Voc.' Like I was stupid. He doesn't get it that the main reason I go to the Voc isn't because I can't cut it in regular school, but because a musician's life can be unpredictable. Maybe there are years I'll want to take a break, just let the creative juices percolate a little. And you got to do something. And Jesus, everyone needs mechanics. You can always work, and you can work anywhere. Not that I'll ever have to. But to treat me like I'm nothing——"

"You're not nothing," Suzanne said so fervently she surprised herself a little.

"And my mom—all I hear from her is she can't come because she's busy—but busy doing what? Shopping for more clothes? Playing bridge and eating party mix?"

"That sounds like my mom," Suzanne said quietly. "Not the bridge or the shopping, but I mean I could be exploding in flames and she would still be looking for her good earrings to go out. The only things she knows about me is how I do the laundry, how I take care of the house and my sister."

Ivan looked over at Suzanne. He held her gaze. "See?" he said, quietly. "We're more alike than either of us could ever know. It's like fate, you and me."

By the time he pulled up in front of Suzanne's house, he knew all he needed to know about her. That Suzanne didn't have a boyfriend and wasn't allowed, under any circumstances, to date. That she liked him. And that they would start seeing each other every chance they both got.

Ivan courted her. Every day he managed to sneak from the vocational school into her high school and leave a love note poking out of her locker. All she had to do was see that wedge of white and her legs turned to jelly. Her breath stopped. His notes sounded like songs to her. *You're like a wild bird in my heart. I'm missing you like a long, lonely river.* She wasn't sure what half of the notes really meant, but she carried all of them in her purse and sometimes all she had to do was touch the paper to feel a thrill. He poured out his heart and he not only liked it when she poured out hers to him, he expected it.

He waited for her after her classes. Walking down the corridor with Ivan was like being with a god. Kids parted to let them pass. They stared admiringly. They acted like Suzanne was something they couldn't ever hope to aspire to.

He always had money in his pocket from doing gigs. He bought her things. A soft red angora sweater. A book of poetry wrapped in tissue, and better than that, he wrote her love songs. "I told you you were my muse and I meant it," he told her. "We're both going to be famous." He swung a rope of her hair. "I can see it now," he said. "My first album cover." He let go of her hair and looked dreamily into space. "Best. That's what I want to call it—something simple, you know? Something people can hook on to for a review—like Best is the best. Or Pneumonia. Like once you catch it, you never get cured! And on the cover—" He grinned at her. His eyes gleamed. "You. Your beautiful face." He touched her cheek, making her shiver. "Just a head shot, with your black hair hanging down, and then in each of your pupils, clear as day, will be my face. Me in you. Get it?"

Suzanne nodded. He could have told her that he was putting a plucked chicken on the album cover and she would have thought it was wonderful. She couldn't visualize the album cover the way he could. All she could think of was, *Me, he wants me on the cover,* and to her, that seemed like everything.

He sang the songs about her at the gigs where he played, the school dances, the sweet sixteens kids hired him to play at, and he always brought Suzanne, whether she was invited or not—and usually, she wasn't. It was always the same thing. Girls swarming around him, screaming, carrying on, throwing their bracelets at him, their car keys, and sometimes their panties, and there was Suzanne perfectly still in the thick of it. And Ivan singing his love songs right to her, for all the world to see.

The first time they made love was in the field behind the high school, hours after school had shut down. Ivan bought a soft blue blanket and a bottle of wine. He brought along a tape player and clicked it on, and there was his voice singing to her. "I would have brought my guitar but even I can't do two things at once," he apologized. "Hope that's okay." He treated Suzanne like a piece of fine silk, lowering her onto the blanket, slowly taking off her clothes. He knew it was her first time. When she was naked, shivering and embarrassed, he shook his head, admiring. "I have never seen anything so goddamned beautiful in my whole life," he said. "And that's a fact." Behind him, on the tape recorder, his voice crooned, "My life is you, you, you—" and Suzanne shut her eyes.

"Okay?" he said. "Is this okay?" He kept asking her questions as he touched her breasts, as he slid her pants down over her thin hips, but she wished he would just be quiet, that he would just hold her. She had heard enough about sex to know the first time wasn't supposed to be so hot, and she hadn't expected much, and she hadn't really cared, because all that mattered was that she was with Ivan. He took his time. He pushed into her. "Me in you," he whispered, and before she had time to think whether she liked this or didn't like this, Ivan rolled off her, flopping on the ground beside her. It was way faster than she had expected, and she wasn't sure if that was a good thing or not. She snuck a peek at his face, wondering if he was disappointed, if it hadn't been any good for him. His eyes were moist, and she sat up, alarmed. It hadn't been a good thing. She had been too clumsy.

She hadn't known the right moves. Maybe she should have moaned more or something. Been more encouraging. "Did I do something wrong?" she said, and he shook his head, swiped at his eyes.

"*You're* a song. The most damned important song of my whole life."

Then he reached up for her, and pulled her to him, and the tape recorder suddenly clicked off so all you could hear was a whir.

Ivan made something happen to her mind and she couldn't control it. She forgot everyone and everything but him. She came home and heard Molly weeping in her room, and for a moment her heart ached. She headed for the room to see what was wrong, before her heart hardened. Was her sister's happiness always going to be her responsibility? Didn't she deserve some fun herself? She was finding her own way; why couldn't Molly make friends or find a boy or simply rely on herself instead of Suzanne? Suzanne pivoted and left the house.

She didn't go to class, but stood outside, waiting to see Ivan. She forgot to get the dry cleaning, including an important business suit Angela needed for work the next day. She forgot that she was supposed to pick up Molly's prescription after school. Instead, she waited until Angela and Molly were out of the house, and then she called Ivan to come over and as soon as he stepped in the house, they were taking each other's clothes off, they were heading for her room.

"Where have you been?" Angela screamed at Suzanne when she came back to the house at four in the morning, Suzanne's mouth all swollen from kissing Ivan, her clothes rumpled from taking them off and putting them on again. "What is wrong with you?" Angela shouted when she came home to find the house looking like a cyclone had swept through it, no groceries in the cupboards, no dinner made, because this time, it was Molly who forgot. "What is going on here?" Angela shouted. But Suzanne knew that the answer wasn't what, but who, and that there was nothing she or anyone could do about it. "The school called me about you," Angela accused her. She was angry that she had to take time off work to go talk to Suzanne's principal because Suzanne had skipped so many classes. She was even more furious when she had to go to Woolworth's to talk the manager out of pressing charges because Suzanne had shoplifted ten dollars' worth of gold-tone earrings because she had been thinking about Ivan so hard, about how lucky she was, that she had walked past the register, the money fisted in her hand, and no matter how Suzanne had explained it to the store, they hadn't believed her for a minute. "Why can't you be good like your sister?" Angela raved.

Their fights got worse and worse. It wasn't about her taking care of Molly anymore, who was nearly thirteen now and certainly able to take care of herself. Suzanne knew it wasn't even about her taking care of the house, which Molly was starting to do anyway. It was about all those people looking down on Angela again, thinking she wasn't handling things well. It was about Angela having to cancel important dates with Lars because she had to stay at home and make sure Suzanne was going to be there, too. And it made Angela furious.

"Shoplifting!" She struck Suzanne on the shoulder. "Skipping school!" She whacked at her again, hitting Suzanne's arm. "Do you think I kill myself so you can screw up?"

"All you care about is you!" Suzanne shouted. Angela lifted a hand to strike her again and, cowering, Suzanne grabbed her mother's wrist. "Don't hit me!" she cried and Angela struck her again.

Suzanne whipped around, bumping right into Molly, pasted by the doorway, acting as if she were drowning in misery and trying to pull Suzanne down with her. Suzanne couldn't look at her. Molly was smart enough to get all As in school, let her be smart enough to figure her own way out of the house. Suzanne headed for the door. She wasn't going to be pulled down. Not anymore. She had had enough. "Suzanne, don't go," Molly cried.

"Yes, go," Angela said, her voice steely. "And when you're eighteen, you go for good. Because I've had it." She looked at her raised hand as if she was just noticing it, and then lowered it.

Suzanne turned and walked out the door, slamming it behind her. She walked all the way to the Giant Eagle and the pay phone, where

she called Ivan, weeping so hard she could hardly catch her breath.
"Oh, man," Ivan said.

"I can't go back there!" Suzanne sobbed. "I can't take it another
minute!"

Ivan was so quiet for a moment she was terrified he might have
hung up. But then he sighed. "Don't you worry, I have a plan," Ivan
told her, and two days later, she and Ivan left for California and their
future together, and neither one of them, especially Suzanne, looked
back even once.

They rented a tiny studio outside of La Jolla, where she had grown
up. The beach was just a block away, but Suzanne never got there.
She had to work every day, even weekends, as a cashier at the local
suprette, just to pay the rent and buy groceries, just so Ivan could
practice with the new band he had put together, Pneumonia.

And then it felt like she had a second job. She tried so hard to
cook meals for Ivan on just about no money, to decorate the apartment
with curtains from Woolworth's. She washed and ironed his clothes
and picked fresh flowers from the window box on the bottom floor
when no one was looking and put them in a glass on the table. It
wasn't like the way it had been with Angela, when she was forced to
clean and cook. She wanted to do this. She wanted Ivan to see what
a good wife she'd make. She wanted him to marry her.

She couldn't wait for him to get home. She fussed in the kitchen,
stir-frying canned crabmeat and packaged noodles. She had even set
the table with a lively paper cloth that she had gotten with her discount
at the suprette, but when Ivan walked in, he didn't look at the bright
blue cloth or the dishes. Suzanne thought the apartment smelled wonderful and spicy, but he just rolled his eyes. "A lot of work for something that's done in ten minutes," he told her. He went right to his
guitar and plunked down on the sofa and started playing that stupid
Joni Mitchell song she hated. "We don't need no piece of paper from
the city hall—" he sang, looking at her meaningfully, making her

wince. And when she set out the meal, he picked at it, and the first time the phone rang, he jumped up and was on the phone talking to a band member for so long that by the time he came back, his dinner was too cold to finish, and only Suzanne seemed to care.

She tried. She'd point out happily married couples, the way they held hands on the street, the way they looked at each other. "So? You need to be married for that?" Ivan shook his head. "I don't think so."

"It's—it's the next step. The next level." Suzanne hated herself for how desperate she sounded.

"Look. You're my forever," Ivan told her. "But marriage. Oh, man, that's the kiss of death for love. I ought to know. I lived with my parents long enough."

But Suzanne couldn't stop wanting marriage. It was something real. Something permanent. It told the world something good about you, that someone loved you enough to let everyone know it. And what else did she have? The rare times she called home, Molly seemed guarded to her, or too needy, like she expected Suzanne to come rescue her, when Suzanne was doing all she could to rescue herself. And Angela was impossible—even Angela's invitation to her ridiculous marriage to Lars was offered with the hope that Suzanne could start to behave. Behave. Like she was twelve years old or something.

Suzanne waited until she couldn't wait anymore. She went out and spent half the food money on a bare black minidress and fresh flowers. She lit scented candles all over the apartment. She put on some low, jazzy music she knew Ivan liked. She tucked one of the flowers behind one ear, and when he walked in the apartment, startled, she got down on her knees, smiling up at him as playfully as she could. "My, my, my," he said. "What have we here?" He bent to kiss her. He reached for the ties at the back of her dress, but she took his hand, stopping him. She stroked his fingers and took a deep breath. "Marry me," she said.

She didn't know what she was thinking. Maybe that he'd laugh. Maybe that he'd tease her. Maybe that he'd actually say yes. But Ivan stiffened. He grabbed her shoulders and jerked her to her feet. His mouth got mean. "Don't push it. You hear me?"

She stepped back from him, reeling. She could still feel his fingers on her skin.

"I love you and I'm never getting married. That's all you have to know. Those two things. And this. I don't change my mind." He walked through the candlelit apartment, knocking over one of the candles, and grabbed his guitar and went into the other room. She picked up the candle and sat on the couch, unable to move. She could hear him playing, one song, and then two, and then he came out, acting as if everything was back to normal. As if nothing important had happened. "Let's have some lights around here," he said more cheerfully, and flicked on the switch.

"Come on, Suzanne, I want to play you something I just wrote." She sat down on the couch beside him while he sang, but she couldn't concentrate. She couldn't hear a single note. All she could think about was the future. She told herself that maybe he'd feel differently when life wasn't such a struggle, when he made it big and things weren't so rushed. Ivan stopped playing and put one hand on her leg. He looked at her. "What a pretty tune," she said.

He leaned forward and kissed her tenderly.

One Friday, Pneumonia was playing a small club called the Ozone Parade for the midnight show. Suzanne was curled up on the sofa with a hot water bottle on her belly for her period cramps and didn't want to go. "Baby, you have to go," Ivan said. "I need you to be there! You know if I don't see you there, I can't play right. I have to sing *to* you."

Suzanne burrowed deeper into the couch.

"Come on. You're my inspiration! I can't do this without you!" He sat down on the couch with her and tickled her under the chin. "Suz-anne," he sang. "Pretty little Suz-anne!"

She got up. She smiled weakly. "That's my love," Ivan said happily.

She'd take a few aspirin. Have a drink. She'd get through the evening.

Eleven-thirty and the Ozone Parade was packed and dark. The noise, never mind the bodies, could knock you right down. Suzanne had been to the Ozone Parade a few times before and each time she vowed it was her last. She didn't know what it was, what had changed for her. She used to love going to the clubs in high school. She loved everything about it. The pulsing noise, the damp heat of all the bodies, the blare of the music, and the haze of smoke. The way you'd stay out all night and then go get french fries at the all-night diners at four in the morning. Now, all of it just made her think how tired she was going to be going to work in the morning. She used to love bands, too. Musicians. It seemed so exciting back in New Jersey. But she didn't love the other guys in Pneumonia. They drank too much and didn't talk about anything except music and when they came to the apartment, they made a big mess, using the floor as an ashtray, treating Suzanne like she was their slave, like all she was good for was bringing out iced tea or more beer or looking good. All of them seemed to have a different girlfriend every week. "Why else go into rock and roll?" Stan, the bass player, leered. He twanged a chord. "Sex and drugs and rock and roll!" It made Suzanne feel creepy, and she always looked at Ivan to see if he was laughing. She always felt relieved when he wasn't.

A cramp shot through Suzanne. She rubbed her stomach. Ivan leaned over and kissed her. "I'm going backstage. Stand where I can see you, honey."

He left her. Whose bright idea was it not to have tables or chairs or even standing room? What was so great about this dingy space? The walls were gray cement block, the floor scuffed linoleum. There wasn't room to dance, let alone to stand. There wasn't air. She wanted silence, the couch, her hot water bottle, and two more Midol. She pressed against the wall. Already, she was sweating. The music they had piped in was so loud, her ears were starting to ring.

A woman in a black apron snarled something at Suzanne and then disappeared. Everyone was moving around, drinking beers, shouting at one another. A woman in a short, tight red dress stepped hard on Suzanne's instep, making her yelp. A guy in jeans and a T-shirt that said FUCKING A tapped his cigarette ash on Suzanne's forearm. How was she going to last?

Pneumonia didn't come on until quarter to one, and by that time Suzanne was ready to scream. It had taken her half an hour just to get to the ladies' room, where two girls were snorting coke in the one free stall and wouldn't get out, even when Suzanne begged them. "I have my period!" she said, and the girls laughed. "Tough break," said one. A woman finally came out of the other stall and Suzanne fled into it. The toilet paper was gone. There was pee all over the seat and on the floor. The door didn't work and she had to hold it shut with one free hand. She peed and changed her tampon and when she went to wash her hands there were four blond hairs spread across the sink. She pushed her way out again.

Kids swarmed toward the stage, jostling Suzanne, who swore. "Hey! Where's Tod?" screamed the boy next to Suzanne. Suzanne looked at him. The band Ivan had put together used to be called Tod, after its lead singer, who left to go to school back east. "Tod!" the boy screamed. "Where's fucking Tod?"

Pneumonia played three songs, and then four, and all around her, the crowd got noisier and noisier. Ivan locked eyes with Suzanne. He sang to her. "You suck!" screamed a voice by her ear, making her flinch back, and then a beer can whizzed by, hitting Ivan on the thigh. He looked stunned. His voice faltered. He looked away from Suzanne. He kept playing.

"Man, know what Pneumonia's singer needs?" a boy breathed against Suzanne's ear. She tried to move away.

"A dose of antibiotics to wipe him out!" He laughed, chortling. He put one hand on Suzanne's shoulder in a too-chummy way, and she jerked away from him.

She suddenly felt sick. Ivan sounded good to her, the way he had always sounded good to her. In New Jersey, everyone had treated him with a kind of reverence. But this wasn't New Jersey.

Pneumonia played for a half hour and then abruptly stopped, jangling a final chord, punching their fists up toward the ceiling. The crowd shouted and stamped their feet. Suzanne tried to move, but everything seemed a tight tangle of legs and arms and by the time she managed to push her way backstage, she was exhausted. Her T-shirt was pasted to her back with sweat. Her cramps had dulled, but she felt sticky and wet and uncomfortable. "Excuse me," she said, and the girl in front of her glared at her. Suzanne was too tired for this. Too crampy. "Move," Suzanne ordered in a new hard voice and the girl stepped aside. Suzanne pushed her way into the back room and as soon as she did she knew something had happened.

The other band members of Pneumonia were whooping and giving each other high fives. A guy she didn't know, who seemed older than everybody else, in a black T-shirt and jeans and silver glasses, was clapping the drummer on the back. Ivan was by himself in a corner, angrily packing up his guitar, while the bass player was intently talking to him. "Hey, man, what do you want me to do? What would you do? I said I was sorry—"

Ivan snapped the guitar case shut. "Fuck you. Fuck all of you."

Suzanne looked from Ivan to the bass player, who gave her a helpless look, who lifted up his hands.

Suzanne looked at Ivan. He didn't say a word to her, but stormed out the back room. Suzanne knew Ivan enough to wait until he was ready to speak. She followed him through the club, struggling to keep up. She walked with him onto the street, and as soon as they were outside, he began to walk faster and faster. Finally, she grabbed his arm. "Ivan! What's wrong?"

He stopped. She threw her arms about him. "You were great!" she cried. "You were so fabulous!" He stepped back from her, glaring, furious.

"Who was that guy? What was going on back there?" she asked.

"Oh, that guy? That slimy little toad? You noticed him? A & R guy. Just happened to be in the club. Heard we were great," Ivan said bitterly. "Only one little problem. He wants all the band except for me."

"What? How can that be?"

"Says he sees a real future for them, that they could go far. Just not with me."

Suzanne tried desperately to think of something to say. "But it's your band."

"Right, Suzanne. Good thinking."

"You're too good for them anyway," she blurted.

He glared at her. "What? Why'd you say it like that?"

"Like what?"

"Like you don't really think so."

"I do think so! You're really good!"

"Good," he said flatly. "Just not great. That's what you think, right? That's what everyone thinks."

"I didn't say that!" she pleaded, but he glared at her and then she saw the hopeless flicker in his eyes. She tried to grab his arm, but he wrenched it away.

After that, it was as if something had changed and she was powerless to do anything about it. He practiced more and more, but it seemed to make him angrier and angrier. He'd throw the guitar down and storm out. She'd wake at three in the morning to find him strumming it in the living room, looking so fierce and determined and sad that she'd go sit beside him and listen, even though she was exhausted. She rested her head against his back. "You want to talk?" she said, but he kept playing and she grew more and more silent. She didn't care whether he could play the comb, let alone the guitar. It didn't change the way she felt about him.

Money began to get tighter and tighter and they had to move three times in one year. Each place was cheaper—and worse than the next. They had roaches and mice and once Suzanne saw a rat running down into one of the burners, which scared her so much she couldn't go near the stove for a week. The walls were so paper thin she could hear it when the next-door neighbor sneezed. Worse, Ivan had to get a job, working as a mechanic at a local shop.

She tried to come up with solutions, and everything she said to Ivan sounded dumb. "Maybe I can work two jobs," she said. "Get something at night. Maybe I can go back to school. I've been thinking maybe I'd like to do something with hair."

"Hair? Oh, that sounds exciting."

"I do the other girls' hair at work. People seem to think I have a talent."

He looked at her as if she had two heads. "For hair," he said. He shook his head. "How are you going to go to school? On what money, Suzanne?"

"Well, can't you work more hours, too?"

Ivan looked at her as if she had struck him. "Sure, Suzanne, what a good idea. Then I won't be able to practice at all."

She bit her lip. "All you need is one break."

He walked to the kitchen table and picked up some of the bills. "Yeah. A break," he said. "Look at this light bill. How hard is it, Suzanne, to turn out a light when you leave a room?" He walked from the room, clicking off the light, to show her, leaving her, alone and shocked, in the dark. She wasn't sure what to do, and then suddenly he came back in and grabbed her.

"I love you so fucking much and I am so fucking sorry," he said. He held her head in his hands, he kissed her mouth, her chin. "I know I can do this," he told her. "You just watch me."

She started working double shifts at the suprette. She was so wrung-out at the end of the day that she never wanted to see a cash register again. Her feet killed her. Her mind felt dead. People treated her like an idiot. One woman was so annoyed at the way Suzanne was packing the groceries, she grabbed the paper bag from Suzanne and began packing it herself. "Eggs do not go on top," she informed Suzanne coolly. "I would think you'd know that."

The man who came next sighed loudly at Suzanne when she gave him his change. "You gave me all pennies. Don't you know what a quarter is?" The man looked at the person standing behind him and rolled his eyes. "This place gets worse and worse."

Suzanne wanted to scream, to tear off the awful blue smock they made her wear and just walk out of there, and she would have, if she and Ivan hadn't needed the money so desperately. So instead, she smiled. She was polite. She kept her mouth firmly shut. And she soothed herself by thinking about a different sort of future. She kept thinking more and more about going to Beauty Culture School. And the more she thought about it, the more excited she became. The suprette aisles receded. She didn't see the irritation in her customers' faces. No, she saw a gleaming salon, heads of glossy hair, a secretary who had to book Suzanne's appointments months in advance because that was how in demand Suzanne was. "No one does it like you do," her customers would rave.

That night when she got home, she tried to talk to Ivan about going to school. "I think we could swing it," she told Ivan. "We could take out a loan—" and then Ivan cut her off with a thrum of guitar chords. He banged his hand against the bridge of his guitar. "Oh, hair, that's really interesting," he said.

He got his jacket and went out without her. "I just need to be alone for a bit," he said. "Don't take it personally."

In a million different ways, she tried not to. She lay on the couch, running through the channels of the TV, and she thought of the other girls at the suprette. One girl's boyfriend had smacked her because she had dared to flirt with another boy. Another girl's boyfriend never told her he loved her. The girls at the suprette all complained, they all swapped horror stories and joked that they were just slaves to love. "You never say anything bad about your Ivan," one girl said to Suzanne admiringly. "You're so lucky." And Suzanne dipped her head down just so the girl couldn't see how unsure Suzanne really felt, how the real reason she didn't say anything bad about him was because it would just end up making her feel worse.

He loves me, she told herself. *It's just a bad time.* Suzanne clicked onto another station. An old sitcom from the fifties. The laugh track blared. She watched the sitcom and an old movie and then just before it was over, Ivan came home. "Hey, you're up!" he said, pleased, and she stretched and got up and kissed him. His breath smelled like wine, but he kept kissing her. He rolled her to the floor with him. "I'm sorry, I'm so fucking sorry," he said, and then he not only told her how much he loved her, he showed her. All the rest of the night. And when he fell asleep, and she was still up, she lay with his arm wrapped about her and she made lists in her head to reassure herself.

He still wanted her. He still wrote songs for her. He held her when she was lonely. He held her the terrible night Lars called to tell her Angela had died. He was there beside her holding her hand when Molly called wanting to visit and Suzanne turned her away because who knew what a third person might do to the mix. Right now, he was so *there*. How could anything be wrong? She wouldn't let it.

She didn't think anything of his behavior until he began coming home later and later, more and more, and then suddenly it was three in the morning and there she was alone in a cold apartment listening to the man next door arguing with his wife.

Those nights, she went looking for him, hating herself. She found him playing his music in the park, only a few young girls around him, and Suzanne recognized the look on all those young girls' faces, she knew it wasn't the music they were hungering for. And she saw the look on his face. He was playing all right. And to an audience. His face was dancing with light. And when he saw her, he acted as if she were interrupting. He blew out a breath. He thrummed a chord. "Let's call it a night," he said. He put his guitar away. The other girls gave Suzanne sly, measured looks, and Ivan didn't bother to introduce Suzanne to any of them.

He was silent the whole walk back, though she tried to talk to him. "You sounded good out there," she said, and he nodded and dug his hands deeper into his pockets. "Maybe you should start playing outside more. Free concerts in the park—" she said lamely, and his mouth tightened.

"Think you can be a little *more* condescending, Suzanne?" he said.

As soon as they got back into the apartment, he started packing his things. She put one hand on his back, and he moved away from her. "It's no good anymore," he told her. "I'm going to sublet Del Bronco's pad for a while."

She blinked at him. "Who?"

He shot her a disgusted look. "See that? That's just what I mean about you. You don't even know the people in my life anymore. God. We used to talk and talk, Suzanne. But now you don't even know what I'm about." He zipped the suitcase shut. "I need to be able to concentrate on my music. To focus."

"But I let you concentrate! And I want to talk! We can still talk!" She reached to touch him. "It's just a matter of time before you get something! You're so talented only an idiot couldn't see it!"

He looked at her. Never had she seen his eyes so flat. "You bore me," he said.

After he left, she went insane. She couldn't eat, couldn't sleep, couldn't go to work. She called in sick and stayed in bed with the covers over her head. She kept expecting him to come back, to show up, just like that. And when he didn't, she got the phone book and looked up the address for D. Bronco. She could go there. She could bring him back. *You know me*, she could say to him. *We know each other. We can make this work.* She was rummaging around on the pile of laundry on the floor for something clean to wear when buried under a T-shirt, she found a brand-new pack of his guitar strings. She held it up, astonished. Didn't that mean something that he had left them here? Wasn't it true that there were no accidents, that everything was somehow meant to happen?

She dressed as carefully as she ever had in her life. In things he had bought her, the angora sweater, a pale rose-colored skirt, turquoise earrings shaped like tiny hearts. She went to his apartment. The front door was broken. It let her right in. She walked up two flights and stood outside his door, her heart thumping. She heard music playing. He was singing something and she leaned against the door. "Black hair to heaven," he sang. She touched her own hair, feeling a heady pulse of relief. He couldn't get her out of his mind any more than she could get him out of hers. And oh. He sounded good. Real good. As good as she had ever heard him. She shut her eyes, trembling. She knocked, and he opened the door, beautiful and laughing, and then just as she started to laugh, too, she saw the woman sitting cross-legged on his couch, a woman with long black hair like hers, in a short skirt, smiling at Suzanne like nothing in the world was wrong.

Suzanne froze. "Suzanne," he said and she swore for a moment, he looked sad. Or at least she wanted to think so. And then the girl who looked like her laughed, a low steady peal like a roller coaster, and Suzanne pivoted, and ran back down the stairs, throwing the guitar strings onto the dirty pavement.

Suzanne fingered the locket. She remembered how she used to feel wearing it, like love could protect her. Family love. True love. She was smarter now. She felt jittery and angry and sad, which might feel worse, but at least it was real. *You bore me*, Ivan had said. She tasted metal in her mouth. Abruptly she took off the locket and shoved it back in the box, along with the sweater. She pushed the box back in the drawer and closed it. End of story.

She had to get out of the house. Gary had told her to go shopping. Well, that's what she'd do. She just wished she didn't have to take the baby with her.

He was stirring when she went into his room. He blinked up at her, as if he were waiting. "Chop chop. Time to go." She bent to him. He blew a glistening bubble of saliva at her. She lifted him up carefully. She checked his diaper, which was dry, thank God, and put a fuzzy coat over him. And got him into the stroller, wrapping a blanket about him. What had Gary told her to pack for him? She couldn't remember. A bottle maybe, his pacifier to keep him quiet. She grabbed a bottle from the refrigerator. It wouldn't kill him to have it cold. She took the keys and money and then glanced outside. Gray and cold and all she had was her thin coat.

She rummaged in the hall closet. There wasn't much here. A blue cloth coat that wasn't much better than hers. And this puffy orange down thing with a hood. She glanced out the window again and pulled out the down parka and put it on.

She felt like a baby rhino. Feathers kept escaping, floating about her like snow. Well, tough. At least she'd be warm.

The streets were empty. She forged ahead, the stroller jerking on the bumpy sidewalk. Gary had told her the supermarket was only a short walk, but already it felt like she had gone a mile. Next time he wanted her to shop, he'd better leave her the car. It was so freezing, she pulled on the ugly hood and tied it tight. Any moment she expected the baby to do something she would be unprepared for, but every time she came around the front of the stroller to check on him, he blinked at her placidly.

There it was. The Thrift-T-Mart. As soon as she got inside, she realized she had left the list Gary had left her. She tried to remember what it was she was supposed to get. The baby made a babbling sound. "You want to tell me what I'm supposed to be looking for?" she said.

She'd go aisle to aisle. She'd figure it out. She bought cheese and cookies and cigarettes. She went to the baby aisle, which seemed like a foreign country to her. There were five different brands of diapers in six different sizes. Ready-made and powder formula. Nipples and pacifiers. Her mind went suddenly blank. What had Gary said to get? She frowned, perplexed. She felt suddenly exhausted. She took the Simulac, and then headed to the bread aisle where things were more familiar.

The groceries fit nicely in the bottom of the stroller, but it made it harder to wheel the thing. Halfway home, she felt hungry, and she pulled out the cheese and wolfed a few slices. It was the kind of makeshift dinner she had had many times before in California. She was used to it.

The baby was sleeping and Suzanne was lazily thumbing through a magazine when Gary came home. It was just after seven, and he looked exhausted and tense. *Too late for me to go to the hospital tonight, anyway,* she thought. She couldn't help feeling relieved.

"How's Molly?" she asked.

He shrugged. "The same."

He picked up some of the baby's toys and put them in the toy bin in the corner. He stopped, as if he were considering something, and then he abruptly went to the thermostat, frowned, and turned it down, but he didn't say anything to Suzanne, and then he went into the kitchen. She heard the refrigerator open and then close. "Suzanne?"

She put the magazine down and went into the kitchen. He was leaning against the counter, facing her. "You didn't have a chance to go shopping?"

"I shopped."

"There's no milk. No fruit." He looked in the cabinets. "You didn't buy pasta?" He turned to her, irritated. "Did you get formula?"

"Sure did."

He looked around and then suddenly picked up the Simulac on the counter and his frown deepened. "I told you Alimentum. He's allergic to Simulac."

"How was I supposed to know that?" Suzanne said.

"Because I told you." He looked at her. "Did you get diapers?"

She stayed perfectly still. Oh, damn. Diapers. She knew she had forgotten something.

Gary turned and wearily pulled his jacket back on. "Fine," he said, annoyed. "I'll get them. I might as well get the other stuff we need." His mouth tightened. "I know we have eggs and cheese. Could you make us a cheese omelet? A salad, do you think?"

Fuck you, she thought. Who was he to make her feel stupid? *Ordering me around.* She wasn't even that hungry. "Sure," she said. At least she didn't have to go out again. She waited until he was gone, then turned the thermostat up and broke eggs into a bowl. She tore the cheese apart with her fingers and dropped it into the bowl. *It's not my fault. I went shopping, I'm taking care of a baby, I'm doing this.* She felt like crying. She angrily ripped at the lettuce.

He came back in a slightly better mood. The salad was made, the eggs and cheese were sizzling into a mess in the pan. As he unloaded the groceries, he seemed to be giving her a kind of tour. Get this kind of milk. Don't get this kind of bread. Otis likes this. I like that. Fine.

Good. She'd remember. Just stop ordering her around as if she were a slave. Just stop treating her as if she were stupid. That didn't seem too much to ask.

They ate in silence.

The next day, Gary gave her the car to drive to the hospital, and the whole time she was driving, all she could think about was how easy it might be to keep going, past one exit and then the next. She could be clear up to Canada before Gary realized she was gone. But then what? It hammered into her head. Then what? Well, Gary's car was kind of a junk heap. It made an odd knocking sound and the brakes pulled. It'd probably never get anywhere anyway. She turned up the radio, blasting it. Oh, good, she liked this song coming on. She'd think of something.

As soon as Suzanne stepped into the hospital, she nearly turned around. People were either grinning like lunatics or looking like they'd lost their best friends. Make a left at the elevator, Gary had told her, and she did, and there was the SICU. Suzanne stalled, looking around, not sure what to do. Gary had told her that Molly was in bad shape, that she wouldn't hear or see her, but it was still important to talk to her anyway. But what could Suzanne say? *I would have called but you didn't seem to want me to.*

A nurse appeared, a blonde with a ponytail. "Yes?"

"I'm Molly Goldman's sister."

"Oh, yes, Gary told me." She touched Suzanne's shoulder. "She's over there. By the window."

Suzanne suddenly couldn't breathe. She stared. She turned to look at the nurse, to tell her there must be some mistake. This woman couldn't be Molly. This woman's face was almost hidden by tubes. Her mouth, her nose, were filled with them. Machines whirred and clicked and green neon numbers flashed. Molly's hair had been this bright shiny red, but this hair was faded, threaded with white. This skin was gray. *This woman is dying.* The force of the thought knocked into Suzanne so hard, she sank into the chair by her sister's bed. She had never imagined this. She had never seen this coming. It was a plane crash. A fall down an elevator shaft. "Molly, it's me—Suzanne—Come on, Molly. You talk to me." She ordered her around, the way she used to. "Let's go. Now." Molly eyes opened. They rolled upward and around and then the lids fluttered shut. Suzanne jerked back, terrified, and then burst into tears.

She had been so sure it wouldn't be as bad as Gary had told her. And she was right. It was much worse.

Suzanne stayed for only an hour. She didn't talk to Molly. She didn't move from the hard plastic seat. She didn't look up when a nurse came by to check one of Molly's machines. When she walked out of the room, she walked like a ghost. When she came home that night, Gary was waiting for her in the living room, reading a magazine. He stood up and walked over to her and had both of his arms around her before she had even started to cry.

That night, Suzanne couldn't sleep. She couldn't stop thinking about Molly, the way she had looked. It made her numb with terror. And she couldn't stop thinking that she would have to go back to see her tomorrow. She kicked the covers off and bolted upright. TV. If it didn't put her to sleep, as least she'd have something to concentrate on. She threw a robe about her but once she got to the living room, she turned the set on and then clicked it off again. Maybe food would settle her down. She made herself an egg but as soon as it was done, she threw it into the garbage. She got back into bed and stared at the ceiling. Next shopping trip, she was buying Nite-all.

Oh, God. Grocery shopping. Housekeeping for Molly all over again. People counting on you, wanting more and more, and no matter what you did, at times it wouldn't be good enough. Sometimes you just had to make yourself botch it because there was just too much pressure. Too many little things to tend to. You had to give so much of yourself, you risked being erased. And she wasn't sure she could pay that price again.

In the morning, she couldn't get up. She pulled the sheet over her head, shutting out the light, the sounds of the baby, all the noise Gary was making. She had had days like this after Ivan had left. She didn't answer the door. She let the phone ring and ring.

All she could think about was Molly in the hospital bed.

There was a knock on the door. *Go away*, she thought, but the door opened and Gary poked his head in. "I'm leaving now."

She nodded and didn't move."

"Can you get Otis?"

"I'm on it." He took his sweet time shutting the door. She made a few sounds, as if she were getting up, but as soon as she heard the front door slam, she burrowed back in bed. Let the baby cry first. Then she'd get up for real.

All that day, she didn't feel like doing anything. Luckily the baby slept late, and when he woke up, he seemed in a good mood. She fed him a cold bottle even though Gary had told her not to, and when he didn't fuss, she nodded at him. "Good going," she told him. She set him on a blanket in the middle of the floor, with a few rubber toys. "Amuse yourself. Be independent." He gummed happily at a yellow duck.

When he slept, she slept, and she didn't realize until Gary came back and gave her that pinched look that she was still in the same clothes she had slept in, that she had forgotten to do a wash and the baby had no more clean clothes left.

Suzanne had been living at the house for only three weeks, but Gary was starting to panic. He had made a serious mistake bringing Suzanne here. She was no help. He couldn't count on her to do the simplest things. The laundry was never done, and when it was, the whites were streaked with pink because she never separated anything, his shirts shrunk or were dappled with bleach. And the house—the house was a wreck. Dust swept across the floor like tumbleweeds. Cracker crumbs speckled the bathtub and soda cans were stacked in almost every room. This woman was inescapably messy. He found bits of Suzanne everywhere he looked: mascara wands in the kitchen, her socks in Otis's stroller, who knew how they got there. Her long black hairs drifted onto the living-room chairs, onto the kitchen table. She used up all the gas in the car and didn't bother to refill it.

And worse, she was always moping. He didn't need that—and Otis didn't need it, either. Hadn't he read somewhere that babies mirrored the faces presented to them? Otis had enough to contend with with Molly not being there with him without seeing Suzanne's sour face. Why couldn't Suzanne behave? Why couldn't she do what he himself did—put herself on automatic pilot, do what she had to just to get through the day? He was depressed, too, but he had Otis and Molly to think of. And so did she.

He hated that he had to bang on Suzanne's door every morning to get her up, and even then, he wasn't so sure that the minute he felt, she wouldn't crawl right back to bed. Sometimes during the day, he'd go to a pay phone and call her. "I just wanted to ask if there was any mail." He was lying. He wanted to make sure she was up and about. He wanted to see if he could hear Otis crying in the background. "Oh, and I forgot, could you add cheese to the grocery list?" They didn't need cheese, but he thought it would nudge her memory, it would make her remember to go shopping. "Can do," she always said, and her can dos always turned into didn'ts. More and more lately.

Gary was always exhausted. One evening, he was walking across the road, not thinking, when he heard a shriek of brakes, and he froze, staring at a blue car slamming to a stop. The driver, a woman in her twenties, flew out of the car, her hands waving in the air. "Oh, my God!" she screamed. "What if I hadn't stopped?"

Frozen, Gary let himself be led to the sidewalk. A few people stopped, staring at him. "Why weren't you looking?" she shouted, suddenly furious at him, her face full of blame. "What's the matter with you?"

Gary sank onto a bench. Horrified, he gripped onto the wood. He felt the hammering of his heart, the raw scratch of his breath. "You're not hurt, right?" the woman said. She studied him, and then turned, getting back into her car. "Next time, watch where you're going!"

He heard the roar of her engine, the way she peeled out into the street again. He planted his hands on his knees and hunched forward, suddenly reeling with nausea. He lifted himself up, sucking in air, forcing himself to breathe normally, to calm. *I can't be killed,* he thought in sudden amazement. *I have to be all right. If I died, who would take care of Otis?*

He got up, stricken. Suzanne was Otis's next of kin. He'd be leaving Otis to Suzanne. *I'm alone in this,* he thought.

He'd have to do something. He'd have to be more careful. And he'd have to have a talk with Suzanne. He'd be calm, since she got so testy if he so much as asked her to wash a dish these days. He'd lie and tell her what a great job she was doing—on the whole. She'd have to rally. She'd have to be more help because the truth was, he couldn't do this alone. And she was all he had.

But the night he decided to talk to her, he came home to find her sprawled on the sofa, quickly stubbing out a cigarette. Otis was lying on a blanket, in the same romper he had been wearing that morning when Gary left. "I asked you not to smoke in here." Gary felt something boiling inside his stomach. He lifted up Otis. "He's wet," he accused. "How long has he been in this diaper?" Suzanne gave him a sullen face.

He took Otis into the bedroom to change him, grabbing for the blue plastic wipes box, flicking it open with a finger. Empty. "Suzanne!"

She came into the room, leaning against the door, her arms folded. Molly was right to have put Suzanne's number in that acrylic puzzle. He had been the fool to break it open with a hammer.

"Where are the wipes?"

"They're not there?"

"You're here all day with a baby and you don't know?"

Suzanne drew herself up. "Look, I have a lot to do around here——"

Otis began to wail and Gary hastily picked him up and rocked him. "I am so sick of this."

"Fine. So am I."

She was leaning against the doorway, sulking. It made something rush through him in fury. "And I'm sick of you! You were brought here to help, not to be another baby I have to take care of! What do you think is going on here? I can't take care of everything myself! I need you! Otis needs you! And so does Molly!"

Suzanne snorted. "Molly doesn't need me. Molly doesn't even know I'm there."

"Shut up! Don't you say that! Don't you ever say that!" Flustered, he carried Otis to the bathroom and wiped the baby off with a washcloth. He came back into the baby's room and set Otis down, grabbing for a clean diaper. Otis screamed. "You're upsetting Otis!"

"*I'm* upsetting him?" Her face tightened with anger. "This is hard for me, too, you know. Molly's my sister. How do you think I feel?"

"You can't just sit around here and be depressed!"

"Fine!" Suzanne whipped around. "I won't." She stormed out.

"Wait! Where are you going?" Otis began to wail again, his voice rising in pitch. Gary heard Suzanne slam the door of her room. He heard her opening and closing drawers. He was so scared she'd leave that he was frozen. What was he going to do now? What was any of them going to do? And then Otis began shrieking, but it was a different kind of shriek, one he had never heard before. Otis flailed in his arms. His face was red, coiled up. And suddenly Suzanne, her face white and scared, came into the room.

"What's wrong with him?" she whispered.

Gary sat in the rocker. Otis screamed even louder. Gary put one hand on the baby's head. "He's not hot." Otis shrieked and balled his hands into fists. Gary looked helplessly at Suzanne.

Suzanne warmed a bottle but when she tried to give it to the baby, he angrily batted it away. "Otis! Otis!" Gary called.

Otis stiffened and caught his breath and screamed.

"That does it. Something's wrong!" Gary handed Otis to Suzanne and reached for the phone. "I'm calling the doctor."

He was on the phone for only five minutes. "Colic." He shook his head in disbelief. "He says it will pass."

"How does he know without seeing him?"

"He said it's common."

"What causes it?"

"Nothing. They don't know."

"I don't believe it," Suzanne said. "There must be something we can do."

Otis screamed and kicked against Suzanne.

"Gerta! Maybe Gerta knows." He grabbed for the phone again. "Gerta?" he said. His voice was tight, desperate. He nodded at the phone.

"Oh. All right." He looked defeated. "You're sure."

"What? What did she say?"

"She has never dealt with colicky babies. She told me that babies know better than to act that way with her." He shook his head. He gave a half laugh.

"Give me a break. What else?"

"The baby—he—" Gary made his voice accented the way Gerta's was. "The baby—he know his mother is ill and this is the way he pray for her." Gary's voice bubbled up. "She thinks Otis is praying for Molly!" He started laughing, doubling over. "This baby, he understand!" Gary laughed so hard he started to cough. Suzanne stared at him, and Otis shrieked and flailed and then, as abruptly as it started, he stopped laughing.

It was Suzanne's idea to take the baby for a drive. The baby screamed and thrashed in Gary's arms the whole way outside. "Sit in back with him," Gary told Suzanne. She opened up the baby's car seat and stepped aside while Gary fit him in. The baby's arms beat like propellers against the seat. His shrieks were like a siren. *This is how people go nuts,* Suzanne thought. Even with her fingers poked into her ears, she could still hear him.

Gary twisted in his seat and surveyed the two of them anxiously. "Go," she said.

They were only a block away when the baby snuffled and suddenly stopped crying. Suzanne took her fingers out of her ears. Gary turned and stared at him and then stared at Suzanne in amazement. He stopped the car. His eyes met Suzanne's. The baby's eyes flew open. His face reddened and he began to wail. "All right, all right, you're the boss—" Gary said, and started the car again.

He had gone only half a mile when Suzanne tapped him, pointing a finger toward the car seat. The baby was asleep.

"Let's just drive." Gary said. He wound around the same route over and over again. Suzanne didn't mind. There was something hypnotic about being in the backseat. Then he started driving farther out, past the diners, the dance joints, the bowling alleys. She looked at everything from a dreamy distance, as if she had never lived here at all. "It's still one big mall out here, isn't it?" Suzanne said. "I never figured Molly would stay in New Jersey." Suzanne shook her head. "At least she got out of Elizabeth."

Gary turned the wheel. The baby's mouth flopped open. "She wanted to stay in Elizabeth. Then we found our house here."

"No way! She was miserable in Elizabeth!"

"Not when I met her."

Gary fiddled with the dials. Surprise, oh, surprise, some good old down and dirty country blues, the kind she had listened to night after night. She used to wail along to it. Gary kept talking. She was barely listening to him. She couldn't have cared less how he met Molly and fell in love, how they found the house—all that mind-numbing suburbia life story stuff that he was telling more for himself than for her.

"I sky-dived a few times."

Suzanne sat up. This was halfway interesting. "You're kidding. You?"

He half smiled. "Ah-ha, the truth comes out what you think about me."

"Why'd you stop? You got scared?"

He shook his head. "Being scared was the point. I was testing myself. Trying to see if I could really do it. And I could. If I had money, I'd do it again."

Gary kept talking, changing the subject now, and Suzanne began to listen to him with a little more interest. His shtick still was pretty boring, the usual stuff about college and travel, but every once in a while, like a bright jewel in the sand, he'd say something that surprised her out of her stupor—that he had learned to drive when he was a little kid. That he liked kung fu movies. And then she would start to listen a little harder to him.

It was four in the morning, they were both exhausted. "I guess we can go home now," Gary said.

The baby was still sleeping when Gary parked the car. Suzanne quietly got him out of his car seat and out of the car, and as she was standing, she suddenly felt Gary beside her. "I'll take him," he said, and she felt his hand, broad and smooth, along her back, and as soon as he took it away, she circled both her arms about herself. She followed Gary into the house. "I can take it from here," Gary whispered, leaving her standing alone in the living room.

By six in the morning, barely seconds after Gary left to go see Molly, the colic was back. Well, so what. Suzanne didn't mind driving the baby around all day. He slept and she got to just go, she got to pick the music she wanted to blast, and she kept her cigarettes nice and handy on the seat beside her. Driving was the perfect excuse. She didn't have to do the laundry or the shopping. Even Gary knew taking care of the baby's colic was more important. The baby would sleep enough so she could haul him into a fast food joint with her so she could grab a burger and fries, eating quickly before he woke and started cranking up all over again. And then they'd go home and wait for Gary and he'd take over for an hour while she went to see Molly, and then before she knew it, she'd be back in the car and on the road.

She had to admit that she liked the night drives better than the day ones. She had always thought of herself as a night person, and maybe her idea of that wasn't exactly riding inside of a car, but at least she was out.

Gary could drive like a pro when he wanted to, sliding in and out of lanes, speeding here and there. You had to admire driving like that. He talked and talked about a million different things, and he began to ask her questions. Not about her life with Molly, thank God. Nothing that would make her feel guilty or want to jump right out of the car. He asked her these weird questions, almost like school essays, or those dopey *Reader's Digest* things: My Most Unforgettable Character, by Suzanne Goldman. "Tell me the worst customer you ever had," Gary insisted.

Come on, she thought. But she found herself talking to him, telling him about the high-priced call girl who paid extra to have her pubic hair dyed, about the biker who wanted KILL FOR THRILL shaved into his hair. She had never talked about her work all that much to Ivan. She used to cut his hair, taking extra pains, making sure it looked good because she knew how important that was to him. But afterward, he'd get up and fuss with it. Once, she saw him nicking at the sides with a nail scissors. "A monkey could do what you do," Ivan had once said. But Gary paid attention. He whooped and laughed and asked questions. He was such a good audience that he made her want to talk even more. He made her remember an eighty-year-old woman who wanted her hair spiked and punky, a kung fu teacher who kicked in her wall when she refused to take a free lesson instead of payment. Gary laughed and hit the steering wheel in appreciation.

"Hold on." Gary pointed to a diner. "I'll be right back."

He wasn't gone long, but when he came back, he had an ice cream cone and an ice cream sandwich. He handed her the cone, strawberry, her favorite.

"How did you know I liked strawberry?" she said.

"It's the only ice cream you buy."

She looked at him, checking to see if he was being sarcastic, but all he was doing was taking bites from his sandwich.

Gary drove, half paying attention, bopping one hand on the steering wheel to the music. Suzanne began to like best the times around three or four in the morning, when there was hardly anyone in the road, when it seemed like there was hardly anyone in the world except for them, sitting in the car, telling stories to each other and laughing. She could have driven all night then.

The baby had the colic for two weeks. And counting. And then one afternoon, when Suzanne was driving around, when she stopped to try to get a hamburger, the baby woke up and for the first time in a long while, the kid wasn't crying. He blinked at her, as if he were awakening from a very long dream. "Well, if it isn't Rip Van Baby," Suzanne said. He was good in the stroller. He was good when she wheeled him into the diner, and good while she ate her burger and fries. He was so good she decided to go check out the record store next door, and he didn't cry there either.

All that afternoon, Suzanne braced for the baby to start screaming again. She drove for an hour and then, as a kind of experiment, took him home. He yawned and batted his hands against her. She set him in his playpen and he cooed at his toys. And when Gary came home, the baby was calmly examining his toes, blinking up at Gary as if he didn't have a care in the world.

Gary crouched down beside the baby. "Does this mean what I think it means?" Gary looked at Suzanne.

"Well, hallelujah!" Suzanne said. But her voice sounded hollow to her, like the inside of a metal can.

chapter

six

S uzanne began to feel as if all her senses had been thrown right out of whack. Her morning coffee tasted like straw. Her favorite perfume smelled so much like oven cleaner, she instantly scrubbed it off. Gary could be at his computer, but she swore she saw him in the doorway, watching her, waiting. She swore she heard him right behind her, saying something to her in a low voice that made her shiver.

Usually, she could sleep until noon, but suddenly, without even trying, she jumped out of bed at six, the same time Gary did. Coincidence, she tried to tell herself, as she rushed to dress, pulling on her prettiest dress, grabbing for her brush, and snapping it through her locks so fast she brought up small sparks of light. Just whom did she think she was brushing her hair for? Why was she slashing on lipstick, coating on mascara? What in the world was she doing?

Gary was her sister's husband, a man so not her type it wasn't even funny.

She was scared about Molly, the same way he was. That was all it was that was bonding them. She was lonely. Sleep-deprived. Sex-deprived. Love-deprived. Look at Patty Hearst. Women fell in love with their captors all the time. Maybe this wasn't the same thing, but it almost was. This was a crush, and she'd just have to get over it the same way she'd get over a cold, and that would be that. She'd have to find more things to keep her busy, to keep her mind off him. She had the house under control. She and Otis were doing fine, working on a kind of schedule. Maybe she could get clients, cut some hair. Get her mind on work instead of Gary.

Besides, Gary loved Molly. Any fool could see that. The way she sometimes caught him staring at Molly's photo, his face so soft and sad, it was all she could do not to run over to him and throw her arms about him. Every time she walked into Molly's hospital room, there was another gift from him. He couldn't afford anything, but what he bought was always simple and beautiful. So perfect, it got her in the gut to see it. Butter-yellow cashmere socks. A sea-blue vial of lotion. Such kindness, such thought, made her just love Gary even more. And she wasn't the only one.

The nurses couldn't stop talking about him, singing his praises. "Your brother-in-law's a jewel," one nurse told Suzanne. "Lots of men would just leave. I've seen it more times than I care to comment on. The wife gets sick and the husband starts visiting less and less, and then one, two, three, you see him in town with a tootsie on his arm." The nurse shook her head with approval. "Gary's a good guy. A really good guy."

"I know," said Suzanne.

One day, Suzanne was coming out of the shower, when she realized all she had with her was her towel. She was freezing. An old blue flannel shirt was hanging on the hook by the door. Gary's. As soon as she touched it, she smelled Gary's pine aftershave. She grabbed the shirt. She put it on. Buttoned it tight against her.

Gary was having his own problems. He looked everywhere for work. Every morning, he spent hours on the phone, calling his friends, his business contacts, always insisting to everyone he spoke with that no job was too mundane, too beneath him or too boring, as long as he could do it at home, and on his own time. He made blind phone calls to agencies he culled from the Yellow Pages, but without much luck, and every day, on his way to the hospital, he stopped at the gift shop and bought four different newspapers, one from New Jersey, one from Connecticut, two from New York. He sent off résumés and he even called a few headhunters. His résumé was impressive enough that people called him back, but after that, he was in trouble, because as soon as anyone heard that all he was looking for was part-time, off-site work, the atmosphere turned suddenly cool. "That's not what we're really looking for," people told him. "We're looking for someone who can be part of a team. Someone more committed."

It made Gary feel hysterical. Committed. Jesus. What was more committed than going to the hospital every day to see the woman you loved most in the world not recognize you, and not letting yourself give up hope? What was more committed than being a single father?

Gary sat in his kitchen and stared at the telephone. *Don't give up,* he told himself, just as the phone suddenly rang, startling him so that he dropped his pen, rolling it across the floor.

"Gary."

"Ada!" He scooped over, grabbing up the pen.

"Guess what? I've got something for you."

"Oh, thank God, thank God. I really need the work."

There was a clip of silence. "Gary, it's not work." Her voice brightened. "It's for Molly."

"For Molly?"

"I was in the bookstore the other day, and I picked up this absolutely amazing book. *The Magic Healing Power of Mushrooms.* It's all about how the mushrooms help the body release this special chemical and how it affects immunity—"

"Ada—" Gary cut her off. He felt suddenly exhausted. "Molly can't eat."

"Well, I know that, but you could boil up the mushrooms and give her the liquid—"

"In her IV?" His voice tightened. "She's comatose. She can't eat."

Ada was quiet. "I was just trying to help."

"I know you were."

"Well, if I hear of anything, I'll call you."

Gary hung up, feeling sick.

He could hear Suzanne in the kitchen noisily washing dishes. At least she was cleaning up. He heard the mail slapping in through the slot and he crouched to leaf through it. Bills. Junk mail. Cards he never had the heart to open because they always made him feel worse. They reminded him too much. He usually just threw them away. He was almost finished with the mail when he found something addressed from the hospital, and he tore it open.

Five pages of pale blue paper with deep blue ink. Columns and explanations and a total on the very bottom. Eight hundred thousand. He stared at the pages again as if there were some mistake, an extra zero, a wrong comma or decimal, a misprint. Operations. Procedures. CAT scans and MRIs and nuclear medicine. A single blood test was two thousand alone. Gary started to laugh. Eight hundred thousand! He looked at the service dates. These were all for last month! The bill didn't even cover the last three weeks! He was laughing so hard he was crying, snuffling his tears, hitting the table, making so much noise, Suzanne ran in, her hands still damp. He flapped the bill in the air and handed it to her.

"This is a joke?" she asked, and he shook his head. "Insurance will cover this, right?"

He leaned along the wall. "What am I going to do?"

Every day now, another bill came, and the totals were always so astronomical, they took his breath away. He didn't recognize the names of the doctors billing them, the procedures all seemed to be in a foreign language, and after a while, he simply stopped looking at the bills altogether, but stuffed them into clean envelopes, stamped and addressed them and sent them off to insurance and tried not to think about them at all.

As soon as he mailed a bill off, another one arrived, and with them began to come the insurance denials. A twenty-thousand-dollar procedure was above what insurance usually paid and so insurance would only pay fifteen thousand of it. His insurance wouldn't cover Molly's hospital stay because they said that it was beyond the normal stay after a C-section, which was only three days. Astounded, Gary called the insurance company. "What can you mean talking to me about normal stay? How can you do this? This isn't a normal C-section! Surely, if you look at her file, you'll see the blood work, the tests, the diagnosis—"

"Hold on," the voice on the other end said. "My computer just went down."

He had to call back five minutes later, waiting through the tinny Muzak rendition of the Beatles' "Got to Get You Into My Life" before a real person got on the line, and even then it was a new person, and he had to tell his story all over again. "Reapply then," the woman told him. "Contest. Tell the doctors to send supporting information."

"What if I don't know exactly who the doctor is or what sort of supporting information you might need?"

"Well, if you don't know, sir, then we certainly don't."

Gary leafed through another bill, denied because Molly had not gotten precertification. "Precertification! What do you mean asking about precertification? My wife was comatose!" Gary shouted into the phone. "How could she precertify anything? Was I supposed to stop the doctors, to say, 'Wait, don't try to save my wife yet, let me call insurance first, make sure it's all right for you to do whatever the hell you're going to do'?"

"I know you're upset, but you don't have to shout at me."

"No? Who do I shout at then?"

"Sir, I don't have to take this call."

"No! Don't hang up. You're right, you're right, I'm sorry." But what was he supposed to do? The people he spoke to on the phone were just clerks. They weren't responsible, they didn't know him, they needed to look up the information and his wife's file was so large, it might take them a while. "Can you call back?" the clerks kept asking. He called back three times in half an hour and each time he got a different person, and none of them knew what exactly was the problem, why the bill hadn't been paid to the hospital by insurance. "Send it in again," they kept telling him.

Gary tried. He kept track of the bills as best he could, but nothing seemed to make sense. He bought two big file envelopes and stuffed the bills into them. He called the doctors, desperate.

The doctors, thank God, were sympathetic. Dr. Price waved his hand in annoyance. "Insurance companies practicing medicine. What a world. As if you don't have enough to think about. I'll have my office call them."

Dr. Kane, the surgeon, told Gary he'd put a note in his file that payment might be delayed. "Pay when you can," he said. "We'll work it out."

And to his astonishment, Karen told him not to pay at all.

"Let's just say that if, when, and whatever insurance pays me is enough," Karen said. "As far as I'm concerned, you don't ever have to worry about it."

Gary blinked at her and she slowly smiled. He was so grateful he could have wept.

But the bills kept coming. From more and more doctors he didn't know. From the hospital and the labs, who weren't so understanding as the individual doctors, so willing to be a little flexible and wait for him to fight with the insurance company. Collection agencies began to call. "Wouldn't you like to pay and get this taken care of?" a smooth voice always asked him. "Why don't we just do it over the phone by credit card?"

"Which tapped-out credit card would you like?" Gary said wearily.

"Sir," the voice said, cooling, "you don't want to let this go too far."

Gary stepped up his search for work, clipping ads from the paper about nighttime proofing, calling, and to his dismay, everyone he called asked about his last job, and then they didn't want to see him. Next time, he told himself, he'd lie.

He had the want ads spread on the floor when Suzanne came into the room. She was wearing a green dress, her arms and legs bare. She was watching him as if she expected him to say something. "You look nice," he said.

She smiled and then sat down, watching him again. "No luck?" she said, and he shrugged.

"You know, I could work. I wouldn't even have to leave the house."

"You work already. You take care of Otis."

She waved her hand. "The baby runs like a little clock. I could do hair right in a corner of the kitchen. It wouldn't be any trouble. I'll schedule people when he sleeps. Or he can sit in the playpen and watch. Learn a little something."

"I don't know—"

"I need to work," she blurted. "I need something to take my mind off—things."

She looked away from him.

Who was Gary not to understand something like that? "Sure. Go ahead," he said. "The money will come in handy."

A CUT ABOVE.
SUZANNE GOLDMAN: LICENSED BEAUTICIAN.
COLOR, CUTS, STYLINGS. IN THE COMFORT OF MY
HOME. THE LOOKS YOU WANT AT PRICES YOU'LL LOVE!

With the baby in the stroller, Wood You, the unpainted furniture store, was Suzanne's last stop of the day. The store was cool and smelled like cedar, filled with soft pine shelves and tables and chairs, some of them stained and stenciled so you could see how beautiful they could become with just a little loving care. Wood You had a big community bulletin board by the front. The store was crowded with people, running their hands over the furniture, peering at the shelves of stains. A good sign. Every one of these people could be a potential haircut.

She had already set up a little work corner for herself in the kitchen. She took the mirror from the hallway and hung it on the wall. She moved a swivel chair from Gary's office in front of it, and put a smock on a hook by the basement door. She set up a small shelf full of supplies, the special shampoos and conditioners she made herself, some vials of color, and small gleaming bowls with scented candles. To give the place atmosphere.

She lifted a flier out from the bottom of the stroller and tried to find a good place on the board to tack it.

"Here, let me help you."

Suzanne turned around. A man in a flannel shirt, a leather apron about his jeans, leaned up and helped position Suzanne's sign on the bulletin board. "Nice-looking sign."

Suzanne looked at him to see if he were making fun of her. He was about her age, with a face like a soup dumpling. Receding brown hair, belly folding over his belt. But his smile was friendly enough.

"Anyone comes in here with raggedy hair, you point them to my sign," she said.

He laughed, and then she felt embarrassed because just look at *his* hair, flying off in every direction. But he didn't seem to take offense. "Bob Tillman," he said. He waggled his fingers at the baby and then squinted up at the sign again. "Suzanne Goldman. Wait a minute here. You're not related to Molly Goldman, are you?"

"You know Molly?"

"I know *of* her. A few of my customers were talking about her." He shook his head. "Terrible thing."

Suzanne stiffened a little. "She's my sister. I'm staying with my brother-in-law helping out. Taking care of the baby."

"I'm so very sorry." He gave her a considering look and then, abruptly, he took down her sign.

Suzanne's hand flew up to stop him. "Hey! What do you think you're doing?"

He dug into his pocket and pulled out some tape, and then he took Suzanne's sign and taped it to the front window. Then he turned back to her, smiling. "That's better."

Suzanne smiled back at him. God, she thought. This guy was *nice* with a capital N. Why didn't guys like that ever look like anything?

"Come back. I'll give you a good deal on some furniture. I'll show you how you can make an unpainted chair look like an expensive antique."

"You got any pickled stains?" A woman tapped Bob Tillman on the arm.

"Come back," Bob Tillman repeated to Suzanne and turned his attention to the pickle stain lady.

Suzanne wheeled Otis out into the sunny street. She felt a little better seeing her sign posted in front like that. She took a moment to admire it.

"He looks just like you. The very image."

Suzanne looked startled. A woman was standing beside her. She looked like Bob Tillman?

"He does. Look at those eyes. That mouth. That coloring. Is he your first?"

Suzanne followed the woman's eyes down to the baby. "Yes," Suzanne said.

"Lucky you." The other woman fretted her hands through her hair. She leaned forward and drew out a pen and began copying the number on Suzanne's sign.

Two breadwinners without bread, Gary thought. No one had called for Suzanne. No one had called for him. Gary tried to stay optimistic, but he felt worn down. He stopped dressing in a shirt and tie and wore only his jeans, his battered leather jacket. He stopped carrying his briefcase, his portfolio. He told himself he was saving wear and tear on his good things, that if he got an interview, he'd shave, he'd have Suzanne trim his hair. He'd spruce up and make his step have spring. He'd make himself look like he knew what hope was.

That evening, when he was coming home from the hospital, he saw Bill sitting on his front porch. It was an odd sight, since it was neighborhood policy not to sit on the stoops until it was good and hot outside, until you could parade out plastic chairs and refreshments and one of those small portable radios. Bill waved one hand in greeting, which surprised Gary even more. He stopped, hesitating.

"How's Molly?"

Gary shrugged. "The same."

Bill took out a cigarette and lighted it. "And how are you managing?"

"You know. As good as can be expected."

Bill drew on his cigarette. He tapped the ashes onto his porch. "I see you around the house a lot more."

Gary nodded. He looked at Bill, who was looking quietly down at the ground. Giving him room. "I got fired," Gary said.

Bill nodded, shaking his head. It was a little disconcerting to Gary that Bill didn't seem the least surprised. If anything, he looked as if he had known already. "What kind of bastard fires someone when his wife is ill?" Bill said finally.

"A bastard who wants you there nine to five, I suppose."

"I know that kind." Bill flung his cigarette away and dug for another in his shirt pocket. He lit it and then looked back at the street, considering. "You know, my cousin Larry runs a warehouse over in Newark. Plumbing supplies. He never trusted those automated security systems. He needs a night watchman. Midnight to six." He looked past Gary, at the cars. "You interested? All you have to do is be there. You can sleep, read magazines, do nothing. It's peace of mind for Larry. I mean, who's really going to break into a plumbing supply place?" Bill stubbed out his cigarette. For the first time, he looked straight at Gary. His face was even, breathing, his eyes a deep, bright blue. "It's money under the table. One hundred a night."

Gary felt a strange light shining from the sky. His mouth was dry. "When can I start?"

Larry's Plumbing Supply Warehouse was on a dark side street in Newark. Larry was a lean, horse-faced man in his fifties with a shelf of sandy hair and straight white teeth and an odd resemblance to Bill. He pumped Gary's hand. "Bill told me all about you," he said. "Good people, Bill and Emma."

"They sure are."

Larry gave Gary a quick tour, down the gray hallways, into the storage rooms, and back to the front desk where Gary would sit. "Every few hours just walk the halls," Larry told him. "Phone's right here. Any trouble, just call the cops. That's your defense." He patted Gary on the back. "You're welcome to bring in a radio, if you want. The last watchman had a portable TV. And you're not totally alone here. We've got a cleaning man who comes here nights, too. A college kid.

Son of a friend of mine, so you'll have a little company, if you want it. At six sharp, the day security man comes in. You punch in and out. And every Friday, I'll come here and pay you."

Even though Gary wouldn't be seeing anyone, he still had to wear a uniform. "Makes it more official," Larry said. The uniform was a long-sleeved shirt and pants, both in stiff, dull brown, with a gold insignia that said TOP SECURITY. "I made up the name," Larry confided with a grin. There was a cap, too, with a plastic brim, that Larry popped onto Gary's head.

The first time Gary put on the uniform, he stared at himself in the mirror. He looked ridiculous. An image flashed into his mind: another kind of uniform, the scrubs he had put on to watch his son being born, the exuberant way he had tied on the mask, the gown, how he had loved the whole green starchy smell. He remembered, too, Molly's face, shining in pleasure at the sight of him. He saw her. He felt her joy. And then he saw Molly, swollen, gray, and sick, a johnny gown tied on. Molly not seeing him at all. He shut his eyes and opened them. He adjusted the hat. It nicked at the back of his ears. The shirt collar itched. It was money. It was one hundred tax-free dollars a night, and taking such a job required no more thought than that.

He walked past Suzanne, who was feeding Otis. Her face changed. "Don't you dare laugh," Gary said.

"I think you look great," she said.

The day security man, tall and thin and pale, met Gary at the door. "Nothing going on tonight," he said, and tipped his hat, walking past Gary. "It's all yours."

Gary's first night, he sat at the desk, a magazine in front of him. He leafed through the pages so roughly, he tore a few. He couldn't see the bright gleam of photos, he couldn't read a line of copy. He couldn't focus. He looked up at the clock. Only a half hour had passed. The night swung out before him.

Larry was right. With this job, he didn't have to concentrate on anything, but in a way, that was part of the problem. Freed, his mind flooded with Molly. It replayed his days at the hospital, the way her face looked. He kept thinking about the moment she had gotten pregnant, if there had been something about her he had missed, something that might have warded this off, something he could have done, and it all made him so crazy, he got up and stormed down the halls, just to have something to do. He checked doors to make sure they were locked. He checked windows and shone the flashlight they gave him into every dark corner. He felt an odd satisfaction, a kind of dull joy in making the building secure.

He was making a circle back to his desk when he heard the hum of a vacuum. He turned a corner. There was a young man, his black hair in a ponytail, in jeans and a white T-shirt, running the machine over the floor. He grinned when he saw Gary and clicked off the vacuum. "Well hot dog! Company!" he called. He wiped his hand on the back of his jeans and thrust it out at Gary.

The man's name was Marty. Marty was twenty-two and in college at Rutgers, paying his way by a variety of jobs. He wanted to be a movie director and he had all these ideas. *"Night job,"* Marty said, making his hands into a frame. "That's the title of my movie. It's about a janitor at night and how he begins to suspect the building he's in is somehow alive and haunted and out to get him and what he does about it. It's sort of like that great Danish film about the hospital, *The King-dom,* you ever see that?"

"I haven't seen any hospital movies lately."

"Well," Marty said, considering, "you should."

Marty went off to finish his vacuuming and Gary wound his way back to his desk. The building had a kind of music, a low, steady hum, a vibration maybe. He had read once where everything had a soul, even machines, even concrete and steel. He tried to keep himself still, to listen deeper to the building, to try to feel what its soul might be like. Benevolent, he decided.

The time passed and then Gary punched out and came home. The morning light seemed unnaturally bright, the air too still. He went inside the house, which was quiet, and the first thing he did, before he got out of his uniform and into his jeans, was look in on Otis, who was sleeping.

He should sleep, too, but he wasn't tired. He didn't want to risk sleeping through a minute he might share with his son, so he kept awake.

He stayed awake so he could check with Suzanne about what kind of a night Otis had had. He stayed awake until Otis cried and then he dressed his son and strolled him to the park and back. He stayed awake on the drive to the hospital and beside Molly's bed. "I'm here." He would have gotten up on the bed with her, if there weren't so many tubes, if his jostling might not harm her. He looked at her and felt himself coming undone. He would have taken her illness into himself. *You live, I live.* It was as simple as that. He took her hand. Her skin was warm. Her pulse beat up against his. *You die, I die.* His lids floated shut. He slept, deep and dreamless, his mind closed tight as a building.

At the end of his first week of work, Larry showed up. He slapped Gary on the back. "You're doing real good," he said seriously, though for the life of him, Gary couldn't figure out how someone did badly at a job like this. He could walk the halls or not walk the halls, he could fall asleep the whole night at his desk and no one would notice, except for maybe Marty, and he was too absorbed in his own future to notice anyone else's. Larry handed Gary an envelope, thick with bills. "I put something extra in there for you," he said, lowering his voice. "Bill told me how things are for you." Larry patted Gary's shoulder.

Suzanne tried to gauge her sister's progress by the way the nurses acted. If they stopped to talk to Suzanne, it was a good sign. If they breezed by, it meant Molly was getting worse. She could tell, too, how her sister was doing by the number of times Gary called the hospital to check on Molly's status. By the number of photos he left on her table. But she didn't begin to be really terrified until Gary stopped calling the hospital altogether, until one Saturday morning she woke up at five and found him sitting in the living room, staring at the window, not moving.

She was afraid to call out to him, to ask what was wrong. She was suddenly terrified Molly might not make it. She turned around and went back to her bed. She bundled herself up in the sheets and stared into the darkness.

She began to be more and more afraid in Molly's house. At night, when Gary was at his night manager's job, she couldn't sleep. She didn't know what she was afraid of. Gary had installed new locks, even on the windows. He had an alarm system.

Now she took a shower with the door wide open, and halfway through, she stepped out of the tub, dripping wet, and locked the door, and even then, she felt uneasy. She knew money was tight, but still, she switched on lights as she moved from room to room. She turned on the television and the radio and the baby's monitor so it buzzed. She sat in the living room half hoping Otis would wake just so she would have company.

She went to the phone and called the hospital. "Molly Goldman," she said and waited.

"Critical. The same," the voice said, and Suzanne hung up. Critical was still alive, she reminded herself. So why then did she see razor-edged dominoes, falling, all pointed toward her?

One day, Suzanne was putting the baby to bed when the bell rang. She raced down and there was a woman standing there, a kerchief about her hair. Suzanne opened the door. "Theresa. From next door," the woman said. She waited and then sighed as if Suzanne were being rude. "Carl's wife."

"Oh, yes," Suzanne said doubtfully. "Theresa." She tried to think why Theresa was here, what had happened, but she felt blank.

"Is everything all right?" she asked and Theresa drew off her kerchief.

"You take walk-ins?" she said.

She gave Theresa a smock. Theresa fingered the material and put it on. "Tea? Coffee?"

Theresa considered. "I like Sanka."

Suzanne sat Theresa in the plastic chair she used and touched Theresa's hair. It didn't feel real. Stiff with spray, dry from bad coloring, and the wrong kind of perm.

"It's still keeping its shape, but I thought a touch-up, a trim, couldn't hurt," Theresa said.

Suzanne lifted her hands from Theresa's hair and nodded.

Usually when Suzanne worked, she filled up the silences with patter, making jokes, asking her clients questions, but there was something about Theresa that made her keep her mouth shut. Every time Suzanne looked in the mirror she saw Theresa watching her, like she was about to have her appendix taken out without anesthesia. When Suzanne touched Theresa's hair, Theresa winced, and all Suzanne could think was: *She's afraid of me.*

She washed Theresa's hair with the good shampoo. "Smells nice," Theresa said. "What's that green stuff floating in it?"

"Fresh mint. It gives the smell."

"Fresh mint. Who'd have thought?" said Theresa doubtfully.

Suzanne combed color through Theresa's hair and set it the way she knew Theresa would like it, a stiff brassy muffin about her head, and popped her under a dryer. It killed her to ruin hair like that, but she was desperate, she needed the money, Gary needed the money, and she wanted to be working, even if it was working badly. Theresa could have told her she wanted hair like a topiary, and Suzanne would have done it.

She let Theresa's hair fry under the dryer, and then took her out, carefully removing the hard pink curlers one by one. Theresa blinked and as Suzanne worked, Theresa's face began to change. Her mouth loosened up. You could see her lips now. Her eyes widened. By the time Suzanne was spraying her hair, making it hard and shiny as a beetle shell, Theresa was smiling. "You did a great job," she said.

"You're surprised, right?" Suzanne didn't tell her that she knew exactly how to do hair like this from her days at Beauty Culture School, when the only people fool enough to let her work on them were all the little old ladies coming in for the five-dollar student cuts.

Theresa beamed and touched her bright helmet of hair. "You know, I decided to do this for Gary. It was the only way I could think that he might accept money from me." She swiveled in the chair, studying the back of her hair. "Isn't it funny, it turns out I did this for me." She smiled at Suzanne. "I have many friends," she said.

Suzanne began to get more and more clients. Many were from her signs, but a lot were from Theresa, too. She was nerved up about how it was going to work with the baby, but to her surprise he put on his best behavior. Not only was he quiet, but he began to look especially cute, even to her. And just seeing him seemed to relax her clients. "Oh, a baby!" they said, as if it were the biggest surprise in the world.

It was strange, but Otis relaxed her, too. It made her feel good to see him. Sometimes she swore he was courting her. She walked into his room mornings and his whole face lit up. "It's just me, Otis," she said, but he couldn't stop wriggling, and she couldn't help feeling pleased. He made cooing sounds when she picked him up, making her laugh, and as soon as she did, he cooed some more.

It killed her the way his eyes followed her around the room now, the way he'd get all nervous if she so much as stepped away for a minute. Some nights, when he was asleep, when she didn't have clients, she told herself she was just checking on him while he slept. She stood by his crib watching him, and some nights it was almost impossible to tear herself away from him. Every night, before she went to sleep, she read two whole chapters of Molly's baby book. She kept a notebook handy. She jotted down things that seemed useful.

She started buying Otis things, too. A pacifier shaped like a pair of big red lips. A terry-cloth lamb. And when she noticed him scrunching his face when she smoked, she suddenly made a decision. She stubbed out the cigarette. She threw out the pack. "Cold turkey," she told Otis.

Her favorite times were sometimes the quietest ones. Midday. She sat in Angela's rocker and rocked Otis, listening to the quiet of the house, the calm. She thought about what she might cook for dinner. She thought about Gary coming home soon. She sighed. Sometimes she couldn't help imagining that this was her life.

Gary left work and stopped at the all-night supermarket to pick up milk and bread and wipes with protective aloe and diapers size two. Seven in the morning. Too early for the Muzak, a syrupy rendition of a Frank Sinatra song he used to like before he heard this version. "The Summer Wind." There were only two cashiers, young women with too much makeup, their eyelids frosted blue, their scratchy hair pulled back into ponytails, yawning, propping themselves up against the registers to lazily gossip back and forth, punctuating the air with their long lacquered nails. There were a few stock boys in bright red aprons swinging metal pricers. He glanced around. Who else beside him would shop this early? A ragged-looking woman in a blue dress shuffled down an aisle. Two teenaged kids giggled by the ice cream, holding up frosty pints and pressing them against each other's heated skin. *Losers and outlaws, all of us,* Gary thought. *The disenfranchised.* He scratched at his arms through his uniform. He still had his hat on, out of habit. He was wheeling the cart, staring sleepily at the fresh fruits, when someone said, "Gary?" He looked up. Brian was standing there, staring at Gary's uniform, at his cap, in pure astonishment. Gary felt hot with new shame, defiant with rage.

"Hi, Brian."

Brian leaned on his cart. Canned puddings, doughnuts, instant coffee, and paper cups. Work food. Single man food. "How's Molly?"

"The same."

"So. You got a job, I see." Brian's gaze slid up and down Gary, stopping at the cap. His mouth moved and he suddenly snorted. "Sorry to laugh, but that cap—that insignia! You gotta admit it's kind of funny."

"It's not funny, Brian. It's a job."

Brian nodded again. He waited for Gary to say something, but Gary was resolutely silent. "Well, that's good," Brian said lamely. "I guess." He looked at Gary's uniform again and shook his head, grinning.

Gary wanted to shove Brian, he wanted to scream at him that everyone knew his girlfriend Candy was made-up, that she probably was a man masquerading to get some free things that only a complete idiot would give her, that no one liked Brian, least of all his made-up girlfriend, but instead, Gary said nothing. He turned, wheeling his cart so roughly into the next aisle, he toppled a display of diaper wipes, clattering them onto the floor.

He was so furious, he drove for a while. By the time he got home, it was nearly nine. He came into the house to hear music playing, an opera aria. The house was clean, and not too warm, and fragrant with mint. Then he heard a woman laughing and he followed the sound into the kitchen. Suzanne was washing a strange woman's hair in his sink. Suzanne wore red rubbery gloves. Suzanne had on a short black smock, the same one the woman was wearing, her legs were long and pale, her feet bare. She smiled at him and kept talking to the woman. The air was tangy with lemon. In a rocker on the floor was Otis, happily batting a plastic toy. Suzanne beamed at Gary. "Two more coming today," she mouthed. She flushed and watching her, for a moment, he felt suddenly stricken. She looked glowing, content. Her hands, long and delicate, moved like pale, exotic flowers. He felt a pull in his stomach, a yearning. The woman getting her hair washed waved. "Hi there," she said.

Gary changed and left the house to go to the hospital. Suzanne was noisily blowing the woman's hair dry, so intent, she didn't see him leave.

At the hospital, Molly lay motionless, her face turned from him. He lifted up her hand. The skin was starting to bruise. He gently put it down again and stroked her fingers. "Come back," he said.

Someone came to take blood twice. A nurse came and bathed Molly. Two orderlies lifted her up into a rubber stretcher to weigh her and lowered her again. He stroked her hands and sang her two songs. The entire time Molly didn't move.

He didn't know what to do. Sometimes he thought he wanted to talk, but he didn't know whom to talk to. He couldn't afford a shrink. Everyone at the hospital was too busy. His friends just tried to make him feel better, to give him hope, or they got so upset, he ended up comforting them. "Everything's going to be fine," he said.

He read the newspaper by Molly's bed, scanning the ads, leafing through the pages. FREE HELP LINE, he saw. He looked back at Molly. Her lids fluttered and didn't open. She didn't move. It was ridiculous, but he found himself getting up, walking over to the bank of pay phones, and dialing.

"Help line." It was a woman's voice, soft and soothing and very young.

Gary cleared his throat. He couldn't speak.

"Help line. Take your time. I'm here for you."

Here for you. Gary felt his throat expanding. "Three days after my wife gave birth, she went into a coma."

The woman was silent.

"They don't know if she's going to make it."

"That must be so hard for you," the woman whispered.

"I feel like I can't do this."

"That's understandable."

Gary suddenly felt a buzz of frustration. "You can't help me, can you?" Gary said sadly. "You don't even know what I'm talking about."

"Of course I can help you. I can listen."

"Have you been in anything like this yourself? Do you know how it feels?"

"Don't you think I can know how something might feel without feeling it myself?"

"No."

"Well, that's just not true. I—"

"Can you make my wife well?" he interrupted.

"I can be here for you. I can listen."

Gary hung up.

Stay calm, he told himself. *Believe things will turn out all right.* But how could he believe in anything? How could he not worry? It suddenly seemed to him that phobics were the true seers, that even the craziest phobia might be a perfectly rational response to a terrifyingly irrational world. And when everything was so upside down, there was nothing left to do but look for miracles.

He bought a fake fur rabbit's foot and kept it in his coat pocket. Once, when he was looking through the want ads for jobs, he saw a Saint Jude's prayer. Say the prayer nine times in nine days and then thank Saint Jude publicly and whatever you want to happen will. He did it, he learned it. He asked for Molly to be instantly healed, and when it didn't work, he told himself, well, maybe it would work later, maybe something still might happen.

He couldn't afford to hire a psychic healer, but he began to buy books. He remembered the crazy mushroom title Ada had suggested; he vaguely remembered other titles she had suggesteded; when he couldn't find any of her books, he found others. *The Mind Can Heal the Body. Heavenly Healing. Mysticism and Health.* He was vaguely embarrassed buying the books, but as soon as the cashier looked up at him, he turned defiant. He slammed his money down onto the counter.

It was the weekend, he didn't have to work, and that night, he sat up poring through the books, underlining passages. Suzanne came back from the hospital and, passing by him, stared at the titles. "Look—" he started to say, but Suzanne suddenly sat down and picked up the other book, leafing through it. "There's something on this page about charging the atmosphere with energy," she said quietly.

He looked up at her to see if she was laughing at him. She still had her coat on. Her face was grave. Her eyes were red, as if she had been crying, her body posture was as exhausted as his own, and he felt suddenly moved. "You think this is stupid?" he asked finally.

Her eyes met his. "I'd like to look at that book when you're done."

He was desperate. He could believe in anything. That fairies lived in the woods. That ghosts haunted houses. That people could travel in time. There were lots of things that people had thought were insane at one time that had turned out to be true. At one time no one had believed in germs. No one had believed in other planets. Who knew what was possible? Who knew what could and couldn't be done? The thing was, you had to risk everything, you had to try.

He and Suzanne studied the books. They memorized the testimonials, which were his favorite part. A woman with inoperable cancer had been healed by the faith of her friends. A man with a rare and disfiguring skin disease had healed himself overnight by imagining his own private healer, which in his case, turned out to be a great white rabbit singing Jefferson Airplane songs. Gary and Suzanne learned a few healing exercises, how you could rub your hands together and charge them with energy and lay them over a person and cure them. How you could think of a silver cord connecting you to the earth, a power line you could tap into to boost your healing capacities. At night, he bolted awake. He calmed himself by practicing, by telling himself that, yes, he did feel his hands heating with healing energy, that, yes, he did think he might have seen a wisp of energy right there in the air. Yes, he could do this. Yes.

The next day, he walked into Molly's room just as the doctors were leaving. Good, he thought, good. You had to be grounded, the books had said. You had to feel strong. He sat by Molly's bed. He tried to imagine, to see and feel and hear the silver cord, vibrating and sparkling, and instead, he felt himself tense because all he could concentrate on was the noise of Molly's machine. He rubbed his hands together, trying to imagine sparks of energy the way the books had said. And then he held his hands up over Molly as if he were doing a massage. He moved them in slow circles, in swoops and dips. The movements were almost hypnotic. He felt himself relaxing. Put your belief in your hands, the books said. Make them heat like an oven. *I believe*, he thought. *I believe, I believe.* He felt something shifting inside of him, giving way. His hands, he told himself, were getting hot. His energy was setting off sparks. "You're getting well," he told Molly.

The door swung open. A nurse came in, and Gary turned to her, trying to act ordinary. His hands hung in the air. He didn't want anyone telling him not to do this. He put his hands by his sides.

The nurse bent and touched Molly and whipped back up. "Oh, my God."

"What's happened?" Gary felt a flash of hope. He could tell the nurse what he was doing. He could come in and do this twice a day, three times. Suzanne could do it, too. "She's better, isn't she?"

"She's burning up, spiking another fever," she said. "We'll have to pack her in ice."

Molly shivered uncontrollably. Her mouth flew open. The ice melted against the sheets and then her fever broke and two other nurses came in and changed the bed, rolling her carefully from one side to another, tucking her back in, and all the while Gary leaned against the wall watching in terror. "She's fine now," the nurse said, giving the sheet an extra pat.

After the nurses left, he sat by her bed. He took her hand, which was cool and dry. He told himself one mistake didn't mean anything, that he'd try again. He didn't care how crazy anything was, he'd find the thing to make her well, to protect her.

At work sometimes, he began to help Marty with the cleaning. "It passes the time." Marty shrugged and leaned along the wall, smoking a joint, a goofy grin spreading across his face. "Jesus. Be my guest. Whatever floats your boat."

Gary found he liked mopping the floors, liked seeing the water sliding across the dark linoleum. He liked the sound of the vacuum, the backdrop of Marty's voice rambling on about plot points in his horror movie, about actors he hoped to get. "Jack Nicholson," Marty insisted. "If I can just get to him, I know he'd want to do it. It's his kind of showcase role." Marty was so lost in his reverie, Gary never even had to respond. Gary liked, too, seeing the building shining and clean and perfect. He stepped back sometimes, sweating, his muscles stretched. He felt himself and the building almost purified.

To Gary's astonishment, Suzanne began to get more clients. The phone would ring and he would brace himself, expecting the clipped tone of a doctor, the worried voice of Karen, and instead there would be a female voice, wanting Suzanne, asking for an appointment. He'd come into the house and a strange woman would be sitting in his kitchen, a blonde or a redhead or a brunette, there would be hair dusted along the floor, and Otis, sunny and happy in his seat.

Suzanne got a bankbook and a checkbook. Having a bit more money made things easier, and it did something to Suzanne. He watched her cutting a woman's hair. She had told him customers didn't like to be watched, that hair was a private thing, so he leaned along the hall. She changed while she worked. He almost didn't know her. The skittishness went out of her, she became calm and sure, as if light were glinting off her.

One day, he heard a woman weeping. He quietly walked by the kitchen. Suzanne had her arms about a woman's shoulder, she was speaking in a low voice. "Forget him," Suzanne said. "You're too good for that. You don't need him."

"Yes, I do."

"No, trust me. What you need are highlights."

The woman came out with reddish glints. She stopped short when she saw Gary. She gave him a doubtful look. "You look beautiful," he said, and the woman suddenly relaxed. Her whole body seemed to beam. Suzanne, behind the woman, grinned triumphantly and gave

Gary the thumbs-up. "Now, just because a guy likes it, doesn't mean that's everything," Suzanne said. "Remember, I told you it was gorgeous, too."

The woman straightened. "That's right," she said. "Damn right. And you know what else, I like it now, too."

"That's the spirit," Suzanne said. "Come on. I'll show you out."

When she came back into the room, she sat opposite him. She didn't ask him anymore how his day at the hospital was, but he knew that she didn't have to. He felt her studying him, gauging his mood. She was as silent as he was, and for the first time, he realized he didn't feel like he had to fill in the silences with her, that he had to say anything. They were in the same place.

"Now you," Suzanne said.

"Oh, no—"

"Yes. Come on. You're a bad advertisement for my work. Clients take one look at you and they get nervous." She laughed. Her smile was friendly.

He ran his fingers self-consciously through his hair. Then he laughed and sat in the chair. "Lean back," Suzanne said. His neck arched and then he felt warm soapy water over his head, around his neck. He felt her fingers massaging his scalp, a shock of feeling. The shampoo was lemon and pine. "What is that?"

"I make it myself. Commercial brands are too harsh." She bent over him, her hair a satiny brush against his arms. "People don't give beauticians the credit they deserve. There's a whole science to it. I can look at hair and tell things."

"What things?"

"I can tell if a person's sad or in love just by the shape of their hair. If it's dry on the ends or at the top. If it feels rough. I can tell if they're drinking enough water, eating enough protein."

"What can you tell about me?" he said.

She was quiet for a moment. Her fingers stilled against his scalp. "I can tell that you're exhausted. That you aren't eating right. That—"

"That what?"

Her fingers began moving again. And then he felt a sudden pour of cool water. He smelled wintergreen. "That you need a rinse," she said.

She bundled him in a towel; she faced him toward the mirror she had hung up. She stared at his face in the mirror, frowning, and then she picked up the scissors.

"Oh, no you don't—"

"Oh, yes I do. You have great long hair, but it has no personality to it. Just a trim. Trust me."

She worked around him, bending, her long hair brushing against him. She smelled of cinnamon, and every time she leaned closer, the scent grew stronger. "Done." She put both hands on his shoulders and lifted them off, light as paper wings, and he looked over at her, meeting her eyes.

Gary began to find that Suzanne now made it easier for him. He came home and found her singing to Otis the way he did. He found her dancing with his son, her face a map of delight. She worried about Otis the way he did. She bolted up when the baby so much as sighed. She stood over his crib watching him. It was Suzanne who came home with the side sleeper. "It prevents SIDS," she told him.

The house smelled different with her in it. Like cinnamon. Like lemon soap. It used to bother him before, finding bits of her all over the house, but now he somehow liked it.

One day, after Gary had gotten paid, he decided to thank Suzanne by taking her out to dinner someplace fancy.

"You don't have to do that—" Suzanne started to say, but Gary held up his hand.

"I want to."

He waited for her to change, busying himself with Otis. He was tickling Otis's belly when Suzanne came into the room. She was in a soft, pale blue dress, barely grazing her body. Her hair gleamed around her. Something moved deep inside of him, startling him. He felt as if he were waking from a dream. "You're staring." She looked pleased and shy.

He lifted Otis up. He turned from her. "Let's get going."

*   *   *

They went to Patsy's, a new place fifteen minutes away. It was a small, bright place, with yellow chintz curtains and tablecloths and a menu scrawled on a big blue blackboard. "They're supposed to have the best desserts in town," Gary said.

He set Otis in his carrier down on the floor beside him and plucked up a menu. Suzanne took off her coat.

"You look nice," Gary said.

Otis slept in the carrier beside them while they ate pasta and chocolate pie and cheesecake, and halfway through the dessert, Suzanne turned to him and speared a strawberry from his plate. "I couldn't resist," she said.

Gary felt a sudden restless knocking in his head. He glanced around the restaurant, at the other customers noisily talking, gesturing, shaping the air with sound. There was a pale, balding man sitting by himself in a corner, staring at Suzanne. There was a buzzing in Gary's ear. Gary looked from the brown-haired man to Suzanne, who was busy taking another strawberry from Gary's plate. Her hand brushed his. She looked up at him. Her eyes were clear and full of light. He felt out of breath. He felt something tingling along his skin, something wrong. "What?" she said.

"That guy over there is looking at you." Gary nodded to the man who lifted his glass of wine in a toast to Suzanne. Suzanne looked from the brown-haired man to Gary. "Oh, the guy from the unpainted furniture store," she said calmly.

The man stood up and came over to the table. "Hello Suzanne," he said. He nodded at Gary. "Bob Tillman," he said, holding out his hand to Gary. "I own Wood You. The unpainted furniture store?"

"Oh, yes, I know that store," Gary said, shaking Bob's hand.

Bob looked from Suzanne to Gary and back again. "Half the numbers from your sign are gone. I keep repositioning the sign, making sure it's getting noticed."

"That's so nice," Suzanne said.

Bob waited, and then his smile deepened. "Well, it was nice to see you again, Suzanne. And it was nice to meet you——?"

"Gary," Gary said.

"Gary."

Bob went back to his table. Gary felt his smile hardening. He felt a prickling of jealousy and he turned back to his cheesecake. "Nice guy," he forced himself to say. "He seems really interested in you."

Suzanne shrugged. "He's so not my type." She stared down at her plate and then she looked up, draining her glass of water. "Let's order more dessert," she said.

Gary told himself it was crazy, what he was feeling. It was just loneliness. Just pure human need. And maybe, too, it was just having someone know what he was feeling, someone going through it with him.

"You should call that guy from the furniture store," he told her.

"That dodo?"

Gary felt a flicker of relief. *Cut it out*, he told himself. "He seems interested in you. You should call him. He seemed nice enough."

"Yeah. Right," she said.

He tried to keep more and more to himself, going up to his office as soon as he got home, taking Otis out alone in the morning instead of inviting Suzanne to go with him. *It's fine, it's under control.* He told himself that a million times a day, and then he went in to take a shower, and there, in a silky puddle of the floor, was Suzanne's peach-colored slip and it hurt him so much just to look at it that he strode out of the room again.

He had a dream. He was walking through a field with Suzanne, holding hands because the grass was so high and rough. "This way," she said, pointing her free hand to the back of a field. "See? There she is." Suzanne pointed out Molly, all that red hair, burnished in the sun.

"Molly!" Gary called. He felt exuberant. Molly was alive and romping through the high grass toward him. His heart was skipping. And then he turned and saw how happy Suzanne was, and he turned and kissed her full and hungry on the mouth and Molly disappeared.

He bolted awake. He was sweating, horrified. He grabbed for the phone to check on Molly. "Critical," the woman said, and then he stumbled down to the kitchen. He leaned against the sink. He grabbed for a bottle of wine and poured himself a glass. He had to calm down. He had to sleep. *It's a dream,* he told himself. *A dream.*

He was on his third glass, drunk, woozy, terrified. He had done this to Molly, this was his punishment. He hadn't been vigilant enough, hadn't been a good enough husband. Thinking about Suzanne had been the easy way out, that's all it was. He was disgusted to have ever imagined kissing her, to have thought about what her skin might feel like.

He was sitting on a chair in the living room when Suzanne came into the room. She had a short blue dress, her hair spilling down. Her beauty was so intense and real, it felt like a wound. He stood up. He hadn't really slept in days. He was always afraid. And here she was.

She walked toward him, stumbling, so that he had to catch her, and then he wasn't thinking at all anymore. He was kissing her, sliding one hand up under her dress. And she was kissing him back.

She grabbed him closer and he kissed her again. Longer. Harder. He bit her lips. He put his hand into her hair, against the back of her neck. He wanted to put his whole self up inside of her. He moved one hand up against her breasts. She moaned, and then abruptly he saw Molly, the way she liked to tilt her neck back for him to kiss, and he wrenched himself free. He shoved Suzanne roughly away from him. Panting, he stepped back. *"No."*

For a minute, she didn't move. He heard her ragged breath. And then she stepped toward him. He had never hated anyone more in his life than he hated himself. He had never wanted anyone more than her.

The phone rang. He could hardly breathe. He couldn't see. But he made his way to the phone and yanked it up. "Yes." His voice was cracked. He listened and then he hung up the phone.

He couldn't bear to look at Suzanne. She grabbed at his arm, and he recoiled, as if she had burnt him.

"It's Molly," he said. "She woke up."

chapter

seven

Molly woke in a strange high-rise apartment, unable to move anything but her eyes. The room was boxy, with a wall of windows that looked out on a skyline jagged with tall, silvery buildings. Metal and steel and glass and all that impossible blinding white. She didn't know what city she was in. She didn't know how she had gotten here or why she was lying flat on her back, a starchy sheet pulled over her. Her head felt cloudy, stuffed with tissue. She tried to find a memory, something, anything that might explain this. She strained, concentrating through the fuzz, and then an image shimmered and bloomed and made her catch her breath. *I had a baby. His eyes were wide open. I had Gary.*

The past tense upset her.

She scanned the ceiling. It had a swirling pattern of half scoops to it, like pearlized shells, and planted in the very center was a decorative white fixture that threw out lines of light. She had never seen any of this room before and yet she couldn't help feeling that everything felt sickeningly familiar, as if her other life had been just a dream and now that layer had been peeled roughly back.

Around her, organ music whined to a crescendo. She shifted her eyes from the window to the right side of the room. Her breathing, harsh and raspy, reverberated.

And then she saw someone. A woman with a curly blond ponytail. She was washing dishes noisily in a kitchenette in the corner. Another woman, with a black bob, was talking to a man with glasses, throwing her head back and laughing, flirting hard. He dug in his pocket and handed her some bills. "Fifty dollars," he said, narrowing his eyes. "But I want the whole night."

I have roommates, Molly thought. She hadn't shared a room with anyone since she had been living with Suzanne, but that was another life, another time. Where did these roommates come from? And where were Gary and her son?

She heard people clapping. She felt as if she were being suddenly watched by a cheerful audience, scores of people all dressed up and leaning forward, wanting to catch her next move, and the joke was on her, she was the punch line.

I know this, Molly thought with desperation. *I've been here before.* It felt like a horrible mistake she had to somehow rectify. *Help*, she said, but there was no sound.

But the blonde heard her. She turned and smiled at Molly in recognition. "There you are," she said happily. The blonde came over, brushing her damp hands along her dress. "No, don't do that," the blonde said with sudden alarm and leaned over Molly. *Do what*, Molly thought. Something jammed deep into Molly's throat. A fish hook. A probe. Smooth and sharp and metallic-tasting. Molly felt herself choking, heard herself cough. Something snaked down her nose, down her throat, deep into her. She wanted to scream, to punch the blonde in the face. She couldn't speak. She couldn't move. The blonde bent closer to Molly, smiling larger, showing her teeth, bright white, sparks glinting off them. She had a laugh like a cracked bell. She was insane, Molly decided. Molly would have to do everything she could to protect herself against her. Molly stared frantically past the blonde at the woman with the black bob, thinking maybe that woman could help her if she only could stop flirting and see what was going on, but the woman was passionately kissing the man in glasses. "I paid, I get to do what I want," the man said. Maybe they were crazy, too, maybe it would be worse for Molly to attract their attention.

She heard the laughter again, a smattering of applause. A bright light shone in her eyes, a clapboard banged shut.

Molly struggled to gesture. "No, you don't," the blonde chirped, tightening something over Molly's chest. The woman with the black bob was leaning over, touching the top of her forehead to the forehead of the man with the glasses. They bent together into another kiss. Steam hissed up between them. They were less than ten feet away. Molly shut her eyes, thinking when she finally opened them, all the craziness would be gone, everything would be back to normal.

She woke again, this time drifting up through winter. Everything was in black and white. Hard white snow shot against her face. Ice formed on her lids. Something pulsed about the length of her legs, squeezing and releasing, tightening its grasp.

Abruptly, her sight cleared. Color returned. She was in an open room. Not the high-rise apartment. Someplace newer. Different somehow. Molly struggled to get up and as soon as she moved, the snowstorm suddenly vanished without a trace. The floor was clean and dry. Green linoleum. The air was clear and silent except for a forced hiss of heat. She looked at the window, at a skyline she still didn't recognize. The tall, silvery buildings were replaced by stubby brick ones, by a network of telephone wires. And then there, taped up on the far window, was a huge black and white Xerox. She squinted and then felt a shock. It was a photograph of Otis, a picture she had never seen before, blown up so many times it was blurry. He was lying in a bassinet, his baby hands, like stars, stretched out to her, his eyes half shut. "Mommy, I miss you," was scribbled underneath. "Get well soon." *He misses me*, she thought vaguely, and then she began to feel panicked. *But where have I been?* Get well, she thought, but what was wrong with her? What had happened?

She shut her eyes, trying to remember. She shivered. "Cold," she said out loud. "Cold." She could hear her voice, but it sounded different to her, as if part of it had been scraped away.

"Do you know where you are?" She heard a voice, deep and

sonorous. She felt something wet on her face. She thought of this movie she had once seen, a Pilgrim girl was lost in the snow, and the only thing that guided her was the voice of the kindly Indian who was leading her to rescue.

"Snow," Molly said and opened her eyes again.

A man's features swam into view. Dark eyes, dark hair, a thin line of a mouth. Glasses and a white coat. A stethoscope. "Doctor," she took a guess, and he nodded.

"Dr. Price. Your hematologist. One of the doctors who has been taking care of you." He paused. "Do you know what's happened to you?" She shook her head.

He spoke to her quietly. She heard his voice. She saw his mouth moving, his brow knotting. But she couldn't seem to concentrate, she couldn't seem to grab hold of anything he was saying. It all rushed by her, like paper driven by wind. She glanced at the door, and there was the insane blonde bopping by, snapping her fingers to invisible music. She looked at Molly and winked broadly.

"It's very, very serious." Dr. Price put his hands in front of him. He frowned, as if it were her fault. "You've been out for some time."

"No. You're wrong." She looked at the Xerox of Otis. "I had a baby," she said.

Dr. Price perked up. "Yes, you did."

"Where is he?" Molly blurted. "Where's my husband? Are they all right?"

Dr. Price stopped. "Your husband? He was here this morning. I imagine your baby's at home with him."

Panic flamed within her. *Liar,* she thought. She would have re-membered seeing Gary.

"Are they alive?"

"Of course they're alive! What kinds of questions are those?" He looked around the room. "Why would we keep your baby's picture up if he were dead? Wouldn't that be a little sadistic?"

Molly was silent, considering, which seemed to irritate Dr. Price even more.

"You're on morphine. You don't remember."

Molly's legs pulsed and she glanced at them, hidden under the sheet. Three different IVs were attached to her, feeding blood into her, feeding something chalky and thick and yellow, feeding something clear. She was attached to a machine. Molly ordered her arms to lift up, and in astonishment, she saw they did. She turned her head back and forth, and felt a pulse of rapture. "I can move."

"Yes. Of course you can."

Molly tried to pull down the sheet to look at her body. Dr. Price stayed her hand. "That's not a good idea."

"Why not?"

"One piece of information at a time."

Stubbornly, Molly continued to draw away the sheets. When she got to her belly, she stopped. Her skin was crisscrossed with stitching. Her belly button was on her right side. She was wrapped in layers of gauze, taped up, and her belly, blue and purple and white, shimmied like lake water. Five clear small plastic bubbles were attached to her by tubes, swimming with blood. She looked back at the doctor in horror.

"Drainage tubes. You've had quite a time."

Molly tentatively touched her belly. She couldn't feel anything.

"It will go down some. We had to cut through muscles. And nerves."

She curled the sheet farther away. Her legs were encased in something rubbery and blue, like a cocoon.

"Those are for your circulation." He straightened, clearing his throat. He replaced the sheet, tucking it in at the bottom.

"I heard music."

The doctor looked at her quizzically.

Molly waggled her fingers and turned her head, looking around the room. Suddenly, behind the doctor, she saw a slice of yellow, and then the blonde suddenly appeared, in a white dress and a lab coat and chunky-soled white sneakers. Molly drew back, alarmed.

"Are you in pain?"

"She's crazy," Molly whispered, nodding at the blonde.

"Who is?"

"The blonde."

"Molly. She's your nurse."

"I'm telling you she's crazy." Molly looked back at the blonde. Behind her the woman with the black bob was talking to the man with the glasses. "They're even crazier. He gave her money! They were kissing!"

Dr. Price followed her gaze. "Dr. Booth is a critical-care specialist. Dr. Schiff is a surgeon. Both of them are highly respected, married, and not to each other."

"Seeing is believing," she said.

"Ah," he said, "but not when you're on morphine." He gave Molly's legs a gentle pat. "You'll need to stay here for a while. And then we'll see. Do you understand?"

"No. What's a while? You can't be serious. I just had a baby."

He fingered his stethoscope. "I'm serious and what you have is even more serious. Do you know how sick you are?" He surveyed her calmly. "I can tell you, you're alive because of me. No one else could have diagnosed you, I don't think."

"And am I getting well?"

"Let's take one thing at a time."

Panicked, Molly tried to sit up again. One thing at a time. What did that mean? What was he saying?

Dr. Price put one hand on Molly's arm. "Try to be still. You don't want to hemorrhage."

"Hemorrhage? Where?"

"Anywhere."

"My brain? My eyes?"

He nodded and she recoiled.

"Well, you *asked*." He looked annoyed again. "And it's your body. You should know what's going on."

She felt herself growing more and more desperate. She didn't know what was going on. The more he told her, the less she felt she knew.

Behind Dr. Price, the blonde and the doctor with glasses laughed. "Please, could you just tell me again what happened to me," Molly said. "Could you just tell me slowly."

He told her again, and this time, she heard him. This time she was even more afraid.

"Call my husband," Molly begged.

Dr. Price nodded at her. "I will come back to see you later," he said.

There wasn't a phone in Molly's room. Even if there was paper or a pen, her hands couldn't work well enough to write. She scanned the room, trying to figure out what she could do. Every time a nurse came in Molly begged her to call her home. "Tell Gary I have to see him," she cried.

"You just talked to him," one nurse said pleasantly. She bent and folded a towel with a snap, dunking it in water and washing Molly's face.

"When?" Molly cried, trying to avert her face. The water hurt. The cloth felt rough. "Where?"

"Why, right here. Dark long hair, light eyes, cute guy. Right? He brought you two tapes he played for you and he held your hand." She daubed the cloth against Molly's nose. "Honey, it's the painkillers you're on. I couldn't remember my own name if I was on those things."

"I can remember my name. Molly Goldman. And I want to see my baby! It's terrible to keep him from me!"

"Honey, what would be terrible is if your baby got sick. Now your baby's immune system is too new to come traipsing into a hospital full of sick people. You yourself are too ill. Don't you want your baby to be safe at home?"

"How do I know he's safe?"

The nurse finished washing Molly's face and stroked the cloth along Molly's arms. "Look at these grandma arms! We've gotta get you some lotion for those grandma arms." She shook her head. "Want to know something? My sister's baby was a preemie. A girl. As small as a minute. She was in an incubator for seven weeks and my sister didn't get to hold her or even look at her through the glass because the baby was just too sick. No one thought that the baby was going to make it except my sister, probably because she couldn't bear to think anything else. And you know what else? That girl is now a happy, healthy five-year-old, and no one's the worse for wear. You wouldn't know for one second that Mom and baby had ever been apart."

"I'm not going to see my baby, am I?"

"I'm just telling you. You have to try to understand." She finished washing Molly and snapped the towel about her arm. "Come on now. There's a lot of depressed doctors walking around here because of you. What have they ever done to you that you should make them so miserable? Why don't you get better and put some smiles on their faces?"

She patted Molly's arm. "I'll be back later."

Molly stared around her. She knew where she was now. Surgical Intensive Care. There were two other beds she hadn't even noticed before. One of them was empty; another held an old man, his mouth slung open.

She heard the creak of wheels and then three orderlies pushed a gurney into the room, a stern-faced doctor following behind them. A Chinese girl was propped up, clutching a yellow bucket, a line of clear tubing pulling up out of the lid like a straw, circling on the bed like a long ring of rope. The girl stared expressionlessly at Molly. "One, two, three—and up," said the orderlies, and they lifted her and the bucket and the tubing up onto the bed. The doctor snapped the curtains shut and then all Molly saw were shadows moving about and then she heard a sharp intake of breath, a long, gurgling hack, and then a shout. "No!" Horrified, Molly tried to make herself as small as possible. She drew the sheet up over her, she tried not to even breathe. *Don't do it to me. Don't do it to me.*

The curtains pulled open. The girl was sitting up, staring straight ahead, the tube running from her nose into the bucket, which was now on a chair by her bed. There was a suctioning sound. Golden liquid spurted from the tube in her nose and flowed into the bucket.

"Mrs. Goldman?" Two nurses approached the bed, carrying what looked like a black rubber sling. She heard the clank of metal and instantly Molly recoiled. "Get away from me—" she yelled. "Don't you dare touch me."

The nurses looked at each other. "We're only weighing you," one of the nurses said.

Molly looked at them doubtfully.

"Relax," said the nurse.

They shifted her onto a black rubber pad. It hurt. She screamed. They hooked the pad to a metal contraption that looked like a huge meat scale. "One, two, and three—" said one nurse, and suddenly Molly was lifted up, suspended over the bed. The scale needle jumped and danced. "One hundred and sixty-five," said a nurse.

"That's not possible," Molly insisted. "I weighed only ninety-eight when I got pregnant. I gained only twenty pounds my whole pregnancy!"

"It's just blood, honey, not fat. Think of it that way."

"Blood!" Molly was terrified.

Every half hour, it seemed that someone was giving her pills. Pink and blue and clear, all lodged in a tiny paper cup. "Down the hatch," the nurse said, waiting, making sure Molly took them. She slept, deep and dreamless.

Someone was shaking her awake. She didn't know if it was day or night. She blinked. It was still dark in the room. She could hear the gurgling from the Chinese girl's bucket and tube, making her clap her hands to her ears. Molly sat up. Six doctors were in a horseshoe about her head and she didn't recognize any of them. All of them looked her age, except for the one coming toward her, who had a thatch of white hair.

"What time is it?" she asked.

"Five-thirty," said the white-haired doctor.

"Who are you?" Molly said.

The doctor stepped forward and pulled back her sheet. He pressed against her stomach, making her jump. "Sorry," he said, but he kept pressing. He opened some of the gauze padding while Molly averted her face. The other doctors stared and murmured at her. "There," the doctor said, motioning for the other doctors to come closer. "Take a look at this." The doctors studied Molly.

"Ah. I see it," one of the doctors said excitedly. He pointed, "There."

"What is it?" Molly said uneasily. "What do you see?"

"Old blood," said one doctor.

"No." Another doctor shook his head vehemently. "New blood."

"What?" Molly said. "What?"

The white-haired doctor looked at her and then back at his students. "Let's talk outside," he said.

"Wait! What do you see? What does it mean?" Molly cried, but the doctors were filing out, talking among themselves.

All that day, Molly waited for Gary. She drifted in and out of sleep and every time she woke, it was to something terrible or strange or both. She woke to see the Chinese girl trying to yank the tube from her nose, pulling out so many yards of tubing it was filling the floor. She woke to hear a man walking by her room, calling "Morning, people!" making her wonder what kind of a hospital would hire someone to greet people, what would be the purpose of that? And she woke to see a woman in the corridor watching her, a locked safe on her head, and then the woman lifted up one arm and spun the combination around and around in a kind of tune.

Around dinnertime, Molly woke to find the Chinese girl was gone and a tall, stern-looking man was standing over her. "You look better," he said.

"Who are you?"

"Dr. Kane. Your surgeon."

Dr. Kane was in a bad mood. His dark eyes squinted. His mouth pulled down. His sandy hair was slicked back. He opened her covers and when she looked away, he sighed. He pressed down on her stomach. "Boggy," he decided.

"Boggy?"

He ignored her and pressed again. "You feel this?"

She shook her head, and then he stood up. "You might. Later." He pulled her sheets up over her again. "No one knows what to expect with you. No one, not the surgeons, not the hematologist, not the critical-care staff, and certainly none of obstetrics ever thought you'd make it this far." He gave a lean, hard grin. "I saved your life so far. No one's been in your belly more than I have."

He waited, and for a minute Molly wondered if he expected her to thank him.

"But all is not out of the woods, by a long shot. You're still very, very sick."

"Is my baby all right?"

"Yes, of course."

"Where's my husband?"

"I spoke with him this morning," Dr. Kane said. "And so did you."

"No, I didn't."

"I'm not going to argue with you," said Dr. Kane, as calmly as if she had asked him to make her a cup of tea. "Has Dr. Swetzer been in to see you?"

Molly looked blank.

"The infectious-disease specialist. Your uterus was badly infected. We couldn't risk anything spreading so we had to take it out."

Molly stared at him in horror.

That night, they took the tube out of the Chinese woman's nose and moved her to another room. That night, the nurse told Molly they were lowering her morphine dose. All that night she didn't sleep. She sat up in her uncomfortable bed and watched the door. She saw a strip of dotted swiss cloth sweep by the doorway, blown by an invisible wind. She heard an echoing tap of shoes. She heard the strains of Isaac Hayes melting and then moving into silence. She heard the click and whir of the monitors about her, the snore of a man next door, the soft cat sounds the white shoes of the nurses made.

She heard something and tried to sit up straighter. A shadow crossed the room and then Dr. Price strode in. She had to look at him twice because something seemed different about him. "Mrs. Goldman," he said in a low voice, and she saw for the first time how exhausted he looked; she felt how gently he handled her arm when he lifted it up to examine the swelling. He leaned in closer, and she smelled something cherry, like a cough drop. She saw a dot of what looked like tomato sauce on the lapel of his white jacket. "Oh, my God." Her voice was raspy with effort.

"Am I hurting you?" He looked at her, concerned.

She shook her head. It was incredible. He really seemed to see her this time. And for the first time, she really saw him.

She couldn't sleep after he left. She stayed awake, listening to the sounds the hospital made. The soft slip of the nurse's shoes, the whir of the machines, the beep of the IVs. The morning light was starting to slant in the room when she heard a voice. "Morning, people!" Molly tried to strain for the door to see who the greeter was. "Morning, yourself!" she called, and this time a small, wolfish-looking man in a plaid shirt strode into the room, waving a stack of newspapers. "Morning paper," he said emphatically, handing one to her.

"I don't have money—"

He waved his hand and tossed a paper on the bed. "Don't worry. They'll put it on your bill."

She didn't know which part of the paper to look at first. There was a small drawing of a happy-faced sun in the corner. *Sunny today. 60 degrees.* She stared at the headline. STATE OKAYS NEW HIGHWAY. It was mundane. It was probably boring. But suddenly it seemed like the most interesting thing she could ever read.

She read everything in the paper, even the sports page. When she turned the last page, she was suddenly tired. She felt like she could sleep for days, deep and uninterrupted. She slid down into the bed and shut her eyes.

*　*　*

It woke her, this feeling that someone was standing over her. Well,
she was used to waking up and finding a face hovering over her, hands
ticking through her bedclothes, probing her body. She yawned and
waited for the face to shimmer into focus. *Do it and go,* she thought,
and then she looked up again and there was Gary.

chapter

eight

Molly was afraid that if she said Gary's name he'd disappear. She kept herself still. She tried to be detached so she wouldn't be disappointed if this was just another mirage, another hallucination. *Wait*, she told herself. *See what happens next.*

He smiled at her. This hallucination was really good, she thought. The details were so exact, so precise, right down to the small gold flaw in Gary's left eye, his curly cowlick. There was even the scar on his thumb where he had once cut himself with an X-acto knife.

She couldn't help herself. She reached for his hand. It was warm. There was a pulse. It was Gary.

"Gary? You're alive?"

His smile deepened. "You, too."

"You're really alive! You're really here!" She touched his face, his cowlick, his scarred thumb. She had thought and thought about him, had seen his face in her mind a thousand times, but here, before her, he seemed to glow. She was so excited, so happy, she could hardly speak.

"I've been here every day. I came here just about all the time."

"You did! You really did! I haven't been able to remember. They kept telling me you were here, but I never remembered any of it." She touched his hair. "I wish there were room in this bed. I wish you could just get up here with me and hold me. Or better yet, I wish I could get up and come home with you. Right now."

He laughed. "You don't know how much I wish that, too."

"I had a baby, didn't I?"

"Yes."

"Is the baby alive?"

His face changed. "Of course he is. He's great."

"Otis." She had a brief flash. Big light eyes looking up at her. His damp mouth against her breast, nursing. Her arms around him. "Where is he?"

"Home." He hesitated.

"What's the matter?" She felt a clip of alarm. "You said he was okay, right?"

"Honey—"

"What? Tell me."

He looked down at the floor and then back at her. "Suzanne is here. She's watching him."

"Suzanne?" Molly tried to sit up. "Not my sister Suzanne?" She shook her head.

"I had to call her, Molly. There was no one else."

Molly was silent for a moment. "I guess I can't believe she came."

"She came right away. And she's great with Otis. And he's crazy about her. And she's been here every day to see you."

"She has for real? What's she like now? What does she look like?"

Gary looked uncomfortable. "You can see for yourself. And you look so sleepy. Should I come back?"

"No, no, what if I sleep and then wake up and you're not here?"

"I'll stay. You sleep and I'll stay. I promise."

"You will? You'll really stay?"

"Try to keep me away."

She reached out her hand and took Gary's. "I love you," she said.

She shut her eyes. She kept opening them, sneaking peeks, making sure he was still there in the orange chair beside her. He was there, watching her. Every time she saw him afresh, she felt a shiver of pure delight. "Gary." As soon as she said his name, he turned his attention to her, he leaned closer, and she drifted into sleep.

A bad dream woke her, fading instantly as she bolted awake.

"Honey—Molly—" Gary was sitting beside her, watching her.

"I'm not supposed to be here! I'm supposed to be home with my baby—with you!"

"You will be soon. I promise."

"I'm missing everything! I don't know what Otis looks like anymore! I don't know what he did when he first came home! I don't know what his first bath was like! I don't even know how he is with you, what you two do!" She caught at her breath.

Gary was silent. "We go to the diner a lot."

"What?" She laughed, swiping at her drippy nose.

"We like the soup."

Gary stayed beside Molly past visiting hours. Molly heard the nurses ushering people out, hurrying them along. "You can visit tomorrow," they said, but when the nurses passed by Molly, not one of them so much as raised an eyebrow. They kind of half smiled. They left Gary and Molly alone.

The floor was quieting down. Finally, Gary rose up slowly. "I'll call you as soon as I get home."

She watched him leave but as soon as he was out of the room, she felt terrified. She knew Gary wouldn't be home yet, but she still wished he would call.

She couldn't stop thinking about him, wondering where he was right that moment, still in the car, driving a little wildly, singing along to the radio the way the two of them used to do together, stopping to get a quick bite at the diner they used to like? Or was he already back in the house? What was he doing, making up Otis's bottle or talking with Suzanne? What was that even like, the three of them together? She tried to imagine Suzanne being good with the baby, tried to imagine Suzanne in her house, and it made her vaguely uncomfortable. What was Suzanne like? She had asked Gary, but he hadn't told her. For the first time, it struck her: Why hadn't he told her?

A half hour later, the phone rang, jolting her. She grabbed for the receiver. "Hello?"

"Someone wants to talk to you," Gary said, and then suddenly she heard a breathy sigh, a babble.

She sat up straight in bed. Her fingers gripped the receiver. "Otis!" She gasped his name. "It's Mommy! I love you, I miss you. I wish I could be there!" she cried. "Forgive me. Can you ever forgive me?" She heard him yawn, slow and sweet, and then the phone tumbled and Gary picked it up.

"Well?" he said.

She was sobbing so hard she could hardly speak. "He's alive."

"Of course he is. You get some sleep. I'll see you tomorrow."

"You promise?"

"Try to keep me away."

She was wiping her nose on the sleeve of her johnny when she suddenly realized Suzanne hadn't asked to speak to her. Suzanne was right there in her house, and she hadn't even picked up the phone.

"Molly?"

She blinked awake. She was used to this. Blood tests, transfusions, medications, doctors. "Go away," she said flatly.

"Molly?" the voice said again, and then she looked up and there, like a shock, was Suzanne.

Suzanne was glowing, pretty, and her black hair was hanging in two thick braids across her chest.

"You look just the same," Molly said, amazed. "Like time just stopped."

"No. I don't. But thanks for saying it." Suzanne gave her a funny half smile. "Was it okay that I came back? I know things ended kind of crummy for us."

"Gary said you're helping out a lot," Molly said carefully.

Suzanne put her hands in her parka, a bright orange one that Molly suddenly recognized.

"Hey. That's my parka."

Suzanne looked down at it as if she were just noticing it for the first time. "I borrowed it. I don't own anything warm." Suzanne sat down and leaned forward. She had trouble meeting Molly's eyes. Molly felt as if a kind of radar had suddenly been turned on, as if she knew something about Suzanne, only she wasn't sure yet what it was.

"How long can you stay?"

"As long as you guys want."

Both women were silent and then Suzanne awkwardly cleared her throat. "Hey. You want a Life Saver? I've got chocolate." She dug in her pockets, rummaging around, and then she grinned and lifted out a bright purple pacifier, wagging it in her fingers.

"I keep extras for Otis," she said. "He likes the round kind. Can you believe it, a baby has pacifier favorites?"

"I don't know—"

"You should see his taste in music. A little James Brown. A little hip-hop."

"Hip-hop. I used to sing him the Beatles."

"Oh, he doesn't like that now. Now, he goes nuts for rap," Suzanne smiled. "Wait until you see his personality!"

Molly smiled weakly. She could only remember what carrying him had been like, and she wasn't sure that counted right now. She could only remember three real days of her son. How the maternity nurses wheeled Otis and her roommate's baby into her room in a kind of parade, both babies swaddled in blue and rose blankets, tiny caps poised on their heads, and what she remembered most of all was the way the other baby always seemed to be sleeping, his eyes squinched shut, the way Otis's dark eyes danced, the way he seemed to be laughing, as if this life was a great and wonderful joke, and he was about to add to the mischief. The other baby woke up with a wail, and Otis would be looking around, in a mood so good, it was contagious. "That baby, he's some firecracker," one of the maternity nurses said to Molly, "he's got himself an *attitude,*" and Molly had laughed. "I remember he was fantastic," Molly said to Suzanne, but Suzanne shook her head.

"I mean *now,* Molly. Wait until you see how big he is. Every day he looks like he's different. He's learning everything. We play all these games. Find my nose. Bat the toys. He makes a sound and I make it back." Suzanne grew more animated. "Gary and I sing to him all the time. You should see how nuts he goes!"

"Gary's wonderful, isn't he?"

"Sure," Suzanne looked down at the floor, but not before Molly saw her sister flush.

"He said you two were getting along."

"Well, you know, we have to. We share the same house. We both look after Otis."

Something about the way Suzanne was talking bothered Molly. The tone in Suzanne's voice nipped and buzzed at Molly like a small insect. She tried to shake it off. This was Suzanne, after all, Suzanne who had run away with the handsomest, wildest boy in school, Suzanne who had never wanted anything Molly had ever had. Suzanne was quiet. She wasn't looking at Molly. Outside Molly could hear the squeaky wheels of a gurney, some nurses joking and laughing. "He's so cute for a resident," one said.

"Was it okay that I came back?" Suzanne repeated.

"I never thought you would."

Suzanne shrugged.

"Gary said you're really helping. You can take off your jacket, you know. Stay a while," Molly said, and then Suzanne did, and Molly saw the sweater Suzanne was wearing.

"That's Gary's."

Suzanne looked slowly down at the sweater. "God, just like the jacket. Isn't that funny. I just grabbed whatever was there." Suzanne laughed nervously. "I'm not used to this cold. Especially at night. As soon as Gary leaves, I crank the heat up."

"What are you talking about? Gary's not there at night?"

"Well, he's not exactly a *day* watchman."

"A what?"

"Oh," said Suzanne, flustered. "I shouldn't have said anything."

Molly looked at Suzanne, astonished. "What's going on here?"

"What do you mean what's going on? Nothing—I mean—look—Gary will tell you."

"No. You're here. You tell me."

Suzanne chewed on her lip. "Gary kind of got fired. Right after you got sick. Luckily, one of the neighbors got him this job."

"Brian fired him?"

"I wasn't there, I don't know the whole story." Suzanne brightened. "But, Molly, it's been working out. He gets to be with you all day, it's not too taxing, it's money under the table. And with me working, too, we're doing just fine."

"You're working?"

"I'm just doing hair in the house—and Otis is right there beside me. Unless he's napping."

Molly looked stupefied.

"I thought you knew that, too."

"I'm calling Gary." Molly reached for the phone. The line rang and rang.

"He won't be there," Suzanne said patiently. "He had to take the car in before he went to work."

Molly slowly lowered her hand. "I knew that," she said defensively. "He told me that about the car."

"He probably didn't tell you about the job because he just didn't want to worry you. That's all it probably is."

Suzanne kept shifting in her seat. Molly couldn't stop thinking about Gary having lost his job and not telling her. It wasn't an important thing about the car, but still, she and Gary used to tell each other everything, no matter how stupid or insignificant. She couldn't help thinking: *If he had kept this from her, what else wasn't he telling her?*

"Suzanne shouldn't have told you—"

Gary was sitting beside her the next morning, trying to explain.

"We never kept secrets from each other," Molly accused.

"It wasn't a secret! I just don't want you to worry. I was going to tell you—"

"When?"

"When you were better."

"Aren't I better? I'm better now."

"Of course you are." He wouldn't look at her, and it made her chilled.

"What else aren't you telling me?"

"Nothing! You know everything!"

"I know nothing! I have no way of knowing what's going on! I'm stuck in here!"

He reached over and took her hand and when she tried to wrench it away, he held it tighter. "It's not a big deal," he insisted, but Molly shook her head.

"Why does Suzanne know things I don't?" Molly asked.

That night, Molly lay in bed awake and terrified. She heard the nurses gossiping, the occasional cry of a patient. She reached for the phone to call Gary. It was so late, she'd probably wake him. His voice would be drowsy with sleep, but they could talk, the way they used to when she couldn't sleep. She remembered once she was tossing and turning, he had dragged her out of bed and made her come into the kitchen. He had made popcorn and put on an old movie. "If you're going to be up, you might as well have a good time," he had laughed, and ten minutes into the movie, she had fallen soundly asleep against him.

The phone rang and rang. *Where could he be at this hour on a weekend? And where was Suzanne?* The machine suddenly turned on, and there was Suzanne's voice, jarring her, lilting, as if Suzanne were in a good mood and couldn't wait to talk to whomever might be calling. "Hi, please leave a message for Gary, Suzanne, Otis, or Molly at the beep." Molly hung up the phone. Suzanne was speaking on her machine. Suzanne's name was on her machine. And Molly's name was last.

She told herself she was being stupid. Of course Suzanne's name was there. She was working out of the house. Clients might call her, it was only businesslike. And what difference, really, did it make that Suzanne was saying the message? Gary was doing enough without worrying about a message. If it bothered her so much, she could always ask him to change it, to put his own voice to it. To ask Suzanne to get her own private line.

Molly lay in bed watching the open door, the occasional nurse whisking by. She wasn't tired. She had woken up, but to a whole different world, a place where her husband kept things from her, her sister cut hair in her kitchen, and her own baby was a stranger. And she had no idea what to do about any of it.

Now that Molly was awake, more and more people came by. Orderlies bringing her water leaned against her bed to watch her TV. Nurses picked up the photos of Otis Gary had brought in and swooned over him. "Those eyes! You must be in heaven!" they told Molly. They said Otis looked like Gary. They said he favored Molly. Sometimes they said he looked like neither one of them, and no matter what the nurses said, no matter how expectantly they looked at Molly, Molly didn't know what to say to any of them.

"You're amazing," one of the day nurses told her. "You fought so hard to get back to your son."

Molly was struck silent. She didn't feel as if she had fought to get back to Otis. It had just happened,

The nurse adjusted Molly's IV, staring at it critically. She flicked the tubing with a nail and then frowned and flicked at it again. "Well, when he's a teenager and starts to act up, you can tell him, 'Hey, buster, I went through hell for you, now you'd better just behave if you know what's good for you.'"

Molly looked at the nurse, shocked. "I would never tell him that! This isn't his fault!"

The nurse laughed and dropped the IV tube. "Ah, spoken like a true mother!"

But Molly didn't feel like a mother, true or otherwise. She didn't feel any connection to this Otis. The baby she felt a part of had been the one she had carried inside of her.

She had known everything about Otis back then. How a sweet biscuit could make him kick, how he preferred to bunch up on her left side, how orange juice made him hiccup so long and hard she felt as if he were percolating inside her belly. She didn't know anything about this baby now. She had heard other mothers say they could pick out their babies from two rooms away just by their scent, just by the sound of their cries, but Molly couldn't have picked Otis out if he was right there in front of her, banked by two other babies.

"I have to see my baby," she told Karen when she came by on rounds.

Karen frowned, "Molly, we've been through this before. I still don't think that'll be great for the baby. There's too much infection on this floor. Let his immune system get a little stronger. Wait a bit."

"What, two years? Three? When he's getting married?"

Karen smiled. "Atta girl, keep up that sense of humor."

But Molly didn't think anything was funny. If Karen didn't think it was a good idea, she'd just find a doctor who did. She lay in a kind of wait in her bed, and when Dr. Price strode in, Molly cornered him.

"It'll exhaust you and you need all your strength," Dr. Price said.

"But I'm stronger now."

He lifted the sheets and gently prodded Molly's belly. He pulled the sheets down again. "Kids are astonishingly resilient. You'd do best not to worry."

She thought of Suzanne hoisting Otis high in the air, the two of them laughing. She thought of Otis grabbing on to Suzanne's long hair. And then she thought of Suzanne and Gary, taking Otis to the park the way Suzanne said they did, sitting on the grass on a blanket so that anyone walking by might think they were a family. "Let me see my son," she said.

"I'll see you later this evening," he said.

Each day, they tried to get her to do a little more. A therapist came in and made Molly stand, which made Molly so dizzy she was sure she was going to throw up. They showed her exercises she could do in bed: flexing her feet, making arm circles. Not too much for fear she might hemorrhage, not too little or she'd never get strong. "A devil's bargain," Molly groused. And they began to let her eat. First Jell-O, rationing it out to her a teaspoon at a time, and then a list of soft, bland foods that Molly considered as carefully as if it were a four-star menu. Never had Jell-O tasted more delicious. She swore the green had a different taste than the yellow. Never had oatmeal seemed like such a feast.

No matter what she ordered, they brought her something different. She checked off cereal and they brought her French toast. She checked off soup and they brought her steak. "I didn't order this!" she told the woman bringing the food. "I'm supposed to have bland food!"

The woman looked at her wearily. "You're not going to make me argue with the kitchen, are you?" she asked Molly. "You do that, and by the time I get you your breakfast it'll be dinnertime. Why don't you just save us all some trouble and eat what's there?"

It became a kind of joke, and she began to have Gary bring her food so they could eat together. She made requests, hoping he'd get what she wanted, trying to gauge how far he'd go for her. Soup from the Kiev. Chinese cold noodles from Chinatown. He always came, and after two bites, her appetite was gone. "You have the rest," she told him. The one time she asked Suzanne to bring her plain pasta, Suzanne came with a tuna sandwich, greasy with mayonnaise, and after that Molly never asked her to bring anything again.

* * *

Later, when Dr. Price came by, he had a strange secretive look play-ing about his face. "What?" she said. She could sit up now, like an expert.

"I see you're eating. Not much, but you're still eating. And your blood levels are getting a bit better."

Molly looked at him, waiting.

"Does that mean I can go home?"

"Well, no, of course not. Not by a long shot—" he admitted.

"So what does it mean?"

He grinned again, the first real smile she had seen on him. "It means you can see your son."

Molly started. "Are you kidding?"

"You have to be in a wheelchair. It's just in the solarium and just for a short time. I discussed this with Karen and the other doctors and we all think it might be good for your state of mind. And good for the baby."

As soon as Dr. Price left, Molly started crying. A new nurse walked into the room, young and coltish, carrying a thermometer, and she looked nervous when she saw Molly weeping.

"What's the matter?"

"Please, will you buy me makeup?"

"What?" The nurse stood beside Molly.

"My son is coming. Please, I haven't seen him in three months. I have to look good. I need mascara. Brown eye shadow, some sort of glossy lipstick in a brownish red. Blush. A mirror. And—" Molly sobbed. "Gold hoop earrings. Tiny ones."

The morning Molly was to see Otis, she woke at four. She grabbed her bag of cosmetics and spread them across the sheet. She brushed her hair, putting it up and then taking it down. She put on the gold hoops, and struggled with the makeup, squinting critically at herself in the hand mirror. Her skin looked ashy to her. Her lips were chapped and her eyes seemed like pin dots in her face. She did the best she could, but she felt as if she were readying herself for a blind date, for a meeting with someone everyone had told her about and all she could think of was, *What if he doesn't like me? What if I make a bad first impression?* She swept the makeup back into the bag and into a drawer. She waited. her hands tensely folded.

It seemed like years before a nurse came to get her, pushing a wheelchair, smiling broadly at her. "Hey, you look good. Your color's better. The meds must be doing their job."

"It's Maybelline," Molly said, and the nurse laughed.

She wheeled Molly lazily toward the solarium, the IV pole squeaking alongside her. Molly was so tense, she wanted to scream at her to hurry, hurry. She couldn't wait. "Here we go," the nurse said, wheeling her into the room. "Not too long now."

The solarium was a misnomer. Molly didn't know what she expected, but the word made her think of green plants and new light spread out like a fresh summer sheet and gleaming wood floors. Instead, the solarium was a small, boxy room with a blue linoleum floor and orange padded chairs. It was filled with magazines and a card table and not a single plant. There was a woman in a red suit whispering to a man in a hospital gown. There was an elderly woman with her eyes shut. And there in the corner was Gary, and next to him, sitting close, was Suzanne, rocking a baby who seemed three times the size of the one Molly remembered. She stared at the baby, trying to find something familiar. He had hair now, dark like Gary's. She knew his eyes, she thought. And maybe his mouth. But would she have known him if he wasn't on Suzanne's lap?

Suzanne bent down, whispering something to Otis, looking up at Molly with a look that made Molly suddenly scared: guilt.

"Hey, look who's here!" Suzanne said to Otis. Otis stared at Molly.

Gary picked up the baby and gently settled him in Molly's lap. Otis fussed. He stiffened, arching his back.

Suzanne crouched down beside Molly, repositioning Otis. Otis's hands clung to Suzanne.

"Say Mommy," Suzanne urged Otis, who said nothing.

Otis looked at Suzanne. She tickled his chin, making him shut his eyes in pleasure.

"He loves this," Suzanne announced. She was talking really fast. She grabbed the baby's little finger. "He likes this, too."

"And stuffed animals," Gary said. "Oh, I think he wants his pacifier." He reached for the baby bag, just as Suzanne did, brushing her hand, jolting his back as if she had burned him. Molly stared from one to the other. Gary and Suzanne both seemed uncomfortable. They were talking without looking at each other. Suzanne rummaged in the bag and popped a blue pacifier in Otis's mouth, and when she sat back down, she angled her body toward Gary. Gary bolted up from the couch. Molly felt a prickling of fear. What was going on here? "Gary?" Molly said, and then Otis spat out the pacifier and began to wail.

"I'll take him—" Suzanne said, but Molly pulled back.

"No. Leave him be," Molly said.

"Let me just get him to stop and then I'll hand him right back—"

"No." Otis wailed louder. Molly felt desperate.

"Oh, not like that—" Suzanne said, and Molly swiveled her body away from her sister.

"I can do this," Molly said sharply. "I can comfort my own baby."

Suzanne put her hands up and took a step back. "Be my guest."

Molly tried to rock him, but it made Otis cry louder. He flailed against Molly. "What's wrong with him?" Molly cried. "Is he wet?"

"He just wants a hug." Suzanne picked Otis up from her arms, and Otis instantly calmed down. "You get to know these things by instinct," Suzanne said.

They didn't stay very long after that. A nurse came to wheel Molly back to her room, letting her linger at the elevator. "Say bye-bye." Gary lifted up Otis's hand and waved it. The baby blinked at her. His lower lip flopped open. *He's trying to tell me something,* she thought, and before she could figure it out, the elevator door opened and the last thing she saw before the door closed were Otis's dark eyes, staring out at her.

*   *   *

She fell asleep almost as soon as she was back in bed. She heard a voice and looked up, trying to rouse, and there was Dr. Price shaking his head at her. "It was too much for you," he said, and then before she could argue with him, she fell asleep again.

chapter

nine

G ary stared at his computer, his hand motionless on the mouse. Downstairs, he could hear Suzanne moving around, shutting doors a bit too loudly, turning up her music too much. Some punk rocker wailing about his cheating heart that was slashing him like a blade.

Gary slammed down the mouse and clicked off the computer. That was it. He'd get out of the house. Get away from her. It was Saturday night. He could go see a couple of movies. Or he could go to the diner. Stay there until he knew Molly would be up and he could go to see her. Anything as long as he wasn't within ten feet of Suzanne. He bolted up from his seat, determined, and came out of his room and as soon as he did, he smelled something wafting through the house, winding its way up to him. Garlic. Tomato sauce. His stomach rumbled and growled. He was suddenly starving.

When he got to the stairs, Suzanne was waiting for him at the bottom. Her lips looked glossy, like she'd shined them up. He stared at them, stricken.

Suzanne smiled. She tucked her hair behind one ear. "Want some dinner?" Suzanne said. "I made pasta."

"I ate," Gary lied. The last thing in his stomach had been a stale piece of Juicy Fruit he had found in his pocket. He was so hungry he could have eaten six bowls of pasta, he probably could have eaten the cardboard box the pasta came in, but he wasn't going to take the chance sitting at a table with her.

"I made garlic bread, too. And salad."

"I said I wasn't hungry," Gary snapped. He hurried down the stairs, intending to walk right past her, but she didn't move. He had to brush past her.

"Everything go okay at the hospital today?" Suzanne said.

Gary nodded and headed for Otis's room. He was going crazy. If he was so anxious to hold someone, it had better be his son. He leaned over the crib. Otis kicked his legs as Gary picked him up. He nuzzled Otis, but then he looked up, and for a moment he was sure he saw Suzanne, leaning in the doorway. He blinked. The doorway was empty. He'd have to get out of the house. And he'd take Otis with him.

Gary got Otis into his jacket. He got the baby carrier and had his hand on the door when he heard Suzanne call to him.

"Hey, where are you going?" Suzanne said. Her voice moved in a funny way. Her expression looked complicated. "Can anyone come or is this a private party?"

"We'll be right back," he said quickly, and then he stepped out into the cold, shutting the door even as she moved toward him.

He headed for the Tastee. "Well, look who's here!" the waitresses said when they saw him. Otis slept on the leatherette seat. Gary nursed his chocolate milkshake and fiddled with his french fries, swiping them through the ketchup and laying them back on his plate. He hardly ate anything. A couple came and sat in the next booth, holding hands, leaning over the table and kissing. "Maybe we should just go home," the woman said, laughing, deep and throaty. Gary was suddenly furious at the couple. They made him feel heartsick, they were so happy. He put down money for the check and picked up Otis. He opened the door and walked outside.

*　*　*

The neighborhood was dark except for a small square of blue light in Suzanne's room. He carried Otis into bed, and when he came outside, there was Suzanne, in her blue robe, sleepy-faced and miserable, her hair rumpled, staring at him. "Are you just going to avoid me forever?" She grabbed for his sleeve. "Nothing happened."

"Everything happened." Gary freed his sleeve and looked past her. "And it's not going to happen again."

"Don't you want to talk about this? We live in the same house. You can't just keep sidestepping me forever."

"I've got tons to do," he said curtly, cutting her off, and then he went upstairs to his office, turned on the computer, and fell instantly asleep in his chair.

He woke with a start and stumbled into bed, and as soon as he hit the sheets, he was wide awake. He put the pillow sideways, the same way he did every night, to trick himself into thinking he was sleeping with Molly. He shut his eyes. "Molly," he murmured, and suddenly he smelled Suzanne's perfume. He saw her eyes, her hair. He felt her body, lowered beside his, the slide of her hair across his back. He bolted up from the bed, kicking the sheets to the floor. The bed was empty. The house was silent. He sat down in the chair by the window.

He'd sit here until morning if he had to.

The next day, on his way to see Molly, Gary, so sleepy he was stumbling, stopped and bought her vegetable soup from the Kiev. Her favorite. He was broke but he stopped at a jewelry store and bought her a silver bracelet, slim as a wedding band. "Someone's quite a lucky girl," the store clerk told him.

When Gary walked into Molly's room, she was turned away from him, looking out the window. Her skin looked gray and it hurt him to see it. Her hair was matted on one side and her face was puffy. "I come bearing gifts," Gary said, forcing cheer, and Molly turned toward him, perking up, putting on a smile, too. He put down the cardboard cup of soup and opened it for her. Steam curls floated in the air. Potatoes bobbed on the surface.

"Oh, my favorite!" she said.

Gary reached in his pocket and then set down the present in front of her. "And what's this?" she said.

He stood back from her, watching her take the gift from the bag and unwrap it. He had heard that lovers could smell betrayal on each other, that you couldn't help but give faithlessness away with a glance, a look, a certain tone in your voice. But Molly's face was glowing with surprise and pleasure. "Oh, my God!" She lifted the bracelet up, admiring it. She held up her wrists helplessly. "Got mine already," Molly joked, showing him her plastic band on one wrist, the coil of IV tubing on the other. She set the bracelet on the dresser by the bed. "Well, I can look at it and love it for now. It's something to aspire to."

"Have some soup," he urged.

Molly tried, but she could only finish half the soup. She yawned and stretched.

"You sleep and I'll stay here," he told her.

She shut her eyes and he sat there watching her for a while. He took the bracelet and opened the clasp and studied her arm. He couldn't believe there wasn't a place for it. Her arm was now so thin, the bracelet would probably fit on a lot of places beside her wrist. Finally, he slipped it on just under her right elbow. He felt a weird, hot kind of relief. He stepped back and looked at it. When Molly woke up, she'd see the bracelet, a silvery gleam on her arm. She'd remember he had given it to her.

When Gary got home that afternoon, Otis was in the Portacrib in the living room, batting irritatedly at the colored plastic toys suspended above him. "What's the matter, you don't like your toys?" he said. Otis whacked a plastic yellow butterfly, sending it spinning. Gary could hear Suzanne in the kitchen, the rush of the water. He knew her routine. She must be doing Otis's bottles by hand. "Let's take a walk," Gary said. Gary quickly got Otis dressed and into the Snugli. And then, as he was ready to go out the door, he called out, "Suzanne, I'm taking Otis out."

"Gary?" she said, but he shut the door. He went out into the street.

He walked around and around, waiting for Suzanne to leave for the hospital, but as soon as he saw the car moving down the street, her head bent forward, her sunglasses on, he felt even worse than before. He didn't want to go back in that empty house and feel the walls closing around him. He didn't know what he wanted. He looked down at Otis, who had fallen fast asleep against his chest. He suddenly felt so lonely he didn't know what to do with himself. He walked around the block twice, the baby bouncing against his chest, just in time for the paperboy, a scrappy little kid in a baseball jacket, to zoom the papers willy-nilly at everyone's door. Gary's landed on the side-walk and he plucked it up.

He found himself at Emma's door. He felt like a foundling that had put himself on her stoop. He didn't know what he wanted, what he'd say, only that he didn't want to be alone another minute. He looked up at her house. A light flickered on. He could hear her TV blasting from the open window. She was up.

He rang her bell.

It took Emma a few seconds to get to the door. She was already dressed and when she saw Gary and Otis, she looked surprised. "Is everything all right?" she said worriedly. "Do you need me to sit?"

He handed her his paper. "The kid knocked it in your rosebushes. I thought I'd deliver it by hand."

She looked at the paper curiously. "But this isn't mine. I don't get the paper."

"Oh, my mistake," Gary said stupidly. He stood there like a fool. Of course she didn't get the paper. On paper recycling days, his was the house with the stacks and stacks of boxes and newspapers and magazines. Her house barely had a flyer. Even so, he couldn't manage to move.

"Well—" Emma said, glancing at her watch. Gary didn't know what to do. He didn't want her to close the door. He didn't want to go into his house, didn't want to go into a coffee shop by himself, and he was so exhausted, he didn't think he could walk another aimless block. And then, like a sparkler going off, he had an idea.

"Would you have breakfast with me? With us?" Gary blurted. "My treat? We could go to Josie's down the street. I hear it's pretty good."

Emma looked perplexed for a moment. And then she suddenly relaxed. "Don't be silly. I don't believe in paying for food when you can make it just as good at home. You come in here instead."

She held open the door and instantly he smelled cigarette smoke and coffee. It struck him suddenly funny. All this time he had lived on this block and he had never once been inside Emma's house before. He had never been inside any of the neighbors'. Had never caught more than a glimpse of the houses because they all kept heavy curtains on the windows, drawn even in the hottest summer days.

Once inside, Emma didn't even bother to give him the tour, the way he would have. She didn't tell him what anything was, or what it might mean. She didn't apologize or brag about a thing. He followed her through the living room. The walls were all dark wood-paneled. The rug was green shag, the furniture heavy and upholstered, some of it covered in white plastic, and dead center on the wall was a badly painted seascape with churning blue water. White checkmark seagulls. Yellow circle sun. Gary blinked at it, astounded.

Emma followed his gaze. "Isn't that beautiful?" Emma said. "My cousin did it. Very talented girl."

Gary nodded. "Very," he said, trying to sound sincere. He had never in his life seen anything like it.

"Right this way."

She led him past the dining room.

The kitchen was papered in a garish big blue and red plaid. Here were the photos, plastered all over the refrigerator. Kids' faces, round and soft as apple dumplings, grinning up at him. Emma followed his gaze. She pointed out the faces. "Theresa's grandniece. My cousin's kids. Bill's nephew. There's Maryann and Betsy and Robert John." She tapped out the photos with her fingers.

"Sit," she ordered. He sat at the table. Emma slid an apron over her and tied it in back. Then she went to the refrigerator and started taking things out, humming to herself. Eggs. American cheese. Butter. She got up and took out a bowl from the cabinet and cracked two eggs into it. She sizzled grease in a pan.

He liked sitting there, listening to her cook. He felt warm. Comfortable. Companionable. He didn't want to move an inch. He stroked Otis's back.

She poured orange juice from a can into polka-dotted jelly glasses. She warmed Otis's bottle for him in case he woke up, and then she set out extra butter and toast and napkins. She scooped the eggs, nubby yellow chunks, onto plates and set them on the table with a flourish. "Hard scrambled. Better than any diner, if I say so myself."

"Molly and I met in a diner," Gary said, and as soon as he said it, he felt a knot in his heart. He felt suddenly exhausted. His shoulders dropped. He felt Emma's eyes on him.

Emma pulled up a chair and sat down carefully next to Gary. She placed one hand over Gary's. He stared down at her hand, at the web of wrinkles, the peach-colored nails, the tiny diamond wedding ring. "We're all praying for Molly, Gary," Emma said quietly. "We've got a very good priest over at St. Ann's and he says special novenas for Molly every Sunday. We even have a prayer circle. Molly's got so many prayers, I'm sure she must be hearing them."

"Really? You all pray for her?"

Emma looked so concerned and motherly that Gary suddenly wanted to fling himself into her arms, to have her pat his back, to tell him it was all going to be all right. He wanted to say something to her, but he couldn't think what to say. Emma folded her fingers over his, and patted them, and then released his hand. She looked at him as if he were a child. "Gary, we pray for you and Otis, too."

Suzanne sat in Molly's hospital room. Sometimes it was hard to look at her sister. Molly had that pallor sick people did, as if illness took away your skin tone. She had gone all puffy, and Suzanne could only

imagine what her sister's hair must feel like. But what she hated the
most was the way Molly acted around her, the way she stared and
stared and wouldn't look away, as if she were trying to figure something out.

"So what did you and Gary do today?" Molly said.

"I was on my own today."

"Uh-huh. I bet you can't wait to get back to California," Molly said.

"No—it's okay here, it's fine."

"Yeah, I bet."

"Why are you talking to me like this?"

Molly stared at Suzanne, considering. She gave her that stare again
that made Suzanne feel like jumping out of her skin. "Are you in love
with Gary?" Molly blurted.

Suzanne stood up. "Why would you ask me that?"

"You're not answering. Is Gary in love with you?"

"Molly, this is ridiculous—"

"No, it's not ridiculous. I'd ask him myself except he probably
wouldn't tell me. At least not now, not while I'm stuck sick in here.
But you, you tell me."

"There's nothing to tell."

"It's my husband. My baby. My house." Molly swallowed. "My
life. I have a right to know."

"Molly!"

"I know something's going on."

A nurse breezed in with a wheelchair. "X rays, honey," she said.

Molly didn't even look at Suzanne when Suzanne left.

Suzanne drove home feeling sick. *Are you in love with Gary?* Molly
had asked. Love. The heart was a lying little muscle that didn't know
the difference between good and bad, between being wanted and un-
wanted. You could fool yourself a million ways when it came to love,
and she had probably gone through all of them. *Is Gary in love with
you?* She saw Gary in her mind, sifting through Internet printouts about
Molly's illness, she saw Gary swaying Otis to sleep, she saw him
looking through the photograph albums filled with Molly. She felt him
touching the side of her own face, tugging her roughly to him. *What*

kind of question is that? she should have asked Molly. And it was true.
What kind of question was it?

The next morning, Molly was already unhooked from the IV and in
the wheelchair, protective plastic taped to her belly, a towel, shampoo,
and soap in her lap, when Gary arrived. "I'm getting a shower this
morning!" she said, triumphant.

Gary shook his head. "No. That can't be right. The hospital's
letting you do that?"

"Yup. There's one right on this floor."

"Do you think that's a good idea?" he said doubtfully.

"Whose side are you on?" She felt suddenly angry. He wasn't the
one stuck in here. He was outside. With Suzanne.

Gary looked offended. "What kind of question is that? Your side."

"Then let me take my goddamned shower."

He flinched at her tone. He held up his hands. "All right, fine."
He wheeled her out into the hall. "Left, and then right," she told him,
until he led her to a door along the wall. SHOWER, it said.

"I'd better go get the nurse now, right? To go in with you. Or
can I just come in with you?"

"Oh, I forgot," Molly said. "No, the nurse would be better. You'd
better get a nurse."

He hesitated and then started to wheel her with him. "No, no—" she
said. "I don't want to lose my place in line. I'll wait here."

She watched Gary winding his way down the aisle, looking back
at her three different times to make sure she was all right, but it didn't
make her feel safe. It made her feel closeted. Eight o'clock. The nurses
were all busy making their rounds, and they were short-staffed today.
Molly had had to badger the nurses three different times just to get
the wheelchair. It would take Gary awhile, she bet, to get a nurse to
leave a sick patient just to help Molly take a shower no one seemed
in a hurry to let her have.

She wheeled closer to the door. No one was in the corridor except
a patient struggling to walk, one hand braced along the wall, not even

looking at her. Molly opened the shower-room door and stood up, using the door handle for leverage. She stepped carefully into the shower room, shutting the door behind her. She looked down. *Oh, my God. A lock.* She hadn't seen a lock since she had gone into the hospital. *A door you could shut and keep people out. Privacy. Oh, what a simple, blissful thing.*

She locked the door with a satisfying click.

Molly looked around. The shower room looked like one big single bathroom. There was a sink and a tub with a kind of rubber chair built into it, with chrome handrails and a handheld shower nozzle. There was a blue tile floor, a toilet, a wastebasket, and an extra bench. Guardrails circled the room. Well, she'd have to work fast. She already felt tired.

Molly turned on the water. She shucked off her clothes and eased herself onto the rubber seat, and as soon as the water hit her, she felt jolted. "Oh!" She gasped. She couldn't imagine anything feeling like that. The water was a shock. The heat an embrace. Her skin seemed to vibrate. The water hummed. She couldn't help laughing. Her mouth dropped open. She threw her head back, gripping the handrails of the chair. She shut her eyes with pleasure. She braced her feet against the rubber bottom of the tub. The water beat down on her, intense and blissful. She sighed. She held on tight. It felt as if all the heat and damp were loosening something up all over her, sliding it off. Layers of hospital. Coming right off in a rush. All the endless morning rounds and medicine in tiny paper cups. The noisily beeping IVs, the food that tasted like paper. The goddamn blood takers and nurses and med students who woke her up at three in the morning. She reached up one hand and grabbed the soap in the tub and used it on her hair. Instantly, her head tingled. Instantly, she felt lighter. Another layer sloughed off. She felt her scalp, alive and tingling. She felt electrified. She laughed out loud.

"Molly?" She heard him outside the door, faintly muffled. Gary. But she wasn't moving. Not for anyone. She wasn't leaving this bliss. "Molly!" His voice boomed. He tried the door and Molly turned the water hotter. She made more steam. "Molly? Are you in there? The door's locked! Molly!" She turned the water pressure up. She sang loudly.

"Molly! Are you crazy? You can't be in there alone!"

"La, la, la," she sang through the door, her voice rising in sudden rage. "I'm singing, I can't hear you!" She felt suddenly powerful. Nothing could hurt her now. Nothing could even touch her.

"Molly, open the door now! What are you doing? I have to be in there with you!"

"La, la, la. I know about you! I know about Suzanne!"

"Molly, it's not true—Molly, nothing happened. Molly, open the goddamned door!"

"Fuck you," she shouted. "I'm washing you down the drain!"

She kept singing. La, la, la. Louder and louder, and the angrier she got, the more powerful she felt. A thousand times stronger. Water cascaded down her in warm sheets, intoxicating her, making her dizzy with the pure bliss of it. She gripped the sides of the chair. Gary banged on the door. "I'm getting somebody!" he shouted. But this time, she didn't bother to shout back at him. The banging stopped. All she heard was the hiss of the water, the rough tag of her own breathing, and then she slowly leaned forward and turned off the water.

She still felt great. Her whole body was buzzing. Everything seemed more intense. The white of the tub was blinding. The blue of the tiles shimmered. Even the air seemed somehow electrified.

Here we go, she thought. She didn't think she could pull herself up, but she didn't feel terrified. *Take it one step at a time.* She tugged herself up. Beads of water fell from the plastic over her gauze covering. Her legs were butter, startling her. *Easy. You can do it. You can do it.* The same words she told herself when she was giving birth. It made her laugh out loud. She shuffled, smiling to herself, holding on to the wall, making her way slowly to the sink. *One baby step at a time. You can do it.* She grabbed at the sink. She caught her breath a little and this time looked frankly at herself in the mirror, at her eyes, sparkling as if they had chips of mica in them. As round and enormous in her face as dinner plates. Her skin flushed pink. Her hair was fat with the steam, curled in damp wisps. Her heart was beating like a bird's heart, fast and thin and fluttery as wings. She felt like she could fly away. She slid on her dress, stepping into her stretchy shoes, and then she took the three steps to the door and unlocked it. She opened it up to Gary.

His face changed when he saw her. He was scared and then he was something else. His eyes widened. His mouth opened. She felt herself coloring. Something sprang between them. He stared at her, astonished, and then suddenly he grabbed her and kissed her deep and passionately on the mouth. He took her arms and wrapped them about his neck. "You are so fucking beautiful and I am so fucking insane for you," he said. And then, right before she could start kissing him back, she fell, collapsing against him into a narrowing cone of black.

She woke in a dark room. She blinked, adjusting her eyes to the dim light. Nighttime. Hours later, she thought. A shadow moved, and then came into focus, and there was Dr. Price in his white coat, hovering over her, glaring.

"You did a very stupid thing," Dr. Price scolded. "What if you had fallen? What if you had hemorrhaged? You must think about these things." He frowned, shaking his head at her. He left the room.

Molly smiled. She'd think about it all right. She waggled her fingers. She flexed her toes. Oh. That wonderful feeling was still there. The pleasure, so keen she could have skated along it. She still was feeling lighter. The hospital's grip was really loosened. She had done it. She had really done it. There was more of her now than there was of the hospital. And she was just going to have to find ways to tip the balance even more.

chapter

ten

Suzanne's last appointment had left minutes ago. Otis was still sleeping and she was sweeping up the last of the hair, contemplating a quick bath, when the doorbell rang.

Suzanne wiped her hands along her smock and grabbed for the door handle. She bet it was a walk-in, or the postman with a package, or Gary, who forgot something, who maybe she could convince into staying in the same room with her long enough to have a simple conversation, a talk, which was a long time coming. She couldn't bear the way he looked past her as if she wasn't even there.

The bell rang again. "Hold your horses," she called. She opened the door, and there, like a dream, was Ivan.

She couldn't move. Her hands flew to her hair, which was bunched into a sloppy tail, to her jeans, speckled with color. In all the times she had fantasized running into Ivan, it had always been when she was prepared for it, when she had been dressed in something tight and shiny and low-cut, with high heels and her hair gleaming like a mirror. Perfume on every pulse point. She had imagined him spotting her on the arm of a gorgeous, adoring guy, a big shimmery ring on her finger, and Ivan staring at her with all the regret and desire she had felt for him these five years since he had walked out on her. But she had never once imagined this.

"So, can I come in?" Ivan said.

She had forgotten his voice, how even his speech could sound musical. But she could never forget his eerie blue eyes, his long, beautiful black hair. He looked as if no time had passed, as if nothing had ever happened to him. She nodded and stepped aside.

The air in the room changed as soon as he was inside. Her knees were collapsing, changing to gum. "What are you doing here?"

He sat down, not taking his eyes from her. "Something I should have done a long time ago. Looking for you."

"How did you find me?"

"Followed your trail. One phone number led to another and when I finally got to the end of the line, I remembered your sister. You told me she taught, and I even remembered where, so I called the school, but they wouldn't tell me anything. Just like a school, right? Still got to show you who's in control. Anyway, I had to practically beg just to find the town she lived in. I figured your sister would know where you were." He shook his head, looking curiously around the house. "But God, Suzanne, of all the places you could go to, I never thought you'd come back here. It really surprised me."

"Molly's sick in the hospital. I'm helping out. Taking care of the baby."

Ivan shook his head. He acted as if he hadn't heard her. "I knew if I could just see you—if we could just see each other."

Suzanne shut her eyes for a moment. Her throat was dry. "How could you have left me like that?" she said finally.

He frowned. "Suzanne. I was a kid. I didn't know anything. Not until I didn't have you."

"So all this time you've been alone thinking about life," she said bitterly.

"Suzanne." He wavered. Then he said, low and quick, "I got married. I had a kid."

"What?" Suzanne felt something rupturing inside of her. Married. How could he be married to someone who wasn't her? She tried to frame a picture, but the only face beside Ivan's that she could see was her own. The only baby was Otis. Suzanne's breath narrowed in her chest. Her heart felt tight and small. Suddenly, she couldn't breathe. "How could you be married? You never wanted that. If I even mentioned it, you were out the door—"

"Was married," Ivan interrupted. "Patty and I got divorced about six months ago."

Suzanne swallowed. Patty. He had married someone named Patty. Had divorced her, too, but that didn't make her feel one single bit better because divorce still meant that you had cared enough about someone to marry them in the first place. Cared enough to have a kid. And cared more than he had about her. She felt suddenly shamed and angry. It was hard to look at him. Hard not to.

"Suzanne," he said, his voice pleading. "Listen to me. When I quit on you, everything turned right to shit. All my dreams. Everything. I tried to make it in music, Suzanne. For the longest time, I really tried. All these new bands I put together. All these crappy gigs. But nothing took. And then by the time I met Patty, I was doing nothing but being a mechanic. She had this old Datsun that nobody could fix right. But I did, and she looked at me like I had just about cured cancer. When I was playing music, I got that kind of feeling all the time. It was like it came with the territory or something. And even a mechanic's got to have things to make him feel like his life's worth something. Like it's special. So I married her. And a year and a half later, we had Ann."

Suzanne flinched. Ann. She looked away from him. She wouldn't let him see how much he had hurt her—was hurting her, still.

"Suzanne. You're not saying anything."

"What do you want me to say? That you should have married me?"

"You're not listening to me. You knew me as this rock star. Patty knew me only as a mechanic. I knew you'd end up hating me. Like I hated myself. And I couldn't stand that."

"You're stupid," she said quietly. "You think I gave a shit about any of that? You could have been a goddamn busboy and I would have loved you. You could never have sung another note your whole long life and I would have loved you. Do you know what it was like for me? How I suffered? I couldn't even look at anyone else, that was how nuts I was about you. How pathetic. I used to cross the street just hoping a truck would run me over because then I wouldn't have to think about you anymore. You left me alone in the world and I still loved you. But you—you went ahead and loved someone else."

"You got it all wrong, Suzanne." His voice rushed past her. "Patty was white noise. She kept this buzz going so I couldn't see, I couldn't hear, I couldn't think what was really important to me. She blocked it all out just by being around. And I didn't see it until after I quit her."

Ivan took Suzanne's hands.

"Fuck you," Suzanne said, breaking his grip. She didn't want him touching her. She couldn't stand it another minute. "Fuck you."

"Suzanne, listen to me. My marriage didn't work out because I never loved Patty. I loved you."

Suzanne looked at him. "Stop. Don't you dare say things you don't mean."

"Remember when I first met you, when I said it was fate—you and me?"

"Ivan, don't—"

"I thought about you night and day, Suzanne. I wanted to call you a million times. I tried to forget you. I know I was a shit the way I left you. I was a cruel bastard. I took it out on you because I couldn't face that maybe I didn't have what it took to make it in music. I couldn't handle it. And I couldn't stand it that you knew it." He sighed. "You were the thing that made my life work, Suzanne. I couldn't even get close to Ann because it reminded me how far away from you I'd come. How I'd probably fucked up any chance to ever have you again."

Ivan's words were like a reel pulling Suzanne out of herself, toward him. She felt as if she were losing her own thoughts. She couldn't even remember what her own thoughts were anymore.

"I thought you'd come back to California," Ivan said. "I kept looking for you everywhere. I'd see someone with long black hair, and zoom—I was off on their trail, just hoping it was you. How could you stay away from me? Why didn't you come back?"

"I told you. I'm helping out here."

He looked at her, nodded, but she got the feeling that he wasn't even listening to her, he was just drinking her in.

He leaned forward and touched her knee, jolting her. As soon as he took his hand away, God help her, but she wanted it back.

"Remember the way we used to stay up all night just talking?" he asked. "Sometimes I wouldn't even have to say a single word and you'd know what I was feeling, you'd understand. You just *knew* me, Suzanne."

He stared at her so hard that even if she tried, she couldn't have looked away from him. "After the divorce, I had a lot of time to think, and what I thought about was you. And I don't know, it unlocked something in me. I hadn't touched my guitar in years, but I thought of you and suddenly I picked it up again, and just as suddenly, the songs just started coming again. Some of them are pretty good. That's your doing, whether you know it or not." He tilted his head back. "Su-zanne of my heart," he sang.

"You sound just the same," she said, pained.

"No, no, I got this new raw quality now." He fanned his fingers over his chest. "From the heart, Suzanne. The broken heart."

Suzanne swallowed. "You never told me why you're here," she interrupted.

"I thought I *was* telling you. I came back for you."

"Ivan."

"You used to tell me you love someone once, you always love them. That's how you tell real love. You told me and you were right." He fished in his pocket and pulled out a key on a green plastic tab and handed it to her, smiling hopefully. "I got us a suite at the Ramada Inn. Room service. Champagne. A great big bed with clean sheets every day. I can sing you those songs there, Suzanne. All those songs about you. We can leave here together. Rent a little beach house in California."

"I can't just leave," she blurted. "I take care of Otis while Gary's at the hospital. I help them out."

He nodded. "Oh, yeah. The baby. So when, then?"

She folded her hand around the key and then he folded his hand around hers, so for a moment, she couldn't think straight. "I don't know when. Or if."

"When can I at least see you?"

"Tomorrow." She thought about Gary's schedule. "At three."

He was suddenly happier. He bounced up. "Jesus, look at me. I'm shaking. I haven't felt like this since I was fifteen. Since I first saw you. I'm like a little kid, I'm so excited. I can't believe I get a chance to make everything right."

Suzanne stood up. His walk to the door was like a dance. He pulled it open and then stepped back and kissed her, hard on the mouth, so that when he pulled away, she felt a little breathless. "Three," he repeated, and whistling, walked down to his car. She watched him leaving, and for a moment she wanted to run out after him and grab him around the legs and stop him. She pressed her hands to her mouth, as if she was holding his kiss in. She was afraid he'd leave her forever this time, but just as much she wanted to lock herself in, to forget that he had ever come back for her. She couldn't let go of the bad times. It was too dangerous. Something so terrible could happen all over again.

All that day, she felt on fire. She felt his hands on her. His eyes. His breath at the back of her neck. She heard his whisper against her ears.

She couldn't stay in the house another second. She looked at her watch. Gary would be home soon. Then it would be time to go see Molly.

Suzanne kept busy so she wouldn't think. She was hoping Otis might wake, but even when she crept into his room, he was sleeping so soundly for a moment she got worried. She placed one hand on his chest, feeling it rise and fall. His eyes were rolling in dreams. He made a low, soft moan. There was a bubble of saliva on his mouth and she daubed gently at it with a finger until it was gone. Then she left his room and started to clean. She got on her hands and knees and scrubbed the kitchen floor. She cleaned both bathrooms and did a wash. She wouldn't allow herself to stop for a minute, because then she would think. Then Ivan would flood her like a tidal wave, drowning her in minutes, not giving her a second to catch her breath. She was just about to scrub the burners on the stove when Gary walked in.

Usually, just the sight of him would charge her. Her breath would clip. Her heart would feel stapled. But after seeing Ivan, Gary suddenly looked faded. Like he belonged to a whole other world that she no longer inhabited.

Gary squinted at her. "Everything okay?" he said. "You look kind of frazzled."

"No, no, I'm fine. Otis is really napping." Her hands were so sweaty, she wiped them on her jeans. The back of her neck prickled and she lifted up her hair to cool it.

"You want to order a pizza?"

She studied him, surprised. She wasn't sure why he was being so friendly. Just a while ago, she would have killed for an offer like that from him. But now all she could think about was Ivan. And in any case, Suzanne could no more eat than she could breathe underwater. "I just want to get going to see Molly."

Gary looked at her curiously. She felt nervous, as if he could tell something might be going on. Something she didn't want to tell him about yet. She didn't want to hear his opinion until she was sure of her own. And she certainly didn't want to hear Molly's. For a second, she almost felt like she was sneaking around, the same way she had been when she was a kid. All that dangerous living, when you felt like you were standing on the edge of a volcano, and all you had to do was shift your weight and you might topple right in. Well, this was different. She was being careful this time, really careful. She was going to wait, to be sure what she wanted to do before getting Gary and Molly all upset. They'd probably think she was going to leave them in the lurch.

"You sure you're all right?" Gary said.

"What could be wrong?" she said, more sharply than she had intended.

Suzanne pointed the car in the direction of the hospital, but it was as if the car had a mind of its own. She started to turn left, and then she missed the light and turned right instead, thinking she'd back around. She started to go east and ended up west. Every light, every turn, led her to Ivan.

The Ramada Inn was off the highway, tucked beside a bowling alley and a diner. She parked the car, her heart hammering, staring at it. *I should visit Molly,* she told herself, even as she got out of the car, as she walked to the Ramada and pushed through the revolving glass doors, even as she headed straight for the elevators and rode to his floor.

The elevator doors whooshed open. She stepped out, walked to his door, and stood in front of it, waiting, unable to move. She couldn't hear anything from outside. No TV. No music. She sucked in a breath and then she knocked on the door.

"Hang on!" she heard, and then Ivan, in jeans and a black T-shirt and bare feet, his black hair wet from the shower, making pinpoints on his shirt, opened the door. As soon as he saw it was her, he grabbed her, tugging her in, tumbling her to the floor. He kicked the door shut with his boot, kissing her so hard she almost stopped breathing.

She couldn't keep her hands off him. She grabbed his shirt and tore it open, popping the buttons. She slid her hands deep into his pants. She wanted to put her whole self inside of him and never come out, never be free. He moaned and bit her shoulder and she shut her eyes, and then he slowly began taking her clothes off, unwrapping her like a treasure.

Suzanne began spending every spare moment she could with Ivan. He was a fever in her blood. As soon as Gary got home, she was out the door. All she could see, all she could think about, was Ivan. She breezed in to see Molly and then as soon as she was in her sister's room, she felt Ivan's hands on her, she smelled the woodsy soap he liked to use, and it drove her crazy. She had just gotten here, but she was dying to leave again. She shifted in her seat. She stood up and sat down again. "So, how you doing today?" she blurted and Molly looked at her curiously.

"Something's different about you," Molly said.

"What? What's different?"

Molly shrugged. "You just seem different, is all."

Suzanne shifted in her seat, got up and sat down.

"You don't have to stay," Molly said.

"No, no, I want to see you." Suzanne couldn't meet Molly's eyes.

"It's okay. I'm feeling a little tired anyway."

"You sure?"

Molly yawned. "Go. You're keeping me awake."

"Nap," Suzanne urged. "I'll sit right here and watch you. Go ahead."

She waited for Molly to sleep. She watched her sister's eyes fluttering, then shutting. Her chest rising and falling with breath, slowing down. *Come on, come on,* Suzanne thought. *Sleep, sleep.* She thought it like a hypnotist. *Sleep.* And then, Molly stilled. "Molly?" Suzanne said softly. No response. "Molly?" Suzanne said again, gently tapping her shoulder. Molly didn't move. Suzanne bolted up. Let Molly think she had been here for three hours instead of ten minutes. Let her tell Gary tomorrow what a shame it was that she had slept through Suzanne's visit. Suzanne grabbed her purse and her jacket and was gone before anyone could stop her.

She knew she was leaving with Ivan before she even dared to say it out loud. Before she even told him. It felt as if an old skin had been peeled from her, as if she could suddenly breathe. What a fool she had been to think she could stop loving him. She felt dizzy with excitement, with things she had to take care of. Otis, for one. "Know any good sitters? Any good, cheap live-in help?" she kept asking her clients. "My friend is looking," she lied.

Nobody knew anything. "I've got expensive, bad live-in help," one client joked.

"I've got an apartment I need to sublet," another said.

Suzanne looked through the ads in the newspaper. She was going to be responsible about this. She was going to do it right. As soon as she had someone good lined up for Otis, she'd tell Gary she was leaving. She'd go and explain it to Molly herself.

The next day, Suzanne was folding Otis's laundry when Ivan showed up. She flung down the laundry and wrapped herself about him, kissing his neck, his shoulder, the side of his face. "Hey! Ow!" he said. "You're attacking my face!"

"Let's go for a drive," she said.

"Let's go to the motel." He kissed her neck.

"No, no—I can't go to the motel now. I've got Otis, remember? I told you that."

He sighed theatrically. "Yeah. You told me."

She pulled back. "I'll just get him ready. We'll take my car because it has the baby seat. We can drive to New York. Maybe go to Central Park. How about that?"

He nodded. She went to get Otis, bundling him into his blue coat, packing his bag, and then she brought him out, presenting him. "Da-duh," she said.

Ivan and Otis blinked at each other. There was something strange in Ivan's smile. "Well, what have we here," he said. He didn't ask to hold Otis. He didn't reach out one hand to touch him. And he quickly looked away. Well, Suzanne thought, maybe it reminded Ivan of his own daughter. Maybe it was painful to see another child when you weren't there with your own.

It took Suzanne a while to put Otis in the car seat. Ivan tapped his finger on the glove compartment, singing a little. "Oh, I was drowning in ree-gret—" His voice looped up. "And you showed up, my safe shore—" He stopped, considering. "You like that line, my safe shore, Suzanne, or do you think I should say something about the rocky shore instead? Maybe rocky is more traumatic-sounding. What do you think?" He paused. "You showed up, my rock-ee shore," he sang. "Which do you like better?"

Suzanne struggled to tighten the buckle. It was stuck and she tugged harder.

"Suzanne?"

"Oh, um, the safe, I guess—" Suzanne said, concentrating on Otis.

"The safe shore? Really? Personally, I think rocky is better."

She nudged at the car seat. "Yeah. Rocky." She was preoccupied with the buckle. She hated that the car seat had to face back. All that drive and she wouldn't even be able to see Otis's pretty face in the rearview mirror. She'd have to rely on any sounds he might make to know how he was doing. It killed her, but at least it was safe.

She took her time driving. She stopped at every intersection, even the ones without stop signs, without a car in sight, because you never knew.

"Anytime you're ready," Ivan kept saying mildly, but she ignored him. She wasn't going to drive crazy. Not with all the kids who were around. She waved other cars in front of her. She let everyone pass her, and every once in a while, even though there was nothing to see, she still looked in the rearview mirror at the back of the car seat. "How you doin', sugar?" she said.

"I'm hungry," he sulked.

She laughed. "Not you. Otis."

"Oh, ex-cuze me."

Once they were in the city, Otis began crying. "Oh, sweetie," Suzanne said, waggling her fingers at him. She dug in his baby bag for a pacifier. "Oh, don't tell me I forgot—" she said. She lifted up on one hip so she could check her pockets.

"I'll do that—" Ivan teased, trying to wedge his fingers in her pocket. She brushed him away.

"We have to stop so I can get him a pacifier."

Ivan sighed and fumbled in his pocket. "I'm out of cigarettes. Can I bum one off you?"

"No way. Not with Otis in the car. And anyway I quit. It's bad for Otis."

Ivan gave her a cool stare that she did her best to ignore. She drove to a Rite Aid and parked on the street. "A parking space! That's a small miracle!" she said.

"He's not the only one who needs a pacifier," Ivan said. "Can you pick me up some Luckies?"

"You're not going to smoke around him."

He rolled his eyes. "Suzanne, you're killing me."

"Leave the radio on, he likes it," Suzanne said. "And there's an extra bottle in his bag if he wants it. And a clean burp cloth if you need it."

"Yes, ma'am." He saluted her.

She wanted to tell him the songs Otis liked, the ones that always calmed him down, especially if you sang them in a silly voice. She wanted to tell him that Otis liked to be tickled, that he liked to hear a voice talking to him, but she stopped herself from saying more. Ivan had a kid. He probably had his own things that he liked to do. So instead, she turned to Otis. "Be a good boy, now. I'll be back in a flash. I'll give both you boys time to get to know each other. Just don't talk about me when I'm not here to defend myself."

"Hurry back," Ivan said.

Suzanne leaped out of the car, running into the store. She ran to the baby aisles like a pro. She knew just what to get. Big white and purple can of Alimentum. She'd better get two cans while she was here. A bright blue pacifier. Maybe two of those, too, because you couldn't have too many the way Otis liked to hurl them into space. It made her smile, just thinking about it. She hightailed it to the checkout, just in time to see the cashier, a young girl with bad skin and a frizzy blond perm, getting all flustered. The cashier held up her hands apologetically. "The machine's jammed," she said in a tight chirpy voice, and Suzanne looked at her watch. Great. She hoped Otis wasn't fussing. She hoped Ivan had pulled out that extra bottle. "Where's the other register?" Suzanne asked.

"What other register?"

Suzanne sighed and looked at her watch again.

The register pinged. The drawer slid open. "Fixed it!" said the cashier, slamming it shut with the flat of her hand. "Next!" Suzanne stepped forward and someone gave her a smart tap on the shoulder. "I was here first," a man said, plunking down a red basket on the counter. He was in an expensive business suit and had on shades inside, which always irritated Suzanne. "I had to exchange a damaged can and I came right back. She knows."

"Like fun you were—" Suzanne said, but the cashier was picking items out of the man's basket, ringing them up. The man gave Suzanne a smug smile that irritated her so much she could have hauled off and whammed him. "Excuse me—" Suzanne said crossly.

"Oh, sorry. I already started the ring-up."

Suzanne waved her hand. Fine. Fine. What did it matter now? But although she knew it was impossible, this girl seemed to be going slower and slower, taking her sweet time counting out the money twice, just to be sure, stapling the receipt to the man's bag slowly, once, twice, three frigging times.

"Okay, now your turn." Unapologetically, the cashier looked at her. Suzanne would have snapped something at her, but she knew how that worked. You made a dig at someone and they took it out on you. You got punished but good. She could be waiting here all day to get the things she needed. She pushed the formula and the pacifiers toward the cashier. She tried to smile pleasantly, while inside she was thinking daggers.

"No bag—" Suzanne reached to stay the cashier's hand.

The cashier looked confused. "But I have to staple the receipt to something—"

"No, no you don't." Suzanne grabbed the cans, the pacifiers, and the receipt.

The cashier blinked at her. "You have a nice day," she said finally.

You eat dirt, thought Suzanne.

She ran out of the store and there was the car, all four doors wide open, just like a mouth telling her something. There were two cops, one of them holding Otis who was screaming, his little face bright red. There was a purple mark on his forehead, like an exotic blooming flower, which made Suzanne stop short. There was glass sparkled all over the street. The side of the car was bashed in. And Ivan was nowhere in sight.

Suzanne looked at Otis in horror. "Oh, my God, is he all right?" Panicked, she reached for Otis and the cop pointedly stepped back from her. Otis screamed louder. "What happened? Who hit the car?" She looked around. "Where's Ivan—the man in the car?"

She tried to reach for Otis and again the cop stepped back. She felt her panic accelerating. "What are you doing! I need to look at him!" She looked wildly around. "What is going on here? Why won't you let me take him?"

"Is this car yours?"

"No, my brother-in-law's, but I—"

"And is the baby yours?" the cop interrupted.

"Yes. No. I'm his aunt. I take care of him." Something cold and damp prickled along Suzanne's spine.

"Where's his parents?"

"His mother's sick in the hospital. His father's visiting her. What's going on here? What's happened?"

He looked at her with disgust, like she was the gum stuck on the bottom of his shoe. "Maybe you should tell me. You leave an infant alone in a locked car with the motor running?"

"What? I didn't do that—he wasn't alone—"

"You got a little sideswiped. Hit and run. Nobody saw anything. You're lucky there wasn't more damage. Even luckier this baby wasn't hurt seriously."

Suzanne's heart jumped. "I want to take Otis to a doctor. Right now." Suzanne tried to sound firm.

"Doesn't look like this car is going anywhere. We can call an ambulance, get the paramedic to take a look at him, but once we do that, you got to take him to a Pediatric ER. Let the doctors there check him out, too."

"Call."

One of the cops went back to the police car. She watched him and then there at the end of the street, she saw Ivan walking toward her, smoking a cigarette. "There!" she said to the cop. "I left Otis with him!"

"Jesus Christ, what's this?" Ivan said when he got there. He frowned, taking another drag before tossing the cigarette. "Who the hell did this?"

"You left him!" Suzanne cried. "There was a car accident! They're calling an ambulance! You left the baby!"

His face changed, working itself into something she didn't recognize. He glared at her. He acted like it was her fault. Otis screamed louder. She looked at the car and then back at him. She tried to imagine such a thing, and then, she felt herself turning desperate. She waited for him to tell her that of course he hadn't done such a thing, he was a father, too, for God's sake, he was responsible. She waited for him to deny it, to make an excuse at least. She looked helplessly at Ivan again and he looked away.

"Endangering the life of a child," the cop said flatly.

Ivan shook his head. "I ran to get cigarettes—I was gone for all of two minutes."

"Ten from when we got here," said one of the cops. "Who knows how long before that."

"Ten?" Suzanne looked at Ivan in astonishment. "Ten minutes?"

Ivan glowered at Suzanne. "For Christ sake, everybody is acting like it's World War III here—look, the kid looks *all right*." He stayed back. He didn't touch Otis. He didn't even look at him, the same way he hadn't back at the house, and suddenly Suzanne felt something uncoiling in her, springing up, sharp as a wire.

She shoved Ivan, so roughly he stumbled. "A car banged into him! They're calling an ambulance!" she screamed.

Ivan stepped away from her. "You"—he angrily pointed at her— "are nuts."

The cop wrote up something on a pad. "What are you doing?" Suzanne said, panicked.

"This goes to Child Protection. They'll be paying you a nice little home visit. Checking for neglect."

"Child Protection! You can't be serious!"

"Do I look like I'm laughing?" the cop said. "Could I have your license?"

Suzanne fumbled in her purse and handed it to him. It unnerved her the way the cop wasn't looking at her, the way he kept writing. She knew what he must think. That she was disgusting. That she didn't care. When the truth was, she cared more than anything. She couldn't swallow. Her breath seemed stuck in her throat.

"When will they come?" Suzanne asked, and the cop shrugged.

"They come unannounced. That's the whole point. And they could keep coming that way for oh—three months, I think it is. Right?" He looked at the other cop.

"Three. Or maybe four," the other cop said.

"No, you're wrong," Suzanne whispered.

"I've seen cases where they even take the kid away." He gave Suzanne her license back. "If there's neglect."

"Give me Otis," Suzanne said. The cop holding Otis looked at her. "Give me the baby." She was practically in tears now, about to hurl herself at his feet and beg him. "Please." Her voice sounded strangled.

He handed her Otis, who burrowed against her. "You be careful," the cop said.

She cradled Otis, talking to him in a low, soothing voice, checking his bruise, his limbs. "It's all right now," she said. "I'm here. We're going to a nice hospital, see a nice doctor, make sure you're okay." She kept talking, repeating the same things over and over, not taking her eyes from him, and when she finally looked up, the ambulance had arrived, and two paramedics jumped out, staring at the car and her and the cops.

Ivan was leaning along the building, his hands in his pockets, staring at her. The paramedics took the baby from Suzanne and opened up the back of the ambulance. "Step on up, ma'am," one said. He held out his hand. He was so sweetly polite to her she felt like crying. The other started talking to the cops, nodding his head, looking right at Suzanne in a way that made her feel shamed. Ivan took a step toward her.

"Don't," she said. Her voice was steel. He stopped. "Don't you come near me." He leaned against a storefront, watching her, his eyes hooded.

She got into the ambulance. She looked straight ahead at Otis, who was screaming, sitting up. His small face was terrified. The paramedics were busy tying him to a small padded chair with bands of white cloth. One across his small chest. One across his legs. One across his feet. "What are you doing?" she said, alarmed. "Don't tie him!"

The paramedic took a strip of white cloth and wrapped it about Otis's head. Otis screamed and looked at Suzanne. "Don't!" Suzanne cried.

"It's for his own good. Keeps his head steady. Just in case. It's not hurting him."

Suzanne leaped up, and the paramedic held up a hand. "Ma'am. We need you to stay in that seat over here. Buckle yourself in. He's not being hurt."

"Where are you taking us?"

"Mt. Sinai."

One of the cops jumped into the ambulance. "We have to come, too," he said.

Mt. Sinai. The same hospital as Molly.

There were three mothers with kids in the Emergency Room, but she was the only woman with a baby who also had a cop beside her. Doctors swirled around her. Any minute she expected one of Molly's doctors to appear, to frown at her and Otis in sudden recognition, to see the cop and then ask pointedly, "What's going on here, exactly?" and she gripped Otis tightly to her. He had stopped crying finally, but his small shoulders shuddered. He sucked in snot. She patted his back, making small constellations with her hand. "You're okay," she promised, but she couldn't help being afraid. Couldn't help wondering, what if he wasn't? What would she do then? She held him tighter to her. She felt her heart beating up against his.

A female doctor in a white lab coat walked toward her and as soon as she saw the cop, she looked at Suzanne differently. "He ever have bruises like this before?" the doctor asked Suzanne pointedly. There was something in the tone of her voice Suzanne couldn't bare.

"It was a car accident," Suzanne said. She tried to make her voice sound firm, controlled.

"I'll take care of the paperwork," the cop said, and left her side, and as soon as he did, Suzanne felt more vulnerable than before.

"He ever have bruises like this?" the doctor repeated. She looked at Otis's eyes.

"No. Of course not."

The doctor looked up at Suzanne with a measured gaze that made Suzanne want to disappear. The doctor checked Otis's signs. She felt his belly, and then she turned to Suzanne. "He looks okay. Just watch him for a few days. Any unusual things, like vomiting or grogginess, you get him back here." Then the doctor dismissed Suzanne, turning from her with a kind of disgust. The doctor looked to another woman holding a child. "Hello," the doctor said, and her voice was so suddenly warm, so richly sympathetic that Suzanne wanted to run over there and start pounding at the doctor's back screaming, *How dare you. How dare you. How dare you.*

She had to call a cab to get home. Had to sit in the backseat with her arms locked about Otis because the seat belts were broken, terrified that any second another accident might happen. She had to call Triple A to tow the car. And then she had to wait for Gary.

All that afternoon, she cried. She sat by Otis's crib while he slept, unable to move. Endangering the life of a child. They were right. It was her fault. Her fault for trusting Ivan. The phone rang and she jumped. She'd have to tell Gary. She'd have to tell Molly. They'd never speak to her again. And the horrible thing was she couldn't blame them. She deserved this, leaving Otis with Ivan.

She cried a little more and then she gave Otis a bath, cried again, stopping only when she thought Otis looked a little sorrowful himself, and then she put him to sleep. The phone rang four times but she didn't pick it up once. She turned off the answering machine. If it was Ivan, he could rot. And if it was Gary, well, she wanted to tell him in person. She didn't deserve the kind of distance the phone could provide. She didn't deserve to hide.

At six, when Gary was due home, she was sitting on the front porch, and when Gary came up the walk, she stood. Her eyes were puffy. Her nose was red.

"What's wrong?" Gary tilted his head and looked at her. "Where's the car?"

"I have something I have to tell you," she said.

For a long while, he didn't say anything, and to Suzanne that was scarier than if he had screamed at her or struck her or hurled her suitcase out the door. Instead, he simply waited until she was finished, and then he slowly stood up. He looked a hundred years old suddenly. He looked at Suzanne as if he didn't know her, as if she were a stranger who had just come into his house and now he didn't want her to touch anything. "I want you out," he said. "I don't care where you go, where you stay. Get a motel room. Stay on the street for all I care. Go with your Ivan. You just get out."

Gary sat in Molly's room. He had cabbed to the hospital. The whole way in he had debated with himself whether or not he should tell her. Would it make her worse? He hadn't been sure what he was going to do, even when he took Otis over to Emma's and begged her to watch him, so upset that Emma didn't say anything, but just took the baby. He hadn't been sure driving to the hospital. Not until he stepped into Molly's room and saw her face and knew that he couldn't lie to her, he couldn't keep secrets anymore.

The whole time he had told Molly, she had stared at him, and by the time Gary finished talking Molly was so furious she swept one arm across her dresser, crashing books to the floor. "You get her out of our house."

"She's gone," Gary said.

That evening, when Gary came back to the house, Otis in his arms, the house was empty. There was no sign of Suzanne. He wandered the rooms. Where were the long black hairs in the tub, the mascara in his office, the glass half filled with now flat soda making rings on the counter? Where was that funny hair color smell, the citrusy perfume of the shampoo she sometimes used? He walked toward Otis's room to get a few things for him. Emma had offered to sit again tonight. "No problem," she said. He wasn't even in the room when he saw it. A clean sheet spread on the floor. Every one of Otis's toys were damp, drying on the sheet. His blankets and drool cloths were neatly folded on his changing table, and a tiny blue pillow that he had never seen before was propped in Otis's crib. Gary sat down with Otis in the rocker and rocked him. He kept his arms tight about him. "Nothing's going to happen to you," he promised. Otis began to rustle in Gary's arms. "I know," Gary said to him. "And I'm so sorry."

Suzanne had no place to go. Not yet. But that didn't mean she was going to stay with Ivan. She had packed all her stuff and left it with a client. There wasn't much. Just a suitcase. Much less than when she'd arrived. She'd left a few things with Ivan in the motel room—things she couldn't afford to just let go. She looked at her watch. Would he be there or not, and what did that matter to her now? She could whisk in and whisk out, and that would be that. She remembered her one client who had the sublet. Suzanne could move in tonight. She had some money saved now. She had work.

She let herself into the motel room. Ivan was sitting on the bed watching an old black-and-white movie on TV. He snapped it off as soon as he saw her. He sprang to his feet. "I've been going crazy waiting for you." He stood up, awkwardly smiling, and for a moment, she felt the old pull. All she'd have to do is let him touch her and she'd be lost. She'd believe anything.

"Feels like Alaska in here all of a sudden. You still pissed at me?" he said.

Suzanne ignored him. She opened a drawer and pulled out her sweater, her good sunglasses, her good wool pants. He cocked his head, watching her quizzically. "What are you doing?"

Suzanne turned to look at him. At one time, it used to almost hurt her to look at him. She had fallen in love with him the first second she had laid eyes on him and he was still the handsomest man she had ever seen in her life. "I'm not going away with you."

"Don't be like that. Don't keep punishing me. I can only take so long off from work."

"I'm not punishing you. And I didn't mean I wanted you to stay with me." Suzanne was exhausted. "I want you to go back to California or wherever else you're going. Without me."

Ivan tried to touch her, but Suzanne pulled back. "No," she said.

Ivan blew out a breath. He leaned against the bureau, watching her. "Come on," he said quietly. "Don't do this. Is it the kid? You want me to apologize about the kid again, I'll apologize. But he's *fine*. You want to get mad at someone, go get mad at the son of a bitch who rammed your car, who hit and run and didn't look back. That's whose fault this really is. That's who's the terrible person. You scared about those cops? They were just blowing smoke at you. They walk away from robberies, you think they're going to go after this? You think they're really going to call that agency? Believe me. I dealt with an ex-wife. I know how these things work and it's all smoke screens and mumbo jumbo to get you good and scared so you'll toe the line."

"I am scared." Suzanne bent down to make sure she hadn't left anything under the bed. She found a pair of shoes and pulled them out, and then stood up again. "You didn't even ask how he made out at the hospital. If he's all right."

Ivan looked impatient. "Okay. How did he make out?"

She shook her head. "He's fine," she said curtly.

"How long are you going to hang me out to dry over this, Suzanne?

You want me to admit I fucked up? Okay, I fucked up. Now can we just get past this? The kid is fine. You just told me so. God, you didn't used to hold a grudge like this. It's not good for you, Suzanne. It's not good for us."

Suzanne got on her jacket from the closet. "His name is Otis," she said. "And it's not just him." She slung her bag over one shoulder. She looked at him. "What's Ann's favorite toy? What's her favorite bedtime story?"

Ivan stared at her. "What is this? Why are we talking about Ann?"

"I'm talking about her. Your daughter. You never do. Do you have a picture of Ann? What's her favorite food? What's her favorite TV show? You don't know, do you?"

"I know you." Ivan's voice was quieter than she had ever heard it. "And I know you don't really want to do this. You and me. We're the same person. All these years. You couldn't stop loving me now. No matter what I did. What you *think* I did."

"You don't know me."

"Oh, no?" He got a strange smile on his face. "Aren't you the woman I'm going to marry—the woman I should have married back when we were seventeen? Aren't you my muse?"

"You're not listening to me."

"You want to live in Jersey? Hell, I don't care. We'll live in stinking Jersey. You want to have a kid? Okay, we'll have a kid."

"I don't want a kid with you. You don't even carry a picture of your own daughter. You never talk about her. At first I thought it was because it hurt you not to be with her, but now I think it's because you don't care. I bet you don't call her, either. You don't know the first thing about her, and she's your own flesh and blood."

He reached for her and she shoved him away.

"I'm so stupid," Suzanne said. "Screw me for not paying attention to how you treat the people who love you. Screw me for not seeing how you don't love anyone back, except maybe yourself. Screw me and screw you."

"What is with you? What is it you want?" he said.

Suzanne put her hand on the doorknob, turning it. "I know what it is about you, now. You're right. I do know you. I know you can't stand to be alone. You never could. I had to come with you to every gig. You couldn't go to sleep unless I was there in the bed with you. We were always together, but it had nothing to do with love. It didn't then and it doesn't now. You have to have an audience. That's why you married Patty, I bet. And that's why you went to find me. You don't really see people, do you? You don't really care."

"Suzanne, it worries me when you talk crazy like this. Maybe you should just calm down a bit. You want me to go out and get you something? Hot tea? A drink of something?"

"You don't know the first thing about me. I only thought you did." Suzanne opened the door.

"No, it's not good-bye." Ivan's voice got quieter and quieter. "You'll call me. You always do. I know you'll call me. You could never stop loving me, no matter what I did," and then Suzanne walked out of the room, shutting the door quietly behind her.

Suzanne stopped at the pay phone to call her client who had said she had an apartment to unload. She was so drained, she leaned her head against the phone. She shut her eyes. "If you like it, you can take over the lease," her client told her.

Suzanne saw the apartment a half hour later. It was the worst apartment she had ever seen, maybe even worse than ones she had had in California. One big dark and musty room with a slanted floor. The one window in it was small and it looked out on a parking lot. She heard a sneeze, as loudly as if it were right in front of her.

"Tissue-paper walls," her client said apologetically. "The neighbor had allergies, but the bright side is they're seasonal."

Suzanne looked around. She didn't have much choice, or much time. There was enough space for a small single bed, a table, a chair for her work. Well, what else did she need? It was available immediately and it was so cheap even she could afford it.

"I'll take it," Suzanne said. "I'm moving in right now."

The woman gave her an odd look. "Well, I guess you can do that. It's your place," she said cheerfully and handed Suzanne the key.

After the woman left, Suzanne sat on her floor and tried to think what to do next. She couldn't stop thinking about Otis, about Molly. Already she missed Otis so much she thought she was going through withdrawal. What could she have been thinking to think she could leave with Ivan and not look back? She kept thinking she heard Otis crying. She kept feeling Otis's breath, warm and sweet and soft as a cat's. Who was watching him? Who knew him better than she did? Who spent more time with him? Did they know what songs he liked to hear? Did they know he liked to be burped on the left shoulder and not the right, that he didn't like strained peaches, but apricots were okay? She had been thrown out of Gary's and Molly's lives for jeopardizing Otis, and maybe she could understand that, maybe she would have flown off the handle the same way, but the bottom line was she loved that kid. He loved her. And she couldn't do without him.

She looked at the corner of the room. The Portacrib might fit there. She looked at the tiny kitchen, with the tiny stove. It still could boil Otis's bottles. No matter where she looked, she thought of Otis. She swore she heard him in the room.

Suzanne stood up heavily. She couldn't stand it. She didn't have a phone yet, so she walked outside, two blocks to the pay phone. She rested her head against the silver phone and dialed.

The line rang three times. She tried to slow her breathing, to ease up her grip on the phone. *Please,* she thought. *Just let me get a word in edgewise.*

"Hello?" said Gary. His voice sounded tense, exhausted. In the background, she heard Otis crying, which made her grip the receiver tighter.

"Please. I told him to go, to never come back. Can I just come over and explain? Can I just see Otis?"

Gary hung up the phone. Static popped and fizzed in her ear.

*   *   *

She knew Gary wouldn't let her see Otis, but he couldn't keep her from walking in the neighborhood, from seeing the baby by accident. *Accident,* she thought. *Accident.*

Accident. It hummed in her mind. Every day, she took her time. Every time she saw a blue stroller, she dashed over, checking to see if Otis was inside it, but it was always a baby she didn't know at all. A mother who would look at her curiously, and then Suzanne would have to retreat. She kept thinking maybe she could run into him and his new caretaker, she could explain and the woman would let her just hold him. "It'll be our little secret," she might say.

She was even desperate enough to think she might appeal to Molly. They were sisters, after all. They would always be sisters, no matter what. You couldn't change that. She used to be able to talk Molly into anything—even forgiveness. But as soon as she got to Molly's floor, she felt a chill. She got halfway into the door when Molly rang for the nurse. "Get out," Molly said.

"If you want to see me, I'll be in the solarium." Suzanne's voice seemed a wisp. "Every day. From ten to two. Just so you know."

"With Ivan."

"I'm not with Ivan anymore."

"Until when?" Molly asked wearily. "Why did you even come here in the first place? What was it? Money? A place to live? To hide out? It wasn't for me, was it." She lay back on the pillow.

"It was for you," Suzanne whispered.

Molly shook her head. "Just go already. I'm tired."

A nurse came in. "Something you need?" she said.

"This visitor's disturbing me," Molly said. "Don't let her in here again—"

The nurse put one hand on Suzanne's back. "Please," she said, and Suzanne turned around. "Ten to two—" Suzanne said quietly. "And I did come for you."

Suzanne sat in the solarium for hours at a time, nursing hot tea, reading magazines, waiting. Every time a nurse came in, she felt a spark of hope, but the nurse never came for her. She didn't dare go back to Molly's room, but some days she simply stood out in the hall by the elevators waiting for Gary. When he saw her, his face set. "She doesn't want you here. She told you that. I'm telling you that. We don't want to see you. Just go back to California. Go back to Ivan."

"Ivan's gone. I told him to go."

"Good. You go, too." He turned away from her.

"I'm not going anywhere!" Suzanne screamed after him. "I'm here every day!" She shouted so loudly a nurse came over to shush her.

It made Suzanne crazy not to see the baby. She kept walking Molly's neighborhood trying to catch a glimpse of him. She walked and she walked until her feet hurt, but she never once saw anyone. She never even saw a curtain flutter.

Not seeing Ivan was a different matter. For a while, she braced herself every time the phone or the doorbell rang. She half expected to see him following her. And it was strange. She expected to feel more wrung-out about all of it, but instead what she felt was this odd kind of relief, almost like closing a book she had loved and read and now was finished with. Ivan didn't really love anyone. He ran out on her. He ran out on his wife. And he ran out on his little girl.

It was only sometimes, late at night, when she did think about him, and then it hurt. But the Ivan she thought about then was the boy she had fallen in love with at fifteen, the rocker who held her in his arms and made her feel like she was worth something, like she was special. The boy who sang to her and told her she was his only one forever. And that Ivan had been gone a long time ago. And so had that Suzanne.

She began coming to the hospital at different times, hoping to catch Otis there.

She had no pride. She didn't care that the nurses saw her sitting in the solarium every day, not moving, completely alone.

*   *   *

Gary was trying to stop Otis from crying. Otis was shrieking and carrying on, flailing his arms and legs, and nothing Gary was doing seemed to help. Gary tried the bottle and Otis batted it away. He checked the baby's diaper and gave him a bath and even put on music, and still Otis wailed. "What's wrong?" he kept asking, and Otis kept crying. "Think of how I feel," Gary coaxed.

Gary had a lot to do today, too. He had the names of three women who might work as baby nurses, though Emma, thank God, had told him not to worry, that she would be more than happy to watch Otis. Theresa had piped in, saying she'd be happy to help out, too. "Just ask," she said. He had to go food shopping and do a wash and clean the house a bit, it was such a pigsty. He looked like hell himself. He was wearing the same flannel shirt and jeans he had been wearing for two days. He hadn't even taken a shower, let alone shaved, and he knew without even looking in the mirror that there were big dark circles under his eyes, like bruises. How had Suzanne managed? How did anyone? The doorbell rang, and Otis screamed louder and Gary cursed, peeking out the window. No one was there. Already this morning, a messenger had come by, carrying a small red thermos. "What's this?" Gary said, looking at the thermos.

He opened the note. *I got you Holy Water! Don't even ask how I did it! Love and kisses, Ada.* Gary sighed and rolled his eyes. Ada. She meant well but this was too much. He had taken the thermos and tossed it right in the trash, and then two minutes later, he fished it out again. Well. You never knew. He was just about to try to figure out some lunch when the phone rang. "You got it?" Ada said.

"Thanks." He was too exhausted to explain.

"Listen, Gary. I have something else to tell you but I have to whisper because I don't want to get caught—"

"Ada, I'm really busy—"

Her voice singsonged. "Guess who's getting fired because he sent his girlfriend a top-of-the-line computer setup that belonged to the company? Guess who racked up a long-distance phone bill so high he was hauled into the head honcho's office and dragged over the coals for it? And guess whose girlfriend, when asked if he could come out there and live with her while he tried to start fresh, said thanks but no thanks, she liked things the way they were?"

Gary was surprised how blank he felt. He didn't care anymore about what Brian had or hadn't done to him. It didn't matter anymore.

"And guess who management's talking about taking his job? Go on, guess."

"Ada, I don't know—"

"You—" Ada said breathlessly. "They're talking about you!"

"Me? They fired me!"

"No, they didn't fire you, Gary. Brian did. I didn't want to tell you, you had so much on your plate, but you wouldn't believe the things he was saying about you. That all your ideas were his. That you were lazy. That they were better off without you. Ha. Things have been hitting the fan since you left. He hasn't been able to produce a thing and everyone knows it's because you're gone and he can't steal your ideas anymore."

"What?" Gary felt amazed.

"His job, Gary. I bet you can have his job."

Gary tried to think straight. "No. That can't be right. And anyway, how can I work now?"

Ada's voice turned even more conspiratorial. "Gary, I'm like this little fly on the wall. No one notices me half the time because I'm a secretary, but I see things. I hear things. You don't know what they're willing to do to get you back. You could tell them three days a week to start and they'd go for it, I bet. Things are shit here! Everything's crazy. Brian really fucked up but good. They're going to call you. I heard them talking. And you take the job and then get me as your secretary and give me a nice raise. Now how about that?"

Gary felt suddenly light-headed. Brian's job. They could have money in the bank. Paid health insurance, not that COBRA shit. And even if he only had the job for half a year, it would be impressive enough so he could quit and freelance anywhere he wanted. "I don't know. Maybe," he said. "Maybe I just will take it."

"Atta boy," Ada cheered.

He hung up. He felt better. Now he'd take his shower. Maybe he'd make some lunch. Call Molly. Maybe things were turning around.

The doorbell rang again. It had better not be Suzanne.

He pulled open the door. A prim-faced young woman in a nondescript blue dress, carrying a clipboard, nodded at him. He was used to this. People canvassing for city council or school board or God knows what else. People wanting you to contribute money to causes he had never heard of. He'd cut her off before she could even open her mouth. "This is a bad time—" he said curtly, but the woman shook her head.

"Gary Breyer?" she said, and he nodded. How'd she know who he was?

"I'm Tonette Thomson, the caseworker assigned to your file and this is an unannounced home visit. As you probably know, a complaint has been filed against you and I'm here to speak with you and visit with Otis in his home." Her voice was formal, stiff.

Gary felt as if he had been struck. His case. A complaint. He couldn't move. He was suddenly super aware of his dirty clothes, his matted hair; his growth of beard suddenly itched. And, of course, Otis was wailing.

"State law requires that you have to let me in to check Otis's safety," Tonette said quietly.

Gary abruptly stepped back, trying to soothe Otis. He saw suddenly the way Tonette was looking at him, taking him in, narrowing, as if she were looking for fault. She stared at Otis so long, and with such concern, that Gary felt suddenly scared. "He isn't usually like this—" Gary said quickly.

"I'm sure he's not," Tonette said, but she looked at him and frowned. She came into the house, looking around. "You understand the seriousness of the allegation? Leaving a child unattended in a locked car? And then with the accident? He suffered—" She flipped through some paper on her clipboard and then frowned. "Contusions," she said finally. "Head abrasions." She shook her head, scolding him. "Tsk," she said.

"My sister-in-law was caring for him that day. She's not caring for him anymore."

Tonette nodded, but she didn't look less disturbed. "And who is caring for Otis while you're at work? Who do you leave him with?"

"Next door. A neighbor. She's raised a daughter."

Tonette seemed to shift gears. "Let's start in the kitchen," she said pleasantly. Otis snuffled and cried louder. Tonette opened the refrigerator and peered in.

"I was just about to go shopping today," Gary said desperately.

She checked the sides of every carton of yogurt. "Expiration dates," she said. She opened the covered bowls and sniffed. She opened cabinets and looked in the dishwasher and held up the cans of formula and then she took out her notebook and wrote something.

"What did you write?" Gary said, terrified. "Is something wrong?"

She looked around. Her mouth pursed into a line. "And the child's bedroom is where?" she said.

Gary led her into Otis's room. He couldn't stand the way she opened Otis's drawers, making them squeak, the way she lifted up his tiny jerseys and studied them, and he couldn't figure out why. He hated when she looked into the crib, when she even checked the wastebasket full of dirty diapers Gary hadn't had time to toss out. "I'm on my own here," he blurted.

Tonette kept moving about the room. She looked at the shelf of baby books and CDs, at the toys, and then she looked at Gary. "I'll take him," she said, and he tightened his grip. "No," he said.

"I just want to take a look at him."

"He'll cry more," Gary said, desperately, but Tonette came toward him and as soon as she reached for Otis, to Gary's shock, Otis stopped crying altogether. The baby blinked and stared gravely at Tonette. Otis let her pick him up.

Tonette lay Otis on the changing table. It bothered Gary the way Tonette didn't even talk to Otis, the way Otis was so suddenly silent. She unsnapped his duck-printed coverall. She opened his diaper and studied him, for what seemed to Gary to be an eternity.

"Is that necessary?" Gary asked, pained.

"Yes, as a matter of fact, it is." Tonette studied Otis's arms and legs. She turned him on his belly and checked his back and then turned him over again.

"Everything looks fine, right?" said Gary.

Tonette began dressing Otis up again, putting his diaper back on, snapping up the coverall, and handing the baby back to Gary.

"Will there be another visit?" Gary asked.

"I can't tell you that. And if there is, it's unannounced. Just as this one was. I can tell you that we leave your file open for three months."

My file. Gary couldn't stand it.

"My wife is ill in the hospital. I hope you're not planning on talking to her."

"Well, I'll have to at some point."

"Please. She needs to stay calm. She's just starting to get better—"

Tonette wrote something on a new piece of paper. "You might want to consider taking a parenting class," she said. She handed him the paper. "This one is very good." She put the cap on her pen and tucked it away in her purse.

Gary was so upset, he could barely speak. A parenting class. Just as if he was the one who had left Otis alone in the car, who had let something bad happen to him. And in a way he had. He had left him with Suzanne.

Gary showed Tonette to the door. She held out her hand to him. "This has been most informative," she said. He wanted to kill Tonette. He could have put both his hands about her neck and snapped it in two. Instead, he shook her hand. He opened the door, he let her out, but he couldn't bring himself to say good-bye, to show the least courtesy to a woman who was barging into his home like this, looking at him as if he had committed murder and she would like to be the one to pull the switch on his electric chair. He double-locked the door.

Gary took Otis and sat in the chair, away from the window. He was lost. He couldn't protect his wife. And now he couldn't protect his son. And he would have to live with both those unlivable things.

*   *   *

That evening at work, Gary couldn't concentrate. He sat at the desk and stared at the four walls and if someone had broken in, he would have let them take everything, and welcome to it. He didn't even bother to turn on the radio.

Marty came around the corner, leaning on the electric broom, a Danish in one hand. He looked as terrible as Gary did. Unshaven. His hair matted. His face glum.

"You look like shit," Gary said matter-of-factly.

"Yeah, well."

Marty turned off the broom and sat beside Gary. "I feel like shit." He waved the Danish in the air. "It came today. My rejection from film school. No explanation, no try again, no we think you're talented anyway. A fucking form letter." He sighed. "I'm getting so tired of all this. It's like you work and work and hope for something. You do everything you can and it all just doesn't happen. Making films is what I've wanted all my life. It *is* my life. I do everything I can to have it and I can't figure out why I can't have it. I can't figure out what I'm going to do now."

Gary looked at Marty. "Sometimes it's really tough," Gary said, his voice so swallowed, Marty looked up.

"What did you say?" Marty asked. He studied Gary. "Hey, what is it? You don't look so hot yourself."

"My wife is in the hospital. My baby was in an accident. A social worker came by today to see if there were grounds to take my baby away from me."

Marty leaped up. "Oh, *fuck* me. Jesus, I'm sorry. Why didn't you tell me? Here I am going on and on like some moron—"

"I know film's your life," Gary said, "My family was my life. Now I can barely get myself up in the morning."

Marty blinked and was silent. And then he suddenly held out the Danish to Gary. "It's cherry. My favorite," he said. "Go ahead. Take it. Please. I want you to."

Gary wasn't hungry but he took the pastry. "Take a bite," Marty urged. Gary bit into it. It was sweet and sugary and delicious. He chewed and then Marty awkwardly put one hand on his shoulder.

"You need anything, you let me know," Marty said.

* * *

Molly was watching an old movie on the television when Gary came in for his visit the next day. She clicked off the TV, smiling faintly at him, waiting for his kiss.

"*She's* not here today, is she?" Molly asked. She couldn't bring herself to even say Suzanne's name.

"I told her to leave. I tell her that every day."

Molly lay still. Suzanne was right outside, staying for hours even when no one would see her or even talk to her.

Gary took Molly's hand. "The case worker showed up yesterday. It was awful, Molly."

"They came to the house?"

"She looked at all the rooms. She went through the kitchen. She even looked at expiration dates on the cans. And she looked at Otis." He swallowed. "She took off his diaper."

Molly shut her eyes for a moment. "What did she say?"

"That's the whole thing. She said nothing. She might come back or she might not. I couldn't tell anything. She said she has to talk with you."

"I could murder Suzanne," Molly said.

"The house was a wreck, Molly. I wasn't even really dressed. There wasn't all that much food in the house. I hadn't time. I wasn't prepared." He looked helplessly at her. "I'm so sorry."

Molly shook her head. "You have nothing to be sorry about."

"Maybe it won't be a problem. Maybe this is it."

They sat silently for a while. "Is anyone lined up to take care of Otis?" Molly asked.

"I'm working on it. Emma and Theresa offered. Even Belle, though I don't know if I trust her." Gary shrugged. "Maybe I can afford a cheap nurse."

Gary stood up. "Hey," he said cheerfully. "Who knows? Maybe you'll be home soon and we won't have to worry about it at all. Right?"

Molly tried to smile. He bent and kissed her. "Come on, chin up," he coaxed.

"Right," she said, smiling, struggling to look optimistic.

As soon as Gary was gone, Molly sank, terrified, into the bed. She looked at the hospital walls, at the brown-and-orange-striped curtain surrounding her bed. It was all sickeningly familiar. Sickeningly safe. Sickeningly known right down to the whole horrible routine. Outside suddenly seemed more dangerous than anything inside. What would she do if they took Otis away? It didn't seem likely but unlikely things happened all the time. Hadn't she read about birth mothers who came back to claim their kids from adoptive families four years after the adoption, and they won? Who would ever think that was reasonable? What would she do then? And even if that didn't happen, there was still another problem: Who *would* take care of Otis? She couldn't stand it. She tried to sit up and felt instantly woozy. She lay back on the pillow and her IV machine beeped and then was silent. Even with the neighbor's help, there were bound to be times when no one was available, when Gary had to work. And even if she ever did get home, she didn't have a clue how to care for Otis herself. She could barely lift her water pitcher, let alone a baby.

Molly and Gary and Otis were in the solarium. Mornings almost no one was ever there. Suzanne never came until the afternoon, and they had the whole place to themselves. Molly held Otis gently on her lap. He stared up at her, batting at the tag ends of her hair with his fingers.

"Look how he can't take his eyes off you," Gary said.

"I think he likes me."

"Come on, what are you saying! Of course he does!"

Molly was tickling Otis's chin when he suddenly began babbling and kicking his legs. She looked up and there was Suzanne, in an awful red coat and sneakers, standing in the doorway, waiting, like a specter that wouldn't go away.

Gary stood up.

"Please," Suzanne said. "Just let me see Otis. Just for a minute."

"Just go," Molly said wearily, and then Otis suddenly began babbling. Molly looked down at him. Otis smiled and waved his hands;

he kicked out his legs. He was looking right at Suzanne. Molly took a second look, too. She saw Suzanne's red-rimmed eyes, the circles under them like stains. She saw how Suzanne had even misbuttoned her blouse.

"Please." Suzanne started to cry, swiping at her eyes. "I love him."

Molly studied her sister's face. She always knew when Suzanne was lying, which was nine times out of ten, but this time, she wasn't.

"I can't stand not seeing him," Suzanne wept. "Tell me what you want me to do and I'll do it. I'll apologize five hundred times. If I could take back that day and do it differently, I swear to God, I would. I don't know what else to do."

Otis made a burbling noise. He kept looking at Suzanne, veering his body toward her. "All right," Molly said finally. "You can see him."

Suzanne came into the room. The closer she got to Otis, the more he squealed with delight. She bent and crouched down beside Otis. She tapped Otis's nose, making him laugh. "How you doing, champ," she cried. "You okay? I missed you so much." Otis grabbed for her finger and popped it into his mouth. He sighed and shut his eyes.

Molly watched her sister and Otis together. Otis didn't act like that with her. He didn't strain to reach her; he didn't light up like that.

Suzanne bent and showered Otis's whole face with little nipping kisses. Otis laughed.

"Well, maybe you can hold him."

"Really?" Suzanne carefully picked up Otis. She cuddled him and rocked him and kissed his hands and face.

"Give him back now," Molly said, and Suzanne settled Otis into Molly's lap.

"Thank you," Suzanne whispered. "Thank you, thank you."

Molly tickled Otis's stomach.

"I'm staying. I got an apartment."

"For how long?" Molly finally said.

"I want to be near you and Otis. Like family."

Molly was silent for a minute, considering. She suddenly felt more tired than she ever had before. She could barely move her mouth to say anything, even if she knew what to say. She couldn't think anymore what was the right thing and what wasn't.

"You look exhausted," Gary said to Molly. "Let's get you back to bed." He looked around. "I'll get a nurse."

Molly shook her head. She looked at Suzanne again, standing there, waiting. "Suzanne can take me. I need to talk to her, anyway."

Gary gently lifted up Otis. He kissed Molly. "I think that's a good idea," he said.

Molly tried to get comfortable in bed and then gave up. She bunched a pillow by her back. She kicked at the sheets. Suzanne pulled a chair close and sat down.

"You've been coming every day," Molly said.

Suzanne nodded.

"Ivan really left?"

Suzanne made a zipping sound. "Gone. I threw him out this time." She leaned closer to Molly. "Molly, I know I fucked up."

"Otis was in your care. Not Ivan's."

"I know. Don't you think I think about that all the time? You can't say anything to me that I don't say to myself. But, Molly, I love you. I love Otis. And I'm not running away."

"You hate New Jersey."

"I hated it when I was unhappy. When I felt like I had nothing here."

Molly was silent for a moment. Suzanne picked up the ends of Molly's hair and started smoothing them with her fingers. Molly recoiled.

"Oh, don't—" Molly said, trying to move away. Threads of hair drifted onto Suzanne's hands. Suzanne stared down at them and then looked back quizzically at Molly.

"My hair is falling out!" Molly cried. "It's all the drugs. I just touch it and handfuls come out." She rubbed at her eyes.

"I can fix it, Molly. I can cut it a little, make it look fuller."

"You can?"

"Sure I can. That's what I do for a living. You sleep and when you wake up, we'll make you gorgeous. They must have a scissors in this joint."

Molly slid down in the bed. "These beds. I think their motto is if we're comfortable they must be doing something wrong." Her eyes dropped shut, she yawned. Through half-closed lids, she saw Suzanne starting to stand, to gather her things.

"Don't go, Suzanne."

Suzanne sat back down. She leaned in toward Molly. Molly touched Suzanne's hair. She began combing it out with her fingers, the way she used to when she was a little girl, when she had to stand on a kitchen stool just to reach.

"I'm not going anywhere," Suzanne said.

Suzanne, in overalls and T-shirt, her hair in a scarf, was perched on a ladder, roller in hand, finishing painting the walls of her apartment. Pale, creamy peach. Soft and refreshing. She had paint all over her overalls and all over the newspaper she had spread on the floor. Peach color speckled on her hands like freckles. Next door, the man with allergies was sneezing, but she didn't really mind. There was almost something companionable about it.

She surveyed the studio. There was still lots she wanted to do. She wanted to sand down the floor, give it a sheen. Those ugly brown cabinets in the kitchen would have to go. Maybe she could paint them. Or strip them down, give them some kind of finish. And photos. She wanted to hang photos. Sort of like Molly's photo gallery, but her own. A big picture of Otis would look great right over there by the window.

She ran the roller up the wall again. She felt content and happy, and she started to sing. "You Shoot Me Down," she sang, and then she realized, with a start, it was Ivan's song. The first song he had ever sung for her, a song he said he had made up for her. Well. So what? It was pretty. It was just a song now. It didn't have to mean a damn thing. She could put her own meaning into it. She eased the roller over the last bare spot on the south wall when the door-bell rang.

Suzanne hopped off the ladder. She hoped it was the super come to fix her leaky toilet. She wiped her hands on her jeans and there was Bob Tillman, a potted green plant in his hand, smiling at her. "Heard you had moved. Brought you a homecoming gift."

She took the plant, pleased.

Bob Tillman cleared his throat. She noticed suddenly he had on a shirt instead of his usual T-shirt, that even his jeans looked pressed. "Come in." She swept her hand. "So, what do you think?"

"The peach is peachy."

She laughed.

Bob smiled at her. "You need any shelving, or a table. You come see me. I'll give you a nice discount." He waited and then put his hands awkwardly in his pockets. "Can I take you to dinner?" he said abruptly. The way he was looking at her made her suddenly self-conscious. Her mind hadn't been on anything but getting her apart-ment in shape.

"I guess that's a no—" Bob Tillman shrugged matter-of-factly.

"No—no—" Suzanne lifted up her hands. "It's just—it's just that I haven't been thinking about that." She looked around the apartment. "This is the first time in my life I've ever lived alone and wanted to. I kind of want to see what that's like." She hesitated. "You're a nice man."

Bob Tillman winced. "The kiss of death! Nice!"

"Well, you are."

"Well, at least you didn't say no. At least it sounds like maybe there's hope."

Suzanne smiled at him.

"So can we go out to dinner once in a while? See a movie?"

"I don't know. Maybe as friends, we can."

"As friends."

"Call me and we'll see."

He stood up. "I like the way you look now."

She looked down at herself, surprised. "Like this? I have paint on my clothes, I haven't washed my hair, and I don't have makeup on."

"I like it."

Suzanne showed Bob to the door. "So, I'll see you," he said cheerfully. "*Friend.*"

She shut the door and turned back to look at the paint job. There, over on the far wall, was a tiny spot she had missed. Humming, she got back on the ladder and carefully filled it in.

Molly lay in bed fiddling with her lunch. She had asked for fish, and here was baked macaroni and cheese and Jell-O. She was just about to call Gary, to ask him if he could bring her something from the Kiev, when Dr. Price came in. He frowned.

Molly slid lower onto the bed.

"Well," he said heavily. "You still are not well. Not by a long shot."

Molly braced herself.

His face seemed to grow darker. "The clotting inhibitor is still in your blood. We'll up the steroids you're getting. We'll watch the inhibitor levels even more closely. If they don't keep going down, we might want to try chemo again."

At the word *chemo,* Molly sank lower in the bed. She pulled the sheets up to her chin.

"I didn't say we'd do the chemo now. For now, you need a great deal of rest."

Molly shut her eyes. Still the hospital.

"But perhaps you can do your resting at home."

Molly opened her eyes. She looked up at him, stunned. He gave her a faint smile. Molly swallowed. She found her voice. "Are you serious?" she said.

"You have to stay in bed. You have to take your meds. You have to get a home nurse for yourself to come in and check on you every single day, twice a day, without fail. And you have to come in and see me three times a week for blood tests. In a wheelchair. No walking. No real movements. Nothing that could cause an accident. No lifting. No cutting with knives. Nothing that could make you bleed. And you must promise to call if you feel anything unusual. Immediately."

"Am I getting cured?"

He was silent for a moment. "Let's just leave it up to rest and luck, shall we?"

Luck. Molly hesitated. "Am I getting cured?" she repeated.

He shrugged. He waited a moment. "We don't know," he said finally.

Molly swallowed. She couldn't let it go. "But wait, wait, if I *am* getting better, then is that it for the inhibitor? Does it mean that once it's out of my system, my blood is normal again, does it mean I can never get the inhibitor again?"

Dr. Price put his hands in his pockets. He studied her for a moment. "We don't know," he said finally. "We don't really know what causes it, and we don't really know what makes it leave. Only that it sometimes does."

After Dr. Price left, she couldn't move. Molly looked at the walls of the hospital room. *We don't know.* Could she live with that? *We don't know.* She thought of going home. She thought of all those months she had been at the hospital, nearly as helpless as a newborn. Then she thought of what it would be like when she was home with the baby. Suddenly, she was terrified. Her body felt like a tire with the wrong amount of air filled into it. If she even pricked her finger, she could be in danger. She could die. Nowhere felt safe to her. No one knew what was going to happen. Except that she was going home.

She thought suddenly of all those people she had read about who had supposedly had near-death experiences, who had seen white lights, long tunnels, been transformed. Molly didn't remember seeing anything. The memory blockers had taken care of that. Had she been transformed? Did she have a new insight? Only her body felt different. The rest she'd have to live to find out. And then she reached for the phone to call Gary.

* * *

Gary hung up the phone with Molly. He went into Otis's room, even though he had just put Otis down for a nap, and picked him up and held him while he cried and cried and cried.

That evening, Gary walked around the neighborhood, Otis strapped against his chest. This was family, an extra heartbeat strapped against him. Lights began going on in the neighborhood. Doors began slapping open, cars came home. Otis yawned and snuggled deeper against him. He thought about Molly coming home. Ada would have said it was destiny. That it was fate. But to him, it seemed that Molly's coming home was as much a fluke as her getting sick. As mysterious and open-ended. She still had the inhibitor. She still was in danger. He could make himself crazy thinking about it. He didn't really believe that things were meant to be, that fate might come through for you. Events didn't turn out the way you always hoped they would. But the thing was that sometimes people came through. The most unexpected people in the most unexpected ways.

It was fall again in the neighborhood. A clear and cold Halloween. Paper ghosts flung themselves off the rooftops. Pumpkins grinned from porches. The streets were crowded with kids and parents, and everyone was dressed up in shiny store-bought costumes, in elaborate handmade outfits. Ghost and goblins, pizzas and refrigerators all wound their way in the annual Halloween parade. Girls in skimpy red uniforms high-kicked their way down the street. The mayor waved ferociously from a car.

Right in the thick of the parade, Molly clung to Gary's arm. She took baby steps down the street, stopping to rest every few minutes, bracing her hands against Otis's stroller. Each step felt awkward, like she had doll feet that any moment might not support her.

This walking business was still new to her. This was the first time she could walk more than a block, and already she felt drained. Her doctors wanted her to walk a little more now, but they still cautioned her, a catch-22. Too little activity, and her muscles would atrophy. Too much and she could tear a muscle. A tear could bleed. A bleed could hemorrhage. She had to think about how she moved, find the happy medium. One foot lifted, planted down and lifted again. But she was determined. Danger or not, she was going to walk this parade with her family. "You want to sit?" Gary asked. He had painted blue stars on his face and Molly's. Otis, in the stroller, had on a mini Harley jacket and shades. Her weight on the stroller knocked it a little and Otis cried. She reached to soothe him and he twisted, ignoring her, looking for Gary, not calming until he saw him. "All right, all right," Gary said. Stung, Molly retracted her hand.

Gary looked at her and ruffled her hair, which had started to grow back in curly tufts. Just last week, when the tufts were poking through her old ruined hair, Suzanne had talked her into a short, wild cut, a boost of color. "Live a little," she said. Molly had never had short hair in her life, had always hated it, and the whole time Suzanne cut it, she had kept her eyes squinched shut. Suzanne worked quickly and efficiently. She kept up a patter of talk. She put on music. But Molly cried as if even the sound and slide of the scissors hurt her. But now, all she knew was she could tilt her head and not feel like people were staring at her hair. Her head felt impossibly light. She could feel almost normal. Gary toyed with her earrings, big complicated tin pieces Suzanne had surprised her with, so she wouldn't feel so shorn. "Want to keep going?"

All Molly wanted to do was go home. "Sure I do," she lied, trying to sound jubilant. "This is great!" She didn't tell him she felt more than a little lost. There were too many people here, and she didn't know any of them. She didn't recognize a few of the stores on the street, either. Had things changed so fast? When had that Italian restaurant opened up? Where was the pastry shop she used to buy their breakfast Danish from? There was new red brick lining the sidewalks. New bright red benches. She stumbled on a stone, but caught herself, trying to cover it up so Gary wouldn't worry. She quickly looked down to make sure she wasn't bleeding.

"Am I going too fast for you?" Gary asked.

"I'm fine," she lied. Neither one of them ever mentioned she was still sick.

Three times a week, Gary and Molly and Otis trooped back to the hospital. Every time Molly saw the hospital, she burst into tears. "Don't make me go back there," she begged. "We can turn around now. We can go to the movies. We can go to a restaurant. Come on. My treat."

Molly hated going back inside the hospital. She felt as if any moment the door would slam shut and they would never let her back out again. As soon as she was inside, a man she had never seen before said, "Molly, you're looking better."

"Who was that?" she asked but Gary just shrugged.

A doctor passed by and said, "Molly, how nice to see you up and about! And what a big boy Otis is." Molly smiled weakly as the doctor passed.

"I don't have a clue who he is, either," Gary said. "Come on, let's get your blood drawn and get out of here." The last time she had gone for her blood test, they had sat her in a little room, papered with signs. *Plant Ps. Peace. Prosperity. Prayer.* There was a poster of an alarmed kitten hanging on to a high branch by its claws. *Lord, with your help, I can hang on.* There were two fluffy puppies sitting in a vat of mud. *Some days, Lord, we need a little help.* If she were well, she would have laughed and made fun. Now, she just quietly studied the posters. "Everyone loves those," the person taking her blood told her.

It took ten minutes to get the results, ten god-awful minutes that felt like ten years, while she sat in the waiting room with Gary and Otis, pretending to relax, stiffening every time someone came out with the reports and mispronounced someone's name. "Molly Goodman!" someone shouted, "Molly Guttman!" and Molly waved her hand. Who else would it be? She didn't even bother to correct his pronunciation. She didn't relax until she saw the numbers on her report, which she could read like a pro. Some days, she had a reprieve. Some days, when the numbers were bad, when her hematocrits hovered dangerously low, she knew the doctor would start talking to her about chemo again. "You can feel fine and still be sick," he told her.

She saw the surgeon and the hematologist and neither one of them made predictions for her. The surgical wounds had healed into angry red scars, raised across her torso like Braille. Sometimes, at night, she woke to find Gary awake, sitting up, looking sorrowfully at her, and when she sat up, his face suddenly changed. He got cheerful. He pretended he was up for some other reason. "Had to pee," he said, but she hadn't heard the toilet flush.

The band perked up. And out-of-tune rendition of "When the Saints Come Marching In." She took Gary's hand and held it. The high-stepping girls pranced backward and forward. Her legs didn't feel like they belonged to her. She had this funny, weird walk, as if everything were off-kilter. Her lungs didn't feel big enough for the breath she needed. And everything seemed too bright, too noisy.

Gary coughed. He bopped his fist against his chest and coughed some more. "Get something to drink," Molly said. Gary looked around. A bench near them was covered in kids. "Go," Molly ordered. "I'll wait right here. I'll lean on the stroller and be just fine."

He hesitated.

"I can do this," she said quietly.

"I'll be two seconds," he promised.

She watched him disappearing in the crowd. She leaned on the stroller. Otis sputtered crankily. Lately when she and Gary talked about the future, she had begun to mention that maybe they could adopt a child. A newborn. She knew that in the shape she was in, no one would even think of giving them a child, it was purely a dream, but it made her feel good to think about it. To have those months back that she had missed with Otis, to start from scratch with a new baby who might love and need her right away. To have a future.

"Otis!" someone called, and she craned her neck, but she didn't see anyone. But Otis cocked his head and burst into tears. He kicked his legs.

"Oh, don't," Molly pleaded. "Please, please, please. Can't you wait until your daddy gets here?" She looked wildly around, but Gary was gone. A little kid in a green dragon suit zipped by, nearly toppling her, jostling the carriage so Otis screamed louder.

"Hungry?" Molly tried. She bent and got his bottle. She tried to pop it in his mouth but he batted it angrily out of her hand, so it rolled under some feet. She grabbed for the pacifier clipped to his sweater and tried to get him to take it, but he spat it out, wailing at her. His lovely little face was turning a violent crimson. His eyes were slits. She felt herself getting desperate. Two women walked by and gave her pointed stares, and Molly flushed, hot with shame. They probably thought she was a terrible mother.

She couldn't just stand here and let him cry.

She still wasn't supposed to lift. She didn't know what else to do. She bent and unbuckled Otis. She put both arms around him. And then she started lifting him up. He kicked against her, and every muscle in her began to scream. "I won't drop you, I promise," she said, but the truth was, she wasn't so sure. Her hands felt like claws gripping him. His weight loosened her fingers. Her breath came in gasps, and then she hoisted him up, so he was resting against her shoulder. She hadn't known anything so small could feel so heavy. She waited in sudden terror for pain. For any sign that meant bleeding, that meant she had to go back into the hospital. But nothing happened. Not this time. Not yet. She waited for Otis to scream even louder. She didn't think she had even a chance of lowering him back into the stroller. If he kicked and thrashed against her, she didn't know how long she could even hold him. "Okay, is that better?" she said, almost pleading, and abruptly, to her astonishment, Otis stopped crying. His face was inches from hers and she locked eyes with him. He stared at her gravely for a moment, unsure. He opened his mouth and she braced herself for his screams. She looked wildly around for Gary again, and then Otis grabbed at her collar and began sucking on the edge of it, all the while carefully watching her. Molly felt a strange new exhilaration. She held on tight to Otis, she swayed a little to keep her balance, to keep him close. She looked down at Otis again, and this time, his eyes were closing. He lifted one hand drowsily and rested it against her cheek.

And then she saw Gary winding his way through the crowd toward her, holding two sodas, flagged with straws, aloft. And then she saw Emma, leaning toward Gary, patting him on the shoulder, and then they both looked up and saw her holding the baby, and Gary suddenly looked struck. Molly, determined, gently hoisted Otis higher. The pain was less this time, or maybe just more familiar. She shifted Otis so that he was nuzzling her shoulder now. She saw Theresa, calling, "Molly! Otis!" She saw Suzanne, in a French maid's costume, winding her way through the crowd, looking around until she suddenly spotted Molly. Otis yawned and burrowed deeper against her.

Molly felt a rush. She rubbed the baby's back. She was like any mother holding her baby, being out in the world. She didn't know what was going to happen to her, but did anybody? Gary, Theresa, and Emma were almost to her. Suzanne was halfway there. Otis yawned and snuggled deeper against her. Right now, right this minute, Molly didn't feel so terrified. She felt like she really belonged in this sea of people, like she was a part of them. Right now, she lived here in this neighborhood. Right now, she lived.

about

the author

C AROLINE LEAVITT is the author of six novels: *Meeting Rozzy Halfway, Lifelines, Jealousies, Family, Into Thin Air,* and *Living Other Lives.* Various titles were optioned for film and condensed in magazines.

Caroline Leavitt has written essays for *Parenting, Parents, Redbook, More, Salon, McCall's, Mademoiselle,* and *New Woman.* Her essays and short stories have also appeared in the anthologies *Father, Forever Sisters, A Few Thousand Words About Love,* and *The Most Wonderful Books.*

She won first prize in *Redbook* magazine's Young Writers Contest in 1978 for her short story "Meeting Rozzy Halfway," which grew into the novel. The recipient of a 1990 New York Foundation of the Arts Award for Fiction for *Into Thin Air,* she was also a judge for the 1990 Fiction Competition for the Writers' Voice Awards in New York City.

Caroline Leavitt lives in Hoboken, New Jersey, with her husband, the writer Jeff Tamarkin, and their four-year-old son, Max.

READING GROUP GUIDE

1. Gary and Molly are drawn together because they both feel orphaned. When they move into New Jersey, they find a tightly knit community that perceives them as outsiders, which makes Gary and Molly so uncomfortable that they draw even closer together. What is Leavitt saying about the notion of community? How and why does this notion change throughout the book?

2. On page 301, Gary thinks: "Events didn't turn out the way you always hoped they would. But the thing was that sometimes people came through. The most unexpected people in the most unexpected ways." Who were the unexpected people for Gary, and how did they help?

3. A cornerstone of the book is two memories of the same event: Molly's version and Suzanne's version of the time when Suzanne ran away from home with her boyfriend Ivan and how it affected the family, especially the relationship between the sisters. Why do you think the author gave us two versions of the same incident?

4. The theme of memory crops up again when Molly is in the hospital and has been given memory blockers and can't remember seeing her family at all. What is Leavitt saying about how and why we remember what we do? Are there ever things people need to forget?

5. Some reviewers noted a surprisingly dark worldview while others focused in on the healing element of hope. Molly, after all, survives her ordeal, but when she asks a doctor if she's cured, the answer is "we don't know." The last sentence of the book says that Molly lives, but it's prefaced with "Right now." What do you think this says about destiny and fate and our ability to plan for the future, and why is this hopeful?

6. Why do you think the characters in this book are so accessible to the reader? How do you think the author made sure you would care about the characters, even the ones like Suzanne who are behaving badly?

7. *Coming Back to Me* is told from the perspectives of three different people. How would the book be different if it was told by just Gary? Or by just Suzanne?

8. Molly and Suzanne both had a missing-in-action mother, a woman who was there, but who was more intent on finding a husband then attending to her daughter's needs. Why do you think the author made Molly a missing-in-action mother, too? What is the significance of the way Molly finally bonds with baby Otis?

For more reading group suggestions visit
www.stmartins.com

Get a **Griffin**

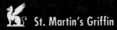 St. Martin's Griffin